PYRESOULS APOCALYPSE: REWIND

PYRESOULS APOCALYPSE, BOOK 1

JAMES T. CALLUM

Copyright © 2020 by James T. Callum

All rights reserved.

No part of this book may be reproduced in any form or by any electronic or mechanical means, including information storage and retrieval systems, without written permission from the author, except for the use of brief quotations in a book review.

ALSO BY JAMES T. CALLUM

Pyresouls Apocalypse Series
Pyresouls Apocalypse: Rewind

Beastborne Chronicles Series
Beastborne: Mark of the Founder (Book 1)

Beastborne: Exiled Lands (Book 2)

Beastborne: Mist Wardens (Book 3)

NEWSLETTER

Want to get notifications when there's a new book out? Are you interested in keeping abreast of the latest sales and new series I've got cooking?

Then you'll want to sign up for the mailing list! I'm no fan of spam myself, so you can expect to only get occasional updates once or twice a month unless there is a major event.

You'll also get exclusive access to early access chapters for upcoming books!

Sign Up Today!

INTRODUCTION

When Pyresouls released, it was a brutal new virtual reality game with a twist. Be the first to beat the game and win billions of dollars. But after the Burgon Beast couldn't be defeated, Pyresouls turned very real and unleashed an apocalypse of undead, monsters and a System of levels and stats onto the world.

For many years since, Jacob Windsor has fought with sword and shield to survive Post-Collapse Earth where only ancient, Guilt-soaked weaponry can harm the monsters from Pyresouls.

While defending his bunker with some of the last refugees of humanity, yet another friend loses his life to secure one final hope. An enigmatic artifact capable of sending one person through time.

In a cruel twist of fate, Jacob becomes humanity's best chance for survival. He takes the plunge into the past of the terrifying, fractured realm of Pyresouls, where every player is out for blood, and the monsters are more vicious than anything on Post-Collapse Earth.

Armed with knowledge of game mechanics, secret loot and enemy weaknesses, along with well-honed swordsmanship from years of battle, Jacob has every possible advantage against the competition. But the choices he makes have long-reaching ripple effects on the timeline.

Can Jacob beat the clock while grinding out Levels and manage

Introduction

to avert the apocalypse, or will his every action darken the timeline even further?

From the #1 Bestseller author of Beastborne Chronicles comes the first book of a new grimdark litRPG / progression fantasy series. This post-apocalyptic gamelit includes battle, leveling and gear enhancing mechanics inspired by the Dark Souls games.

Start your time travel dark litRPG adventure today!

As always, if you find any typos or errors feel free to drop me an email citing what chapter they're in at: typos@jamestcallum.com. I update the manuscript whenever an error is found, so make sure you allow your reading device to update your ebooks! That way you will always have the best version.

DEDICATION

To all those struggling against insurmountable odds who never give up, this book is for you.

1

May 7th, 2045 – 10 Years Post-Collapse.

The air rang with the sound of Jacob's deflection. He raised his cracked lucidian brass shield just in time to fend off a second blow from the wheezing undead. As he did, he drew his notched and battered sword from its sheath.

Jacob stepped forward and swept his sword beneath the angle of his raised shield using the Sword Form, *Wind Parts the Grass,* to strike into his opponent's gaping ribcage.

His blade split the bone of the decaying creature and swept clear through its spine, blasting the brittle bone and desiccated flesh into the dry hot wind. Another lost soul took its place, providing only a moment for Jacob to recover his Stamina.

The [Vacant Human] *takes 470 damage from* **Wind Parts the Grass.**
You consume 20 Stamina.
You defeat the [Vacant Human].
Awarded 50 Souls.

A wisp of white mist lifted from the fallen creature and into Jacob's chest. A chill spread through his chest and his Souls went up by 50, bringing his total in the bottom right quadrant of his vision to 97,120.

The number didn't matter. Without the Pyres, Souls were useless.

Jacob focused on the upper left quadrant of his vision, taking a step back up the dusty mountain trail as he did. Stamina management was one of the most important aspects of fighting the hellish creatures that all but destroyed the world.

His green Stamina bar filled slowly as he kept his shield up, but he didn't dare drop his guard. There were too many. And he had been fighting for too long. With less than a quarter of his Health remaining, he couldn't afford to take any risks.

Down below, clad in tattered black robes hemmed in bright blue thread, Caleb held up a hand and called down fire into his palm. Jacob was less than fifty feet from the man but couldn't get to him through the narrow switchback that descended into the clearing the sorcerer was in.

Even if he had more Health, taking the fast route down would be suicide. The fall alone would take most of his Health and the undead would be on him before he could recover from the impact.

Jacob, with only a passing understanding of sorcery, didn't understand what Caleb was doing. Surrounded by the undead – called Vacant, due to their empty unseeing gaze – he couldn't see how Caleb would be able to extricate himself.

But Alec understood.

"Caleb, no!" Alec cried, his voice raw with emotion. Like Jacob, he was situated up the side of the same sheer cliff face. The narrow stony paths prevented them from getting rushed, forcing the Vacant to come at them single-file. It also prevented them from reaching any allies caught in the clearing below.

That didn't stop Alec. He didn't understand the meaning of the word "can't."

Clad in full medieval plate mail stolen from the Smithsonian well over four years ago, Alec raised his shield and charged down the switchback trail. His heavy greaves crunched the long-dead sere grass beneath his rust-splotched boots.

It would have been comical, seeing all the Vacant thrown to their deaths, if Jacob didn't know how close Alec was to joining them among the dead. All it took was one slip, one Vacant that got a lucky strike, and Alec would lose his footing. White wisps rose from their broken bodies and entered Alec's charging form as he built up speed.

Each of them had once been a brother, sister, mother, father, son, or daughter to somebody. Now they were empty. Vacant. Stripped of all humanity, they were nothing more than vicious beasts.

Clapping his hands together, Caleb condensed the flame in his hand into three small beads. Jacob's heart fell at the sight. He may not know much about sorcery but he knew that spell. *Sorcerer's Breath* turned their body into one massive explosion of fire.

In the game of Pyresouls Online, that wasn't a big deal. It was a final spell that would kill you but also had an equally good chance to kill your opponents. You would simply respawn at the last Pyre you visited.

But there were no Pyres on Earth. Death was final.

"Get down!" Jacob cried out.

Caleb's dark eyes looked up at him, then drifted to the still-charging form of his brother, Alec. Amid the deepening sadness in the sorcerer's eyes, he clapped his hands together for one final time, triggering the spell.

Half a dozen heavily armored men and women in ancient hauberks, chainmail, and plate mail fell to the hard, dead earth just as the wave of white-hot fire flashed across the clearing. Dozens of the Vacant were incinerated in an instant.

Jacob covered his head with his shield as he hit the rocky trail with a bone-rattling jolt. The wave of intense heat washed over him but he was high enough along the trail that it did little more than make him break out into an uncomfortable sweat.

He was on his feet in a moment, ready to meet the attack he feared was coming. Instead, he stared at nothing but the half-dozen blazes Caleb had set off down below at the forest's edge.

There was nothing left of the man and nothing left of the raiding force of Vacant and other monstrosities.

They were able to sniff out the last dregs of humanity no matter how far they ran or how deeply they hid in their holes. More monsters would pick up their trail.

Up in the once-green Appalachian mountains of North Carolina, it had been safe for a while. Then they found them. They always did.

Caleb was their best sorcerer, and through his sacrifice, dozens of horrendous monsters were defeated. White wisps, Souls, flew in every direction, split evenly among the survivors. But other abominations would find them before long. And when that happened, they would be one man down.

It was a war of attrition played out again and again in scattered pockets across the dying world. It was one war the human race couldn't hope to win.

Miraculously, Alec had thrown himself down at the last moment and managed to avoid the brunt of the sorcerous explosion. His surcoat was turned to ash, bits of the ragged cloth still burning. And his armor was blackened in several spots.

"Form up, and fall back!" Alec called, rising to his feet. Jacob shook his head at his resiliency. Not for the first time, he wished he was as strong as him. Or that he at least stayed in the game long enough to level up some more.

Without the Pyres, no matter how many Souls he got, he couldn't level up on Earth. Still, he couldn't complain too much. Skills could still be increased and upgraded through extensive use and intensive training.

Even the weakest of surviving Pyresouls players were better off than those who never played. They were perpetually stuck at Level 0 without any hope of increasing their stats beyond the average human's.

Alec crossed the narrow ledge to Jacob's position, lifting the visor to his helm as he did. His face was tight with barely-held grief. Caleb was his brother and the big man had a habit of putting the fate of the world on his shoulders. Jacob had known him for years now, there was no way Alec wouldn't blame himself for his brother's death.

Jacob lifted the visor on his helm and looked into Alec's bright blue eyes. He didn't say anything. They had both seen death often enough to know that no words could suffice. He placed a comforting hand on the bigger man's pauldrons in a gesture of solidarity.

Alec nodded to him in thanks, then turned his gaze north and hurried off up the trail, his equipment making its customary racket.

A couple heavily armored – now blackened – forms didn't get up. Jacob sighed. They would be down more than just a single man when the monsters returned. He turned to look up at Alec's back.

He wasn't about to ask him to clear the dead.

Jacob raised a gauntleted hand to the woman in a crimson surcoat and a beak-faced bascinet that was coming up the path. "Kat, you're with me."

She was among the most gifted among them. Despite being stuck at Level 2, she took to the training well and showed great promise. Only her weak stats held her back. Like Jacob, Kat had quit Pyresouls early.

Many people had underestimated the psychological weight of a Full-Immersion Virtual Reality (FIVR for short) game with no pain dampeners, no memory inhibitors for death, and horrific fiends straight out of H.P. Lovecraft's mythos. Few stayed logged in past their first death.

While the others followed Alec up the trail to the caves that housed one of the last bastions of humanity, Jacob and Kat picked their way down the smoldering trails to their fallen comrades.

If they were dead, Jacob needed to be sure they stayed that way. And if they weren't, they needed to be brought inside.

Kat lifted her visor, her face was streaked with grime and sweat. Her blue eyes met Jacob's green. "I'll get Daniel and Melissa."

With a nod, Jacob split off and went to the first lifeless form. Sal never did like being crammed into a suit of armor. Nothing they ever found fit the man's rotund frame. And yet, when the enemy was at the gate, he was the first one to squeeze into that uncomfortable armor.

Unlike modern, comfortable fabrics, and flexible nanoweave, the suits of medieval armor they wore were bulky and difficult to move in. But they were the only armaments that offered true protection against the horde of creatures that now dominated the world after the Collapse.

Without Guilt, a force imbued into equipment by its previous wearers over many long years, even the sturdiest steel plates were little better than tissue paper. Replicas didn't work, even melting down the ancient metal failed to produce decent armor. It had been one of Jacob and Kim's first real discoveries.

Raiding local museums and collectors was the only reason their group - diminished though it was - still survived. Guns were useless. Tactical armor a joke. But dress up like you were going to a jousting match, and you could weather blows that would take down a tank.

With Sal's body facedown in the smoldering dirt, Jacob nudged the man with the toe of his metal boot. When he didn't respond, he rolled him over and crouched at his side. Placing his sword to the side, he drew a thin-bladed dagger from his hip and carefully lifted the man's visor.

His stomach churned at the sight of the grouchy, fatherly figure burned to a crisp. With a practiced motion, Jacob tilted back the man's head and drove the thin tip of the dagger from the man's chin into his brain.

The Vacant liked to come back wearing the faces of friends and loved ones. Damaging the brain prevented that from happening. Once they were Vacant, they were much harder to put down.

It was hard work, emotionally and physically taxing. But it was a necessity after the Collapse changed all the rules.

After cleaning the dagger, Jacob picked up his sword and waited. A moment later, a glowing fiery sphere of sapphire light drifted off the man's chest and floated in the air. He reached his hand out and touched it, willing the wisp into himself.

You gain [Stygian Iron Helm].
You gain [Stygian Iron Breastplate].
You gain [Stygian Iron Gauntlets].
You gain [Stygian Iron Greaves].
You gain [Ring of Bitter Dreams].

The words flashed across Jacob's vision and vanished with a mental confirmation. All of Sal's effects were contained in that wispy orb of blue fire.

It was one of the quirks of this new post-apocalyptic reality.

One of the very few benefits of the Collapse was the inventory system that provided everybody with a [Boundless Box] that seemed to hold an impossible number of items without weighing them down.

Any item you had on you – or within your [Boundless Box] – would be contained in your wisp. Unlike monsters, the wisps of people stayed at the site of their death. Long after a person's body turned to ash, their wisp would remain in place waiting for somebody to collect it.

Simply touching a person's wisp allowed you to gain all of their usable items and in rare cases, it might contain a fragment of the Souls they had collected in life.

Jacob turned to Caleb, or rather the blackened blasted stone where Caleb had once stood. All that remained of Caleb was a glowing azure wisp that hung in the air above the charred stone.

Caleb had gone out on some secret mission almost two months ago. They all thought he was dead until the scouts saw him and the horde of Vacant on his heels an hour ago.

Unsurprisingly, the man had little left. But aside from his equipment, which Jacob collected and would give to Alec, there was another item. One he had never seen before.

He summoned the [Ember of Probability] he collected from Caleb's wisp. He watched as shimmering images played out like a kaleidoscope from within the tiny glowing mote in his leather-clad palm. Every so often it vanished, the only trace it was still there was the comforting warmth it spread even through his armor.

With a shrug, Jacob put the item back into his [Boundless Box]. He'd seen stranger things in the ten years since the Collapse. He made a mental note to see Doctor Jasieux, she was the one who sent Caleb out after all.

After the Collapse, a lot of strange things happened. The laws of the world faltered and were superseded by those of a new and obscenely popular game, Pyresouls Online.

Players who managed to survive the First Wave found they had stats outside of the game. Spells and abilities that were impossible just a few days prior were suddenly commonplace.

The bystanders were the first to die en masse.

A world of stats, skills, and levels caught them by surprise. Without any frame of reference or instruction on how to utilize these new gifts, most people were helpless against the flood of undead abominations, hellspawn creatures, and horrors without name.

When they were finished with their grim deed, Kat and Jacob marched up the winding narrow trails to the caverns in relative silence.

"Sent those monsters straight to Hell, did ya?" George asked, standing beside the heavy gates set deep into the walls of the cave on either side. He threw a heavy lever, the rattle of chains echoed deep within the stone.

Somewhere inside the half-foot thick blast doors, there was another lever being thrown that would open the way for them into the bunker.

Kat gave the younger man a tired look. "Can't very well send them to Hell when we're already there."

Without a word more, the pair passed into the opened doors and the guardroom beyond. They passed through three more blast doors until they reached the heart of the bunker. The mess hall. The whole place had once belonged to some ludicrously wealthy family that was convinced the world would end.

It turned out they were right.

Unfortunately for them, money was a poor shield against the creatures that flooded into the world during the Collapse. Whoever they were, they never survived long enough to make it to the bunker.

Just as well. They probably wouldn't have been the sharing kind. And with so few humans left, it would have been a shame to kill them just to secure lodgings. They even had a FIVR pod. Too bad there were no games.

That didn't stop the few scientists they had in their group from setting up shop alongside the thing.

FIVR pods were all the rage back when reality was so predictable and mundane. Using them, people could escape - body and mind - into worlds full of violence, magic, and mayhem for fun.

That all ended the moment Pyresouls turned out to be more than a game.

The dull electric buzz of fluorescent lights gave Jacob a headache as he mentally dismissed his shield and sword. They vanished into a swirl of ash. He could recall them with another thought easily enough.

Kat gently punched his shoulder. The clink of metal reminded him that he still wore his armor. Jacob sent that away with a thought, that too broke apart into ash that vanished a second later, leaving Jacob in a sweat-soaked shirt and pants.

"Gonna grab some grub, you want me to snag you something?" she asked.

Jacob shook his head. "I gotta talk to the Doc. I'll see you at eighteen-hundred for sparring though."

"You got it, Jake. Think you'll finally teach me *Moon Crests the Horizon*?"

"Maybe," Jacob hedged, no longer paying much attention. He finally spotted Alec among the fifty or so people currently in the mess hall. With a wave of goodbye in Kat's direction, he headed toward the only table filled to the brim.

Alec never ate alone, though it wasn't out of preference. He had a way about him that drew people to him. It should have gone to his head but it never seemed to.

There was an empty spot on the bench at the long aluminum table his group was eating at.

Jacob wanted to leave him alone. He knew the man well enough to know he would prefer to grieve in peace. Alec placed the billions of people's deaths squarely on his shoulders. He felt responsible for the Collapse that wiped out half of Earth's population in the first week alone.

The problem was, it was true.

After all, it was Alec who failed to defeat the monster he awoke within Pyresouls Online. That same monster managed to get out of the game and create a breach in reality that caused the Collapse. An apocalyptic event that changed the fundamental rules of reality forever.

Not only that, but he had just lost his brother. Caleb had left on some sort of errand that the Doc gave him. He left with seven others, the strongest and swiftest among them that didn't rely on heavy armor.

When the scouts picked up Caleb's return, he was alone and being chased by a horde of monsters. Alec and Jacob were summoned along with a few others not already on patrols to bring Caleb in.

They had failed. As they had so many times in the past. Failure was an old friend to the dwindling survivors of the human race.

Every week their numbers shrank. Even with food and shelter, every death made the next one that much more likely. Many other groups weren't so lucky. Death came in the form of famine, disease, and even other humans.

Jacob wanted to give the ember to the Doc. But it somehow felt wrong not to include Alec. Caleb was his little brother after all. If he died to get the [Ember of Probability], shouldn't Alec know?

Of all the people Jacob met since the Collapse, he was closest to Alec. He knew Caleb but only in passing. There was a deep wound between the brothers that even the Collapse hadn't managed to heal.

"Got a sec?" Jacob asked, standing at the edge of Alec's table.

Classically handsome, the blonde-haired blue-eyed man looked up at Jacob and pushed away from his meal without a word. Selfless to a fault, he put everybody else before himself.

Once they were out of earshot in an adjacent hallway, Jacob summoned the item he took off Caleb's body, the [Ember of Probability]. "I found this on Caleb, with his effects. Did you...?"

Alec shook his head. "You keep them. He liked you better than me anyway," he said with a dark chuckle. "May I?" He tilted his head to the ember.

Jacob handed it over, watching as Alec's blue eyes danced with the shimmering light of the ember. "Do you know what that is?"

He nodded, something shifted on his features. Fear? Jacob hadn't ever seen it before. For a brief moment, his best friend seemed weary and tired. Aged dozens of years beyond his mid-twenties. "We need to see Alice."

2

Doctor Alice Jasieux shut the door to the once-spacious white-lit room, now cramped with all sorts of tables and devices. "What the *hell* do you think you are doing?" She snatched the [Ember of Probability] from Alec's hands. "Do you have any idea what this is?" She had a lilting voice with a slight Parisian accent that grew more intense when she was upset.

You could tell the Doc was pissed when she began to mutter in French. That was the only warning you'd get to leave the room.

"Some," Alec said, leaning against a metal table.

"Then you should know that either of you two *geniuses* handling this could instigate a Causal Loop if it binds to either of you." She raised the ember in front of her round glasses. "Thankfully it has not."

"Somebody mind looping me in here?" Jacob asked. Ever since Alec dragged him along to the Doc's playroom where she spent most of her time tinkering with the FIVR pod and who knew what else, Jacob had been almost completely ignored.

The Doc set the ember down in a small instrument, a set of thin needles that held the ember aloft. A large magnifying glass slid down in front of it so she could examine it in greater detail. She ran a hand through her long red hair. "You found this, yes Jacob?"

"Technically, it was on Caleb's body," Jacob said.

As if she just remembered, the Doc turned around and furrowed her brow. "Poor Caleb." She turned her hazel eyes to Alec. "I am so sorry for your loss. I know you two were not very close but I know how much you wished that was not so. Things will be different this time, you will see."

What is she talking about? The way she spoke to Alec was remarkably familiar. Was there something going on between them that Jacob missed?

"Thanks, Alice," Alec said, crossing his arms. "Is that it then? Are you done?" There was a hint of hope in his voice.

"It is the last piece," she agreed.

Jacob threw up his arms. "If nobody's going to bother to explain what is going on, I'm just going to get something to eat because you both are having an *entirely* different conversation than I am."

Doctor Jasieux looked from Alec to Jacob. "I am sorry, you are right. Jacob, come over here please." She motioned him beside her. When he stood next to her, she stepped behind him, put her delicate hands on his shoulders, and turned him toward the FIVR pod.

It looked familiar, but then again they all did. "What am I looking at, precisely?" he asked.

He knew what it was but he didn't understand the significance. Even if they had a cluster of servers to run a program to dive into, what was the point? They didn't need an escape from reality. They needed to save it.

"You know what that is." Her voice was too close to his ear for comfort. He could feel her warm breath on the back of his neck.

"It's a FIVR pod. We used them to play games and stuff."

"Correct. When was the last time you entered one?"

"When I joined the competition for Pyresouls Online." Jacob motioned to Alec to his left. "We both did. What's your point?"

"My point, Jacob, is that this is not your normal FIVR. I have spent every day since the Collapse looking for some way to undo it. There is no way we can rebuild humanity from this point going forward. The population... it is too small. We underestimated the Vacant's strength. Do you remember the Day of the Dead?"

Jacob shivered as if she dripped ice cold water down his shirt. He remembered all right. Anybody alive remembered it.

The so-called First Wave was when the reality of Pyresouls became the reality on Earth. The dead did not stay dead in Pyresouls, it was a recurring theme with the game.

That was fine for a game but on Earth, the dead outnumbered the living by many orders of magnitude. When the graveyards began to stir with activity nobody knew what to make of it. By the time people understood the threat, it was too late.

It wasn't a typical zombie outbreak, the dead didn't turn another person. Unless you counted their fervent desire to kill all living creatures. But there was no mutated infection. If you died, you turned. Unless your brain or head was damaged significantly.

Bites from the undead were still dangerous, but they were hardly a death sentence if you had medicine.

However, the Vacant were driven and monstrous in a way nobody was prepared for. Shooting them with a gun didn't do much. They were ridiculously resilient.

Like all of the creatures from Pyresouls, modern armaments were useless against them.

The largest cities fell almost overnight. Every death only added to the horde of monsters. The lucky ones were out camping or trying to "unplug" when it all went down. Like Jacob was at the time.

"I do," he said finally. "Why?"

"And the Red Plague?" she asked without answering.

Jacob spun on her and took a step back, trying to understand where the Doc was going with this. "I remember all the horrible shit that happened. Yes, I remember the Red Plague.

"I also remember the Lowing, the Vile Kingdom's poisoned promise of safety, the Shadowrend, the Hellgates, and every other horrible thing that's happened since the Collapse. I still don't know how I managed to survive it all. Why, what's the point of asking me?"

Dressed in a loose-fitting lab coat, Doctor Alice Jasieux plucked the

[Ember of Probability] and sauntered to the FIVR pod. She slid back a tiny panel on its side. It was a high-end model, a soft white bed encased in a cylinder with the upper half made of glass.

She tapped out a sequence on the panel. When she was done, a small receptacle to the side extended out from the pod.

Unlike every other part of the machine, this looked out of place. Jacob had seen people modding their FIVR pods for illegal dives or to experience things out of spec. The twisted wires and silver traceries that dipped into the hole the size of Jacob's thumb reminded him of that, except professionally done.

This was no kid trying to bypass his parent's sexual content filter with a foil wrapper and some chewing gum.

She slid the ember into the slot as if it was always meant for it. The silver traces shimmered with light and the machine began to hum with power. The lights in the room dimmed as she slid the panel closed. The receptacle for the ember retracted and vanished from sight.

The Doc turned around. "What if I told you, all of this could be undone?" She waved her arms with a flourish to indicate the entire world and all its many horrors.

Jacob chuckled. He'd heard that before.

There was no shortage of groups claiming they could provide safety or absolution from all the horrors around. At first, it was the typical religious fanatics that thought they were being punished. When it became obvious things weren't changing for the better, things took a dark turn.

Many of those people were no better than the demons they promised they could protect people from.

He looked at Alec, surprised that his friend was taking this seriously. They'd run into more than a few of those groups on some of their earlier mishaps. How many horrors did those people commit under the guise of "the greater good?"

"You can't be buying into this," he said to Alec. Jacob turned to Doctor Jasieux. "Then I'd say you've finally snapped because you sound like a cultist."

She shook her head and sighed, removing her glasses and rubbing the bridge of her nose. "*Mon Dieu!* God save me from small minds." The Doc took a deep breath, resituated her glasses, and looked at Jacob. "Do you believe that a plane weighing several hundred tons can fly?"

"Of course. I used to fly all the time."

"And do you understand how it would look to somebody born now – God have mercy on their soul – if you proposed that a metal tube with wings could fly?"

"But that's different. They're ignorant of how a plane works. If they understood the mechanics behind it they wouldn't think it's impossible," Jacob countered. But even as he said it, he was beginning to catch on to what she meant.

"And do *you* understand how a plane manages to stay in the air even though every common-sense rule says something so heavy shouldn't be able to fly?" she asked, tilting her chin up at him.

"Bernoulli's law?" he vaguely recalled. A lot of information from his high school days was dusty and shoved into a dark corner with all the other useless information from his life before the Collapse.

"Principle," she corrected, "but close enough. And if I told you the underlying theories explaining how this is possible, you would still be skeptical unless you saw it work for yourself."

Jacob opened his mouth to object but Alec was at his side in a second placing a hand on his shoulder. "Trust her, Jacob. She's been at this a long time."

"All right," he said, dropping the matter. Alec was more skeptical than even he was. If he believed her, there had to be something there. "So let's say that you *can* undo everything." He jerked his chin toward the panel she accessed. "Presumably that ember is needed?"

"So you *are* brighter than you look," she congratulated. "Think of it as the last piece to the quantum puzzle. The rules of Lormar are not the same as on Earth, that much I am sure you are aware, yes?

"Everything we ever thought we understood about the flow of time is distorted in Lormar, the world of Pyresouls. Now that it affects us, we can use some of its quirks to our benefit."

Jacob looked from Alec to the Doc, then to the FIVR pod. "And somehow you think you found a way to undo everything with that?" he asked, pointing at the pod.

Doctor Jasieux patted the curved glass top. "This is only half of the equation, as you say. We need a person to send back."

"I thought you were talking about sending back a... I don't know, a *bomb* or something to destroy the company that made Pyresouls. You're talking about sending back a *person*?"

Jacob took a few steps to the side to keep both Alec and the Doc in his sight. "Just so we're all on the same page. You're proposing time travel. Like, literal *time travel* by sending some poor soul back in time to... what, fix all this somehow?"

Before the Doc could launch into a tirade about how time travel was a misnomer or something along those lines, Alec stepped between them.

He put a hand up to calm the Doc. "I can hardly understand the particulars, but yes. At its core, that is what she is talking about. This is real, Jacob. How much magic have you seen in the last decade? Are you really going to start doubting *now*?"

Jacob had to concede the point. Time travel was far from the most unbelievable thing he witnessed over the last ten years.

The Doc rubbed her forehead in annoyance. "Not *time travel*," she chided. "But now is not the time to be discussing the quantum mechanics of Lormar's influence on this world."

Doctor Jasieux shook her red locks. "This, it is serious Jacob. No game. We send one soul back." She lifted one finger. "One soul for one ember." She raised another and put them side by side.

You didn't survive very long in the apocalypse without being able to adapt quickly. This was just another thing to adapt to. Whether it was real or not didn't much matter to Jacob.

It didn't have much of an impact on his life. If the machine worked and somebody went back to change the past, good.

He would love if his worst fears and issues were trivial things like scoring well on exams or finding a job. And not securing clean water, shelter, food, and ensuring that they weren't all violently murdered by superhuman creatures.

For a moment, just a moment, he allowed his mind to wander. Wondering what his life would be like if the Collapse never happened. His relationship with Emily would have ended, for sure. You didn't up and betray somebody like that if you truly loved them.

Jacob shook his head to clear the bitter memories of Emily and why he quit Pyresouls only halfway through the competition. When he came back to the present he found both Alec and Doctor Jasieux looking at him. "What?"

"You think you're up for it?" Alec asked, clapping him on the back.

"Wait, you want *me* to go in that thing?"

"Who else?"

"You!" Jacob pointed accusingly at Alec. "You practically beat the damn game already! How many times have you told me the story of how it happened? How, if you had known the Burgon Beast was going to destroy your Pyre, you would have rested at one much farther away?

"Not to mention all the mistakes in your character build and over what equipment to get. If *you* had a second chance you'd beat Pyresouls and be the champion."

Alec's face suddenly aged a decade, his normally bright blue eyes were dark and without their customary light. Jacob had only seen his friend's mask slip a few times before when they were alone and morale wouldn't be affected, this was the second time in the same day. "I can't," he whispered.

"We have spoken on this much," Doctor Jasieux added. "He cannot go. You hear his tales, his stories but you do not feel his pain. The weight bears heavy on his soul. If he goes, the process will kill him."

Alec brightened a bit and nudged Jacob in the ribs. "Besides man, what do you think all my stories have been for? All that nightly sparring and telling you what I would've done differently? It was all to train you as my replacement."

I seriously doubt that. "Are you saying you knew I would need to *time travel* and you were grooming me for that?"

"Okay, fine, you got me." Alec raised his hands in a conciliatory gesture and stepped back. "I had no idea this was a thing until a bit ago, after Caleb left in search of the ember. So, no, not for this *specifically* but in general what I said still holds. People look up to me, Jacob but I'm not the leader they need. That's you. The only reason you're not stronger than me is because you quit the game early.

"Even still, how many other players have you seen running around? Not many! They're dead. Many of them were stronger than you by a country mile. But who was it that figured out the connection between the in-game stat of Guilt and ancient battle-worn armors and weapons having the same effect? That was you.

"If we didn't raid all those museums for these old medieval sets of armor and weapons, we would have died several times over. That's all you, man. You were supposed to be my replacement." Alec motioned to the pod. "Now you can be the hero I couldn't. You know the paths I took, the mistakes I made, the mistakes *you* made. And you know what the Burgon Beast will do. You got this."

Swallowing, Jacob looked at the Doc. "Doctor Jasieux, *you* want me to do this?" Ever since they picked her up back in Charleston three years ago the Doc had been cordial with him but never seemed to pay much attention to him.

"Call me Alice," she said with a tilt to her head as she studied him. "Would you prefer we use Katherine? Maybe Victor? How many souls would you prefer we send before you feel worthy?"

Jacob padded the air between them. "I just don't get why you would want me. I quit, remember? Hell, I nearly quit a dozen times before I got to the point it was too much." He pinched the bridge of his nose, pushing back the gruesome memories.

"I still remember the first time I died. Besides, if you're sending me into the past – if it works – then you're sending me back to when I was a nineteen-year-old kid. I was an idiot and not nearly as fit as I am now. What would my goal even be? Blow up the Altis HQ so Pyresouls never gets made?"

"No, we can only create a link between your self now and your past self once you have calibrated to the same generation of FIVR pods as this one." She motioned to the pod behind her. "You will have to compete."

"And win," Alec added.

He couldn't help but laugh. Jacob was just some idiot kid that signed up for a shot at a ridiculous prize he never stood any chance of winning. He didn't ever have a shot at winning.

At a time when VRMMOs were old hat and everything was stagnating, Pyresouls Online was announced. It was supposed to be the next greatest thing from one of the largest VRMMO titans in the industry, Altis.

They stunned the world by not only promising to make the most brutal and difficult game possible but they also held a world-wide competition for their brand-new game.

Anybody could enter and all entrants vied for the same prize: The first person to beat Pyresouls Online would gain a 49% stake in the privately-owned company, instantly making the winner a multi-billionaire.

Of course, nineteen-year-old Jacob wanted his shot. Millions of people did.

Nobody ever understood the dire consequences of what would happen if they all lost. None of them could even fathom it.

With the chance to go back and fix it all, armed with what knowledge Alec had imparted to him and his own experiences, would he have a chance this time?

Flexing his fingers, Jacob looked at his hand and all the scars it bore. "What will happen to me?"

"You agree?" Alice asked, more than a little surprised. "Perhaps there is more to you than I thought. Come." She motioned him over and placed her hand on his thick bicep. "You will lie down in this pod and you will go to sleep. When you wake up, it will be some time after your calibration tests when you first entered Pyresouls Online."

"I'll keep all my memories of what will happen?"

"You will."

There was something she wasn't telling him. This was too good to be true. "And if I do succeed and change the future... will it be this future? Am I going to split off an alternate timeline and never see you again?"

"No." The Doc paused for a moment, then continued, "At least, I am not sure. I do not think so but this is uncharted territory. It is unlikely, I will say."

"Then what aren't you telling me?" Jacob asked. "There has to be some downside to this."

"You will have memories of a time we do not," she answered. "And the changes you have done, you will not know of past the time we pull you out."

"Pull me out?"

"The human mind can only sustain such a strenuous connection for so long," Alice said, pacing back and forth. "The ember will stop your mind from splintering across each of the possible universes until there is nothing left. But it is an arduous process and the energy expenditure is phenomenal.

"Even should you somehow manage to endure, we can only maintain a connection for a few hours at a time before the machine must rest."

"And what happens to me when the connection ends?" Jacob wanted to back away from the pod but he forced himself to look at the distorted reflection of himself in the curved glass.

"You'll be fine," Alec said. "Alice, Ian, and Clive all agree that there's likely to be some mild time dilation as a result of moving against the typical flow of time. For each jaunt into the past, you should have more than a day's worth of time there, right?"

Doctor Jasieux nodded. "Sometimes more. Sometimes less. It is imprecise. You will need to be examined each time we pull you back. Mental fragmentation is the most likely side effect, where you experience more than one reality at a time. It is only a theory, do not look so worried. It may never happen."

"So I'll have time to see if anything I did made an impact on this future then," Jacob reasoned. "And if so." He motioned to Alec. "You'll have different memories than the ones you told me."

"Exactly. If everything works like Alice thinks, the memories of your past – this future as you remember it – will stay but the world will change. You'll remember the horrors but none of us will. I know it's a heavy burden we're asking you to bear. I'm sorry about that, Jacob. Truly.

"But you'll have downtime when you're back here, and we'll do everything we can to help you get acclimatized. You'll also be able to research anything we might have been able to piece together from survivor stories and secondhand accounts. Assuming you change the game that much. Just try not to kill me in-game, huh?"

With a snort, Jacob shook his head. *I'm really going to do this, aren't I?* "What about my skills? Will I retain those? They're mostly knowledge, aren't they?"

"We do not think so," Alice said. "You will know of them but you will not possess any of the strength or specific skills you do now."

"There's nothing that would stop you from acquiring it again in the game," Alec put in. "You already know the various Sword Forms from years of training. It should be quick to relearn them. Like riding a bike."

Jacob placed a hand on the cold glass of the FIVR pod. "All right. I'll do it." He turned to Alec. "But before we do, I need to know everything you can tell me about the path you took. The abilities you gained, the stats you picked, and the equipment you found. After all, I'm going to have to beat *you*."

Alice squeezed Jacob's arm. "Thank you, Jacob. I will find Ian and Clive, they should have the sedatives mixed already. Take as long as you need."

As she walked out of the room, Jacob turned to Alec. "Tell me how you got through the Asylum of Silent Sorrows."

3

As Jacob laid in the FIVR pod, a potent sedative coursing in his veins, he knew he should be doing as Ian – their resident doctor – asked, namely counting backward from 100 out loud but he kept getting sidetracked.

Some of the things Alec said he did, the tricks he discovered either at the time or after were truly illuminating. And horrifying. "Ninety-five…" The Asylum of Silent Sorrows was the only area he never dared to go. It truly terrified him and it made sense that Alec had charged headlong into the frightening place.

In the past, Jacob took the much longer roundabout path into the Fogdrift Gardens. A veritable maze of darkness and fog, strewn with snakes and animated plants that were indistinguishable from the environment.

It took him a long time to get through it and even looking back through his memories, he wasn't sure if he could navigate it at any speed. Not if he was going to beat Alec's past-self to the Burgon Beast.

"Keep counting," Ian reminded him.

"Ninety-four… ninety-three–"

In between one heavy blink and the next Jacob felt a stab of electric pain arc from the crown of his head to the bottom of his soles. When he opened his eyes, he was standing in a sea of darkness.

August 30th, 2035 – 14 days remain before the Collapse.

A beautiful half-naked woman stood in front of him. Her hair was like spun gold and there was a cloth tied around her eyes like a blindfold. She held a scroll protectively in both hands up to her chest. "I welcome you, Jacob Windsor." She did a little curtsy. "I am here to remind you of the rules of the competition and to attain your signature on the contract. Be aware, that should you disagree with any of the rules, or refuse to sign you will be forcibly ejected and escorted from the premises."

Jacob reeled from the sudden shift but he recovered quickly. He remembered this speech. Only last time, he was so excited to get into the game and get started he hardly noticed the scantily clad woman.

"I understand," he said.

"Excellent," she said cheerily. "The rules are simple. Firstly, all players must commit to full immersion. Any logouts are considered an automatic forfeit. By agreeing to this first stipulation, you will be provided with quality medical care to ensure that your physical self remains in top condition while immersed.

"Secondly, all players are to start at the same time. No new players are allowed once the competition is underway. From this point forward you have ninety minutes to agree to this contract and to complete your character creation.

"You may take more than the allotted time for character creation if you so choose but beware that other players will be released into the game world if they wish it. And finally, the first to reach – and defeat – the final boss is awarded the prize. There is no second place. Do you agree to these terms as I have described them?"

Jacob rubbed his smooth stubble-less chin. *Gonna take a while to get used to* that. "Is there any NDA I need to sign?" He had never thought to ask before.

If he could contact the outside world....

"No, there is no connection to any outside sources from within your gameplay experience. All the information you gain will have to be gathered by yourself or learned from other players within the game. There will be no outside communication. As such, if you forfeit early you may feel free to post about your experiences to your heart's content."

Right. Now, he remembered. Decade-old memories he never thought he would have any use for were beginning to come back to him.

His past self hadn't asked the question but he clearly remembered the forums were lit up with experiences of various players that bowed out early. He learned a lot about the game – probably more than playing it himself – by reading the various accounts of mechanics and how certain magic worked.

Things like stat scaling, soft caps, and Soul farming were entirely foreign to him while he was playing. Things were different now. This wasn't about playing a game. If he could pull this off, humanity itself would be saved. His family would live to see the next year.

The fate of billions rested on his narrow nineteen-year-old shoulders. And it terrified him. *I don't know how you did it day in and day out Alec. Maybe I should've asked you how you could shoulder so much responsibility all the time.*

"I agree," he said to the waiting avatar.

"Then sign here, please." She unfurled the mile-long scroll and held it out. He was also agreeing to not sue Altis for the trauma he would endure in the game, and that it was entirely his choice to subject himself to the torturous experience that was Pyresouls Online.

A quill appeared in Jacob's hand and he signed his name on the empty line. With a snap, the scroll rolled up and the avatar disappeared, replaced by a character creation menu.

Four mirrors materialized out of the darkness at each cardinal direction. Despite the dark all around, he could easily see his reflections surrounding him as if they were lit by an otherworldly source of light.

A ridiculous-looking loincloth covered his modesty. He couldn't believe the lean teenager he was looking at. The man he became was covered with scars and old wounds, with hardened cords of muscle thickening his frame. This kid wouldn't be able to survive a week Post-Collapse.

He paused and chuckled at that because he *did* survive. For years. And if he did things right, those memories would be nothing more than nightmares he had to live with for the rest of his life.

Small price to pay for saving humanity, he thought with a grimace. *Not that anybody would know it was me.*

That was the rub. The ultimate goal was one that, should he succeed, nobody would ever know the horrors that consumed the world. He would return to an Earth that was utterly normal and mundane. It would be foreign to him.

Then again, if he succeeded, he would win the competition. Having a few billion dollars would surely help to ease the transition. Honor, glory, and fame for saving humanity were all well and good. But having a swimming pool of money like those classic Duck Tales cartoons was a decent consolation prize.

The first thing that he had to pick was one of the four races in Pyresouls Online. A small list appeared in the top right of whichever mirror he was looking in at the time.

Reaching out, he tapped the list to bring it to the forefront. After he quit the game, the biggest point of contention between the players was the lack of extensive races.

On one hand, there was a camp of players that believed you didn't need a dozen different races to make a unique character. They believed that the game's mechanics and grueling difficulty was the main draw. Everything else was merely flavor.

The other group thought it was criminal to have any game in 2035 with only 4 playable races. There were hybrids of course. People usually forgot about that – Jacob included. A lot of Pyresouls was like that. Hidden paths, illusory walls, and objectives that were only possible if you went off the beaten path.

From what Alec said, the game practically required you to constantly play "out of bounds" as if the map's suggestions were an obstacle to overcome and not a typical marker on where to go next.

Human, Elf, Fairy, and Karhu were the four races. Each of them had a base set of stats and there was no way to customize them.

In Pyresouls Online there were 8 stats: Vitality (VIT), Agility (AGI), Endurance (END), Temper (TMP), Strength (STR), Dexterity (DEX), Intelligence (INT), and Faith (FTH).

Most people could glean at least a little information from the basic stats of VIT, AGI, STR, and DEX. But few people understood precisely what TMP did, even less understood the interplay between INT and FTH.

VIT was the easiest one that most people understood. It governed total Health, a large red HP bar in the top left quadrant of his vision. Simple.

AGI increased one's speed and physical swiftness while END governed total Stamina and increased Bleed Resist. END was one of the most important stats that few people understood early enough for them to take advantage of.

Pyresouls was largely a game about resource management and Stamina was used to do just about everything. Sprinting, rolling, dodging, jumping, swinging or firing a weapon, everything took Stamina.

Increasing Stamina meant you could go longer between needing to rest, where you were at your weakest and most likely to be killed.

TMP, on the other hand, was unlike anything in any other game. The in-game description – cryptic as always – only said, "Allows you to withstand the burden of Guilt."

Not very informative.

What it really did, was determine your speed and encumbrance. Guilt functioned similarly to weight in a lot of other games.

Each piece of gear had a certain amount of Guilt associated with it. Mostly, this coincided with heavier armor but sometimes special armors, those that were uniquely powerful, had a high Guilt cost as well.

Each point of Guilt slowed you down as its burden upon your soul increased. There were certain breakpoints that people had found out by comparing information.

The general consensus was that each 25% of Guilt you carried incurred another penalty. From 0% to 25% then 25.1% to 50% and so on. Under 25% Guilt, you had full movement and no Stamina penalty. Each tier of Guilt above that slowed you down further and made your Stamina cost higher.

For example, your basic Human started with 5 TMP. That meant they could only have a single point of Guilt before they were penalized. Luckily, most of the starting gear had 0 points of Guilt on it.

Like the medieval gear they raided from collectors and museums, it would stand up to the monsters of Pyresouls, but it wasn't particularly strong. It possessed enough Guilt to make it stronger than even the hardest nanowire weaves back home but not enough to encumber your movement.

But very quickly you could get gear dropped off the various monsters, or find it in chests – if the traps didn't kill you first – and sooner than later you were moving like a fat old man in a girdle instead of some badass knight.

If you couldn't move, you died.

Which made increasing TMP one of the most important things you could do. Especially early game, when you didn't have many stats to begin with. It was the stat Jacob intended to boost first.

On his first attempt, he had found a piece of armor that even Alec didn't know about. But it was so damn thick with Guilt that the first time he tried to wear the breastplate, he was killed trying to swing his sword at the half-armored Vacant he was fighting.

It didn't matter how good the armor was if he was left vulnerable to every attack. Pyresouls wasn't like a typical MMO where you loaded up on HP and armor, tanking everything the game could throw at you.

Even with an incredibly good set of armor and a proper shield, you had to play smart. The weakest enemies in the game could still kill you.

They never stopped posing a lethal threat, even after the hundredth creature was slain.

In that sense, it wasn't too dissimilar from the reality he knew for the last decade. While most skilled fighters could take a Vacant or two in single combat, all it took was a single mistake to die.

The only difference was, in Pyresouls Jacob would respawn at the last Pyre he touched. And for some reason on Earth, there were no Pyres.

Nobody ever quite figured that one out.

There was a theme of balance and picking stats wisely in Pyresouls. Having super high TMP was great to wear the best armor but if you couldn't put down an enemy fast, you were at exponentially greater risk of death.

STR boosted the Attack Rating (AR) of any non-finesse based physical weapons. It was also required to wear certain gear and to wield specific weapons.

DEX boosted the AR of finesse weapons and increased spellcasting speed. Like STR, a lot of armor and weaponry required a specific amount of DEX to wear or use properly.

You could equip the items even without the required stats but there were a host of negative effects that usually didn't make it worth doing.

INT and FTH were two sides of the same coin. They each increased a secondary stat like AR. INT increased Vile Intent while FTH increased Noble Intent.

Both were magical stats but for entirely different schools of magic that did not mix. And that was the reason that Jacob had failed so miserably on his first attempt. He picked Fairy as his race thinking he would be a spellcaster and then began to raise FTH to offset the imbalance.

Big mistake.

The problem was, Vile Intent and Noble Intent were incompatible to the extreme. Raising INT increased Vile Intent just as the game said but what it *didn't mention* was that raising INT also *decreased* Noble Intent.

The inverse happened when you raised FTH.

It didn't completely invalidate the other stat but it severely hamstrung its efficacy. And with each stat point being so hard to get – you only get one per level up – it was a waste of both stats.

You picked one based on the magic you wanted to use. INT for Sorcery and FTH for Clemency.

Jacob took a closer look at the description for Humans.

Human
The most fundamental and proliferate of all the known races. Humans have spread far and wide across Lormar due in no small part to their capacity to take up any role in society and see it filled. As a result, humans are very well-rounded individuals with no inherent weaknesses nor strengths.

VIT: 5 | AGI: 5
END: 5 | TMP: 5
STR: 5 | DEX: 5
INT: 5 | FTH: 5

Curse: Undeath
Boon: Bleed Resistance, Physical Resistance.
Bane: Reduced Speed, Fire Vulnerability.

That was the other thing about Pyresouls that people didn't fully understand. You not only had to pick a race – a difficult enough proposition for most MMO players even without the stakes of the competition – but also a curse. A negative effect that likely caused more deaths than the game's monsters.

Each race had its own curse. Human's curse was turning into the undead. And as Earth was entirely populated by humans, it meant that any dead human would rise up again unless dispatched before they turned.

It gave rise to the Day of the Dead shortly after the Collapse and the proliferation of the Vacant.

In-game, the curse was different. You could influence it to a degree but it was painful and grueling. Most people opted to keep their curses at bay while a select few used them to frightening effect.

Each curse came attached to a specific race, but you could choose any curse from any other race if you so chose. Jacob's first run through, he kept the human's curse of Undeath.

Curses worked pretty simply on the surface, but like most things in Pyresouls there was a hidden complexity to using curses effectively.

As with most MMOs, Humans were the middle-of-the-road race. No stat was larger than the other, making them a solid choice especially when nobody had any clue what each of the stats did.

Despite that, any Human in Pyresouls was several times stronger than their counterparts on Earth. It was one of the primary reasons that players of Pyresouls who managed to survive the Collapse were so integral to the survival of those less fortunate bystanders around them.

What little people could understand after the Collapse suggested that a single point in any stat was equal to an average human. Two points were considered twice as strong as the average human, and so on.

Having 3 points in STR was the equivalent of a world-class bodybuilder. While 3 points in AGI made you as fast as some of the gold medalist sprinters.

Starting at 5 in every stat gave even a first level of Pyresouls a ridiculous advantage.

Alec had chosen human and regretted it. There was a lot of contradiction within Pyresouls and the world of Lormar. It suggested that balance was important but by doing so you were made ridiculously weak. It would take exponentially more Souls to level up and raise all your stats if you spread them out.

At higher levels raising a single stat could easily cost upwards of 20,000 Souls. Most of the dangerous enemies – enemies that when taken head-on gave you a 50% chance of survival – only gave around

800 Souls. And any time spent grinding for more Souls was time another person was progressing deeper into the realm of Lormar.

There simply wasn't time to do more than one thing well and even then it often wasn't enough.

I'll need to decide on what I want to be before I choose a race, he thought, going over all the races for a brief refresher. Based on his discussion with Alec, he already had a good idea for what he wanted.

But he knew he had time and so he indulged himself. After all, he would only get to relive this once.

<u>Elf</u>
Rare and reclusive, elves are known for their superior swordsmanship and archery among the races. They are, however, less inclined to wield heavy bulky weapons and armor. They are also the likeliest of all to view the world through the lens of one who keeps to the old ways. They hold to their traditions well, allowing them unparalleled use of Harmony.

VIT: 3 | AGI: 7
END: 5 | TMP: 5
STR: 4 | DEX: 7
INT: 2 | FTH: 7

Curse: Fractured Sight
Boon: Peer into other realities and gain valuable insight into hidden paths.
Bane: Potential realities have a habit of bleeding into one another, letting in unspeakable horrors.

<u>Fairy</u>
Keen-minded but slight, fairies are renowned for their cunning and trickery. It should come as no surprise then, that they specifically aligned to the turbulent art of Chaos magic and the underlying Vile Intent that empowers it. Their excellent use of magic comes at a cost. They are physically frail and must work harder than other races to bring physical prowess to bear.

VIT: 2 | AGI: 8

END: 2 | TMP: 9
STR: 3 | DEX: 5
INT: 9 | FTH: 2

Curse: Soul Thief
Boon: You gain valuable insight when collecting Souls.
Bane: Memories can be overwhelming, blocking out threats around you.

Karhu

Powerful, nomadic people who keep to their tribalistic traditions. These large hulking bear-like people excel with a strength of arms but due to their past transgressions find it hard to bear the Guilt required of them. What they lack in magical strength they more than make up for in sheer physical prowess.

VIT: 9 | AGI: 5
END: 7 | TMP: 1
STR: 8 | DEX: 8
INT: 1 | FTH: 1

Curse: Ursinthrope (Werebear)
Boon: Increased physical prowess and defense.
Bane: Uncontrollable bloodlust.

Jacob was disappointed with being a fairy but that was because he misused it and could only find two spells during his entire time in Lormar.

Of all the curses available, the two most appealing were Ursinthrope and Fractured Sight.

Jacob had heard of enough people dying from Soul Thief while trapped in a memory that blocked out all senses. Most people didn't even realize they died until the memory ended and they awoke next to the last Pyre they rested at.

If each kill that granted Souls provided some glimpse into that person's life, it would be all but impossible to concentrate in a fight with more than one enemy. An all-too-common occurrence.

I'm good with a sword and shield, if I could use some magic to bolster both of those I might be in a good position. But that would require finding the spells.

Unlike every other MMO out there, spells had to be taught or found. You couldn't make your own, and you didn't get a spell simply for being a caster-type. Something Jacob had found out the hard way.

Every race had specific strengths and weaknesses. Karhu were powerhouses but you'd spend at least the first four level-ups boosting their TMP up so they could equip anything beyond the starter equipment. Which was also different per race and something that even Alec hadn't known much about.

As strong as the karhu were, they lacked any magical prowess and he wanted to try and bolster his physical attacks with magic. Several enemies in Pyresouls were highly resistant to one form of damage or another. That made it incredibly valuable to have multiple weapons and damage types.

And finding a weapon that dealt magical damage was not only incredibly rare, but it also required an amount of INT or FTH (based on the magic of the weapon) to use.

Fairy was already out of the running, he played them last time. Using them well came down to finding spells and Spell Gems. Both of which were difficult to attain. If time wasn't an issue he would have been tempted.

The few fairies Jacob saw at the Crossings often left him awe-inspired at their prowess.

That left elves as his only choice for a full-blooded race. According to Alec, if he picked two races at once he would create a hybrid. It was a little known secret, one that Jacob didn't ever remember seeing posted on any forum after he quit.

While there was no way to customize your starting stats beyond choosing a race, by creating various hybrids you could influence the stats to your liking. Some combinations were simply bad.

Fairy mixed with karhu for example, made something very similar to a human although inferior to what Jacob wanted. Using human as a base worked well to temper the more extreme stat swings.

Human and karhu for example were physically robust and magically weak but not so much to the point of utter uselessness. Of course, their TMP was still quite low.

After playing around with different hybrids, for a grand total of 10 actual race choices when you counted the 6 hybrids, Jacob finally made his choice.

As tempting as being an elf was, he had no understanding of Clemency and its set of Harmony-based spells, which were based on FTH. Despite barely finding any spells as a fairy, he did learn a great amount of information about Sorcery and its set of Chaos-based spells.

Most of his information came from neither his own experience in the game nor from Alec. It came from the various forums after he quit the game, trying to understand what he did wrong. His primary reason for turning his back on Clemency was its effect on other players.

Compared to Sorcery, Clemency was less than half as potent at damaging other players. There wasn't much information other than an overwhelming amount of anecdotes that pointed to Sorcery being designed to harm another person while Clemency was used to soothe those hurts.

The few instances of Sorcery that Jacob was unfortunate to see up close Post-Collapse only confirmed those suspicions. The most dangerous humans he ever dealt with – largely running away from them – were all Sorcerers.

He shuddered at the memories of the charred corpses of both monsters and innocent humans alike.

Pushing the memories from his mind, he selected human and fairy. The resulting stat build was close to what he was hoping for. A capable fighter with good capacity to wield Sorcery.

Unlike most games, you couldn't change your physical appearance into something else entirely. Only changing race altered the way you looked.

Increasing various stats improved your physique but you were still you. Anybody you knew would still recognize you, not that that mattered when nearly everybody wore equipment that hid their features.

Still, it was neat to see the effects of being a human-fairy hybrid. Looking at himself in the mirror, Jacob's green eyes turned bright. They gleamed with an inner-light when he tilted his head, much like a cat's might flash in the dark but without the freaky slit.

His facial features were lifted a little, cheekbones a little higher. He thought he looked a bit more handsome with better facial symmetry but it had been a while since he had seen this younger face before.

Most intriguing of all were the emerald-green shimmering tattoos that curled across his brow and down each of his arms like emerald vines.

A deep resounding *gong* filled the dark emptiness around him and a large ruby-red countdown clock appeared as large as a holoboard you'd see from the interstate. He had an hour left.

I already spent thirty minutes doing this?

Thankfully the curse selection was going to be a lot easier. You couldn't create hybrids with them like you could the races, making his choice easier. Undeath was off the table and as much as he'd like to turn into a hulking bear and rip things apart, he knew it was a trap.

Without control over your actions, you were no better than any other beast, and that meant you were easily killed by any enemy that could strategize.

While he hadn't met many enemies that could do that early on, right before he quit the creatures he faced began to use pack tactics and according to Alec that only increased in the later areas.

That left Fractured Sight as the only contender. At least with what he knew of that curse, he could exert a modicum of control over it. Selecting the curse, he was greeted by a confirmation window for his choices.

It seemed the human and fairy hybrid had a name. He didn't expect that.

Kemora – Fae-touched (Human/Fairy)

Pyresouls Apocalypse: Rewind

VIT: 3 | AGI: 6
END: 3 | TMP: 8
STR: 4 | DEX: 5
INT: 8 | FTH: 3

Curse: Fractured Sight
Boon: Peer into other realities and gain valuable insight into hidden paths.
Bane: Potential realities have a habit of bleeding into one another, letting in unspeakable horrors.
Accept?
Y/N.

Jacob tapped his finger against the mirror, confirming his selection. The other three mirrors vanished and were replaced with rows of mannequins wearing various types of armor and wielding weapons in their wooden hands.

He felt the change settle on his skin like static in his blood. He flashed a slightly feral grin at his reflection and turned to examine the equipment choices.

All that was left to do was pick his starting gear.

4

There were 10 starting load-outs. Calling them classes would be a stretch since Pyresouls didn't actually have any classes. Nevertheless, they were often referred to as classes. Probably for the sake of people coming into the game without any frame of reference.

Warrior, Knight, Rogue, Barbarian, Cleric, Hunter, Bandit, Noble, Sorcerer, and finally Savage. None of them changed your stats or gave you abilities like in most MMOs. It was down primarily to the gear you were given at the start. Gear that had remarkably low Guilt for the parameters they provided.

All of them except the Savage.

It seemed like a joke, armed with nothing but a loincloth – like he was currently wearing – and a crude club, they were sent out into the world utterly defenseless.

He saw a few of them running around at the Crossings. It was funny at first.

They were generally faster than any other player since they didn't have to worry much about Guilt. But the deeper he pressed into the game the more their name made sense.

They were the most erratic players, as likely to attack you as to help you out, most people avoided them like the Red Plague.

It boiled down to the three armor types: Light, Medium, and Heavy. Like most other games each had its pros and cons. Magical damage was resisted most by Light and least by Heavy while physical damage was the inverse.

There were a few exceptions, and far too many seemed to forget that you could use a shield to bolster your defense to a specific type of damage.

The problem was, you couldn't simply look at the armors given because each load-out came with a weapon as well. The magical types; Cleric, Noble, and Sorcerer all came with a Spell Gem that allowed you to use a single spell.

However, none of them came with a spell for said gem.

Warriors and Knights both came with straight swords and a shield. Rogues used daggers, Barbarians large two-handed axes, while Clerics used a mace and shoddy plank shield.

Hunters used a longbow, Bandits had a crossbow, Nobles used a rapier, and Sorcerers used a focus. A tiny crystalline idol that increased the efficacy of their spells when held.

For most people picking a Knight was a trap. They had the heaviest armor but also the highest stat requirements and Guilt. The result was most players were sluggish and awkward when they first came into the game, leading most people to believe that Knight was one of the worst picks.

But that was only if they lacked the TMP to withstand the Guilt. With 8 TMP, Jacob would be penalized for using the armor but not too severely. If he upped his TMP to 10 quickly, he could easily withstand the heavy 4 Guilt the entire Knight set – shield and longsword included – would incur.

He nearly touched the mannequin full of half-rusted, weathered plate mail before Alec's voice came back to him. *"You need a mace. It's a ridiculously underappreciated weapon and you don't get access to another strong blunt-type weapon until far too late in the game. Getting a sword and replacing that pile of planks they give a Cleric is easy. With a mace and a sword, you'll have access to all three physical damage types. Trust me, you'll need them."*

"Fair enough," Jacob muttered, standing in front of the frail-looking parchment-colored robes of the Cleric. "I hope you're right about this." He reached forward and claimed the Cleric as his own.

*You have chosen **Cleric** as your starting Class, please confirm your selection.*

Cleric Equipment

Anointed Robe [Chest]

Physical Protection: 50
    Blunt: 30
    Slashing: 10
    Piercing: 10

Magical Protection: 75
    Arcane: 20
    Fire: 10
    Water: 20
    Earth: 15
    Harmony: 5
    Chaos: 5

Resistances
    Bleed: 12
    Poison: 10
    Curse: 0

Stability: 0

Durability: 300/300
    Guilt: 0

Anointed Gloves [Gauntlets]

Physical Protection: 10
    Blunt: 4
    Slashing: 3
    Piercing: 3

Magical Protection: 30
    Arcane: 20
    Fire: 10
    Water: 0
    Earth: 0
    Harmony: 0
    Chaos: 0

Resistances
    Bleed: 5
    Poison: 2
    Curse: 0
    Stability: 0

Durability: 300/300
    Guilt: 0

. . .

Anointed Trousers [Leggings]

Physical Protection: 30
    Blunt: 15
    Slashing: 7
    Piercing: 8

Magical Protection: 50
    Arcane: 15
    Fire: 10
    Water: 10
    Earth: 15
    Harmony: 0
    Chaos: 0

Resistances
    Bleed: 20
    Poison: 16
    Curse: 0
    Stability: 0

Durability: 300/300
    Guilt: 0

Mace [Weapon]

Physical Damage: 100
    Type: Blunt

Scaling: STR [B]

Magical Damage: 0
    Arcane: 0
    Fire: 0
    Water: 0
    Earth: 0
    Harmony: 0
    Chaos: 0

Status Infliction
    Bleed: 10
    Poison: 0
    Curse: 0
    Stagger: 50
    Break: 30

Durability: 400/400
    Guilt: 1

Plank Shield [Shield]

Physical Damage: 50
    Type: Blunt

Balance: 50
    Physical Reduction: 75
    Arcane Reduction: 30

Fire Reduction: 10
Water Reduction: 30
Earth Reduction: 40
Harmony Reduction: 0
Chaos Reduction: 0

Durability: 300/300
  Guilt: 0

Spell Gem: No Spell Inscribed

The Spell Gem was incredibly useful. He knew of the location of one early on and Alec gave him the location of another somewhere in the Defiled Cistern. He wasn't sure he would have the time - or the desire - to get them, but knowing the location of two Spell Gems was incredibly valuable.

All he had to do was find some spells. *Fairy Lights* was the only spell he ever managed to find, and as the name suggests it wasn't meant for damage.

Without any other spells at his disposal, he figured magical lights were better than nothing considering how soul-crushingly dark Pyresouls was.

Jacob groaned at the defense on the robes. On the upside, the only Guilt the entire set had was on the mace. With 8 TMP he wasn't going to have any penalty to Speed or Stamina.

Both of which he'd have to use to their fullest because any of the early enemies would likely kill him in 2 to 3 hits with the Cleric's armor.

There was nothing for it. According to Alec, the mace was incredibly useful. Jacob's memories backed up his claims of its rarity because he couldn't recall anybody ever using a mace.

And with the mace's relatively high ability to stagger and break bones, he could imagine a few enemies it would be particularly potent against.

Those Stone Gargoyles aren't going to know what hit them.

With fifteen minutes left on the timer, Jacob confirmed his selection. The robes vanished from the mannequin and appeared on his body. They were warm and surprisingly comforting to have on.

A brief tutorial popped up explaining how he could summon and dismiss weapons or gear at will but he already understood how it all worked.

When the game started he would receive his "first" [Boundless Box], it would store anything he didn't put on his equipment panel.

Anything in the [Boundless Box], which was essentially his inventory, weighed nothing. Only the equipment that was currently on him counted toward his total Guilt. There were only four slots for armor: helm, chest, gauntlets, and leggings.

He would have to find a helm soon, hits to the head were particularly vicious. It was worth the reduced visibility to prevent getting easily stunned.

With nothing else to do, Jacob tested out summoning and dismissing his mace. Just like Post-Collapse Earth, the weapon disappeared into a swirl of ash and returned to his grip the same way.

He performed a few test swings, checking the balance of the steel mace and the wooden shield strapped to his left arm. He learned all he needed to know in those swings.

Jacob was awkward and unbalanced with the weapon. He had difficulty controlling it the way his mind knew he could. As a new player, all of his skills would be at 0. And as Alice said, he wouldn't get the benefit of his years of training.

Though he remembered how to use many weapons, his body had no muscle memory and it lacked the strength and speed he was used to. *This is going to take me a while to get acclimatized.*

While practicing wouldn't increase his skills before the game started, it would help him to realign his expectations to what his younger body was capable of. Overextending himself would only leave him wide open to a fatal counterattack.

Before he knew it, the darkness began to break and fade away. The countdown clock hit zero and its gong shivered reality like a pebble tossed into a still pond.

The Pyresouls Online Competition Will Now Commence.
Good Luck.

5

Cold, groggy, and aching all over, Jacob opened his eyes. His cheek was pressed against the cold dewy grass and his gaze looked straight out onto a series of mountains so high up that the land below was hidden beneath a sea of leaden clouds.

This was the beginning of Pyresouls Online. The game's equivalent of a "safe" tutorial zone. The enemies around here were weak and sluggish but could still kill you. He had barely managed to make it to his first Pyre alive.

The forums were filled with the salt and rage of players who managed to die before lighting their first Pyre. They were kicked out of the game. Without a Pyre, whenever you died you didn't come back.

Just like on Earth after the Collapse.

Jacob drew in a deep breath and pushed his gloved palms against the slick grass. He knew what the area was, it was the same for everybody. An equal starting ground.

Same, but segmented. Like most of Pyresouls Online each player inhabited a reflection of Lormar. At first, Altis explained it as a sort of instancing they did to lighten the load on the servers.

But after the horrors that came out of Pyresouls and took over the world... Jacob wasn't so sure that was the whole story. In either case, players were largely segmented from one another. There were likely hundreds, if not thousands of players all standing in the exact spot Jacob was.

They could affect the game world in some ways and it would ripple across the entire world. Cause enough of a change and it reflected everywhere. If a player in another shard (as they were called) caused a large enough rockslide, it would appear in everybody's reflection of Lormar.

As odd as it was, it prevented the beginning from becoming a madhouse of players slaughtering each other or steamrolling the monsters. It made every threat of Lormar much more real and the lonely, oppressive atmosphere of the world was keenly felt without a party of people at your side.

Rising to his feet, he took a look around just to be sure. As he remembered, it was the same scene of aged carnage. He awoke at the edge of a mountain village that had met a terrible end. The houses were cold charred husks. Blackened bodies littered the grassy paths that wound between the broken shells of buildings.

The name of the area flashed across his sight.

Shrouded Village

It was hard to tell how long ago the damage was. It could have been months or years.

Time moved strangely in Lormar.

Was this once a real place, instead of just a game world? He passed by a lump of charcoal in the shape of a young man. He knelt down by it, examining it. Was this once a man who died protecting his village and not just some fancy graphics and code?

Were all the demons and beasts he fought real creatures that lived in this world?

Jacob was just standing up again and about to turn away when he saw a glint of light from the burned husk. He readied his mace and took a hesitant step back, but when nothing happened he lowered it and approached again.

What was that?

As the sun peeked out through the ceiling of iron-gray clouds overhead, he saw the glint again. Jacob crouched and dismissed his shield to ash, reaching out with his left hand to the corpse's chest.

At the slightest hint of pressure the man's body broke apart into ash and blew away on the ever-present mournful wind.

In its place was a familiar sight. A sapphire-blue wisp. He had never seen this before. Alec didn't even know of it.

Reaching out to it, he wondered how many people just ran by the beginning zone without any thought in their mind other than getting to the end as fast as possible? How many secrets and useful items would they have missed?

You gain [Soul of a Loving Father].

Souls like this were different than the typical Souls received from defeating enemies. Named Souls were items that could be stowed away and used later.

Jacob got up and kept an eye out for anything else unusual as he moved deeper into the mountains, keeping in mind the narrow path he would need to traverse to the north and the two Vacant that would be guarding it.

After lighting the first Pyre, death became a deeply frightening (and painful) but common occurrence. When you died, two very important things happened.

First, you dropped all of the Souls and Anima you had on you at the site of your death. Second, you respawned back at the last Pyre you rested at. If you died again, the Souls and Anima you dropped were lost.

Those unlucky enough to die at a Crossing - an area filled with players and no instancing - often found their Souls already claimed by another player who passed by the site of their death.

Losing Souls was the equivalent of losing your Experience Points in other MMOs. To most people, the concept of losing all unspent EXP was so foreign that they didn't understand what happened at first.

It made Named Souls like the one he just picked up all the more valuable. You could choose to absorb the Souls within the item or hold onto it for when you needed them later. It was like being able to bank a small portion of Souls to use when you arrived at a Pyre or one of the very few merchants scattered about the world.

Unlike most games with money and EXP as two different entities, Souls were one and the same in Pyresouls Online. You crafted with Souls at a Pyre, used it to increase your stats – and therein level up – and it was a currency to purchase items both from other players and the rare merchants.

It made the world so much more dangerous. Players were much less enticed to recklessly kill each other or explore areas with all the vicious monsters and cunning traps about.

At the same time, Lormar was rife with ancient treasures just off the beaten path for any brave enough to go searching. So while people became more cautious, those few adventurous souls would often be rewarded for their efforts.

That was the heart of Pyresouls Online.

It professed to be one way, openly showing you a path while hiding a better way just out of view. Players that chose to look and explore were rewarded, often with shortcuts and loot that simply could not be found anywhere else.

Alec was one of those players that explored.

Jacob's first time had been too terrifying for him to risk being adventurous. He stuck to the clearly marked paths like so many others. Everything was so much worse when you were alone. He, like many others, had not expected that, and Altis never hinted at the severe almost solo experience many players encountered.

With certain items, you could invite a person to your shard. Other, less cooperative items allowed you to invade another's world. Aside from Crossings, those were the only two ways for players to play together.

There was no friend list, no UI for guilds, or general chat. So even if you had an item to invite a person over, you first had to find them. And that meant lingering around at a Crossing where you were never sure if the next player was going to kill you or team up with you.

Worse, you could be waiting at that Crossing for hours or days for whomever you were hoping would show up. With the way time flowed in Lormar, you might never meet up with the one you were hoping for.

All the meanwhile every other player was getting more Souls and reaching farther into the game toward the ultimate goal. Jacob had been one of those people to wait at a Crossing.

The game was truly horrifying and without pain dampeners or memory suppressants, every death was a scarring experience.

But after years of having the specter of death breathing down his neck, he no longer let fear control him. When you could die tomorrow, you learned to live for the moment.

As he came upon the town square, Jacob was met by the familiar sight of a ten-foot-high pile of blackened bones. Jacob already knew the penalty for disturbing them. In most games, skeletons were among the weakest enemies you could find. In Pyresouls, they were truly terrifying and insanely strong.

It took specific forms of damage, namely Fire and Chaos, to put them down for good. Otherwise, they would yield no Souls and break apart only to reassemble a few seconds later.

That they appeared in the first area of the game was a stark reminder to the players that Pyresouls was not a typical experience. It set the bar high and kept it there. It was up to the players to decide if it was worth the pain and effort to rise to the challenge.

If it had been just a game, it would have been one of the most popular things in the world. But knowing its sinister nature, Jacob knew he had no choice but to meet and destroy every challenge the game threw at him.

But the skeletons were an unnecessary risk, especially without a Pyre to return to. With no way to kill them, they wouldn't even be worth the effort.

The square split off into four different directions. The one he wanted headed north, into the mountains where the two Vacant were waiting for him. Giving the bone pile a wide berth, Jacob picked the northern path and strolled through the remains of the dead village.

Eventually, he reached the edge of the village where he first remembered encountering the two Vacant on his first time through.

They stood in mismatched rusted and soiled armor with broken swords gripped limply in each emaciated gray-skinned hand. Their vacant stares looked into the village as if waiting for prey. They wouldn't notice him until he got within twenty feet.

Most of the Vacant, especially the lower leveled ones, had poor senses. Many would mill about or stand stock-still like a statue until something attracted their attention.

Many tried to resume their last acts before death. Guards stood vigil over ancient, crumbling throne rooms. Butchers walked between their home and their caved-in shop. Archers patrolled the battlements or towers of ancient defenses.

Unless somebody came too close, they would do little else other than mime out their past life.

With his inexperience wielding a mace, he had no intention of getting that close. Instead, he picked his way carefully between two blackened buildings, heading west of the northern pass.

There was a narrow path hidden by tall grass that switchbacked up the mountainside and overlooked the narrow mountain-pass where the two Vacant stood guard.

Mace at the ready in case anything sprang out at him, Jacob found the hidden path and hurried along it. A humble grave stood lonely vigil at the top. Right next to a pile of rough boulders.

Just what he was looking for.

Setting his shoulder against the largest boulder, Jacob heaved with all of his might. While he was a lot weaker than he was used to, he still had roughly four times as much strength as the average human, and moving the boulder was an easy task.

With a grating rumble, the boulder shifted and tiny fist-sized stones began to tumble and bounce down the side of the trail. The Vacant remained where they were. They only cared for the living, other undead or inanimate creatures didn't interest them. Throwing a rock to distract them was useless, they simply didn't notice it.

Throwing half a ton of rock on top of their heads made sure they wouldn't notice anything ever again.

The boulders careened down into the narrow pass, crushing the two creatures in an instant. The ground shook with the impact and two wisps of white light streaked out of the pass and went straight into Jacob's chest.

You defeat the [Vacant Human].
You defeat the [Vacant Human].
Awarded 250 Souls.

That was about half of what he'd need to upgrade one stat. Taking a quick peek around to make sure he was relatively safe, Jacob pulled up his status panel.

[Status]

Jacob Windsor
Covenant: None
Race: Kemora - Fae-touched (Human/Fairy)
Level: 1
Health: 124
Stamina: 86
Anima: 0
Souls: 250
Required Souls: 673

Parameters
   VIT: 3
   AGI: 6
   END: 3
   TMP: 8

STR: 4
DEX: 5
INT: 8
FTH: 3

Curse: Fractured Sight
Curse Level: 0

Spell Gem: No Spell Inscribed

Maybe a little less than half, he corrected himself.

He needed to get out of the Shrouded Village and into the Razor Pass. Halfway up the winding trails with jagged razor-sharp stones jutting from the mountainside was the first Pyre.

For now, that was his only goal. Everything else came second to that.

Without a Pyre he was vulnerable. While he didn't intend on dying, it was all but inevitable. Pyresouls was designed specifically with the player's death in mind.

Whether these were real places on a real world in some other reality didn't matter, every area in Pyresouls was many orders of magnitude deadlier than even the largest plague-ridden cities back on Earth.

Jacob glanced down into the narrow pass that led out of the Shrouded Village, scanning it for hidden threats. It would be just his luck that the noise brought something other than the Vacant out of hiding.

Everything looked clear.

Time to get going.

6

The Razor Pass lifted high above the sea of leaden clouds below. It progressed northward, ever-twisting, ever-tightening. Nothing was visible save the dark mountain stone that jutted out from the narrow path giving rise to its name and the dark clouds below.

If there was anything below the clouds, nobody had ever wasted their time venturing down there to find out.

Which made the Razor Pass all the more disturbing for their completely incomprehensible size. Everything in Lormar was massive. On a scale that completely dwarfed anything his Earth-styled sensibilities could make sense of.

Several people with megalophobia quit the game early for that reason alone. The mountains were the size of cities, ancient and implacable they rose thousands of feet into the air to tower over everything.

The Forbidden Kingdom, visible from the northern mouth of the Razor Pass, had walls that dwarfed Mount Everest back home. Spires and towers that were dizzying in their size and scope.

Those structures were miles away and yet were visible only because of their sheer size.

The path through the Razor Pass was a narrow ledge less than five feet wide. There wasn't enough room for more than a single person at a time. Jacob edged along, mindful of his footing at all times.

Any creatures he met along the way would need to be dealt with. There was no way to sneak around them. And that wasn't even touching on the sheer drop into the gray clouds below with a single misstep.

Because the pass snaked back on itself with such disturbing regularity, he could cut hours off of his travel time by trying to make the leap from his side to the other.

It was deceptively close, no more than five or ten feet wide in some places. He could jump it with his stats. But he didn't dare.

To prove his point, and to alleviate some of the boredom of endlessly walking, Jacob passed about fifty feet ahead of the closest gap. An area he could have well and truly leaped over with ease.

Dismissing his [Mace], Jacob scooped up a handful of black pebbles from the path. With a rapid-fire flick of his wrist, he sent each of them careening over that gap.

Nearly to the other side, the first pebble disappeared before it ever hit the other side of the pass. It was so fast, Jacob wasn't able to track it.

The next few pebbles elicited a slower more pronounced reaction. Black spiked tentacles snapped out of the roiling darkness between the mountain paths and swatted the pebbles clear.

Nothing would clear whatever that thing was.

He could have leaped the gap, yes. Just as that *thing* could have snatched him out of the air and crushed the life from his bones.

Like the rest of Pyresouls, the Razor Pass was deceptive. He stood again and resummoned his [Mace] before continuing on his way.

The first half of the Razor Pass was uneventful, if incredibly stressful. At times the path narrowed to a ledge barely two feet wide.

It wasn't until the Vacant Archer that things got truly dangerous.

It often seemed to Jacob that the Razor Pass was meant to lull people into a false sense of security and boredom.

The first few empty stretches of U-shaped paths were boring but Jacob knew the fourth was far deadlier. A few Vacant Archers were positioned on the opposite side. They were easy to spot if you were looking for them but after hours of traveling with no threats, most people let their concentration lapse.

Two arrows lodged in his shoulder on his first playthrough. And he was one of the luckier ones. Had they hit him center mass he would have likely bled out like many others had.

This time, Jacob was ready.

He lifted his shield as he crept around the corner. The archers were waiting for him. Before he took two steps around the tight bend his shield quivered with two arrows stuck deep into the wood.

You block the [Vacant Archers] *arrow (x2).*
You consume 18 Stamina.
You take 14 points of damage.

I really need to get a better shield.

The [Plank Shield] he had only reduced physical damage by 75%. Which meant he still took a quarter of any damage he managed to block with.

Most of the better shields – like the [Kite Shield] the Knight started with – had upwards of 90% physical damage reduction. And shields later on were often 100%, only costing a chunk of Stamina to weather a blow.

After the first two strikes, Jacob lowered his shield and walked leisurely down the narrow path ahead. He counted off the seconds, dividing his attention between his Stamina bar, the archers ahead, and his internal counting.

Three seconds. That's how long it took a Vacant Archer to reload and take aim.

Sprinting drained Stamina continually, and having a shield raised significantly reduced the recovery of Stamina. By leaving himself open, he was able to rapidly regenerate his Stamina.

In 3 seconds, knowing the mechanics of Lormar, he would completely regenerate his Stamina. With 124 Health, he could take several more volleys of arrows on his shield.

Provided he had the Stamina. Which he wouldn't if he ran forward with the shield out. With 6 AGI compared to the 8 of his last playthrough, he wasn't quick enough to make it to the archers in between shots.

Like everything else in his life for the last decade, he had to adapt.

Three seconds, and Jacob was only halfway to the archers. He lifted his shield just in time to feel his arm quiver painfully from the twin arrow strikes.

Another 18 Stamina down, and another 14 Health gone. He dropped his shield arm and began counting again as his Stamina rapidly filled.

With a glance, Jacob noted the hiding spot he used the first time he came here. A jutting of razor-sharp stone that he had used to break the archer's line of sight. He wouldn't make it in time and after this next salvo, he wouldn't need it.

Jacob lifted his shield for the third time, pain lanced through his arm as a rusted arrowhead broke through the [Plank Shield] and embedded itself a solid half-inch into his forearm.

With a grimace, Jacob dismissed his mace into ash and took hold of his [Plank Shield] with both hands. With a furious roar, he rushed the final fifteen feet and barreled into the first archer.

He let loose another shout and lifted the archer off the narrow pass, twisted his hips, and threw the light creature into the void on his left without ever breaking stride.

Before the next archer could nock his next arrow, Jacob had his shield back in line. His momentum barely slowed, he crashed into the next emaciated archer with everything he had. Just as his shield made contact with the archer, Jacob came to an immediate skidding halt.

The Vacant went flying through the air and tumbled off the side of the mountain, swallowed by the sea of dark clouds without a sound.

That was the most disturbing thing about the Vacant. They didn't make any sound. Not when they attacked, nor took damage.

There was no typical hissing or guttural sounds like you heard in zombie movies. The only noise they made was the occasional scrape of their weapon or armor. It was incredibly disconcerting to face a group of them.

He took a moment to catch his breath and let his Stamina regenerate. That maneuver nearly bottomed out his Stamina. If he was caught out without any Stamina at his level, he'd be a dead man.

What he just did was reckless. He would have chastised himself if not for the gain it likely brought him. While the other players were discovering the archers for the first time, he was already past them.

If he was going to beat Alec, he would need to take risks. Too many lives were at stake for him to play it safe or give in to fear.

Jacob was already heading down the last leg of the Razor Pass when the white wisps of the Vacant Archers flew into his back, making him 300 Souls richer. Sometimes it took creatures flung over the edge a while to die.

He never understood what the reason was, whether they died from some creature down below - like that black tentacled monstrosity - or merely from the falling damage.

Not that it mattered, but he found himself more than a little curious about what was below that blanket of clouds. How many more of those creatures were down there?

In the distance, he could see the Pyre. Currently unlit, it emitted only a faint orange glow from within the mouth of the cave. The embers, partially covered in ash were a welcome sight indeed.

Jacob's eyes misted up as he drew nearer. They had a distinctive look, a pyramidal pile of ash and ember that gave off a warm orange glow that fought back the general dimness of the world.

They were beacons of hope in a world where everything wanted you dead.

True to Pyresouls form, there was a final test to overcome before he managed to make it to that first Pyre. This wasn't an enemy he could fight, at least not now.

Making his way along the Razor Pass, Jacob slowed to a careful shuffle, keeping his eyes focused on the path ahead. As the passage bowed out the stone below his feet changed, becoming a deep groove. A casual observer would find that the mountainside was also worn down with a half-circle groove nearly two feet across.

As soon as Jacob looked up the side of the mountain, a hulking behemoth of stony sinew peering over the mountaintop saw him and dropped a spherical boulder into the groove. It rolled down the side of the mountain at a speed that defied everything Jacob understood about conventional physics.

The mountain trembled when the two-foot-wide boulder hit the mountain pass and skipped off into the sea of clouds below. Jacob rushed into the dust and debris that the impact threw up, hiding him from the Stone Giant up above.

He breathed a sigh of relief once he passed. Normally it would have taken several throws to get the timing down but he felt confident enough that he could slip through unnoticed.

The path to the Pyre was clear.

Nestled at the mouth of a cave that led deep into the nameless mountain range protecting the Forbidden Kingdom, the Pyre was the first step along a very long and treacherous road.

There were a lot of choices to make once he rested at the Pyre.

Ever since he was a kid he had always been impatient. Everything always took too long. Learning patience had been long and painful.

But with no enemies ahead of him and a fully regenerated Stamina bar, Jacob indulged his younger self by sprinting all the way along the narrow mountain trail until he reached the cold embers of the Pyre.

Breathing hard, he didn't wait to catch his breath or recover his Stamina. The Pyre would do that for him. Jacob reached a hand over the pile of ash and low glowing embers. Something inside him flared with warmth and a spark of light fell from his palm into the ash below.

The embers flared to life, a blazing Pyre leaped into being. And most important, the small ferret-like creature wreathed in fire began to wake up and shake off the ages of ash that coated his thick fur.

Pyre Ignited.
*Your respawn location has been set to the **Razor Pass**.*
The Fire Oppa stokes the embers of your conviction.
Health, Stamina, and Spell Gems restored.

"Well, aren't you a sight for sore eyes!" cried the little fire ferret. He sauntered out of the fire a few inches to sit at Jacob's feet. "How long has it been?"

Jacob stared, nonplussed. That wasn't what the creature said his first playthrough. He couldn't remember precisely *what* the little creature said. Who could after a decade? But it sure as hell wasn't that. He was greeting Jacob like an old friend.

Looking down at the adorable thing beside him, Jacob sat down at the fire's edge. The warmth of it spread throughout his body. And though he wasn't grievously injured, the instant he ignited the Pyre any wounds vanished.

More than the soothing sensation of being freed from his injuries though was the soul-calming effect of the Pyre. He had forgotten how *good* it felt to be warm.

"You remember me?" he asked tentatively, brushing aside his sweat-plastered hair.

The ferret got up on his paws and circled the Pyre before coming over to rest at Jacob's feet once more. "Why wouldn't I?" As if suddenly realizing that this was strange, the creature looked around. "This isn't the first Pyre you've awoken. But that-" The little creature narrowed beady eyes at Jacob as if he was playing a trick the ferret didn't find funny. "Something is wrong here."

"What do you mean?" Jacob asked, doing his best to hide his shock. His heart began to pound in his chest. The adorable little creature called himself Fire Oppa and was remarkably cagey about his origins whenever Jacob had asked in his last playthrough.

At the time he figured it was just a clever way of introducing a cute NPC that was meant to be more utility than story focused. But if Lormar was real, and all the creatures and characters within were also real... then that meant that the Fire Oppa wasn't just an NPC but a real mystical creature.

"This is the wrong order of events," Fire Oppa squeaked. He rose up onto all four paws and padded back and forth, leaving tiny fiery paw prints in the stone. "We have done this before. You and me. Only you... are not you."

He had never hoped to find an ally within Pyresouls or in any of the other players. Briefly, he considered trying to tell people about the reality of Pyresouls and the horrors that were to come but who would believe him?

Either he would seem like somebody trying to spread fear and doubt to get people to quit and increase his chances, or he would be labeled as insane. That was even worse than being a Savage. At least if he kept his mouth shut he might survive some of the Crossings coming up.

If people thought he was insane they'd either attack him openly out of annoyance or they would go out of their way to avoid him. And cooperation was the best way to survive the deadly Crossings.

Even if he told Alec everything he knew about him, how likely was he to listen to him? If he could even find him. Each person had their own shard, a reality that was all their own. Other players could invade or be invited in to help but aside from the Crossings, most players were kept separate.

The large worldwide guilds were screwed over hardest and it was the best-kept secret of the competition. Altis let the best guilds organize all they wanted and prepare to steamroll the content in well-disciplined groups. People studied ancient warfare tactics like phalanxes and shield walls all to no avail.

Group tactics were useless without a group.

The likelihood that you would come across members of your guild was vanishingly small considering there was no way to contact each other. There was no in-game mail or messaging. No way of organizing beyond meeting somebody at a Crossing in-person and asking.

And the risk of approaching somebody was high. Would they kill you for your Souls or would they be willing to hear you out? Nobody really knew and aside from specific puzzles and monsters, most people stayed out of each other's way.

The Fire Oppa was still staring at Jacob as he pulled himself out of his thoughts. "How do you know I'm different?" he asked.

"I'm a mystical creature of fire that can instantly heal all your wounds, recover your Stamina, craft items, bring you back from the dead, and you question how I can tell you're any different?" The Fire

Oppa snorted, twin jets of bright flame flared out of his black nose. "Give me a break."

For the first time he could ever think of in the game, he chuckled. Far from one of the sounds he ever thought he'd make within Pyresouls. "Fair enough little dude, so you can tell something's up with me? What're you gonna do with that?"

The Fire Oppa gasped and paused his pacing. "Why help you of course! That is all I have ever wanted! If you're less of an idiot now then maybe we can *actually* get something done for once."

Jacob rubbed his chin thoughtfully. "Can you tell if anybody else has lit a Pyre yet?"

"Oh, you *are* different! Good, good!" Fire Oppa pranced about the flames giddily. "Yes, yes, I can. And the answer is no. You are the first."

"That's good to hear," Jacob said. "Fire Oppa?"

"What can I do for you, Jacob?" he squeaked. Somehow it comforted him that the Fire Oppa knew his name. He keenly recalled introducing himself to the creature before.

"Are you at every Pyre in the game?" Jacob shook his head. "I mean, in Lormar. Or are there multiple versions of you or something?"

"Not every single Pyre," Fire Oppa explained, lifting a paw to his muzzle and licking it. Gouts of flame erupted from the side of his snout. "I have a few brothers but all of the Pyres that you humans have managed to reach, it's me and only me. Time... works differently for me. The Pyres are all linked outside of the normal flow of time.

"It's what allows me to reset the local area when I undo your hurts or bring you back from the dead. That's why all the monsters come back too. I can't do one without the other."

"Can you... send a message to another player?" Jacob asked hopefully. Maybe he could send a warning to Alec somehow or find a way to coordinate.

The Fire Oppa shook his head. "No can do, Chief. There are rules, and while I'll be the first to leap through a loophole, that's one I've never been able to get around."

"Damn," Jacob pulled his knees up to his chest and thought for a moment. "So you remember everything I did last time?"

"More or less." The Fire Oppa laid on his side lazily. The stone turned black and scorched around him. "I can't follow you outside of the radius of a Pyre. The more Pyres you reignite the more my influence spreads, however." He lifted his head and looked Jacob up and down. "I take it you don't need to hear my spiel about what I can do for you?"

Jacob shook his head. "I'm sure you're tired of it by now."

"You have no idea."

He set his mace down and summoned the [Soul of a Loving Father] to his palm. Suspecting that this was once a living person and not some code in a game changed the way he looked at everything. The sapphire wisp danced in his upturned palm.

"I'm sorry," he whispered to it. "I'll do my best to make your sacrifice mean something." Jacob tightened his grip on the wisp and crushed it. The Soul contained within flooded into his body. It wasn't much, only 150 Souls but it was enough to increase one stat.

Fire Oppa perked up at that. "Looks like you got some Souls to spend."

Stats could only be raised at an ignited Pyre. Jacob didn't quite understand how the Fire Oppa was able to use the Souls to make him stronger and in the end, he didn't care very much.

When the Collapse happened and Earth's rules were rewritten, the Pyres didn't make their appearance. And neither did the Fire Oppa. Without the Pyres, people couldn't respawn and more importantly, they couldn't spend their Souls to become stronger.

"Yeah, I'd like to raise my Temper," he said. A stream of white wispy energy flowed out of Jacob and into the Pyre.

The flames leaped high into the air, licking the roof of the cave and then calmed. An ember flew out of the fire and touched Jacob's robes. It melted into his chest and a brief look at his Status confirmed his Temper had gone up a single point.

[Status]

Jacob Windsor

Covenant: None
Race: Kemora - Fae-touched (Human/Fairy)
Level: 2
Health: 124
Stamina: 86
Anima: 0
Souls: 27
Required Souls: 690

Parameters
VIT: 3
AGI: 6
END: 3
TMP: 9
STR: 4
DEX: 5
INT: 8
FTH: 3

Curse: Fractured Sight
Curse Level: 0

Spell Gem: No Spell Inscribed

One more point and he would be ready to equip the Knight's armor when he found it. According to Alec, he could find a Knight's corpse bearing the armor just after the cavern that led out of the Razor Pass and into the valley beyond.

From there he had three choices. Either he could descend the mountain into the Stalking Wood, go northwest to Weslyn's Watch and the horrors beyond or continue northeast to the Steps of Penance that inevitably led to the dreaded Asylum of Silent Sorrows.

Naturally, that meant his next destination was the Steps of Penance where he'd find the dead Knight and finally get some decent armor.

It was also a path he never took before.

Jacob looked at the Fire Oppa. "Don't you have something for me?"

"I thought you'd never ask!" He got up and scampered over to the fire. Digging through the ashes, he sent embers, and what should have been scalding hot ash all over Jacob.

Rather than hurt him, it felt warm and comforting. Like snuggling under a warm blanket after spending hours in the freezing cold outside.

The Pyre's heat seeped into his very bones. He hadn't realized how much he missed its soothing warmth. From the accounts he read on the forums, more than a few people stayed at the first Pyre until the Collapse happened.

At the time, he had a hard time understanding why.

But after ten long years of the apocalypse, his soul was wounded again and again. Every loss, every final goodbye, every hope dashed.

Sitting in front of the Pyre soothed that pain, it didn't numb it like a drug but made it easier to deal with. He wondered if there was something that the Fire Oppa's fire could do beyond what was useful for survival.

Could the adorable little creature heal the scars on a person's soul if given enough time?

His reverie was cut short as the Fire Oppa found what he was looking for, dragged it out of the flames, and deposited it at Jacob's feet. "There you go! Thought I was going to need to do my whole spiel about ampoules again! I was hoping you weren't going to try and run off without some."

Jacob reached down and picked up the five small glass vials, each one attached to the next by a red knotted waxed cord. Each ampoule contained a tiny glowing red cinder, no bigger than a grain of sand. When the ampoule was broken, the cinder would instantly restore a large portion of Health.

Or try to, if you were clumsy and accidentally crushed the ampoule at full Health.

As Jacob put the [Cinder Ampoules] away they were whisked into his [Boundless Box] by a swirl of black ash. He looked at the Fire Oppa. "I don't suppose you could help me out and come with me?"

The Fire Oppa deflated, though the look in his beady black eyes was eager as always, the fires that flared from his ruddy fur coat dulled and cooled as he laid down. "I would like nothing more. But I am bound to the Pyres. If I leave them, they will gutter and die... taking me with them. I will help you when and where I can if you promise to light six of the Pyres in Lormar."

I don't know if I'll have the time to do that. Jacob bit his lip, mulling over the Fire Oppa's proposal. In any other game, this would have been considered a Quest with a capital "Q."

But Pyresouls didn't work like most games. There would be no minimap – there was no map at all actually – and there would be no bulleted list that explained what steps he'd taken to complete the quest and what was yet left to accomplish.

He wanted nothing more than to help the Fire Oppa. He always had a fondness for the thing even when he thought it was an NPC. Its disappearance from Earth after the Collapse was one of the greatest travesties of all time.

But to go out of his way to light more Pyres would slow him down. And yet... he couldn't just say no. "You got yourself a deal," Jacob said, reaching out his hand to the Fire Oppa.

A flaming human-like hand emerged from the flames of the Pyre and shook Jacob's. "Of all the millions of people who think they're playing a game, this is the first instance any person undertook this task that I can recall. Most people think I'm trying to slow them down or an NPC trying to give backstory. It's so frustrating I can't tell them!"

That set Jacob back. "Wait, why can't you tell them?"

"Because they don't ask!"

"How was it you could tell me what you did then?"

The Fire Oppa gave him the stink eye. For the second time that day, it made Jacob chuckle. Seeing such a tiny, fiery little thing give him such a disgruntled look was so endearing and strange.

"Because you asked," the Fire Oppa responded.

"But you greeted me as if you already knew me," Jacob countered.

"I can do that. But I can't reveal my task to players unless they ask about it or ask for something in return. Most players listen to my 'Pyre Pitch' about what they can do at the Pyre and what I can help them with. Respawn, yada yada, healing, yada yada. And then most of them leave. Few have enough Souls to spend so early to reinforce a parameter like you."

"So if I asked you a whole bunch of questions, you would be able to give me more information about Lormar and the workings of Pyresouls?" Jacob asked, incredulous.

It couldn't be that easy, could it?

"Yes, and no," the Fire Oppa said. "I can only give you information related to the area my Pyre is in. I could tell you the number of deaths already incurred by the Razor Pass. I could tell you the number of people who have made it here already and I could give you some background to the Razor Pass if you wanted.

"For each Pyre you reignite, I grow stronger and my influence – as I've already said – grows. That includes my knowledge of the area and my ability to help you. The more Pyres you or anybody else relight, the better I am able to help. You humans are literally leaving me on the wayside like some annoying sidekick instead of letting me *help you*."

The Fire Oppa turned to the side and blew out a plume of fire in an exasperated sigh. "The Nelana would never treat me like this," he added under his breath.

"What's a Nelana?" Jacob asked.

The Fire Oppa gave him the whale-eye, a thin crescent of white appeared at the edge of his dark beady eyes. Jacob faintly recalled that, at least in dogs, it meant they were spooked or sometimes guarding something they weren't comfortable sharing.

Padding the air between them, Jacob said, "Nevermind, don't worry about it."

That seemed to put the Fire Oppa at ease.

Getting to his feet, Jacob looked down at the Fire Oppa with renewed fondness. He wanted to pet him. In all his time in Pyresouls he never managed to bridge that gap. At first, it was because he thought this was all a game, and wasting time petting a digital creation was silly.

Now, it felt somehow wrong to treat the Fire Oppa like a common ferret. Like some kind of pet, when he was trying to help humanity all while being constantly rebuffed.

Had there been nobody from his original timeline that took the Fire Oppa up on his task? It seemed ridiculous, almost improbable, that millions of people would have all ignored the creature.

Especially considering the obsessive nature of some gamers. Those that, despite the competition going on, would try to find every glitch and every easter egg.

No, he thought. *The likeliest course is that somebody* did *take the Fire Oppa up on his offer but it didn't matter anyway because the Burgon Beast escaped and either killed or forcibly logged out everybody still in Pyresouls.*

Not that he had an inkling of what the Fire Oppa actually was. For all the good the Fire Oppa did for his people, he knew very little of the creature. Without the Fire Oppa there would be no Pyres.

That must have been what happened when Alec released the Burgon Beast and failed to defeat it. The monster snuffed out the Pyres, and with it the Fire Oppa. No Fire Oppa, no Pyres.

And so Earth was doomed from the start.

Knowing that, it was even harder to resist petting him. He was such a good boy.

Next Pyre, he promised himself. *After I light the next Pyre.*

"Thank you, Fire Oppa, for all that you've done for us. I'm sorry most of my kind don't understand what you've really done for them." He lifted a gloved hand in farewell. "But if I'm going to make sure things are different this time, I have to get going."

"May the flames light your path," the Fire Oppa intoned.

"And may they guide me back home," Jacob finished without thinking. It was a popular enough saying Post-Collapse. He never really thought of where it came from. Now that he did, it only made him like the saying more.

7

The twisting cavern wasn't very long, but it was impossibly dark. Luckily, every player had a faint glow around their body that provided a bit of light to see by. Other players would appear as phantasmic creatures wreathed in either white-gold or black-red auras of light depending on their method of entry.

Invited players were white-gold, while invaders were black-red.

The only exception was at the Crossings. Players appeared normally there without any specific aura, but their personal illumination still worked so that when a group of people entered a dark cave it was reasonably lit.

A torch or lantern worked much better and cast a wider pool of light. But then you were giving up one of your hands for light and not defense.

In a world where everything wanted you dead, giving up a weapon hand was not a choice to make lightly.

Even with Pyresoul's inventory management system that allowed you to call an item or piece of equipment you've previously set to your hand in a swirl of ash, that fraction of a second you lost swapping from a torch to a shield mattered.

Pyresouls Apocalypse: Rewind

If you had to swap to a sword instead, you were likely to wake up at your last Pyre.

Pyresouls was not an easy game. It did not cater to the player's whims or desires unless that desire was masochistic in nature.

Even though the initial areas held weaker enemies, they were remarkably deadly. Due in no small part to how easy it was to die.

Though the system did well to impart knowledge of proper stances and footwork, if you knew how to fight with swords, spears, maces, axes, or knew how to use a bow you were far more effective than some random guy off the street several levels higher than you.

Even though skill – such as sword, mace, greatsword, etc. – mattered, it was how you used them that truly set people apart.

On his first time through, Jacob had no idea how to properly swing a sword. The two Vacant back in the Shrouded Village nearly killed him. He had to run, and in heavier armor no less which he had no idea how to properly move in, kiting the creatures around a burned-out shell of a home. He chipped away at their health until the much slower creatures were dead.

That had been his go-to move for most of his time playing Pyresouls. Separate his enemies, lure them one at a time, and then use hit-and-run tactics until their health was whittled away.

It was a remarkably clunky and slow strategy.

Unsurprisingly, it fell apart the moment more than one creature was lured. Or, as was often the case in Pyresouls, when more enemies suddenly descended upon you.

Such as the area up ahead.

The cavern bent and twisted back on itself, eventually breaking into a fork. Down the left path, Jacob could see nothing but interminable darkness.

On the right path, however, there was the telltale glow of an item wisp, its sapphire glow stood out like a beacon in the dark.

But there was more than an item down there. He remembered the terrifying, fatal beating he received. His first death in Pyresouls had been falling for the tantalizing lure.

The creatures that waited just out of sight on a narrow ledge wouldn't make a move unless he got close to the sapphire wisp and the corpse it once belonged to. Unlike the other Vacant, those creatures were far stronger.

With my current physical defense, I doubt I could stand more than a single hit. Last time I had the Knight's Armor set and that only allowed me to take three hits before I died.

He never did beat them or find out what the item was. Alec had resisted the temptation as well and like so many others had kept his eyes on the prize.

Like coming back to a low-level area when you're much stronger, Jacob couldn't resist the urge to test himself against his past tormentors. Pain wasn't dulled or altered in Pyresouls. When you died, it felt *real* and it was both terrifying and agonizing.

Many people quit the game shortly after their first death. Every other game had adjustable pain dampeners as well as a sort of fugue state that allowed you to quickly forget about your death.

Tightening his grip on his [Mace], the flanges catching the faint bit of luminescence from his body, Jacob took the right path.

Pyresouls didn't hold anybody's hand.

Once, that had terrified Jacob. Now, it was a reminder of this world's realism. His mace skill was a pitiful level 1 and he had no mace forms to use. But even without them, he knew well enough how to use a mace.

Far from his favorite weapon, it tended to get stuck and wedged in places a sword could slide out of. But it packed a wallop if you could slip through an opponent's defense.

Every step took him closer to the body half slipped over the edge of the black abyss inside the cavernous room, the sapphire glow of the wisp hung a few inches above the corpse's back. Jacob shifted the straps of the [Plank Shield] farther up his forearm and took his [Mace] in both hands.

He took one step closer, and though he couldn't see the ledges to either side he knew they were there.

As the first Vacant in heavy armor leaped in front of him, Jacob was already winding up his swing.

The best thing about maces was their raw staggering power. While a great hammer could launch a foe several feet, it was slow and unwieldy. In a tunnel like the one he found himself in, he'd never be able to put much power behind the swing.

But a mace? It was small enough to work well in tight quarters – a running theme in Pyresouls – and its heavy metal frame could pack one hell of a wallop.

The Vacant wore a half rusted set of plate mail, its greatsword raised and poised to strike. Already swinging for the fences, Jacob had a clear shot at the thing's rotting, exposed chest.

Crunching through the brittle metal breastplate, Jacob's [Mace] caught the Vacant Knight fully unprepared and the creature's glowing red eyes could only widen in surprise.

You strike the [Vacant Knight] *for 139 points of damage.*
You consume 40 Stamina.
You **Stagger** *the* [Vacant Knight].

Jacob stepped forward with the swing, following through as he had been taught all those years ago. It wasn't the damage of the [Mace] that was impressive – though at Level 2, dealing 139 damage was *quite* an accomplishment – it was the stagger effect.

At that moment the Vacant Knight was staggered, unable to act and with its stability reduced – temporarily – to 0, it couldn't resist the follow-through of Jacob's swing.

Normally when the creature was able to dig in its heels, it might slide a few inches but no more. Having 0 stability prevented it from getting a solid footing. The creature was pushed out past the corpse and its sapphire wisp, right over into the gaping pit beyond.

It was swallowed by the abyss without a whisper.

There was no time for Jacob to celebrate though, the second Vacant Knight landed in the tunnel and this time Jacob was not ready for it. He was too committed to the previous strike and too weak to halt and reverse his momentum in time.

He knew what he had to do. His mind already plotting his defensive posture and the resulting counterstroke. But his body moved like it was submerged in gelatin. He knew what to do but his muscles weren't strong enough, he lacked the speed and adroitness he was used to.

The Vacant Knight brought its rusted longsword up and slashed at him from shoulder to hip in a bright line of pain and blood. With both hands still on his [Mace], he couldn't even slide into a defensive posture.

The [Vacant Knight] *slashes you for 65 points of damage.*

Jacob took the hit full-force, pushing through the pain and readying himself at the same time. More than half his health was wiped out with that single strike. Being accustomed to years of battle and a body that was more scar tissue than anything else didn't make the pain any less but it did make it slightly easier to shrug off the effects.

And so, even as the Vacant Knight pulled back its blade readying what would be a life-ending stroke, Jacob swapped his [Mace] to a single hand and with a shrug of his left shoulder slid the [Plank Shield] into place low on his forearm.

When the deadly blade began to fall, Jacob was there, stepping into the Vacant Knight's arc. He swept his [Plank Shield] up and out in a forceful sweeping blow. It caught the Vacant Knight's hilt and threw the blade out wide, exposing the hideous jerky-skinned creature for Jacob's follow-up attack.

In came the [Mace] with startling speed. It cracked through the rusted breastplate and into the creature's ribs. The sound that emanated from the crumbling ribcage was like somebody balling up a sheet of bubble wrap.

The Vacant Knight doubled over, stunned. Jacob was already turning a complete circuit, building up momentum for the final hit in the two-hit riposte combo.

With a slight upward arc, Jacob's [Mace] hit the Vacant Knight square on the chin, its head burst into a fine silver mist moments before the rest of the monster's body did. A sound like ringing metal accompanied it.

Its white wisp, bearing a hefty reward of Souls, joined its brethren that finally found the bottom of the chasm as both wisps flew into Jacob's chest.

The sensation, as always, was cold but exhilarating.

Parry!
You Riposte the [Vacant Knight] *for 520 points of damage.*
You defeat the [Vacant Knight].
You defeat the [Vacant Knight].
Awarded 1,600 Souls.
Mace Skill increases to Level 2...3...4...5.

For a brief moment, Jacob considered going back to the Pyre to spend his Souls. But by resting at a Pyre any enemies – barring special creatures like these Vacant Knights – would reset and be there again.

The white mist was the telltale sign that they were more than a standard monster. Despite having run into other Vacant Knights a decade ago, he had to admit that these two looked and acted a little differently.

Normally all monsters would reappear in the exact places they were before Jacob's interference if he rested at a Pyre. It made farming for Souls easy. Items wouldn't reappear, and any major events that took place would remain.

The mace skill up message was... strange. He never remembered gaining more than a single skill level, no matter how hard the enemies were or how great his skill had progressed.

But rather than achieving level 2 in mace skill, he was at level 5. Could Alice have been wrong? While he wasn't *skilled* in using a mace, he understood the mechanics well enough to wield one.

Maybe Pyresouls was trying to sync up his innate knowledge with his skill level. He needed to find a sword. If he could, and he was indeed gaining enhanced skill levels to match his knowledge, he would gain tens of levels.

Back on Earth, his sword skill was a lofty 75.

He never would have thought he could take both of them before. At

800 Souls each, they were far more rewarding than the typical Vacant. Too bad they couldn't be farmed for an easy boost to Souls.

Doubling back to the Pyre would waste another hour or more he didn't have and the only benefit would be to raise another parameter. Something he could do at the next Pyre instead, all while gaining ground.

Jacob edged forward toward the broken corpse and touched its sapphire wisp, curious what item it held.

You gain a [Dull Spark].

Now he really was tempted to return to the Pyre.

Which was a shame, because once he found some proper armor he would need [Dull Sparks] to upgrade it.

He had to remind himself that this wasn't the weapon he wanted to continue using. And he most *definitely* did not want to keep these ratty robes on him. One look down at the throbbing gash across his chest and the blood-soaked parchment-colored robes confirmed that.

Jacob turned around, leaving the tunnel behind and taking the other path in the fork. His [Plank Shield] vanished with a swirl of ash, a glowing glass ampoule appeared in his left palm.

Crushing the [Cinder Ampoule], the mote of flame held within bloomed and spread across his entire body. It was a tiny fragment of the Fire Oppa's Pyre and as such, it didn't hurt but healed.

His wounds knit in an instant and for a single moment, the comforting warmth of the Pyre was with him.

All too soon, it was gone, and Jacob was alone again.

That was something he'd need to get used to again. Even after the Collapse, he was always part of some group or another. The lowest points of his entire life were the times he was alone.

You couldn't sleep, couldn't take a break, and even if you tried it didn't work. Knowing what was out there made it impossible. Your brain was constantly in a state of hypervigilance.

At least in Pyresouls the fighting and struggling didn't last years.

The competition hardly lasted two weeks before Alec found the Burgon Beast and inadvertently let it loose upon the world.

If all else failed, Jacob knew exactly where that was and what time. At the very least he could be there, beside Alec to help him battle the Burgon Beast. If he could even find Alec.

By the time the monster began collapsing the shards and destroying Pyres, it would be too late. And if he was already behind Alec at that point, he didn't like his chances of facing the Burgon Beast alone.

Jacob needed to not only get there before Alec, but to do so with more strength and power than the other man.

If things went according to plan, he would beat Alec there and destroy the Burgon Beast himself. Somehow. It wasn't like Alec had beaten the creature and was able to pass on his winning strategy.

As if to contrast his suddenly darkening thoughts, a watery gray light bloomed at the end of the dark tunnel.

After the oppressive darkness of the tunnels through the Razorpass, Jacob had to squint against the ashen sunlight that greeted him as he emerged northward out of the tunnel.

High up in the mountains, he could easily spot the winding switchback that would lead him down to either the Stalking Woods dead north, or into the narrow canyon passage that was Weslyn's Watch to the northwest.

As much as he felt the tug of familiarity pulling him to the Stalking Wood, he knew where his path lay and instead turned northeast along a narrow scree-ridden path that would take him to the Steps of Penance.

There, according to Alec, he would find the body of a Knight and be able to get some proper gear. Not to mention, there was a Pyre nearby that would allow him to rest and recover.

With those 1,600 Souls, he would be able to reinforce a parameter twice. No doubt there were nasty things waiting for him up ahead. The pale daylight that filtered from above didn't make him feel any better.

Something was wrong with the sun in Pyresouls, it didn't warm the way it should. There was a coldness to everything that slowly wormed its way into your very bones. That bleak, gray light promised nothing. No hope. No brighter tomorrow.

Picking his way carefully ahead, the slippery mountain path began to spread and open its arms wide, revealing a vast mist-filled gorge between the towering mountain he was on and a taller one wreathed in a mantle of white snow in the distance.

"The Steps of Penance are inappropriately named," Alec had said. *"It's a massive, half-broken bridge. You'll want to find the narrow paths and long beams on top of the bridge and on the edges.*

"Do not go inside. There are all manner of ghoulish creatures within the twisting hallways beneath the top level of the bridge. They are the stuff of nightmares. You remember asking me why I insisted on finding an alternative route instead of crossing the Arlington Memorial Bridge in D.C.? It's because of the Steps of Penance. Mind your footing, Jacob. And for God's sake, whatever you do: Do not go inside the bridge."

"I hate heights," Jacob muttered as he made his way down to the base of the wide bridge. Drawing near, he could see exactly what Alec had meant.

The damn thing was falling apart. It was as wide as any modern bridge back home, enough for two lanes of traffic in each direction. Only difference was, the stone paving was caved in more often than not and the whole thing was poised over a misty gorge whose bottom was impossible to discern.

In more than one of those darkened pits that fell to the inner sections of the bridge, Jacob could make out faint movement and glowing blood-red eyes watching him.

Licking his lips nervously, Jacob stepped onto the bridge.

<u>The Steps of Penance</u>

The sudden words that appeared telling him the name of the area – which he already knew – nearly gave him a heart attack. He was so focused on everything around him, expecting an attack at any moment that the simple prompt had startled him more than it should have.

Already he could see that less than a hundred feet across, he would be forced into the upper floors of the bridge. There wasn't much activity on the bridge in front of him, a few Vacant were milling about aimlessly.

From time to time they'd bump into each other or a pillar but mostly they stood still. If he moved quietly enough – usually impossible in a suit of armor – he could slip behind them and dispatch them one by one.

Taking another tentative step forward and berating himself for taking so long, Jacob discovered something that the trailblazing Alec never knew. There was a lumbering boulder-throwing giant up on the mountain behind him. And if you stood still long enough, it would notice you.

And Jacob had spent far too much time mulling over Alec's warning and picking out his path carefully.

The giant's echoing grunt that rolled down the mountainside was Jacob's only warning.

He dove to the side, tucked his shoulder, and rolled trying to get as much distance as he could from the sailing missile he knew would smear him into a fine paste across the bridge.

With a mighty teeth-rattling crash, the boulder struck the bridge and skipped a few times before taking out two Vacant too dim-witted to get out of the way in time. Even as the white wisps flew toward him, granting him another 300 Souls, the bridge gave a deep, disturbing groan.

Before Jacob could register the omen for what it was, the surface of the bridge began to buckle and crack. The massive boulder fell into the bridge and then made another sharp report as it fell down another level deeper.

He barely managed two strides before his feet met nothing but dark air and then he was falling.

8

Without any proper armor or even a basic helmet, it was a miracle Jacob survived the collapse of the bridge's top layer. Except, now he was precisely where Alec had expressly told him *not* to venture.

The ride down had been sudden and jarring, luckily the sharp-edged bricks and hard stone broke his fall. He ached in a dozen different places.

Groaning and covered in stone dust and debris, Jacob sluggishly rose to his feet, bracing himself against a rotten beam of wood to his left. The dark was somehow worse than the lightless tunnel coming out of the Razor Pass.

It pressed in on all sides as if it were a living thing. With everything Jacob had seen those last ten years, he wouldn't be surprised if it was.

A quick look at his Health bar showed him that he only lost a tenth of his Health in the fall. Turning his gaze to the ragged dusty hole in the ceiling some twenty feet above him, Jacob knew he wasn't going to be climbing out anytime soon.

Judging by the damage done, he was surprised this level of the bridge hadn't collapsed too. Without any idea where the Pyre was from his present location, Jacob decided to save his remaining 4 [Cinder Ampoules] for when he was really hurt.

The only problem was, with so little Health and defense it would not be hard to imagine a single powerful strike ending his life if he was not at full Health.

Sitting here isn't going to do me any good.

Jacob took hold of his [Mace] a little tighter and double-checked the straps on his [Plank Shield] to see if they still held, before taking his first furtive steps into the dark room.

Crates and barrels – many broken or covered in the recent debris – lined the far walls. Fear and trepidation washed over him as he tried to peer into the dark passageway ahead. There was nothing but a simple stone archway leading out of the room, from which Jacob could hear nothing.

Heart jackhammering in his chest, Jacob forced himself to take steady strides forward. Each footfall was practically a stomp and it no doubt looked ridiculous. But it was the only way to keep going when that primal fear of the dark unknown welled up inside him.

[Plank Shield] lifted up and at the ready to intercept any coming attack, Jacob stepped out of his room. If it brought the attention of any nearby creatures, they didn't show themselves.

The hallway ran to his left and right, barely wide enough for two men abreast. Several holes in the ceiling let in shafts of dusty light. Instead of illuminating, the pillars of light ruined what night vision he was able to acquire whenever he glanced their way.

It only made the dark that much more foreboding.

Inch by inch, Jacob made his way through the halls that created a maze within the upper level of the bridge. Loose stones and rotted planks showed him that there were at least two more levels below this one inside the bridge. The rasping, wheezing noises he heard from below made him test his footing often.

And so, concerned more with his footing than his surroundings, Jacob didn't see the tall lanky figure step out of a shadowed alcove. It tore three lines of nauseating agony down his exposed back.

The [Graceful Penitent] slashes you for 78 points of damage.

Trying to break through the haze of pain, Jacob lurched ahead. His legs buckled more from the pain than his own conscious prompting and he just barely managed to tuck into a roll at the last minute. The swish of air above his head told him he narrowly missed the following deathblow.

He struggled to his feet and brandished his mace, only to see another lanky bandage-wrapped creature with hooks embedded in its skin emerge from another previously unseen alcove.

Jacob cursed and tried to come up with a plan as he slowly backed away from his advancing too-tall adversaries. Nearly seven feet tall, their limbs were unnervingly long and lean with hands that fell past their knees on their too-long legs.

He never heard, nor saw anything about these creatures. They carried flails with three blades at the end of long chains. Their faces were set in a lipless grinning rictus. With their eyes covered in bloody bandages, Jacob wondered how they could see.

With a flash of ash, Jacob called forth a [Cinder Ampoule] and crushed it. The blaze of fire illuminated the section of the hallway, showing at least another half-dozen alcoves. Roused by his use of the [Cinder Ampoule], the other alcoves began to stir.

You use a [Cinder Ampoule] and recover 120 Health.

Focused on those in front of him and the ones off to the sides that he could barely make out, Jacob was on high alert when he heard the shuffling scrape of a bandaged foot behind him. He rolled to the left, hearing the same telltale *swish* of a flail meeting nothing but air.

And there he made his first fatal mistake.

Cloaked in darkness, Jacob couldn't make out when the stone flooring transitioned into dry-rotted planking until he was already mid-roll. He heard the ominous creaking but could do nothing about it.

As he got to his feet he tried to vault forward, hoping to find some sturdier ground. The rotten planks gave way beneath the push and instead of springing forward, he fell once more into the depths of the bridge. Ten feet, twenty feet, thirty feet, until finally, he hit something solid.

Though not quite as solid as he hoped.

His Health dropped a full third and before he could so much as take a breath, the flooring beneath him crumbled to dust.

He fell a long, long way.

The bottom of the bridge arched up above him, growing fainter with every passing heartbeat. He knew it would hurt but Jacob would come back. It wasn't so far a walk from the Razor Pass Pyre and this time he would be better equipped to deal with those *things*.

After a very long fall through a shroud of white mist, Jacob finally found the bottom of the gorge.

You Died.

With a jolt of fear and panic, Jacob sat up. He looked about frantically and then realized where he was and what he was doing. Crossing his legs, Jacob took one steadying breath after the other.

I'll get used to it, he reminded himself.

After so long fearing the day death would finally claim its due, he forgot what it felt like to be revived by the Pyre.

Only now, he would acquire a level of curse. Just to make sure, Jacob looked at his status screen.

[Status]

Jacob Windsor
    Covenant: None
    Race: Kemora - Fae-touched (Human/Fairy)
    Level: 2
    Health: 124
    Stamina: 86
    Anima: 0

Souls: 0
Required Souls: 690

Parameters
VIT: 3
AGI: 6
END: 3
TMP: 9
STR: 4
DEX: 5
INT: 8
FTH: 3

Curse: Fractured Sight
Curse Level: 1

Spell Gem: No Spell Inscribed

"That took longer than I figured," the Fire Oppa said. He trotted over to Jacob and put one paw on Jacob's knee in a gesture of compassion. "You are safe here."

Jacob shook his head. "No, I am not. Every death is a delay I cannot afford." He pushed to his feet, checking his equipment. Ten years without a revival mechanic like the Pyres was a long time. He was still wary that something was wrong.

Something *more* than gaining a level of curse and losing all his Souls.

Kneeling, Jacob reached out to the Fire Oppa and pet along his long sleek flame-licked body. The Fire Oppa let out a low contended series of dooks. "I wish I had more time to speak to you, maybe when this is all over. Hopefully, when I see you next, it'll be at the next Pyre."

Jacob took off at a fast trot.

He sprinted right past the now-empty path that had once led to the Vacant Knights, sticking to the left path out of the tunnel and taking a sharp right along the scree-ridden path. He didn't slow down, not until he nearly slipped.

If he took another fatal tumble, those Souls would be lost forever.

That was one of the iconic things about Pyresouls, it was punishing. When you died you were sent back to the last Pyre you rested at. And at the site of your death, an emerald wisp would form containing all the Souls and Anima you managed to gather up to that point.

At the same time, it gave a level of curse. The first level was more of a warning. After that, the effects of the curse began to kick in. Each curse was different. For Fractured Sight, Jacob would begin seeing things that weren't really there.

If used responsibly, he heard of several players maintaining a mild curse level of 3 to 4. Strong enough that he could pierce through the veil but not so much that he attracted too much unwanted attention from the other side.

Being able to see other paths also meant that hidden pathways, shrouded enemies, and illusory doors and walls, were all visible to him. Pyresouls had a great deal of that, not to mention many traps. Being able to avoid them or take a hidden path altogether would be immensely helpful.

Jacob reached the Steps of Penance in record time.

Staying near the mountain, he looked for a way up to where he thought the giant was, but he couldn't make out a path that wouldn't have him climbing a sheer cliff face.

It was a long shot anyway. He was not sure he would even want to fight a giant at this level. Jacob turned his attention to the massive bridge ahead of him, hoping that the Pyre also reset the damage to the structure.

What little hopes he had were dashed as he saw the state of the bridge.

It was still damaged, though the two roaming Vacant that were crushed were now milling around at the edge of the ragged hole leading deeper into the bridge.

Coming out from the mountain, Jacob hurried to the lip of the hole and jumped down on top of the tallest rubble pile. He nearly lost his balance once or twice as the stone and brick beneath him settled under his weight.

Soon enough, Jacob was picking his way carefully down the pile and into the archway beyond. He sidestepped the archway and paused a moment, wondering if the two Vacant that were above had seen him and would follow.

Several heartbeats later, and without any sign of the Vacant, Jacob continued on.

Only this time, he knew where to look to spot the darkened alcoves. They were easy to miss, shallow dark archways set into the walls that were just a few shades darker than the stonework around them.

Normally considered an annoyance, the Pyre reset the monsters back to their original location before your interference, whenever you rested at it or died and woke up there. In this instance, however, it was a blessing. The Graceful Penitents were sleeping in their alcoves instead of wandering about.

Jacob once more took his [Mace] in a two-handed grip and quietly as he could, sidled up in front of one of the alcoves. As close as he was, he could see the hideous slender creature with limbs that were far too long and dry cracked desiccated skin that was wrapped in bloody bandages in all its gruesome glory.

Hardly daring to breathe, Jacob cocked back the [Mace] and then threw everything he had into the strike right at its head, hoping to cave it in before the thing ever woke up.

Exploited Weakness!
You strike the [Graceful Penitent] *for 332 points of damage.*
You consume 40 Stamina.
You defeat the [Graceful Penitent].
Awarded 350 Souls.

It was a short-lived celebration because the sound of the attack woke the others and soon the hallway was once again littered with the grotesque, half-dead creations.

Curious, Jacob knelt down quickly and picked up a piece of rubble and tossed it clear across the hallway. Disturbingly, several heads swiveled in unison to look in the direction of the sound.

Jacob was all but forgotten.

He grinned, realizing that they weren't like other Vacant. Now that he thought about it, they probably weren't Vacant at all.

Their seven-foot-tall frames should have been a dead giveaway. They were not human, but they *were* blind. The bandages weren't just a red herring but an actual clue as to their weakness.

Gathering up a few pebbles and placing them in a pouch on his hip for easy access, Jacob stalked as quietly as he could to the nearest Graceful Penitent. Gripping his [Mace] in both hands, he snuck up so close to the emaciated creature that he could have spit on it.

Arching his back away from the creature, Jacob gathered all of his strength into that single overhead chop with his [Mace]. The flanged mace head completely obliterated the thing's skull like a hammer to an overripe pumpkin.

Backstab!
You strike the [Graceful Penitent] for 456 points of damage.
You consume 40 Stamina.
You defeat the [Graceful Penitent].
Awarded 350 Souls.
Mace Skill increases to Level 6...7...8...9.

Quickly as he could – and while keeping his feet perfectly still, which was not easy with so many of the ghastly creatures turning his way – Jacob took out a pebble and tossed it across the hall.

Predictably, the stupid creatures were lured by the same sound once again.

One by one, Jacob snuck up on the remaining Graceful Penitents and ended their wretched existence. Such easy tricks would not work for long, and Jacob took full advantage of the simple diversionary tactic.

With the way cleared, Jacob approached the glowing emerald wisp floating a few inches above the ground near where he had died.

While Pyresouls Online was often unfair, brutal, and even downright sadistic, it wasn't impossible.

Despite the fact that Jacob fell a full level down and then through that to the distant chasm below, his wisp wasn't hundreds of feet down in the rocky gorge where he died.

The player's wisp would often be found at the site of where their death originated. Jumping off a cliff – a common way of dying, whether intentional or not – would spawn the emerald wisp at the edge of where they leaped off.

Anything else would be nearly impossible to recover, and in some cases, their wisp would be located somewhere more accessible based on the series of events that got them killed in the first place.

After Jacob left Pyresouls before the Collapse, the boards were beginning to call it the Death Point Origination or DPO.

If a string of events predicated a player's death, then their wisp would spawn just before that series began. Allowing the player to learn from their past mistake and improve themselves.

Jacob leaned forward and touched his emerald wisp.

Souls Retrieved.

There was nothing he could do about his curse level aside from getting lucky and finding some Anima, using that to lower his curse level back to zero.

Just to be sure he double-checked his Souls to make sure they were there. It had been a long time since Jacob played Pyresouls Online. Dying in the real world Post-Collapse was not something that you could come back from.

Including the recently acquired Souls, he was sitting at 3,677 Souls. With so many Souls, he could get a jump on leveling. Despite what Alec had said, the interior of the bridge seemed positively lucrative.

All it cost was a small bit of his sanity and a truly horrifying death that only reinforced his fear of heights.

Satisfied that everything was in order, he looked around the darkened space. Alec never told him anything about the interior of the Steps of Penance. Only that up on the bridge near one of the stairways going into the dark was the corpse of a knight.

From him, Jacob could retrieve the knight's armor and, if he was lucky, a sword. That last part was random chance according to Alec. Some players found a sword, others found extra souls while many more found nothing but the knightly armor set.

Hefting his [Mace], Jacob tried to keep in mind that he picked Cleric for a reason. Not for the paper-thin armor but for the weapon he held in his hand. Having looked at the damage it did, he couldn't fault Alec's opinion of the weapon. It performed admirably for a starter weapon.

Particularly since Jacob was quite weak at the moment. With any luck, he might find a Pyre down in the dark winding corridors.

One of the few benefits to his light armor was the bonus to stealth. He was far quieter in robes than he would be in the knight's armor set.

Stealth wasn't his preferred approach, though. It took time to set up the proper encounters and led to more death than success, in his opinion.

Neither did he like charging head-long into battle, rattling in heavy armor like somebody with a kitchen's worth of pots and pans strapped to his body. Some players went the heavy route and thoroughly enjoyed the "tankiness" of their builds.

That was all well and good, up until it wasn't. The problem with all-or-nothing builds was their over-reliance on their specific strength or gimmick.

A rogue style would be powerful in the right situations. The problem was, Pyresouls had so many different situations that it rarely threw the same one at you twice.

Sneaking around would mean that you would lose out on potential Souls from killing enemies. Relying on backstabs and sneak attacks meant large groups of enemies – a common sight further into the game – was almost impossible.

And then there were the bosses. When you were pitted against one of the many bosses of Pyresouls, there was no place to hide or sneak. The boss *knew* you were there, and while particularly skilled players could still hide, they had to work extra hard at doing so.

Meanwhile, the tanky players could shrug off blows like they were minor annoyances for the most part. Until they ran into a monster that used deadly magic or enemy rogues.

Heavy armor was slow. While it was physically sturdy, its magic defenses were usually pretty weak. That was why Jacob preferred medium armor, the middle-ground of physical and magical defense with the downside that it was almost impossible to sneak in.

Not much of a downside to Jacob. Though as he slid one foot in front of the other, testing the ground for weaknesses, he realized sneaking had served him fairly well in the oppressive halls.

The maze-like hall doubled back on itself more than once, and Jacob nearly slipped into the same alcove as one of the sleeping Graceful Penitents.

For the better part of an hour, Jacob explored those winding passages, felling a waking Graceful Penitent only when necessary and sneaking by whenever possible. Sneaking would hardly be an option for long, he was committed to using it while he had the chance.

Aside from an assortment of Souls, he received a strange accessory off one of the penitents. A [Ring of Blameless Guilt]. It was a simple ring, nothing more than an iron band with a black jewel set in the middle.

With only two ring slots to use, Jacob equipped the ring to his first slot. He felt no immediate difference and decided to give the ring a deeper examination.

Ring of Blameless Guilt
Ring granted to the Penitent who saw fit to take upon the Guilt of the masses to heal the dark heart of the world. Increases Maximum Burden.

Despite himself, Jacob felt that familiar thrill of danger and excitement. The anticipation of what lay around the next bend; treasures, traps, or monsters.

Jacob had to remind himself that this was so much more than a game to him now, the future of everything he knew rested on his unworthy shoulders.

His first time playing, he never took the time to savor the feeling of adventure and discovery. And now, he would be irresponsible to indulge in it.

Ironic, he thought as he came to a crossroads. The hall to his right was partially caved in with rubble, the way ahead seemed clear, and the path on his left held a faint illumination from one of the nearby doors.

Always go left, he thought to himself. It was, after all, the motto he took whenever he had to choose a path ahead. If that path failed, then he'd take the next in a clockwise fashion.

It never steered him wrong before.

Taking the left hallway, Jacob quickly found himself at the side of the door he spied earlier. Faint light spilled out through the cracks in the rough planks, but he could hear no noise from within.

Tightening his grip on his [Mace], Jacob opened the door and immediately lifted his [Plank Shield]. There was a creature sitting in the corner, slumped and likely dead.

But as Jacob approached warily, the thing stirred and drew in a rattling breath. Its eyes glowed in their sockets, and it regarded him mistrustfully at first until its eyes alighted on his ring.

"Ah," it wheezed. "One of the Penitent. Good it is to see you, brother. Come, rest by the fire." The husk of a man waved one shriveled arm toward a measly pile of ashes on the floor.

Still wary, Jacob sat so the man was on his right while he faced the door to his left. He was far from the ideal position of his back to the wall, but a quick look within the medium-sized stone storage room showed no immediate threats and no other entrances or exits.

A stirring warmth pulsed in his chest as he realized this wasn't just any extinguished campfire.

It was a Pyre.

Jacob leaned forward and closed his eyes. He concentrated on the flames of warming life as he held out his hand above the cold ashes. A bead of flame fell from his palm.

Pyre Ignited.
Your respawn location has been set to the **Steps of Penance.**
The Fire Oppa stokes the embers of your conviction.
Health, Stamina, Ampoules, and Spell Gems restored.

Slowly, the ashes began to remember their purpose. Embers peeked through the dust, then tiny tongues of flame danced upon the powder until a small cozy fire sprang forth in a flash consuming his hand.

If it was anything other than a Pyre, his hand would have been burned to a crisp. Instead, Jacob felt only comfort and warmth.

"Well, that sure didn't take you long," Fire Oppa said, making his way out of the ashes and shaking them loose from fiery fur. "Steps of Penance, huh? Not bad, not bad at all."

Jacob noticed the Fire Oppa burned a little brighter, stood a little stronger.

The husk, though he looked like a Vacant, did not act aggressively like one. He sat propped up against the wall watching Jacob with a curious expression. Filthy bandages were wrapped all over his withered limbs, and his expression was one of sorrow instead of the typical blind rage seen on most Vacant.

"Can he see you?" Jacob asked the Fire Oppa, lowering his voice so only the small creature could hear him.

"Nope. He can hear *you*, but I'm beyond his awareness. He is linked to you, however, as are most of the sentient creatures that still possess a spark of their soul still."

"What do you mean by that?"

"Normally, if you rest at a Pyre, every monster comes back, right? Well, those with some shred of sentience still left become... what's the word... *entangled* with you. Their timestreams join your own, and if you kill them...."

Jacob nodded his understanding. If he killed the husk against the wall or any creature that could likely be reasoned with, they would be gone for good. At least to Jacob's reckoning.

It was a tactful warning about taking unnecessary precautions against creatures that might not be aggressive. How many such entities had he taken out on his first playthrough?

Pyresouls terrified him back then. He hadn't yet been hardened by the reality of the Collapse and the edge-of-death that every day brought. Zombies used to be a deep fear of his.

When they became an everyday affair, one that often needed to be violently dealt with, they lost their fearful edge. He hated them, and that hatred gave him the power to push past his fear.

"You got a name?" Jacob asked the husk.

For a long moment, the husk stared pensively at him, gap-toothed and slackjawed. Eventually, he roused from his stupor and said, "Brother Aker. And you?"

"Jacob."

"Brother Jacob, how nice to make your acquaintance. You know, the world's going to end."

Jacob swallowed hard and stared at Brother Aker. "In many ways, it seems like it already has."

"Too true, too true indeed." Aker wagged a desiccated finger at him. "You Penitent, always so perceptive. But enough doom and gloom! I see you have some Souls on you. Seeing as you're a man of faith such as myself, I would consider it an honor to trade with you."

There was nothing he ever read about a man named Brother Aker on any board or in any conversations with Alec. Jacob looked down at his ring, the black teardrop-shaped jewel glittered in the dancing firelight.

Would Brother Aker have attacked him if he didn't wear the ring? Or would he have said something else entirely and refused to trade with him?

In the days before the Collapse, people who had left Pyresouls early or were disqualified had started to put together a repository of information. One of them was a list of NPCs – or what they thought were NPCs at the time – that could be traded with or used to get unique gear and quests.

At the time, everybody thought Pyresouls would open up to the general audience after the competition, and many people – even those who barely left the first Pyre out of fear – were eager to jump in again and explore the dark world of Lormar.

Of course, it didn't happen like that. The game became all too real, and without the life-sustaining Pyres to respawn or improve one's parameters.

"All right, Brother Aker," Jacob said, "what have you got to trade?"

9

As it turned out, Aker had a lot to sell.

[Brother Aker's Shop]

[Repair Powder] -- *500 Souls*
    [Throwing Knife] -- *10 Souls*
    [Firebomb] -- *50 Souls*
    [Repair Kit] -- *2,000 Souls*
    [Dagger] -- *1,300 Souls*
    [Shortsword] -- *1,600 Souls*
    [Hatchet] -- *1,450 Souls*
    [Club] -- *1,500 Souls*
    [Bladed Whip] -- *3,200 Souls*
    [Buckler] -- *1,800 Souls*
    [Arrow] -- *10 Souls*
    [Large Arrow] -- *50 Souls*
    [Bolt] -- *30 Souls*
    [Large Bolt] -- *80 Souls*

[Holy Water] -- *500 Souls*

The prices, while high, weren't particularly surprising. Merchants that were found outside of "safe" areas usually charged a premium. In a world where being without a weapon was synonymous with a death sentence, weapons were always expensive.

With a quick glance at his current stock of 4,727 Souls, he was in a good position to buy anything Aker had for sale. Unfortunately, Aker didn't have any armor. Not that he expected him to.

The nearest merchant that sold armor was quite a ways away. By the time he got to him, he would have better armor than the rusted and flimsy [Chainmail] that wretch sold.

[Firebombs] were useful if he ran into an enemy weak to fire but he had other plans for those types and wasting Souls so early seemed foolish. With any luck, he would have a better weapon than a [Shortsword] soon enough.

Fighting with the [Mace] was a lot harder than he thought it would be. And though his skill continued to rise at an astonishing rate, it paled in comparison to what he expected from wielding a sword.

The weapon was undeniably strong, far stronger than he originally gave it credit for. The problem was its reach was so short that it required him to get far too close for comfort to get in a proper hit.

His preferred weapon, the [Longsword] had a significantly longer reach and could deal two types of damage depending on the way he attacked. Thrusts provided piercing damage while standard swipes dealt slashing.

He always wanted to try a [Bastard Sword], though he never quite had enough STR to swing it properly.

One item did stand out to him, however. He reached forward to the [Bladed Whip].

The coiled leather was wrapped in long jagged blades sticking out at odd angles. Only the handle was safe to touch and as the length of whip unfurled it hit the floor with a rattle, like hail on a tin roof.

Brother Aker giggled, quite disturbingly. "I knew you would pick that one! Penitent through and through, I see. Knew it when I saw that ring. You are a true believer! That price is for one of the Brothers such as yourself, quite a rare and expensive item. You'll bleed out all that Guilt in no time."

Prompted by the husk's words, Jacob examined the item in further detail.

Bladed Whip
An unwieldy item that exceptionally devout Penitents use to self-flagellate, ridding themselves of the Guilt they have borne out of sacrifice to their fellow man. Of poor make, the item is just as likely to turn on its wielder as it is to strike at a foe.

Physical Damage: 87
    Type: Slashing
    Scaling: DEX [B]

Magical Damage: 35
    Arcane: 0
    Fire: 0
    Water: 0
    Earth: 0
    Harmony: 0
    Chaos: 35

Status Infliction
    Bleed: 50
    Poison: 0
    Curse: 0
    Stagger: 0
    Break: 0

. . .

Durability: 200/200
Guilt: 3

The Guilt was heavy but manageable with his stats. Chaos damage was one of the rarest types. Most of the enemies in Pyresouls were mortal or had once been mortal, so Chaos damage did exceedingly well against them.

Technically, the total AR of the weapon was stronger than his [Mace]. The [Bladed Whip] was a grand total of 122. Comparatively, his [Mace] was only 100 damage and dealt nothing but blunt.

Nothing in the item's parameters said it would work particularly well on the enemies nearby except the brief mention in its description. That, combined with what Aker said, made Jacob wonder if there was a hidden attribute to the weapon.

There was some part of him that simply wanted the whip for the sake of owning one. His favorite game growing up had been the VR hit Castlevania: Brotherhood of Shadow. Simon Belmont was one of his childhood idols and he loved the vampire slayer's characteristic weapon.

The world was filled with heroes that used far more practical and versatile weapons like swords, hammers, and spears. But it was just cool the way you could swing from a conveniently hanging branch with a whip or knock off a skeleton's head with a resounding whip crack.

Not that he desired to face skeletons again in Pyresouls.

No other game made skeletons – typically the fodder of any fantasy game – so terrifyingly overpowered and deadly. He would have no choice but to run from them if he stumbled across even a few skeletons.

Deciding he had enough Souls to spare, Jacob purchased the [Bladed Whip] and equipped it. Immediately he felt the strain of Guilt lay a heavy burden on his heart. Together with his [Mace], that brought him to 4 Guilt, a little less than half of his Temper.

He could feel the Guilt of the whip's past owners. Their failure and lamentations over the death of their loved ones. No amount of physical weight could compare to the burden that coursed through his limbs. And yet, when he went to move he didn't feel slow at all.

He should be at the second or third tier of Guilt already, somewhere between a 10% and 25% Movement and Stamina penalty. Except, he was light on his feet as if the feeling deep in his chest wasn't there at all.

Moving around experimentally, Jacob caught a flash of light on his hand and realized what was doing it. The [Ring of Blameless Guilt] said it increased "Maximum Burden" but there was no parameter by that name.

A red light shimmered within the darkness of the black teardrop jewel set in the middle of the iron band. Jacob could guess easily enough that what it meant was that by wearing the ring he could withstand more Guilt than normal.

As tempted as he was to confirm his theory and take off the ring, he didn't. Not only because Brother Aker might attack him – no longer able to tell he was a friend because he took the ring off – but because some rings would break as soon as they were removed.

Particularly powerful rings.

Since Jacob had never *once* heard of a ring that could increase the burden of his Guilt, he was not about to risk it.

The ring itself was a game-changer. At 4 Guilt he should have been slowed at least a little bit, but there was nothing. At the very least, the [Ring of Blameless Guilt] acted like he had +2 Temper. If not more.

Likely, it was a percentage but the specifics didn't matter. What mattered was that the ring allowed him to spend points on other stats. Temper was only useful to keep him out of any serious penalties. He would accept a 10% penalty but once he reached the third tier of 25%, the cost would be too high to fight effectively.

Not with Pyresoul's legendary drawn-out battles of attrition it would become known for. It was not something most people built their parameters for. Even Alec only realized the dire importance of Temper late into the competition.

He accredited his shift to farming Souls later on specifically to boost his Temper as the reason he was able to get past some of the harder areas and get to the main boss of the game itself, the Burgon Beast.

"Anything else catch your fancy?" Aker asked, "No? Well all right, may the Guilt rest comfortably upon your bowed shoulders, brother. I'll be here for a spell if you change your mind."

With a nod, Jacob returned to the campfire and sat down.

He was going to continue pumping TMP so he would be able to wear the knight's armor without much strain but his new ring changed that plan.

Jacob took a look at his stats, mulling over what parameter he should increase next. The plan he had kept in his head all along was altered but it only meant he could skip a few Levels of increasing his TMP.

There was no way the ring was so powerful that he would never need to increase his TMP again.

[Status]

Jacob Windsor
Covenant: None
Race: Kemora - Fae-touched (Human/Fairy)
Level: 2
Health: 124
Stamina: 86
Anima: 0
Souls: 1,527
Required Souls: 690

Parameters
VIT: 3
AGI: 6
END: 3

TMP: 9
STR: 4
DEX: 5
INT: 8
FTH: 3

Curse: Fractured Sight
Curse Level: 1

Spell Gem: No Spell Inscribed

If his memory was right, the parameter improvement after next would be around 700. He would have just enough Souls.

Even with 2 points of VIT, he wasn't going to be much sturdier. Armor would work better than raw Health, especially with his paper-thin robes.

More STR would increase his damage with the [Mace] but the [Bladed Whip] scaled off of DEX, making any increases to STR useless while wielding it. And he had a hunch about the whip that he wanted to test out.

Stronger weapons often required upwards of 10 DEX in order to wield. Something that came as a shock to most players who had built specifically for STR then realized they needed thousands of Souls to move their DEX a single point.

Each parameter increase raised the cost for the next, just like traditional levels would in most other games. He *could* leave his DEX at 5 – many people had left theirs much lower – and continue on his way gaining Souls and increasing his other stats.

But when he came across an item many levels later that required even 7 points of DEX, if he was in his 20s, that'd require 5,000 Souls or more just to move 2 points of DEX.

Hitting the common breakpoints for weapons and gear earlier

meant that he could equip the items as soon as he found them. The rest of his time could be dedicated to increasing his combat prowess.

Jacob spent his Souls to increase his DEX 1 point. He breathed a sigh of relief when the next parameter cost was only 707, just within his amount of Souls. He spent those 707 Souls to raise his DEX another point, to a total of 7.

Unlike most other games, increasing his level didn't make him directly more powerful. On the contrary, the common consensus among surviving players was that the creatures in Lormar actually became *stronger* with each level a player in their shard gained.

Of course, like every other theory about the game, it was just that - a theory. Nobody knew for sure *how* Pyresouls worked. Their best "rules" were little more than anecdotes.

Level was just a useful tracker to know how many times a person's parameters were reinforced. His Health or Stamina would only go up if he raised the appropriate parameter.

While 2 points in DEX may not seem like much, it made him significantly more adroit than most humans. At 7 DEX, he was approaching levels of deftness that even heavily augmented humans struggled to reach. And he was one step closer to the 10 DEX he would need for some of the heavier kite shields he intended to use.

In the meantime, he would get a nice little boost to the damage of his [Bladed Whip], which he took out and uncoiled with a rattle of sharpened metal plates on the stone floor.

"You're going to cut yourself with that," the Fire Oppa said, eyeing the weapon lazily. He crossed his paws and laid his head atop them.

Remembering his earlier vow, Jacob dismissed his shield and reached to pet the Fire Oppa's small head. While he already pet the Fire Oppa once, he was eager to do so again.

Precious few animals - ones that were neither mutated nor violent - existed on Earth. Whenever he touched the Fire Oppa, he was filled with the most soul-soothing sensation. As if the cold corpse of Lormar could rise from the ashes and live again.

He brushed the thing's fiery, rounded bear-like ears back and heard a distinct rumbling sound emanate from the creature. His tail puffed up and thrashed about behind him, fanning the flames of the Pyre higher.

"You like that, huh?" Jacob asked, smiling at the warmth that spread through him and the obvious enjoyment of the Fire Oppa. "Is that your name, Fire Oppa?"

"No, that is what *I am*."

"Then, what is your name?"

The Fire Oppa, whose eyes had shut in contentment, popped open a single dark eye to regard him. "Perhaps later," he said.

Jacob didn't press the point. He was far from well-versed in magic but even he knew that there was power in a name. Clearly, there needed to be more trust between them before the Fire Oppa would consent to give such a potential weapon over.

As always, Jacob wanted nothing more than to sit at the Pyre and pet the Fire Oppa. There was a peace there that he had not known in many years. He felt he was standing on a precipice over a black abyss. The worst was yet to come for humanity, and for himself.

He knew it and yet he could not help but feel a sense of relief. Yes, he may be standing at the edge of a dark, impossibly deep pit just waiting to swallow him and ten billion people up but for now he was safe.

For now, Jacob knew peace and the warmth of a Pyre.

It was better than the perpetual fall, wondering when you would hit the bottom. Knowing, with iron certainty that the gruesome death awaiting you was not a matter of "if" but of "when."

"I have to go," Jacob said mournfully to the Fire Oppa as much as to himself. After resting at the Pyre if he died he would be sent back. His [Cinder Ampoules] were filled and he had a purpose beyond the lofty goal of beating Alec to the Burgon Beast's lair.

"May the flames light your path," the Fire Oppa intoned once more upon their parting.

"May they guide me back home."

Back in the halls outside, Jacob moved cautiously knowing that the last Graceful Penitent he killed would be back. He could have dismissed his [Mace] back to his inventory but chose not to, suffering the extra point of Guilt so he could readily swap between it and the [Bladed Whip].

It took a lot longer to draw an item out of the Inventory, particularly weapons, shields, and foci. By keeping them equipped but dismissed, he still bore the burden of their Guilt but could instantly swap to that weapon.

As much as he felt his hunch might be correct about the [Bladed Whip], he wasn't about to trust it blindly. If things got dicey, he would step in with his [Mace].

Rounding the corner, Jacob came to the first Graceful Penitent. Like the others it seemed to hide in an alcove, waiting to ambush with its lanky limbs and clawing broken nails.

Uncoiling his whip made enough noise to rouse the creature from its hole and it made shambling, sluggish movements toward him. It was loud enough to draw its attention but not enough to make it overly aggressive.

After all, the creatures couldn't see. Filthy rotted bandages covered their heads, splotched with long-dried bloodstains.

Setting himself properly and shifting his shoulder back, Jacob pulled back on the whip and then lashed his arm forward. The hallway echoed with the repeated *tink, tink, tink* of the blades scraping against the stone floor as they were whipped up into the air.

The Graceful Penitent lunged toward the sound, black teeth bared. Jacob raised his shield to guard himself but realized halfway through the automatic motion that it would be unnecessary.

His whip sliced through the air and with a less-than-satisfying *crack* snapped into the creature's chest. The damage wasn't incredible but the creature let out a horrific moaning sound of ecstasy and fell to its knees clawing savagely at its own body.

Jacob's lip curled in disgust. *Oh, man, they* like *it?*

All the while it moaned in a strange tongue, filling the dark hall with indecipherable words.

You whip the [Graceful Penitent] for 164 points of damage.
You consume 20 Stamina.

The [Graceful Penitent] *is afflicted with* **Rapture.**

Jacob wasted no time dismissing the whip and taking a two-handed grip on his [Mace]. He stepped in, lifting the [Mace] high over his head, and with all the strength he could muster he slammed the heavy head of the [Mace] into the stunned creature's bowed head.

The impact splattered the stones with gore and cut off the monster's incessant babbling.

Exploited Weakness!
You strike the [Graceful Penitent] *for 332 points of damage.*
You consume 40 Stamina.
You defeat the [Graceful Penitent].
Awarded 350 Souls.

Your Whip Skill increases to Level 1.
Your Mace Skill increases to Level 10...11...12.

No matter how much he felt creeped out by the Graceful Penitent's reaction, he could hardly argue with the results. The whip practically incapacitated them.

With a quick look at the empty hall, Jacob took a moment to reconfigure his log settings. A few mental swipes of his settings cleaned up his vision. All he would see now was the Souls he was awarded unless he opened up his log and decided to inspect the damage done.

That was one of the things Alec had told him to do first but he wanted to see how much weaker he was without his Sword Forms. The answer was: a lot. He had to resort to exploiting weaknesses, backstabs, and ripostes to get any real damage in.

And in the meantime his vision was filling up with text, making it harder to make out any new threats.

He still could see his Health and Stamina bars. He didn't need to know that he was using 15 Stamina for each light swing and 40 Stamina per heavy swing. The vanishing green bar told him how much Stamina he lost and how much remained without so much clutter.

The most important bit, was that he was correct about his hunch. These creatures were weakened by the whip *in an extremely disconcerting manner*. A single lash and they lost their damn mind, effectively stunning them while he walked up with a [Mace] and delivered the coup de grace.

Although it was early in the game, he could catapult his strength by taking a little time to farm the creatures around the Pyre.

It wasn't something he could do perpetually. Some people got stuck in the grind and while they were likely stronger than even Alec, they hadn't progressed through Lormar at all. Making their vaunted strength useless.

No doubt, if the Burgon Beast hadn't escaped and caused the Collapse, they would have taken to the forums to boast about how high their levels were. But where were these grinders when the world ended and their strength was in dire need?

Strength unused is strength wasted.

Hoarders – both Souls and goods alike – were not uncommon Post-Collapse. He wouldn't be like that. A few rounds of wiping out the creatures with the whip, then he would press on. There had to be a balance and each minute he spent in the Steps of Penance was one he would need to make up later.

Each Graceful Penitent gave him 350 Souls, a large amount even much farther into Lormar. And there were several hallways filled with the things. Not to mention whatever awaited him ahead.

He only needed about three kills to get enough Souls to raise a parameter. Most of them he avoided purely because he didn't want to get overwhelmed, but now he headed down pathways he didn't dare tread before, whip at the ready.

It was time to farm.

10

Soaked with sweat, Jacob caved in a Graceful Penitent's skull. Another came out from its hole in the wall, but he was expecting it. This was a scenario he played out several times already and the sudden emergence of the creature no longer startled him.

Another crack of the [Bladed Whip] sent the thing to its knees, keening with that disturbing ululating tone that he soon quieted with a swap back to his [Mace] and a crunching impact to the thing's sightless face.

Jacob turned, switching back to the [Bladed Whip], ready for the last two Graceful Penitents that would come falling from the dark rafters above.

He thought it was an ancient dining hall since it had a large rotted table in the middle. Though why somebody would build that *inside* of a bridge – even one as startlingly massive as the Steps of Penance – was beyond him.

Just as he saw the creatures fall, darker shadows against the black abyss above, Jacob felt a terrible wrenching feeling behind his navel. He jerked back as if somebody lassoed him with a rope and was giving him a sturdy yank backward.

Everything tasted like blue raspberry for a second and it took him another few seconds to wrap his mind around what was happening. That strange sensation was a common byproduct of FIVR technology, upon connection and disconnection some users experienced nonsensical sensations.

Largely harmless, but jarring all the same.

May 7th, 2045 – 10 Years Post-Collapse.

"Alec, hold him down," Alice said. "He is seizing."

No, I'm not, Jacob tried to say but found his jaw unresponsive.

"Ian, give me the levetiracetam!"

Jacob winced, though his body wasn't responding to him, expecting the sting of a needle. He hated needles. In a world where zombies were real and monsters stalked the dying land, he *still* hated needles.

Slowly, Jacob found himself back in control of his body. His eyes fluttered open and sensation came back to him. And what he felt was a wave of *pain*. He could tell he wasn't injured but every one of his muscles was wrung out as if he overworked himself with intensive all-day training.

"Good, he is coming around," Alice's face appeared above Jacob. "*Bonjour!*" she said with forced enthusiasm. "How do you feel, Jacob? Can you sit up for me?"

Struggling to breathe, in a body that no longer felt like his own, Jacob did as she asked and slowly – so very slowly – sat up. The glass half of the FIVR pod was already opened but he only realized that after he sat up. He would have conked his head like a moron without ever noticing.

"Hey, man, how're you doing?" Alec asked, clapping him on the shoulder.

Jacob felt a small tug on the inside of his elbow and his green eyes were drawn down to the small IV taped there. Of course, he had no reason to worry about needles. He already had one jammed into his arm. They weren't about to poke him again when they could just inject into the IV.

As if suddenly realizing Alec spoke to him, he looked up at his friend's smiling face. "I feel like crap."

"Well you were thrashing around like a madman," Alec said, trying to downplay things.

He wasn't a very good liar. Perhaps that was why he liked the man so much. He rarely lied and when he did it was usually for a good reason, but it was so painfully evident that Jacob couldn't hold it against him for long.

"Yes, yes, now tell us everything," the Doc said, brushing aside Alec and leaning down to inspect Jacob intently. She flashed a small penlight into his eyes, looked into his mouth, his ears, and up his nose with a small black tool. Finally, she straightened and nodded. "So, out with it. Did it work?"

The question made no sense. "What do you mean, 'did it work?' How don't you know?"

"It was pretty scary from this end, dude," Alec said, hopping up and sitting at the foot of the FIVR's bed. "As soon as you went under, the Doc said your brain lit up like a Christmas tree and then you started to have a grand mal seizure. We brought you back immediately. You've only been gone – to us – about ten minutes."

"Whatever happened to putting me in for an hour?" Jacob asked, starting to feel a bit more in control.

The familiar cold sensation of being without a Pyre settled into his bones. All he wanted at that moment was a Pyre to rest at and to have some idle conversation with the Fire Oppa that would wash away all his pains and aches.

"As Alec has said," Alice put in, straightening her white coat, "you began to seize shortly into the process. A calibration error, nothing more. You could have ridden it out but Ian-" She turned to glare at the aging doctor. "He thought it would endanger your health, so we shut down the machine and brought you out early."

Rubbing his head, Jacob nodded to show his understanding.

"If you have had enough of abusing my patient, I would like to examine him for myself," Ian said.

He was a tall man with swept-back black hair that was graying at the sides. Ian was one of those people that aged well, despite the horrors of the world he only looked more refined and handsome as the years went on.

The doctor, one of the two resident physicians in their refugee group, shooed out anybody still left in the room and shut the door with a loud bang. He turned back to Jacob with a fatherly smile.

As always, Jacob's eyes immediately latched onto the man's upper lip. The only thing that detracted from his looks was that ridiculous pencil mustache he insisted on wearing.

"Now, tell me truthfully. How are you feeling Jacob?" Ian placed a hand on his shoulder and looked him straight in the eye.

"I feel like somebody ran me over, realized I was still alive, and then backed up over me again with a truck."

The doctor chuckled. "Seizures can do that, but you don't seem to have suffered any long-term damage. You didn't bite your tongue off, or crack your head thankfully. Though that would be hard to do inside one of these chambers, wouldn't it?" He pressed against the pillowy soft gel padding.

"Aside from that, you feel okay? Do you know what year it is?" Ian said, his soft brown eyes fastened to Jacob's green.

It took him more time than it should have to say, "Twenty forty-five."

Ian patted his shoulder with a broad smile. "Right you are, right you are." He bent down and took out a small cuff. "I'm just going to take some vitals, don't mind me. All very routine stuff."

The doctor kept up a stream of pleasant conversation while he performed his examination. Jacob always thought he had an excellent bedside manner.

Unfortunately, Jacob had seen him do this before. And it was always with terminal patients or those with wounds too great to heal, but to leave the person to die without treating them would be even crueler.

Which meant something was wrong. He wouldn't be constantly talking, trying to keep Jacob at ease otherwise.

He didn't know much about medicine besides what it took to stitch himself or a friend up in the field and keep people alive until they could get proper medical help. But he knew that it wasn't typical for routine vitals to include a blood draw *and* a spinal tap.

That last procedure *hurt*. Jacob was still curled up on his side when Ian said, "There, all done. Nothing a knight like yourself doesn't get out in the field I'm betting! So, you're all set, would you like some time to yourself or shall I let the circus back in?"

As much as Jacob wanted a day – two, preferably – to rest and relax, he shook his head.

His goal was to get back into Pyresouls, to fix all of this. Besides, he didn't like the feeling of being pulled out from Pyresouls. He wasn't sure whether it was his mind playing tricks or some side-effect of the process, but he couldn't get warm.

Everything felt so cold. Colder by far than Lormar. It seeped into his bones, his joints. It *hurt*. The longer he was away from Lormar, the more he yearned for the warming comfort of a Pyre.

"Suit yourself, son. Try not to overdo it though, okay?" With a final pat of farewell, the doctor left, sliding the vials he collected from Jacob into a coat pocket.

Alice and Alec were quick to return and though he could tell that Alec was trying to give him some space, Alice was having none of that. Jacob raised a hand to quiet her down. "It worked," he said, launching into his story.

Technically speaking, he knew he had all the time in the world to tell them every last detail and ask for tips and tricks from Alec in return. But he couldn't shake the sense of urgency within him.

A large part of it – though he didn't want to admit it – was the lack of this cold despair that suffused his every cell back in the past. He forgot how used to it he was and being suddenly pulled back into that was physically painful.

No amount of time would get rid of that feeling. So, while he had all the time he might need – barring an attack that could destroy the machine, bunker, or his body – he kept the conversation as brief as possible and only asked about the exact location of the knight's body and a few other pertinent locations.

Time definitely didn't flow correctly between the two points. It had been hours in Pyresouls but only minutes back on Earth. That meant if they planned on sticking to the one-hour window, he should be beyond the Steps of Penance and into the Asylum of Silent Sorrows by the time they pulled him out again.

Somewhere he never wanted to go after hearing the horror stories of that wretched, dark place. Pyresouls was scary enough on its own without leaning heavily into the horror aspect that seemed tailormade to his fears and phobias.

"You will give us another brief in an hour," Alice said. "We will not know when things change, remember this, yes? Only you will have the memory of how things used to be."

Jacob nodded, ready and eager to return to the past. To a brief period of adventure and a lack of constant pervasive bone-deep pain. Even within the bunker with its heated purified air, there was a chill that lingered as if the warmth of the world had gone out.

Already hooked up to the FIVR pod, it didn't take them long to get Jacob settled in again and ready for his return trip. He shut his eyes and counted back from 100 again, losing track somewhere around 87.

August 30th, 2035 – 14 days remain before the Collapse.

The first thing Jacob realized upon being shunted into Pyresouls once more was that time travel, was not an exact science.

Still tasting blue raspberry, Jacob opened his eyes in the darkness to find himself already on his back being ripped apart by the very Graceful Penitents he had last seen falling down from their hiding spot.

You Died.

"Lovely," Jacob said, finding himself sitting back at the Pyre. At least it didn't hurt.

"Time travel is a tricky business," the Fire Oppa said, grooming one paw. The moisture from his tongue hissed and created tiny puffs of steam. "I would generally not recommend it."

Leaning forward, Jacob pet the Fire Oppa and laughed to himself. The shock of dying so suddenly was more than the pain. He was barely in control of his body, let alone capable of feeling anything when he died.

"Better go get my Souls back," he said by way of goodbye and ventured out of the room into the cramped halls beyond.

Originally, it was his intention to do one more circuit then call it quits. A lanky Penitent came out of the alcove on his right and he snapped the whip out at center mass.

Predictably the creature fell to its knees and began chanting. Without breaking stride, Jacob dismissed the whip into a cloud of ash and summoned forth his [Mace].

He twisted his hip, gripped the weapon in two hands and swung like he was trying to hit a home run. The heavy head of the [Mace] obliterated the creature's skull.

It was almost too easy.

You defeat the [Graceful Penitent].
Awarded 350 Souls.
You gain [Anima].

Finally, he thought.

With that second death, he was at curse level 2. He didn't see anything odd *yet*, but it was just a matter of time now. Using an [Anima] would reset his curse level back to 0 once he was back at a Pyre.

Similar to named souls, like the [Soul of a Loving Father], [Anima] was an item he could store in his [Boundless Box]. It could only be used at a Pyre.

No matter how many you gained, the "Anima" counter on your

status always displayed 0. If he wanted to know his current stock of [Anima], he would have to look into his [Boundless Box].

Jacob could never quite figure that out. Considering how rare [Anima] was, and the pressing need to save it to reverse any levels of curse gained, nobody else ever figured it out either.

And if they did, they never posted about it. That was the problem with relying on second-hand accounts, and archived forum posts.

The next few halls were much the same until he reached the dining room where the creatures came out in a specific order. By that point, Jacob was well used to the quick-swap from [Bladed Whip] to [Mace] and back again to deal with multiple threats at once.

With no more enemies around, Jacob focused on the emerald wisp. Kneeling, he touched his fingertips to the glowing swirl of emerald light and felt the rush of his Souls returning.

Jacob wasted no time clearing out the next room of the two Penitents there, but it was almost an afterthought at that point. Killing the creatures posed nearly zero risk, not with them stunned. And a single heavy blow would kill them.

Malicious spirit Emily Cooper has invaded!

Jacob's heart stuttered in his chest.

The message flashed three more times in quick succession, making sure there was no way he would miss the notification.

There was no way she knew it was his shard when she attempted to invade a fellow player. But now that she was in Jacob's shard, she would know.

And that presented a problem Jacob had hoped to sidestep entirely.

It was because of Emily that he quit Pyresouls early. Her betrayal had stung him profoundly. He had thought they were happy together.

She didn't care about him. And if she did, she cared for him less than billions of dollars. Back then, she had killed him and claimed the creature they were fighting for her own.

In one fell swoop, she set him back thousands of Souls, took the kill they should have shared, and leaped ahead in power.

He never did find out how far she got in the competition. And the Collapse afterward made it all moot anyhow.

She had never searched for him, and Jacob had been too busy surviving day-to-day to look for her.

And here she was, probably thinking to herself that she could manipulate him as easily as she had before.

There was no way she wasn't aware who she was invading now. Like the prompt had displayed for him, she would have seen whose shard she was invading. Which meant he could tell by her aura what her intentions were.

It was one of the few ways he could use his knowledge to turn the tables on her. Emily wouldn't know that a player's body possessed differently colored auras when occupying another player's shard.

Even though she invaded - usually a sign of aggression - it didn't automatically mean her body would be limned in red-and-black. If she chose to help him instead, her aura would be either white or gold.

Steeling himself, Jacob swapped his [Bladed Whip] for the [Mace] and desperately wished he had a sword right then. Even the shoddy [Shortsword] Brother Aker had would be better.

Though his skill was likely higher than Emily's, he could dance circles around her with a blade.

He wandered the nearly empty halls for some time before he spied her peeking into an empty alcove. She moved stealthily, with a tiny dagger clutched tightly in one hand.

Not the same dagger she had ended his life with ten years ago, that would be too poetic. It was a filthy, rusted thing that looked like it was better served to opening letters than people.

But most unmistakable of all was the red-and-black aura.

She meant to do harm and by the way she was sneaking about, she clearly meant to get the drop on him and finish him quickly. Maybe she thought the invaded player wasn't aware of the invasion.

In that case, she could likely get in, gank him, then get out with her spoils.

He tried to remind himself that he wasn't a 19-year-old kid anymore. Once upon a time, she had him wrapped around her finger. He would have done anything for her.

Not anymore.

There was no way to tell whether she was stronger or weaker than him. But considering his recent windfall of Souls so early on, he was willing to bet they were at least even.

Emily slipped inside what he knew to be an empty room with extreme caution. It was hard to make out her equipment from where he was and through her aura, but it looked like the ratty old leathers a player would start with.

As she disappeared into the room, Jacob went over the various ways he could deal with her. Chief among them was a desire to string her along like she did to him, then kill her.

But that was pedantic and petty. Her betrayal was ten years ago and despite the recent reminder, he had let go of it. Hadn't thought about it in years. He would be a small man indeed if he kept that with him all this time.

No, he would let her take her chance. And then, win or lose, he would press on.

This invasion was a reminder that he had lingered too long already.

Stepping out into the hallway fully, Jacob walked halfway down the hall and stopped roughly ten feet from the room. He lifted his mace and clanged it loudly against the stones.

He heard her shuffle and freeze inside the room and then she slinked out of the room, still crouching in an attempt to remain hidden.

Emily looked left, away from him, then right. Their eyes locked and she quickly popped up to her feet and smiled. "Jakey! I was so relieved to finally find you hun-bun. It took nearly all of my Souls just to scrounge enough to get one of those weird lil' helper stone things.

"But I'm here now! I told you I would find you and together we'll win the competition just like we did in Mrs. Trager's science competition!"

Her aura didn't waver in the slightest. It was still red-and-black. Her intent was clear, even if he wanted to believe otherwise.

Despite himself, he was disappointed. In her for betraying him - though it would only be the first time for Emily - and in himself for holding out a shred of hope that she hadn't always intended on stabbing him in the back.

With a world-weary sigh, Jacob shook his head and lifted his gaze to meet hers. Did she always have those dead eyes? Or was he just better at reading people now?

There was nothing behind them, no warmth or emotion. Her face was twisted up into a smile but he could see the way she held her dagger a little too tightly.

So that was it. She had no other weapon then and with such a pitiful weapon she would need to get close to use it to any effect.

Very close.

"Jakey, sweetums? You know I don't like it when you go off into your own world like that!" she cried, quickening her pace.

I'm so tired of this, he thought as he waited for her to get close enough to strike at his heart. He kept his shield close, knowing he would need to time it perfectly if she struck to bat the weapon aside and execute a riposte.

His other arm, holding his [Mace], he let spread wide in a welcoming gesture. He was practically inviting her to stab him.

She came in like she was going to hug him. Emily even said something, though Jacob wasn't paying attention to her words anymore. He watched the telltale sign of her impending betrayal.

The tendons on the back of her hand stood out starkly and she came into the "hug" a little too fast. But aside from that, she seemed genuinely to want to embrace him. She was good.

Her knife flashed out, but Jacob was prepared. Out swept his [Plank Shield] and her arm went wide.

Emily's eyes were as round as saucers. Her betrayal had been reversed. For a brief moment, she was stunned. Jacob had set her up for a perfect riposte. For once, Emily had not disappointed him.

"If I ever see you again," Jacob said, already twisting and pivoting on one foot, raising his [Mace] as it whipped around at her head. "I will kill you."

His words rang out just as his [Mace] connected with her head. He shut his eyes against the scene and Emily dropped to her knees bonelessly.

She was dead before she ever hit the ground. Her body broke apart into fiery red motes and she was sent back to her shard.

Malicious spirit Emily Cooper was vanquished.
Awarded 5,448 Souls.

Dying at a Crossing was much less dangerous than dying while invading another's shard. Only a portion of Souls were dropped at a Crossing. A nod, perhaps, to the fact that Crossings could not be wholly avoided.

Invading was a choice. Emily had lost all of her Souls.

As the blood-red vestiges of Emily's aura vanished, Jacob couldn't help but feel like the whole affair was a *little* cathartic.

While he doubted he would ever be able to fathom why she wanted to betray him, at least he had some closure.

Jacob walked the quiet, deserted halls back to the Pyre to spend his hard-earned Souls. They would make a massive leap in his power. Amassing the 10,828 Souls he now possessed had taken him most of the day.

And, he had to admit, seeing Emily again had somehow left him feeling drained. As much as he didn't want to stay in the area any longer, since it would likely invite further invasions, he needed to spend his Souls and rest.

Time he would need to make up. But at least at the Pyre, he would be safe. From invasions and monsters both.

The upside was, he now had a sizeable amount of Souls. Enough to splurge on some much-needed parameter reinforcement.

Instead of being ahead, he was surely behind the frontrunners now. Not for the first time he wondered if he spent too long there grinding out Souls. As a side effect, he received a few extra items as well. Rare items that he would need later on, so having a few early would only stack the odds in his favor.

As he pushed open the rough plank door to the Pyre room, he wondered if his newfound strength would let him rush through the Asylum of Silent Sorrows. If he could press on quickly through the asylum he could make it back into the lead.

Both areas were major obstacles for most players. Jacob had barely been able to get past the Corpse Garden last time and he had help. Many others had gotten stuck in the asylum, lost in the labyrinthine passages, and the terrifying monsters that lurked its silent halls.

"Back so soon?" asked Brother Aker. "My, you have really put that whip through the wringer, haven't you, brother?"

"Indeed I have," Jacob said with a relieved smile, as the soothing warmth of the Pyre washed away his weariness and fatigue.

That purchase and the happenstance of wearing the ring at the right time had made dealing with the Graceful Penitents a trivial matter. Despite the high cost of the whip, it more than paid for itself many times over.

"Well, if you want another one, I've got plenty. Looks like yours is about ready to snap in half."

A glance at the durability of the [Bladed Whip] confirmed Brother Aker's words. He barely had 50 durability left. He wasn't used to such low levels of durability and hadn't thought to check it.

I guess it was a good thing I came back and didn't try to press on.

Staring into the Pyre, Jacob extended his hand to the snoozing Fire Oppa. He woke to Jacob's touch so quickly that he doubted the little guy was actually asleep at all.

Each parameter reinforcement still cost under 1,000 Souls, except for the 9th increase, letting Jacob boost his power considerably more than any other player should have access to at the moment. Especially not so far back as he was.

When he was playing his first time through, he narrowly made it out of the Stalking Woods at Level 6. This time, he was going to be more than twice that strong.

And with his [Ring of Blameless Guilt] he wasn't going to need to waste as much on Temper, or the other stats he foolishly raised without an idea as to how they worked.

Jacob shook his head, remembering that he raised both Faith and Intelligence at once, trying to raise both magic stats and in effect almost entirely canceling each other out.

It was an odd system that the vast majority of players had underestimated or misunderstood in much the same way. Armed with better knowledge, Jacob spent all of his available Souls.

He reserved 2,000 Souls for the [Repair Kit] which could be used with a scant amount of Souls at a Pyre to restore the durability of his equipment. It was a relatively high upfront cost, but having a merchant repair it was far costlier.

Not to mention, finding a merchant wasn't always easy. To find a Pyre, all he had to do was die. True, he wouldn't have any Souls, but a few kills would likely be enough to fully repair at least one piece of equipment.

After buying the [Repair Kit] and increasing 9 parameters – 3 into DEX and 6 into STR – Jacob still had 1,511 Souls left. He could have pushed himself to Level 14 but he decided against it. Better to have some Souls for upgrades and repairs.

[Status]

Jacob Windsor
Covenant: None
Race: Kemora - Fae-touched (Human/Fairy)
Level: 13
Health: 124
Stamina: 86
Anima: 0
Souls: 1,511
Required Souls: 1,238

Parameters

VIT: 3
AGI: 6
END: 3
TMP: 9
STR: 10
DEX: 10
INT: 8
FTH: 3

Curse: Fractured Sight
   Curse Level: 2

Spell Gem: No Spell Inscribed

It really struck home how important raising his VIT and END was. No matter how much he raised his level, his Health and Stamina would never move unless he reinforced those parameters. For now, he was more than strong enough.

No matter how much he pumped his VIT, his Health would never hit the monstrous levels seen in other games. Having 1,000 Health was a pipe dream, even 500 Health would be a massive achievement.

He would need to do something about his curse level soon though. He did have 3 [Anima] from farming those creatures but it was such a rare and precious commodity that he didn't feel it was worth using just yet.

Jacob had high expectations that he would die - a lot - in the Asylum of Silent Sorrows. Saving the [Anima] for when it hit level 3 or 4 seemed most prudent.

Besides, he didn't notice any negative side effects yet. And if he started to see things, there was a real chance he might find a passage that could make his passage through the next area easier.

Most important were the 2 [Dull Sparks] and 2 [Bright Sparks] he had in his possession. With them, and a payment of Souls, the Fire Oppa would reinforce his equipment.

And upgrading his equipment was of paramount concern.

There was nothing more effective than improving one's equipment. The only downside is that he had no equipment he wanted to be reinforced at the moment.

Which meant he would need to hold his Souls on him until he found the knight's body, retrieved the armor set, and found another Pyre. With so much time to make up, he couldn't waste it backtracking to this same Pyre.

It was a risk worth taking.

Already weary and tired, after increasing so many parameters, Jacob was beat. While you didn't need to eat or drink while in Pyresouls Online, sleep was still a necessity if and only if you reached a new level past level 5.

It probably had something to do with the added strain on the body. But Jacob couldn't be sure, and he realized theorizing about it wasn't a terribly useful expenditure of his limited time.

As much as he wanted to press on, he needed to rest. He took some solace that for 9 parameter increases, he only needed to sleep once. While others would need to rest every parameter increase until a few of the players caught on.

Just another example of the way Pyresouls played the risk versus reward game. Holding so many Souls at once was a huge risk, not only would it attract more invading players but every death risked losing it all.

Spending them as soon as he had enough to increase one parameter was safer, but then he would have to rest more.

Jacob let the weariness wash over him and shut his eyes. Sitting at the Pyre, Jacob's chin touched his chest as his head nodded forward. When he awoke, it wasn't with a start or thick with fatigue but energized and ready for what lay ahead.

August 31st, 2035 – 13 days remain before the Collapse.

Refreshed, Jacob took out his newly acquired [Repair Kit]. It was a simple enough tool. All he had to do was place a piece of equipment within the confines of the wooden box and shut the lid. Even if he had a greataxe bigger than the box, it would fit in what could only be considered game logic.

Though, now that Jacob was fairly sure Pyresouls wasn't just a game, he wondered about the magic behind it. The [Repair Kits] would have been invaluable back on Earth and he had never seen one. Not that they would have been much use.

A [Repair Kit] would have been worthless without a Pyre anyway.

Once the item was in the box, all he had to do was place it in the Pyre. The Fire Oppa looked at him, then at the [Repair Kit]. Rising to his paws, the Fire Oppa walked into the box as if the wood was no barrier at all.

At that point, Jacob needed to supply it with the requested amount of Souls. For his [Bladed Whip] it only took 70 Souls to fully repair its durability back to 200.

After a few seconds, a faint light flashed out between the seam of the lid and the body of the box. The Fire Oppa leaped out, signaling that the item was repaired. Jacob pulled the [Bladed Whip] out, careful not to get cut and dismissed it into ash once it was clear of the box.

The whole process was quick and relatively painless. Souls were still required but he no longer needed to find a merchant that could repair the item. Without a [Repair Kit], the Fire Oppa wasn't able to repair items.

It wasn't as handy as [Repair Powder], which could restore a small portion of durability in the field, but compared to that the cost was low to completely repair a full set of gear.

With the way the Fire Oppa was grinning at him, Jacob had the impression that the little fiery guy liked being helpful.

"You wouldn't happen to know where the next Pyre is, would you?" he ventured to ask the Fire Oppa.

"You're not going to like the answer," he replied.

He could guess well enough but any definitive answer was better than nothing. "Where?"

"Below the depths of the Asylum of Silent Sorrows," the Fire Oppa said, laying back down within the burning Pyre.

Jacob winced. "Yeah, I thought you would say that. But you said the *depths*?"

The Fire Oppa nodded.

"Not going to tell me anything more specific?"

The Fire Oppa shook his head.

With a sigh and a shrug of his shoulders, Jacob went to the door and looked over his shoulder. "See you there, then." He already knew the Pyre for the asylum was far below the first floor from Alec but it was good to have confirmation.

His next task would be to find the knight's corpse and get some proper gear. He was tired of wearing a paper set of robes.

11

Raising his [Plank Shield], Jacob braced for the bull-headed monster's rush. His shield held and he skidded back on his heels across the dusty stone. Just as he was turning aside to swipe his [Mace] into the thing's remaining horn, the Minos lifted a heavy hand and pulled it back to clobber Jacob.

Without the Health to take another blow, he shifted his [Plank Shield] higher, knowing what was coming but unable to see a better way. Predictably, the Minos crashed his fist into the shield, shattering it.

Freed from the shield on his left arm, and seizing his opportunity while the Minos was preoccupied, Jacob swept his [Mace] up and into the Minos' ribs.

He grabbed the handle with both hands, twisted on the ball of his leading foot, and pivoted around behind the Minos, swinging as hard as humanly possible at the back of the thing's knee.

With a roar of pain and rage, the Minos collapsed to one knee. Using the last of his Stamina, Jacob broke the final horn atop the Minos' head.

The binding magic of its heavily enchanted horns dissipated in a flash of blood-red light. Jets of flame scorched its open, screaming mouth. Flames burst from its eyes and the creature fell facedown onto the stone, no longer moving.

Lazy drifts of black smoke curled into the air from its mouth and eyes.

You defeat the [Minos].
Awarded 1,500 Souls.
You gain 2 [Broken Minos Horns].
Your Mace Skill increases to Level 18.

Dammit, Jacob thought.

He looked at his bloodied left arm where his shield had been. He leaned against the wall, pulled out his third [Cinder Ampoule], and crushed it. The healing ember knit his wounds in an instant and he wiped the blood on his arm to reveal unblemished skin.

The large spreading stain in his middle where the Minos gored him as he tried to break off the first horn stopped widening, but his robes remained just as stained and ripped.

When he first heard the telltale sound of a Minos, the massive bull-headed hulking man-thing, he only meant to investigate enough to stay ahead of it. Minos horns were powerfully enchanted – it was both their strength and their weakness – but even with his current prowess he should not have stood a chance against the thing.

Without breaking the horns, he never would have. Knowing its weakness was his only hope since the [Bladed Whip] had barely tickled the thing. Only the increase in his STR and the [Mace's] blunt prowess allowed him to shatter the horns.

A sword, unless it was powerfully enchanted, would never have cut through them. He would need to remember to thank Alec for advising him to choose a mace.

The Minos was meant to be a threat that players ran from.

There was a reason this section of the Steps of Penance was largely devoid of any other enemy. He was meant to be chased by the creature, a constant threat that drove him deeper into the maze within the bowels of the massive bridge.

Jacob turned, summoning a whip to his left hand and his [Mace] to his right. Dual-wielding wasn't his strong suit. A shield was just too useful. But without one, he didn't have much choice.

Without the threat of the Minos, he was free to backtrack to where he first ran into the thing and find out just what it was guarding.

Once he followed the path back to where it had come from, Jacob realized he was closer to the other side of the Steps of Penance than he thought.

He came to a storage room filled with broken barrels littering the floor and light spilling in from a set of stairs going up through a cut section of the roof.

But he found himself drawn to the side by some unknown sensation. He missed something but he wasn't sure what.

Jacob turned back around where the Minos had been standing and looked around. The walls were heavily scraped in long gashes as if the Minos had grown bored and tried sharpening its horns on the stone walls.

Except, there was a five-foot section of unblemished stone that interrupted the gouge marks on the wall. It shimmered strangely to Jacob's eyes, like he was looking at it through a dirty camera lens. When Jacob put his hand to it, the illusion faded entirely and revealed a room beyond the false wall.

He entered cautiously. There was a rattling sound from the far wall. The room was incredibly long with several sets of manacles lining each wall with dark stains on the floor beneath and a small grate beneath whose purpose was abundantly evident.

Before he could muse on the need of a blood drain, a voice spoke, "H-hello?" It sounded hoarse and drawn. "Is somebody there?"

The darkness slowly peeled back beneath Jacob's faint illumination, revealing a series of bodies in various states of decay. Several of them were Vacant, they gnashed their teeth and lunged at him but were held in place by sturdy black chains.

Without conscious thought, Jacob ended their suffering with a swift two-handed strike to their heads, one after the other. They were only worth 100 Souls each but every bit helped.

One, chained to the far wall, was not a Vacant.

Though she looked like it might not take very long to complete the process. A raven-haired woman, she might have been pretty once if she wasn't half-dead from starvation. The thin shift she wore displayed her ribs prominently and the hollows of her cheeks were so deep they were darkened with shadow.

But her eyes… they were very much alive.

Her ruby-red irises burned with intense passion, not hope, not despair, not even fear. Her chains rattled against her straining efforts to get closer to him.

Jacob kept her just at the edge of his light, watching her warily. He never managed to find what he thought were NPCs before, now he had found two in short order. Though, of course, he wasn't sure that they *were* NPCs anymore.

These were people, he was beginning to believe – or had been once upon a time.

"Can you speak?" she asked, and it was obvious the effort cost her greatly.

He wasn't sure how to answer her. He didn't have time to be slowed down by helping her and yet he couldn't live with himself if he could do something to help her.

Jacob tried to remind himself that she wasn't his problem. He could have passed her by – he had in the past – without ever being aware of her presence.

She was not his problem.

As he turned his back on her she let out a strangled cry as she lunged after him. The collar at her throat choked her and strangled her words.

"Don't!" she managed to croak.

Grinding his teeth, Jacob turned back around. "I'm sorry lady, but this really isn't any of my business. You don't understand what is at stake here for me and my people. This world…."

Jacob motioned dismissively around at the dead bodies chained to the wall. No doubt they died a horribly painful death. But how long had they been dead? Decades? Centuries? "This world is already dead.

It's lost. My home still stands a chance. I'm sorry, I have to think of them."

Scanning the room once more, pointedly avoiding her burning gaze, Jacob left. There was no loot there and he had no way of extricating her from those chains. He saw the runes marked on the metal and knew that no normal weaponry could break them.

He found no key. Had no food or water. And the [Cinder Ampoules] he carried were only for himself. Even if she was another player, he could not have given one to her.

Her anguished screams followed him as he fled. Jacob tried to rationalize his sprinting as a means of making up lost time.

But he knew the truth. He had to get away from her screaming. It tore at his heart.

He came out into the dim watery light of midday, as he ascended the steps he came face-to-face with the knight's corpse.

Resting against the low wall of the bridge, the body was encased in basic knightly armor. It was superior to anything Jacob could get for a long while. Once he reinforced it a bit, it would be even better than the suit of armor he used back on Earth.

Not that there was much option on Earth.

Kneeling to the knight's side, careful to stay out of sight of the shambling Vacant that patrolled the top of the bridge, Jacob relieved the knight of his worldly possessions by placing his hand atop the azure wisp that floated over the man's breastplate.

You gain [Knight's Helm].
You gain [Knight's Armor].
You gain [Knight's Gauntlets].
You gain [Knight's Leggings].

Skulking back down into the depths of the bridge, Jacob donned his new armor. As always with the equipment from Pyresouls, he found it fit him remarkably well. As if it was tailored for him.

The Guilt that weighed him down had more to do with his actions with the woman than the stats of his new gear. Not that the knight's set had a minimal amount of Guilt.

As proper armor, each piece carried a single point of Guilt, but together it was a hefty 4 Guilt. Making sure no enemies were around, Jacob checked the condition of the armor.

He had never managed the knight's set before, he had been forced to purchase flimsy chainmail in Hollow Dreams, a sprawling ruined town filled with the Vacant. But among them, there existed a few merchants still that were barely more sentient than the bestial monsters that roamed the streets.

[Equipment]

<u>Knight's Helm</u> *[Helm]*

Physical Protection: 40
    Blunt: 10
    Slashing: 15
    Piercing: 15

    Magical Protection: 25
Arcane: 15
Fire: 10
Water: 0
Earth: 0
Harmony: 0
Chaos: 0

Resistances
Bleed: 13
Poison: 4
Curse: 0

Stability: 11

Durability: 550/550
Guilt: 1

Knight's Armor [Chest]

Physical Protection: 90
    Blunt: 20
    Slashing: 40
    Piercing: 30

    Magical Protection: 70
    Arcane: 30
    Fire: 15
    Water: 10
    Earth: 15
    Harmony: 0
    Chaos: 0

    Resistances
    Bleed: 22
    Poison: 9
    Curse: 0
    Stability: 20

    Durability: 550/550
    Guilt: 1

Knight's Gauntlets [Gauntlets]

Physical Protection: 40

Blunt: 15
Slashing: 15
Piercing: 10

Magical Protection: 30
Arcane: 10
Fire: 10
Water: 5
Earth: 5
Harmony: 0
Chaos: 0

Resistances
Bleed: 10
Poison: 0
Curse: 0
Stability: 7

Durability: 550/550
Guilt: 1

<u>Knight's Leggings</u> *[Leggings]*

Physical Protection: 65
   Blunt: 15
   Slashing: 25
   Piercing: 25

   Magical Protection: 60
   Arcane: 30
   Fire: 10
   Water: 5
   Earth: 5

Harmony: 5
Chaos: 5

Resistances
Bleed: 20
Poison: 5
Curse: 0
Stability: 10

Durability: 550/550
Guilt: 1

Altogether, he was much better protected but he wished he could get a proper shield to replace his destroyed [Plank Shield] which had hardly been worthy of the name.

It wasn't until they raided that mansion's collection of medieval suits of armor back in Charleston, that Jacob managed to acquire a shield that had 100 physical damage reduction. He sorely missed it now.

That was also the day he learned how important it would have been to increase his Stamina while he had the chance. While a blocked physical hit would deal zero damage, it still ate up a large chunk of Stamina to block the attack.

Without enough Stamina to absorb the blow, the rest transferred to HP. With enough Stamina *and* a good shield, it was possible to shrug off an otherwise mortal attack.

At only 86 Stamina, Jacob was far away from making that a reality.

Jacob performed a series of warm-up exercises, getting used to the new armor and its range of motion. By the time he was done, he had worked up a decent sweat despite the cool air of the storeroom.

But something was wrong. He moved just as freely as he did with his robes.

Glancing at his stats, his total Guilt was at 2. A number that didn't add up whatsoever. With everything equipped, he should be at 5.

Each tier of Guilt was broken up into 25% breakpoints. Guilt was divided by your Temper, and that percentage was the amount of total Guilt you had to bear. Possessing 1 Guilt with 10 TMP meant you were at 10% Guilt. Easy enough to grasp.

The first tier, 25% and under incurred no penalty or movement degradation. That was the goal for some but it took too much Temper to reach it with stronger weapons and better armor.

Tier 2 was 25% to 50% Guilt, and it had a slight 10% penalty to movement and Stamina.

Jacob was used to tier 3, 50% to 75% Guilt. At that stage, it was a 25% penalty to both movement and Stamina cost.

He *should* have been at 5 Guilt. With his TMP at 9, that would place him at 55% Guilt, or just into tier 3. After all, 4 pieces of the knight's armor and his [Mace] all added up to 5. Instead, he was at 2.

And despite the fact that he wore a full loadout of knightly armor, he moved around as fast as any Savage would.

Breathing hard from the exercise, Jacob found himself amid the broken crates and barrels that littered the floor. Among them was a shattered mirror.

Jacob saw himself in its broken reflection, the look of a knight but the heart of a coward.

He was glad to be alone at that moment but he wished he had a helm that properly hid his burning face. Try as he might, he could not lower the visor. Alec would have found a way to help her, wouldn't he?

Nothing he ever said to Jacob even hinted that the other man knew the woman existed, nor the Minos down below. The only Minos Jacob ever heard Alec talk about was the one in the torture chambers of the asylum.

It would seem that the creatures preferred to linger in places of deep suffering. That thought only made Jacob feel worse.

Twice, he nearly turned back for the dark hallway that would lead to the woman. And each time he turned for the stairs and the way forward, he never got past the first few steps. His guilt wouldn't let him.

But he still had no way to free her. No key, and though he had a [Mace] it wasn't magical. Not without significant work, though one of the [Minos Horns] could likely enchant it if he strengthened the weapon enough.

Altering the essence of a weapon, making it magical in one way or another required a weapon to be reinforced to at least +10. And he definitely didn't have the Souls or items to reach that level of reinforcement.

The thought of the [Minos Horn] made him curse to himself. If he destroyed one, the resulting impact could *possibly* dissolve the magical bonds that held the woman. Or they would break a single chain and she'd still be chained with Jacob down one very rare ingredient.

Pacing back and forth, he was unable to make up his mind. If Alec had encountered the woman and was too ashamed to admit that he failed, or worse left her to die, would he have buried that truth?

Stuck in the same situation, Jacob wasn't sure if he would blame him.

Jacob looked up to the ceiling above as if he could somehow see across space and time to Alice and Alec. "You picked the wrong person for the job," he grumbled.

Clenching his fists, Jacob stalked back toward the room with the woman. His new armor clanking noisily along the way.

12

When the woman saw Jacob, her eyes widened with hope and then seared him with rage. But behind that was a faint glimmer of fear. He hated seeing that most of all.

"Come back to taunt me?" she asked, her words dripped with venom despite the hoarseness of her voice.

Jacob had tried again on the way there to lower the visor on the helm but found, much to his annoyance, that it was still stuck in the up position, leaving his face open and vulnerable.

Not the best helm to wear, but better than nothing.

"Did you think a change of clothing would fool me?" she asked, a tremor threaded through her voice as Jacob came within striking distance of her.

Up so close, he could see the elven features clearly on the woman. He still wasn't sure what he could do to help her. He hadn't been lying when his goal was first and foremost to his people. To humanity and to Earth.

But he couldn't get her out of his head. He had never been the sort of person who believed the ends justified the means. What good was saving humanity if he lost his soul in the process?

The odds were staggeringly high that he wouldn't be able to help her. But the last sentient person, Brother Aker, had helped him immensely. A merchant so soon was a godsend and the [Bladed Whip] he provided even more so.

It was interesting thinking of all the little changes, the events that rolled downhill like a snowball gathering into a massive boulder to change his course.

Without the bridge being broken, finding that ring, talking to Brother Aker, buying the whip, or the many other leading events he never would have defeated the Minos.

And if he never defeated the Minos, he would never have discovered this woman.

"Are you some kind of sicko?" she asked, her voice strained as it jumped another octave. Unlike the first time Jacob came to her, she was pressed against the wall. As far away from him as possible.

Something twisted in his guts to see her look at him like he might have come back specifically to torture her or worse. With a shake of his head to dispel the thoughts, he said, "How can I free you? I have no magical weapons, but I do have this." He raised one of the [Minos Horns] from his Inventory.

Her demeanor flipped in an instant and she was reaching and grasping for him. Jacob barely slipped out of her reach. "Yes, that can free me! Please, I'll do anything you want. Just loose me from this Hell!"

Feverish ruby red eyes glinted as they locked with his. "I've seen the way you look at me. You want this body?"

She tried, in vain mostly, to push up her scantily clad breasts to look more appealing. It only made her ribs stand out more though and a pang of sorrow lanced through Jacob's heart. "Free me and it's yours. Anything... *just don't leave me.*"

The way her voice broke on those last four words crumbled any resolve Jacob might have possessed. "I'm not going to use your body," he said. To his surprise, the woman didn't act nearly as relieved as he thought she might. "But I will ask for something in return."

She seemed to regain some of her composure as she eyed him curiously, though the woman still attempted to appear sultry and alluring.

The effect she intended might have worked if her thin clothes didn't hang off her twig-like limbs.

Jacob couldn't believe he might have left her to die. At the very least he could have put her out of her misery with a clean death. He'd done enough mercy blows since the Collapse to know it was a kindness, even if it was one of the hardest things to do.

"Clearly, I'm not in much of a position to argue," she said. "You don't want to ravage me on the spot and take whatever you like, so you've at least *some* morals. Even if you did nearly leave me to rot a slow and painful death."

Seeing Jacob's darkening expression and likely presuming he did not appreciate her last words, she abruptly tried to clear her throat and started over, a note of panic in her hoarse voice, "But you came back! That's what matters. Surely no noble knight would-"

Jacob lifted the [Minos Horn]. "How do I use this to free you?"

The woman tilted her chin up, indicating above her head where the chains from her wrists led. Slowly following the path of the engraved links revealed to Jacob the overall design. Everything ran through a single eyelet about a foot above the woman's unkempt, raven black hair.

From there, if she moved her legs, arms, or neck enough it would tighten everything else. It seemed like a security flaw to Jacob but he didn't major in dungeon design so he let it go at that.

He knew well enough the properties of a [Minos Horn] and how he might release its magic to break the magic holding the chains together. That still didn't answer his question. He might free her from the wall but she would still have lengths of chain linking the manacles at her ankles, wrists, and the collar at her neck.

"I don't care what you want," she said as she moved slightly out of Jacob's way when he came forward with the horn raised above his head. He placed the tip of the horn at the base of the wall where the eyelet was anchored. "But, just for my curiosity, what is it you *do* want?"

Jacob paused. What *did* he want? A friend? A companion to help him through that wouldn't be limited mostly to Crossings like everybody else?

Was he hoping to be some white knight come to save a damsel in distress and they'd beat the evil, then ride off into the sunset to create a kingdom of their own with a thousand happy stupid children?

Truthfully, he didn't know.

He would welcome the help, she wasn't a player and so if she helped him he would still win the prize. Most importantly, even if she was weak, he would be greatly strengthened just by having one other person around.

Having Emily by his side in the Defiled Cistern – while ultimately leading to his doom - had been an immense relief.

The fear was cut in half, there was somebody who was *supposed* to watch your back and all the while every monster had to contend with two targets, not one.

But this girl, he didn't know if she was even going to be useful. Rescuing her, only to use her like bait felt sick and cruel. Unlike a player, he had no idea if she would come back if killed.

In the end, he realized she had nothing to offer him. And strangely, that he wanted nothing from her.

He wouldn't turn down an offer but he would be damned if he was going to force her. It was hard enough staying vigilant for enemies, if he had to make sure his "rescued help" also stayed loyal his attention would be split.

And he would never see her as anything else other than an unwilling ally if he demanded she worked for him as some sort of debt repayment. It would be better if they parted ways and he could continue on his own.

"You'll probably want to cover your ears," he warned, a moment before he pounded the [Mace] into the wide broken base of the [Minos Horn] like he was hammering a nail into the wall.

The resulting explosion blasted him back several feet and rained debris and masonry down upon him and the woman. His improved armor absorbed the impacts, though a few chips did get through and drew bright lines of pain across his exposed cheeks.

When Jacob got to his feet, he found the woman huddled in a crouch, hugging her knees and sobbing. He went up to her, offering his hand. "I don't want anything," he said honestly.

"I don't mean it in that cheesy, bullshit way of 'I'm too good to be corrupted.' I mean, what I want is from myself. To be a better person than I was. If you want to help me to repay me, I won't say no. But you're under no compulsion to do so."

She took Jacob's hand and he effortlessly pulled her to her feet. She scrubbed at her hollow, wet cheeks. "You have no idea how good it feels not to be nearly stretched to your limit for weeks on end...."

Jacob motioned toward the exit. "You're free," he told her, then he cast a look at her gathering up the loops of chains she would need to carry around. "Somewhat at least."

Looking at him then at the heavy chains looped in her arms. "You're just... letting me go?"

"Do you want a written letter? Really, lady, I don't have time to sit here and convince you. Your life is your own now, do with it as you will."

She bit her lip, studying him intently.

Jacob gave her one last look and with a shrug left the room, heading back to the storage area with the broken crates. He was halfway up the stairs when he heard the jingle of chains and paused to look back.

The woman stood there, half-naked and staring at him defiantly with those ruby-red eyes that seemed so out of place in her otherwise pale – if dirtied – complexion. "I'm coming with you," she said with just the tiniest hint of uncertainty.

"Listen, lady, if you don't have anything to contribute I'm not sure what good it will be to follow along with me," Jacob said, coming down to the base of the steps to face her. "I'm going to die, *a lot*. I'm not sure if that's a normal feat for your people here but-"

"If I can bind my soul to a Cairn, I can return as well," she said, sticking her chin out at him. "And my name is, Camilla."

"Not a Pyre?" Jacob asked, taken aback by her interruption.

The look she gave him was incredulous. "No. The souls of my ancestors will catch me before I am taken beyond the veil and return me to the Cairn. But I must first find one."

Grumbling to himself, Jacob took out the cleric's set he wore when he first met Camilla. "Here, you need to wear something more than that. You're one nip-slip from turning this into an NC-18 game."

Obviously, Camilla didn't get the joke. She stared at him blankly but accepted the clothes without ceremony. In an eyeblink, they vanished from her hands and appeared on her body.

They hung off her and billowed in the gentle breeze wafting down from the staircase, carrying the carrion stench of Vacant up above. It looked not too dissimilar from trying to dress up a scarecrow. Or a child in their parent's clothing.

That meant, at least to some degree, she could use the same game systems he could. Because there would be no way she could have put on any clothes with those chains still on her.

He wasn't about to give her his [Mace], but he thought about giving her the [Bladed Whip]. It seemed to be approaching the end of its usefulness anyway.

But when he offered it to her, she shook her head. "I am a Sorceress. I do not require a weapon. But it seems like you could use a shield. Is it common, where you are from, for knights to be without a shield?"

Jacob shook his head. "My shield was destroyed recently, getting the Minos Horn I used to free you as a matter of fact."

Camilla nodded, biting her dry and cracked lip. "I know of a supply cache, the weapons are of no use to me but you may prefer them."

"Where is it?" Jacob asked warily.

Secretly glad to have a potentially powerful ally – though one that would be all but useless without a focus – Jacob couldn't get the image out of his head of her roasting him alive with gouts of flame when his back was turned.

With a rattle of chains, she motioned to the stonework beneath the stairs leading up onto the bridge. Jacob stepped aside, keeping her in his line of sight at all times.

Dragging her chains with her, Camilla pressed against various blocks in a particular series. After she pressed into the last one, the stones simply vanished.

In their place was a small half-rotted wooden chest with rusted banding. Camilla stepped back to let Jacob inspect the contents. When Jacob didn't move closer, she retreated all the way to the far corner.

He may have helped her, but he still felt more than a little skittish about leaning down to inspect a chest when she stood behind him with sturdy lengths of chain.

Striding quickly to the chest, Jacob opened it with a loud ominous creak. Inside was a sapphire wisp and as he touched it, two items fell into his [Boundless Box].

You gain [Kite Shield].
You gain [Longsword].

"You'll need a focus," he said, turning back to her. He tried to remember back a couple of hours to Brother Aker's shop. Did he have a focus for sale? The way back was long and winding but it would be clear.

The thought was soon cast aside. Enough time was wasted rescuing Camilla. It may have been a wash after defeating the Minos and not getting lost in the depths of the Steps of Penance but he didn't think so.

"I have my methods," she said cryptically. "Lead on, *brave knight* and I will show you to cast doubt on a Sorceress of Asalin."

In the back of Jacob's mind, he felt a little twinge of annoyance. If Camilla died after he used a [Minos Horn], not to mention the time, he would be sorely disappointed. He immediately chastised himself for the thought.

Was he really criticizing a woman who was chained up and left to die?

Even if she wasn't directly tortured – he didn't see any wounds on her – being imprisoned and left to starve to death would be a *horrible* way to die. And it would, by its very nature, be its own kind of torture.

I'm kind of turning into a dick, he thought sourly. *Was I always this selfish?*

Maybe being back in this time period was causing him to revert in some subtle way to the person he was before the literal and figurative trial-by-fire that was the Collapse.

The notion didn't sit well with Jacob as he equipped both the shield and sword. He summoned the [Kite Shield] with a flash of ash, and accompanied it with the [Longsword] in his right hand.

Both weapons were familiar to him. The weight of each was a comfort. He inspected them quickly.

[Equipment]

<u>Kite Shield</u> *[Standard Shield]*

Physical Damage: 66
    Type: Blunt

Balance: 65
    Physical Reduction: 100
    Arcane Reduction: 30
    Fire Reduction: 50
    Water Reduction: 30
    Earth Reduction: 70
    Harmony Reduction: 20
    Chaos Reduction: 20

    Durability: 600/600
    Guilt: 1

<u>Longsword</u> *[Straight Sword]*

Physical Damage: 80
    Type: Slashing, Piercing

Scaling: STR [B], DEX [B]
Requirements: STR(8), DEX(10)

Magical Damage: 0
Arcane: 0
Fire: 0
Water: 0
Earth: 0
Harmony: 0
Chaos: 0

Status Infliction
Bleed: 70
Poison: 0
Curse: 0
Stagger: 10
Break: 5

Durability: 500/500
Guilt: 1

With a glance over at Camilla in the corner, he rolled the [Longsword] in a smooth series of practice motions.

It felt right to hold a sword again, particularly his favorite type.

Jacob flowed through the Sword Forms that were so deeply ingrained in his mind. Alice was wrong, he remembered them just as vividly as before.

Wind Parts the Grass transitioned into *Stag Rushes Through the Field*, he put a foot down to slow his rush and twisted around, taking a two-handed grip on his sword and drawing sparks along the stone as he swept the blade upward in *Sunflower Faces the Sun*. He ended with a swift downward chop of *Lightning Cracks Stone*.

His labored breath and the quicker drop in Stamina with each

Sword Form told him he was at least at tier 2 of Guilt, meaning he was losing 10% more Stamina and moving that much slower as well.

Checking his Guilt shed some light on the matter. Swapping out his [Bladed Whip] for the [Kite Shield] and adding the [Longsword] brought him up to 3 Guilt. At 33% of his TMP, he was well beyond the first threshold of 25%.

The difference was still curious, but he wasn't about to look a gift horse in the mouth. After ten straight years of nothing but bad luck, he wasn't going to complain when he couldn't precisely anticipate how much Guilt he would have.

"Impressive," Camilla said, raising a dark brow at him.

Jacob shrugged and said, "Thank you for these. It's been too long since I held a proper sword and shield."

Feeling more confident in his chances now that he was properly outfitted, Jacob ascended the stairs. Once more in the watery sunlight, he looked to the north toward the last quarter of the massive bridge.

Dozens of creatures milled about, mostly Vacant of varying types, but there were a few strange beasts among them. In the distance was the start of another mountain range, this one taller and wider than the one he came from. Its peaks wrapped in a thick mantle of snow.

And sitting like a squat toad upon the first mountaintop was the Asylum of Silent Sorrows. A staggeringly large set of buildings with broken spires and narrow bridges between the aging structures.

The nearest Vacant turned to regard them as Jacob's armor made more than enough noise to draw attention. He needed to keep that in mind, the element of surprise would rarely be on his side anymore.

But that hardly mattered when he had a proper shield, a sword, and full armor. All of which – despite the Guilt burden – was exactly what he was most comfortable in.

Years of training and fighting in very similar armor and weapons gave Jacob the confidence to wade into the nearest group of three Vacant.

One shambling corpse stared at him with glowing red lights in the darkened pits where its eyes should have been. Without any armor and wielding a simple broken sword unlike its two fellows, most players would count it as the weaker threat.

It was weak, but it was *fast*.

Jacob took one more step then leaned his weight on his back foot, raising his [Kite Shield] preemptively, knowing what was about to come.

The Vacant twitched, the inhuman motion never failed to send a shiver of revulsion down his spine. In the blink of an eye, the creature *twitched* through the space between them.

There was no other way to describe it. Like some monster from a horror movie, it moved too fast for the eye to see. It was suddenly in front of Jacob, its club raised.

With his shield already in place, Jacob swept his left arm up and out, catching the club just as it fell. One of the downsides of moving so fast was the creature fully committed to each attack.

If you knew what you were doing – or had years of practice as Jacob had – you could block the blow and retaliate. In Jacob's case, his mind was so used to the automatic parry-and-riposte motion that he found his arm moving before he made the conscious decision.

Years of combat experience drilled into him paid dividends as he exploded into action. The familiar weight of the armor resting on his shoulders – lighter than it should be but familiar all the same – the shield strapped to his left forearm and the balanced weight of a [Longsword] in his right hand evoked combat routines and Sword Forms.

Around went the club, thrown out wide. Jacob pulled back on his sword even as he shifted his weight to his left leg, raising his right like a crane standing in water.

His sword thrust out, hips twisted to put his full force behind it. He impaled the defenseless Vacant through the chest. Before the hilt came to rest against the creature's ribcage, his heavy boot was there pushing the dying thing back.

Combat senses told him to expect the other two. One half-armored with a rusted iron cap and half of a breastplate with bare shriveled arms that held a sturdy spear, the other wielding an axe and shield.

Jacob looped his shield out wide, inviting the coming attack from the spearman. With a snap of his shoulder muscles, he brought the shield back in line. Not to block the blow but to knock the spear low enough that he could step out and stomp on the haft with his boot.

In the momentary confusion of the action, as the Vacant tried to recover its weapon, Jacob attacked. *Wind Parts the Grass* tore open the creature from groin to sternum, cleaving several inches through the rusting breastplate.

Releasing his lodged [Longsword] into a swirl of ash, Jacob bent and grabbed at the haft of the spear.

That was a trick nobody had to teach him.

One of the unique aspects – and his favorite – was the way equipment could be summoned or dismissed with a thought. If a weapon was stuck, it was better to dismiss and resummon than to try and extricate it.

During combat, when a fraction of a second could mean the difference between life and death it was a handy trick to learn.

The Fade - as it was called - was his personal favorite. It utilized the mechanic that weapons could be dismissed and resummoned in a different hand to create complex feints or attack a weak point otherwise inaccessible.

Setting his feet, he tucked the spearhead just behind his right bicep, and with all of his might he twisted. Bringing the spearman right in line with the charging axe of its friend.

The falling axeblade was too heavy to stop and the third Vacant cleaved the spearman right through the back of the breastplate. With a wheeze of air leaking from its torn, rotten lungs, the spearman fell away to reveal an overbalanced and surprised Vacant Axe Master.

In a flurry of ash, his [Longsword] came back but before he could drive it home, a rush of black-limned flame shot over Jacob's shoulder and collided with the Vacant Axe Master's head.

Like touching a matchstick to flame, the creature's head immediately caught fire. What little flesh remained blackened as the black-edged flame spread, consuming everything the creature touched. Reduced to ash, only its wisp remained along with the other two.

Seconds was all it took for Jacob – with some help by Camilla – to dispatch the trio, earning 500 Souls.

Jacob's eyes widened as his vision flooded with skill ups for his sword and shield. He "relearned" more than half of the Sword Forms he already knew.

Your Shield Skill increases to Level 19...20...21.
Your Sword Skill increases to Level 1...5...10...20...40.
Sword Forms Unlocked.
You learn Wind Parts the Grass.
You learn Stag Rushes Through the Field.
You learn Lightning Cracks Stone.
You learn Ox Plows the Field.
You learn Sunflower Faces the Sun.
You learn Planting the Flag.
You learn Reaping the Harvest.
You learn Moonlight's Edge.

"I had it," Jacob said, looking over his shoulder at Camilla, surprised to see the woman smirking back at him a playful light in her eyes.

"Did you now?" she asked, brushing past him and sauntering toward the next group as if she owned the bridge. Black flames curled around her fingertips. "Because it looked to me like that last one was burnt to a crisp with *Blackfire*."

As she summoned two balls of curling, rolling *Blackfire*, Jacob caught up to her as she crouched down and began to windmill her arms about. The balls of *Blackfire* streaked through the air, creating spinning circles – wheels – of the magical dark flames.

Cold rushed in around them as if the magic robbed the world of warmth. So transfixed with Camilla's spell that Jacob wasn't sure whether it was dimming the world or a particularly dense cloud cover rolled in front of the sun.

The wheels of *Blackfire* grew until they touched the cold stones, sending up sparks and bits of molten stone that Jacob did well to move clear of.

Camilla brought her arms together with a resounding clap of her palms, rattling her chains and sending the twin wheels of *Blackfire* racing down the bridge.

Jacob watched in awe as the wheels sought out each creature, passing through them and leaving them apparently unharmed. A second later a dark line appeared on the nearest Vacant. It burst into a gout of dark flame and the creatures dropped to the ground neatly cleaved in half.

The wheels raced around the bridge leaving cauterized and bisected bodies wherever they passed. Even the larger monstrosities fell before two passes of those devastating wheels.

The spell clearly had a heavy cost though, as Camilla's skin was now glistening with sweat. Streaks of dirt and soot ran in tiny black rivulets down her face and arms. Though whether it was because of the magic, or moving her arms so much while weighed down with her chains, Jacob couldn't tell.

A bit of both, if he had to guess. The chains were far from heavy, the little he knew of such things would have meant they were of high-quality metal. Likely some sort of precious metal, as those were best suited to enchantment.

Even if the chains weren't particularly heavy, doing a repetitive motion like that over and over again would be tiring with even a pound of extra weight.

Trying hard to get her heavy breathing under control, she looked back at Jacob with a smug expression just as a torrent of wisps flew across the bridge to strike each of them.

Awarded 3,120 Souls.
You gain [Anima].
You gain 2 [Dull Sparks].

Returning her grin, Jacob inclined his head. The bridge was clear of enemies. Even if it burned out all of Camilla's reserves, it saved them time cutting through or dodging so many enemies.

The [Dull Sparks] were useful for reinforcing equipment up to +5. And while it didn't outweigh the [Minos Horn] he lost to rescue her, the time she just saved them both more than made up for it.

Together, they jogged toward the Asylum of the Silent Sorrows.

13

The Asylum of Silent Sorrows was just as creepy as Jacob could have imagined. Inside the looming dark structure was a spell of silence that afflicted most floors of the building. Even though Alec warned him about the area effect, it still shocked Jacob to suddenly be rendered deaf and mute.

Camilla was just as stunned, trying to speak but finding no sound coming out, she pointed to her hands and wriggled them about. After a few false starts, she managed to mime that she was incapable of casting any spells while silenced.

Sound was such a key part of listening for the wheezing, rasping breath of a panting beast, or the shuffling sound of a Vacant that he felt a wave of panic assault him as they stepped inside.

Without a map of any kind, Jacob relied on the memories of rough sketches Alec drew for him. The asylum was filled with creatures that preyed on fear, using hallucination and poison to cripple and render their targets vulnerable.

Luckily, the monsters were relatively weak and would fall with one or two well-placed attacks. Especially now that he had a sword.

While his [Mace] was fine, with his increased skill his [Longsword] was capable of more than double the former's damage. Not to mention that the Sword Forms were more efficient on Stamina than simply swinging a weapon about.

If he took the time to venture to the top floor of the bell tower and ring the bell, it would disable the magical enchantment. Without the silencing effect, they would be free to cast spells and most importantly hear the creatures.

The Patients and Staff as they were called, were quite loud according to Alec. They laughed and chuckled to themselves, making them easy to avoid or sneak up on.

It was, as Alec told him, a great place to farm Souls if he was short. A quick glance at his current reserves made Jacob smile.

He didn't need to waste his time here. His goal was to get through the asylum as fast as possible through the basements, ignite the Pyre there and press on.

The main hall was frigid. Flurries of snow drifted in from the broken, crumbling gaps in the walls. Ice gathered on the exposed surfaces, creating false reflections and shimmers of light that distracted Jacob as they tried to press deeper into the asylum.

Following what he could remember of Alec's directions, Jacob took a series of decrepit tunnels off to the left. Instead of using the stairs, Camilla found a series of rooms so badly damaged by the frost that the outer walls caved in. The damage from the cave-in created broken gaps in the stone flooring. A direct path down several levels of the asylum.

So far they had only seen a few creatures, patients in various medieval torture devices like straitjackets, cages placed on their heads, shock collars, and more than a few with large sections of their skull missing.

The crumbling walls of the asylum grew tighter, the rooms they ventured within, claustrophobic. The deeper they went, the more the asylum seemed to bend in on itself in unnatural ways.

Doing their best to avoid any sort of conflict, the pair tried to stay in visual range whenever possible. But due to the tight turns and narrow halls, it was often impossible.

The number of things that required speech was surprising. Even something as simple as warning Camilla about a bug-like creature skittering up from one of the pits in one of the outer walls required Jacob to physically touch the woman and point out the threat.

They were both so wound up that any touch likely brought up a reactionary attack. Camilla nearly lost a finger when she tugged on Jacob's belt, pulling him back into a room just as a lumbering creature emerged into the hall looking about suspiciously.

That silencing enchantment worked both ways. While they were undeniably stealthier, so was everything else. But it meant that if a creature did not directly see Jacob or Camilla, they were in the clear.

It was slow going for a while, skulking from one ruined chamber to the next, peering out using gaps in the walls or looking both ways and praying something wasn't perched just outside the door.

Jacob sported more than a few bruises from Camilla's surprisingly strong right-cross. Her go-to whenever she was startled. Was it his imagination, or was she growing stronger?

Her first few surprised attacks were weak and feeble but the longer they were together, the stronger Camilla seemed to get. She still looked like death warmed over but she no longer acted like it.

Camilla ventured out into the narrow hall. The hairs on the back of Jacob's neck stood on end, something wasn't right but he couldn't put his finger on it.

The hallway looked different from the others. For one, it led to a clearly visible staircase that would let them go deeper into the asylum.

The last fifteen minutes had them venturing all over the labyrinth of crossing narrow hallways in an attempt to find more holes in the floor to go down deeper. The sudden appearance of what they so desperately needed filled Jacob with more concern than relief.

Pyresouls didn't work that way. If starvation was a mechanic, then the first thing any player would see after feeling the pit of despair in their stomach grow would be a tasty looking apple.

Sure enough, that apple would be poisoned and kill the player. *That is how Pyresouls worked* and so spying a staircase when they saw no other path deeper was more than a little worrying.

Since they were now well into the sub-levels of the asylum, there wasn't much damage to the surrounding structure. Just as Camilla was about to step forward, seeing no immediate danger, Jacob spotted it.

A glint of polished metal that sent his internal alarm bells ringing like crazy. With no time to warn her properly, Jacob reached and grabbed a handful of the chains she had crisscrossed around her robes.

He narrowly managed to pull her back just as her foot fell onto the pressure plate, activating the rows of five-foot-long metal spikes from the sides and ceiling.

They fit together perfectly, creating a mesh of thin spikes. Camilla turned and slugged Jacob right in the face, splattering his nose to his face. A steady stream of blood trickled down over his lips and his eyes watered from the sudden bright spots of pain that danced in his vision.

Purely - stupidly - on reaction, he popped a [Cinder Ampoule], bringing his supply to just a single ampoule left. If they didn't find a Pyre and soon, he would run out. And that was extremely bad.

Camilla tried to mouth that she was sorry, going so far as to place her hands on the sides of his helm to inspect the rapidly healing damage. Jacob shook her off and pointed at the hall.

The spikes were gone now, retreated back into the cunningly worked holes set within the shadowed mortar above. Jacob took the tip of his sword and pressed on the slightly off-colored stone tile.

Spikes sprang out from the walls and ceiling silently.

They looked back at each other and knew that despite the risks they needed to press on. Their options were limited and though they couldn't see the source of the rhythmic vibrations they occasionally felt through the stone, they could guess the size of the beast that might make them.

Neither of them wanted to run into a Minos, or worse. His last run-in with the creature required two ampoules to survive the encounter. Now he only had one and without his sense of hearing a Minos would gore him before he ever saw it coming.

Taking out a small glowing jagged piece of white stone the length of her middle finger, Camilla crouched down and marked the tile with a slightly glowing white X.

It didn't escape either of their notice that the tile was set in the center of the narrow hall. While it would be awkward to sidle along the edge, it might be a decent way of avoiding traps.

Then again, that might make it easier for either of them to end up as shishkabobs.

Forced to tap each of the stones ahead with his [Longsword], Jacob finally understood the old joke about Dungeons and Dragons, and ten-foot poles. He would have killed for one at the moment.

Each trap they came to, he would trigger and Camilla would mark. Thankfully, most of the traps were simple. Spikes were incredibly common, once or twice a bladed pendulum would slide out of a narrow channel set in the wall and sweep across their path.

The darkness of the deeper levels made it impossible to see where a trap might spring. And only an occasional shimmer from Jacob's Fractured Sight curse gave him any clue which pieces of the flooring might be trapped.

And even then it was a coin toss whether it was correct or not.

Without the subtle illumination coming off their bodies, they would have died a horrible death many times over. Thankfully the monsters couldn't see it, or else they would stand out like torches in the dark of night.

Nothing explosive reared its head and there were no trap doors. Still, it took them the better part of an hour to reach the end of the hallway. They took to the stairs immediately, only to find out the horrible truth.

They were an illusion.

Jacob banged his fist against the illusory image of a darkened stairwell, feeling only the hard stone. The hall hit a T-junction where they stood, so Jacob struck off down the left path.

There would be no "Perception Skill" that would highlight things for Jacob if he kept trying to peer into the lightless murk more than fifteen feet out from him. The upside was, the traps were fairly obvious once he got used to them.

While the traps themselves might vary, the trigger plate was always in the center of the room and was slightly darker than the surrounding ones. Not enough that a casual observer would note the difference as being odd but after repeated observations, it was easy to spot them.

Tight corners and long halls made this section of the asylum an ambusher's daydream as they crept deeper in. Focused on the traps, Jacob went around the next corner. Finding it clear, he looked back for Camilla only to find her gone.

A brief glance farther down the hall they came from revealed a door slightly agape that wasn't before. Jacob turned on his heels and ran toward it, heedless of the traps he might have missed.

The door across from the partially ajar one burst open as he came upon it, the heavy impact arrested his movement and even managed to throw him back 3 feet. The wooden door shattered on impact.

Though he lacked the musculature to support the years of training, Jacob managed to stay on his feet. He wasn't as strong as he had been but he was close.

Out of the door came a brute half-again his height and nearly three times as wide with biceps that bulged and ripped its straitjacket. Buckles and straps flailed as the creature squeezed through the open door, its milky-white eyes snapping to Jacob.

Shit.

Overbalanced as he was and seeing the size of his adversary, he knew he was in trouble.

The monstrous creature grinned at him through a horrifying lipless visage with teeth that were filed down to resemble a shark's. With a soundless roar, it charged.

Blocking it would surely take more Stamina than he possessed, and getting his block broken would leave him dazed and vulnerable. Against such a monstrosity, that was a death sentence.

And if Camilla wasn't already dead, she would need his help. Unlike him, she wouldn't come back.

With the creature's bulky shoulders practically scraping the walls on either side of the hallway, Jacob's only recourse was to find a suitable place to stand his ground.

So he turned and ran, flinging open as many doors as he could along the way in a desperate bid to slow the monster down. He had to keep looking over his back to see what was going on because the silence made it impossible to tell if the creature was gaining on him or not.

He could feel the vibrations in the stone floor from each door being smashed apart but little else. Seeing the blind corner up ahead, Jacob had an idea. Back the way they came was a hallway with several traps. Spikes that would erupt from the walls if triggered.

The only problem was, he was running away from them.

An issue he would have to remedy.

Dismissing his shield, knowing it would be useless at the moment anyway, Jacob reached out to grip the wall as he rounded the corner at full speed. Using his arm as a lever to whip him into the narrow hall, he entered the very first door he came upon and shut it quickly.

Heart hammering in his chest, Jacob could feel the lumbering steps of the brute just outside the hall as it made the turn and continued on without sight of its quarry. He hoped it was as dumb as it looked and continued down the hall away from him. Turning around to take in the room he was within, made him instantly regret his decision.

There were four beds, all containing a twisted body wrapped up in barbed wire and stuck through with long iron spikes pinning their limbs to their sides. They lifted their heads, a rusting iron cage fastened over their skull-like heads. Glowing blue fires flickered in their eyes.

Really?

The creatures before him weren't fast, but they rose from their beds with a languid grace that made his blood run cold. They *floated* through the air toward him, the burning blue fires in their eyes froze him to the spot for a heartbeat.

It was nearly enough.

He didn't recognize them immediately and that second of gathering awareness cost him dearly. Vile Insinuators by name, they were foul twisted creatures that invaded people's minds and destroyed them from within.

Back on Earth, during the silent rise of the Vile Kingdom, the Insinuators were a terrifying anomaly. It took many long years to learn the horrible truth of their origins.

The weak were obliterated instantly, nothing was left of who they were. They were the lucky ones.

Those with enough willpower to resist the initial mental attack – signified by the blue flare of fire in their eyes – but not enough to break free were taken and tormented.

Many died horrible deaths and those few that survived the countless mental and physical tortures at the hands of the Insinuators were molded into monstrosities just like their captors. Then they would go out in search of more victims to start the cycle anew.

They became one of the Vile Kingdom's most feared weapons. Luckily, the process to create one was so difficult that killing even one Vile Insinuator was devastating.

To find them so readily, and so many in one place was truly disturbing.

Jacob quickly built up a wall of anger and rage to block out the mental intrusion. Each brick, a memory of a different tragedy. The Red Plague. The lies of the Vile Kingdom. Kim's bloodied teeth grinning up at Jacob as she drowned in her own blood from a wound that should have been Jacob's.

He pushed off the Insinuator's attempt to lock his body up and ripped the door open, rushing back into the hall. They reached out twisted, backward-facing limbs to him. More hands and arms than they had any right to have. He felt more than one scrape against his armor without finding purchase.

Hoping that the brute wasn't lingering outside of the door, Jacob turned back the way he came and ran for all he was worth. The few seconds of idleness had restored more than half of his Stamina.

As he rounded the corner and looked over his shoulder, Jacob knew he wouldn't have the luxury of any more rest. The brute hadn't been far past Jacob's door when he burst out and was fast gaining on him with the four Vile Insinuators close behind, floating in the brute's wake.

Sprinting flat-out, his Stamina bleeding away, Jacob lured the brute down the nearby trap-filled hall. With less than a tenth of his Stamina remaining, he lunged forward and threw himself into a roll, right over the trigger for the spike trap.

Jacob hit the ground hard. Tucking his shoulder and mindful of his sword, he executed the roll and even managed to twist about to face the charging brute. There was nowhere else to hide.

The fear on his face was genuine. It only made the brute grin and snarl silently with greater glee. Standing there took all of Jacob's willpower. The combat training in his brain told him to run or at least ready his sword but he kept the tip pointed toward the stones.

What he needed was the brute to think he was too tired – which was true – and too afraid – that was only partly true – to do anything other than stare at his impending death.

He kept his eyes fastened on the lumbering creature, wary that it may be smart enough to watch its step if he stared at the trigger mechanism less than three feet away.

C'mon, c'mon, just a little more big guy. There you go. The look of fear was washed away by a wide-spreading grin as the monster stepped right on the pressure plate.

The creature took half a step more before it was impaled dozens of times, held in place with a look of abject confusion on its grotesque, lipless face. Dark blood oozed out as the spikes retracted and the creature staggered three steps forward, forcing Jacob to backpedal quickly.

He couldn't go too far though as he glanced over his shoulder and saw the next pressure plate a few inches away. Mindful not to share the creature's fate, Jacob stepped around the pressure plate and put more distance between him and the dying, lumbering thing.

The concern was unwarranted. The lumbering creature fell to its knees, stretched its bloody maw wide in a silent scream, and fell to the ground at Jacob's feet, very dead.

You defeat the [Brute Patient]
Awarded 1,250 Souls.
You gain [Bright Spark].
You gain [Whisper of Insanity].

Jacob's victory was cut short when he saw the quartet of Vile Insinuators round the corner and float down the hallway after him.

In the fear and turmoil, he had lost the mental wall he had erected and had to build it up once more as the blue fires in their skulls flared again. Four waves of mental intrusion struck him at once and he staggered under the assault. His mind worked feverishly to come up with a solution.

While he struggled against the waves of psychic pressure, he noticed that the four were speeding up. Like predators sensing an easy kill, they thought he was ensnared. And so Jacob played along, biding his time and regenerating his Stamina.

As soon as the first Vile Insinuator came close enough that he could smell its rotten reek, he broke the fake trance.

Knowing he would only get one chance, he lunged forward with his [Longsword], mindful of the trap in front of him. Though it was often used with rapier style weapons, Jacob used *Hummingbird Kisses the Rose*.

With a much heavier [Longsword], the blade ripped through the meager defenses of the Insinuator and even managed to tear right through to the one behind. A cruel twist and sideways tug pulled the blade out and tore a mortal wound in the sadistic creatures.

While the [Mace] possessed a higher damage rating than his new [Longsword], his skill paired with the unique attributes of the blade made it the superior weapon. Not only could a [Mace] not impale two creatures as he just did, its reach was drastically shorter.

More than that, even though the physical damage was less on the [Longsword] it scaled off of two stats, DEX and STR. Both of which Jacob had at 10 now. While the [Mace] scaled exclusively off of STR - making it stronger in the long run - for now, the [Longsword] had superior damage.

And it likely would remain superior unless he ran into one of the many monsters resistant to piercing or slashing.

Jacob wanted to back up but knew he couldn't without triggering the next trap. Not that it mattered. He couldn't tear his eyes away from the violent spectacle even if he wanted to.

The two Insinuators, mortally wounded, were unable to control their own power. The blue fires in their eyes raged and spread unchecked over their skulls. The iron cages around their heads melted into slag as their soundless screams filled the air, their jaws stretched wide.

The blue fire flashed out, staining the stones black. In an instant, the two creatures were nothing but bright afterimages on the backs of Jacob's eyelids whenever he blinked.

You defeat the [Vile Insinuator].
You defeat the [Vile Insinuator].
Awarded 2,000 Souls.

Six pairs of twisted hands reached for Jacob before he could recover from the bright flash that had incinerated the two monsters. Desperation drove the creature toward him even though it should have realized its mistake.

A clawing strike ripped a series of jagged rents across Jacob's face, nearly blinding him as he leaned back but refused to move his feet. Accepting the blow in exchange for letting the thing get so close, Jacob reached up and grasped the gnarled forearm of his attacker.

With a growling curse that was immediately silenced the moment it left his lips, Jacob twisted in the tight corridor, bringing the creature practically face-to-face with him as if they were dance partners about to perform a spin.

Instead, Jacob shoved its grasping and clawing hands farther down the hall. It didn't go far, merely floating two feet away from Jacob but it was enough.

A savage grin clued the Insinuator that something was amiss but it didn't have the time to ponder its precarious position. Jacob pressed his foot to the pressure plate.

Once again, spikes sprang forth from the walls and ceiling to impale his enemy for him. Though the Insinuator was smaller, it could not dodge so many at once. Before it could blind him with its dying flash of blue fire, Jacob turned and leveled his blade at the remaining creature, only to find it gone.

Insinuators were not known for their bravery.

Three white wisps collided with Jacob. One from behind, and two through the wall. They caught him off-guard and signaled that perhaps the Insinuator had met an untimely end after all.

Awarded 1,900 Souls.

One look at the Souls given, gave him pause, however. Aside from the number – three wisps instead of the single – the amount was all wrong.

No, that Insinuator was still out and about. Likely waiting for a chance to strike. Judging from the angle of the wisps, they could just as easily been creatures Camilla took down.

And that brought him back to the reason for all of this to begin with. The elf had gone missing. That she had potentially put down two monsters gave him some hope that she was still alive.

Breathing hard, Jacob summoned his shield, stepped around the trap, and took off at a run down the hall. The few hits he took from getting so close to the Insinuator, not to mention the repeated mental blasts had left him at just over half Health.

Turning down the next hall and coming to the ajar door, he thought about exhausting his last ampoule. If Camilla was in trouble he might need that extra Health.

Steeling himself, Jacob opened the door with bloodied handprints staining its dark wood. He was hit by a wall of fetid odor that nearly knocked him off his feet.

Jacob staggered back, forcing his breathing through his mouth, tasting the iron tang of his blood as he inadvertently sucked in the few droplets that ran down his lips.

Camilla stood before him, draped in viscera, and soaked through with black and red blood. She had a wild light in her red eyes, her hair plastered to the sides of her face and a long jagged wound that ripped a hole down her left sleeve.

A stream of blood ran down her left arm as it hung there, limp and lifeless. The steady drip of her bright-red blood down her fingertips to the stone below distracted Jacob for a moment. As her blood mixed with that of... whatever coated the stones and Camilla, it sizzled violently and emitted a red vapor.

Camilla mouthed, "Not a word." And then pushed past him into the hall. Bloody, fetid muscle tissue clung to her foot and dragged a streaking trail after her.

A quick glance into the room made Jacob shudder.

Jacob caught up to her and gently pressed two fingertips to her spine. Partly because he didn't want to risk losing anymore Health from a startled Camilla. The softness of the touch caused her to pause and look over her shoulder at him.

He tried to smile, but the burning pain from the action as it stretched wide the bleeding wounds on his face brought forth a grimace instead.

Pointing, he motioned to the length of intestine on her shoulder. Camilla looked at it with disgust and brushed it off. It made a silent splat on the ground, oozing out some foul thick liquid in the process.

Jacob made sure to give it, and many other hunks of gore and viscera that continued to fall off Camilla's borrowed robes, a wide berth as they ventured deeper into the asylum.

As far as Jacob was concerned, those robes were hers now.

14

Together, the pair made it deep into the dark recesses of the asylum. So far down below the hallways were as much natural cavern as worked stone. Gaping wounds in the stone walls led to expansive lightless spaces of unknowable size.

Strange, lizard-like creatures crawled forth from such spaces, ambushing them at times and at others being caught unawares by the duo. The higher Jacob's skill with his sword grew, the slower the skill up messages came.

He had hoped to be back to 75 Sword Skill by the time they reached the next Pyre but it didn't seem likely.

They were still silenced but despite Camilla's strongest resource being taken away, she made do with a large rusty cleaver. The same one she managed to find when a couple of Patients took her when Jacob wasn't looking.

A slight smirk came to his lips, a light to his forest-green eyes. Camilla was full of surprises and it ended up that she didn't need his help after all. The dynamic between them was becoming more and more like a partnership.

Jacob helped bandage up Camilla's bleeding arm to the best of his ability, enough to stop the bleeding at least.

They developed rudimentary hand signals to alert each other and constantly kept in visual contact to avoid being separated again. The unfortunate side effect was that, at times, they would both be caught in an ambush.

Like right then.

Jacob, in his haste to find a Pyre, went around the next corner without checking it. Something inside him said there would be a Pyre nearby. He felt it in his bones, almost as if he were standing at the farthest edge from the warm flames.

A flicker of movement to the side had him rolling forward, too committed to the motion to reverse. In doing so, he inadvertently separated from Camilla who just turned the corner at that moment.

Out from two holes, one between him and Camilla, and one behind Jacob crawled those sticky-footed lizards. Their mottled red-and-yellow skin shimmered wetly.

Having faced them a few times already, Jacob immediately pivoted on the balls of his feet and at the same time shifted to a two-hand grip on his [Longsword].

As he spun about, raising his blade high and tightening his core muscles to bring it down, the Gekk reared up to bite him.

With a concerted snap of his core muscles, Jacob brought his [Longsword] flashing down. *Lightning Cracks Stone* cleaved the opened fang-filled maw in half. Even as the monster fell, another came at him.

Jacob was already in motion.

Stag Rushes Through the Field closed the gap to the next Gekk, and he seamlessly transitioned his blade, pointing it low and to his left. This lizard was smarter than its brethren, and it managed to back up several sticky-footed steps.

Wind Parts the Grass caught it but only drew a line of yellow ichor from its fast-retreating underbelly as it reared up on its hind legs and backpedaled comically fast.

A quick glance at the corridor walls confirmed that Jacob had enough room. He was at less than 20% of his Stamina, using another Sword Form might deplete it and leave him vulnerable.

The safer thing would be to let the creature back up, take a moment to reorient himself and regenerate Stamina. But if he could kill it quickly enough, they could be gone before reinforcements ever arrived.

That was the problem with Gekks. They would make a reverberating croak he could feel in his belly that summoned more of their kind through the walls. At 78 Health, with his last [Cinder Ampoule] used up getting this far down, he wasn't interested in a protracted battle.

Especially when he was *certain* that there was a Pyre nearby.

So Jacob didn't do the smart or safe thing. He lunged forward, swung his sword out at maximum extension, nearly clanging it off the corridor walls and twisted.

Already raised on its hind legs and unable to move back any faster, *Leaf Circles the Whirlpool* freed the creature's head from its neck. Sparks flew from the tip of his [Longsword] as it skipped off the stone walls.

Exhausted and breathing hard, Jacob paid no more attention to the Gekk's body. It backpedaled a few more steps, not quite aware that it was dead yet before it fell bonelessly to the floor.

Turning back, he saw Camilla split a Gekk in half like she was chopping firewood. Recovering his Stamina, Jacob made his way back one plodding step at a time.

The last remaining Gekk opened its maw wide at her. Jacob knew from personal experience that those dozens of teeth were filled with a poison that continued to deal damage long after the initial painful bite was finished.

Her eyes flickered up to Jacob's. He nodded and positioned the flat of his [Longsword] across his body, a signal to her that she was to stall the creature.

Over short distances, a Gekk could outpace either of them with ease. Provided it was running in the direction it was facing. So backpedaling was useless, and Camilla had to know that because she came forward suddenly raising the meat cleaver, bracing the flat of the rusted blood-soaked blade with her free hand.

Predictably, the Gekk surged to meet her with its maw snapping at her. She managed to fit the cleaver into the thing's mouth, blocking a more potent bite. From the grimace of pain Jacob saw on her face, she still felt the sting of at least a few teeth and the poison that coated them.

Jacob was there, reversing his grip on the [Longsword] and driving it down into the creature's body. *Planting the Flag* pinned it to the stone like a gigantic kebab and dealt a mortal blow all at once.

Freed from the creature's sudden thrashing, Camilla backed up and with one sure swing of her cleaver severed the thing's head. It was a few moments before the body of the creature – now dousing Camilla in yellow blood like a loose garden hose – stilled and fell to the ground.

For their trouble, they received 1,200 Souls and several vials of [Gekk Blood]. Camilla wasted no time in taking out one such vial. Before Jacob could stop her, she put it to her lips and drank. A brief flash of yellow-green light rippled down her body.

At Jacob's incredulous stare, she stepped forward onto the corpse of the creature and pointed at the bite wound on her forearm. The oozing virulent green poison was being pushed out of the wound.

The blood, when imbibed, counteracted any poison or toxin in the body making it a valuable item to have.

Jacob had heard of such items before, Pyresouls Online wasn't particularly specific about their antidotes. If one item cured poison, it cured all types of poison regardless of the source.

Jacob marked that information down. If the Pyre wasn't too far, it wouldn't be a bad idea to come back here and farm for some [Gekk Blood]. The Corpse Garden he would need to go through was particularly toxic, as was the Defiled Cistern where the water itself was poisonous.

As they turned to continue, Jacob started to taste blue raspberries. Fear shot through him like a lightning bolt and he turned back to Camilla, trying to explain what was about to happen.

The look of fear that mirrored on her face reminded him that the enchantment of silence was still active. He must have looked terrified, quickly moving his lips to explain something she would never hear.

Even as he did, his limbs filled with static and he felt that familiar tug at his navel, pulling him back with a violent tug into the darkness.

May 7th, 2045 – 10 Years Post-Collapse.

Darkness still held dominion even as his other senses returned. His body ached and he soon realized he was making a painfully tight fist with each hand. In fact, as awareness continued to assault him, he came to realize it wasn't just his hands. Every muscle in his body was flexed in a painful spasm that wracked his whole body.

"I told you it wasn't safe!" That was Ian. Jacob had never heard him so angry.

"You have the levetiracetam, do you not?" Alice's tone was clipped and slightly accented.

"Yes, but it will only stop the symptoms-"

"Give it to him!"

The darkness pulled back by inches. His body began to relax but the pain seemed to climb higher.

Everything hurt. Worse, it was so *cold*. He felt like those nights he was on watch duty in the winter when they weren't able to light a fire for fear of being spotted.

He was beyond shivering. The cold was bone-deep and it *hurt*. The fierce ache of his muscles was nothing compared to the pain in his entire skeleton. He tried to open his eyes but a cold hand reached up from the depths and grabbed him.

Everything turned so very cold. His breath caught in his chest and it felt like his heart might explode. Jacob cried out as the pain reached a crescendo and then fell off a cliff into nothingness. The icy grip relaxed and he felt like he was falling into a dark abyss.

"Jacob?" Kim called, nudging Jacob in the ribs. "C'mon man, no sleeping on the job. That's soldier duty 101." The lithe form of Kimberly O'Neill sat next to him.

Looking around, Jacob noticed they were sitting on a familiar rooftop on the outskirts of some town in Virginia. He remembered that safehouse. Almost a full year they had been safe and secure. Long enough to start a rooftop garden on top of the old school building.

At first, he thought something went terribly, terribly wrong. But the lack of the blue raspberry flavor that usually coated his tongue, and the dream-like sensation of this place felt more like a memory than anything to do with erroneous time travel.

"Kim?" he asked, incredulously.

Kim was dead. He watched the light leave her eyes. He had helped her pass on himself, making sure she would never turn Vacant. It was the least he could do when she had given her life to save his.

Jacob fought back the moisture gathering at the edges of his eyes and turned away from her to look at the blood-red sky.

"I miss the blue skies," she said, leaning back on her palms. "Do you remember them? The way the shades of blue would differ throughout the day? The white cottony clouds drifting lazily above you on a warm summer's day?"

She groaned in the back of her throat, a deep longing for a better time. "And the warmth of a summer's sun on my skin. *Ugh*, I miss sunbathing. Back when the flame of the world wasn't blown out. When you could get warm – hot even – just standing out in the sunlight."

Jacob let her ramble on for several minutes. It was clear she was lost in nostalgia and he found himself slipping into that younger version of himself.

Virginia... that would mean this is roughly two, maybe even three years Post-Collapse. A year after the Red Plague but the worst is yet to come. We're right on the edge of the Vile Kingdom's territory.

The memory of the sudden betrayal by the Vile Kingdom and the reason they left the shelter of that private school in Virginia came back to him. Jacob pushed the painful images away.

"Jake?" Kim turned her brilliant baby-blue eyes on him. He never told her how he felt about her, but he was pretty sure she knew anyway. The way he blushed and stammered around her. How she could tongue-tie him with just a look.

"Am I dead?" he asked, unable to stop himself. On some level, he knew this must be a dream or something like it. But a small part of him – the shadow of his soul – hoped that perhaps his fight was over. Let some other person be yanked back and forth through time.

Hadn't he lost enough already?

The moment of weakness passed as Jacob crushed it under his heel. No, he wasn't going to just roll over and give up. Who *hadn't* lost friends, family, and loved ones? *Suck it up,* he chastised himself.

Kim giggled and slapped him on the arm. Back in Virginia, it was safe enough that he didn't need to wear armor all the time. Not that he had a full set of medieval armor yet. He wore a leather jacket though, more to ward off the cold than anything.

"No, of course not, dude!" She motioned around to the red sky and the burned-out shells of buildings around them. The streets were filled with strategically overturned cars that created a maze of corridors to slow any approaching threat.

"Then what are you doing here?" he asked. She wasn't *really* there, he knew that. Despite that knowledge, he hoped she wouldn't take offense at his tone and leave.

"I'm kind of... a whatchamacallit... a safe place, I guess," she answered, still thinking of the word. Jacob knew what she meant immediately.

"*This* is my happy place?"

"Yep!" She looped a strong arm over his shoulders and gave him a sidelong hug. "Lazy days on watch, doing nothing special. And for the first time thinking about what could be, instead of what was lost. This was a good time, man. You forget that."

All Jacob could do was shrug. Kim was dead, whoever was talking back to him wasn't her. At best, it was his own subconscious trying to communicate through her or at least doing its best impersonation.

Which, he supposed was pretty good. The freckles across the bridge of her nose were just as he remembered. A flash of a bloodied smile invaded his thoughts and he scrambled to his feet suddenly, pushing off her arm and panting with sudden panic.

"Hey, hey, Jake calm down," she said, getting to her feet and putting up her hands. "You're safe here. Nothing's going to happen to you."

He backed up a few steps and eyed her cautiously. "I'm not worried about *me*."

That gave her pause. She let her arms fall to her sides. "That's fair, y'know."

"What am I doing here?"

"I believe you've already caught onto that."

"Are you seriously pulling some psychoanalytical bullshit on me? You're me, right? So just tell me."

With a shrug, Kim collapsed into a cross-legged position in one smooth motion. "You're unconscious. Stress, or maybe something the docs gave you. I don't know, dude. I'm not *there*. Neither am I *you*. It's complicated and the particulars of it would go right over your head anyway."

He wasn't entirely sure he believed her. In the end, he realized it didn't matter. Kim patted a nearby spot on the roof, a pair of threadbare pillows to sit atop.

It barely rained anymore, so they left out blankets and pillows on the rooftop for people to sit and tend the garden or just to enjoy the little bit of greenery left in the world.

Sitting across from her, Jacob found himself staring at her again. "What am I doing here?"

"Resting," came her answer. She leaned forward, placed her palms on her knees and grinned impishly at him as she always used to. Right before she got them both in trouble. "I have a secret, wanna see?"

"I swear... if you turn into some eldritch monstrosity I will be *sorely* disappointed in you Kimberly O'Neill."

She answered with a throaty chuckle, took her hands off her knees, and raised them in the air between Jacob and herself. "I need your help though. Think you're up for it?"

Humoring her, Jacob nodded.

"Good boy. Stick out your hands like this. No, cup your hands. Yep, now make sure all your fingertips are touching each other." Kim gave him a flat look. "Ya got thumbs, don'tcha? Touch 'em! Good. Now focus on me."

Blue eyes dancing with mirth, Kimberly stared at her own cupped palms in that strange pose. Focused on her eyes, Jacob missed what she was doing at first. It appeared as a faint glimmer reflected in her wide eyes that he mistook for the setting sun.

Then a small fire blossomed in her palms and his eyes were torn from her beautiful pixie features to the tiny flame that shimmered and danced and grew.

Three heartbeats later it was a proper flame, dancing and filling up her cupped palms. She leaned forward, catching Jacob by surprise and planted a kiss on his lips. At the same time, she brought her cupped hands to his and tilted them over his.

Her lips tasted like sunflower seeds and lemonade. Her favorites. Jacob was stunned. He stared, dumbfounded into her baby-blue eyes.

Eyes he could get lost in forever.

She wrinkled her nose and smirked at him, eyes twinkling. "Always wanted to do that. Least I got the chance to see how it felt now. Pretty good, Jacob Windsor. Not gonna lie. Pretty damn good. But you might wanna look at your hands, instead of me. We ain't got long."

The fire in her palms had fallen into his. Instinctively, he moved to pull his hands apart, afraid of getting burned.

Kim's hands were there on his, forcing them together with the same impressive strength he remembered her having. "There, doesn't that feel better?"

No longer panicked, Jacob could focus on the magical flame in his palm. It was warm. Alive.

Cupped in his palms he could feel a faint echo of the Pyre. That same warmth that seeped into his bones and chased away the chill that had settled on the world. A chill that only grew with each passing day since the Collapse.

"How?" he asked, nonplussed.

Kim leaned back and gently, so very gently, released her hands from his, lingering her fingertips on the backs of his hands. "A girl's got to have her secrets."

All he could do was nod dumbly. A spike of alarm stabbed through him as lightning spiderwebbed across the nearly cloudless red sky. "What the-"

Rolling forward onto her knees, Kim cupped Jacob's face in her hands. She smiled through glittering tears in her eyes. "Just remember this, remember my face. Remember the flame, Jacob. It's important. I wish we had more time."

"What? Where are you going? Don't leave-"

A shake of her head silenced him as the lightning sparkled at the edge of his vision and darkness began to fold over everything. "I'm not leaving, Jacob. You are."

15

"He's back in normal sinus rhythm," Ian said, his voice was strained. Tired.

"Why is he not waking up?" Alice asked. "Everything reads normal, no?"

"Jacob nearly *died*, Alice. Give him some time. His body is likely still recovering. Just because he's in stable condition doesn't mean he's going to be up on his feet, walking around."

"We do not have the *time*," she began but stopped suddenly. It sounded like an old argument, one she had made many times and was tired of making.

"I know."

"Let him rest," Alice said wearily. "You will call me the moment he awakes, yes?"

"Very well."

Jacob could hear the door to the room open and shut. A few moments later he felt a hand on his shoulder. "She's gone, Jacob."

He popped open his eyes and stared up at the older man and his ridiculous affectation of a mustache. "Guess I just wanted a few minutes to myself," he said with a pained chuckle, trying to hide the way he actually felt.

Every joint ached. Every muscle felt torn after a day of heavy marching. And despite having been asleep, he was so *tired*.

"You're going to be sore for a while," Ian confirmed. "Can you sit up?"

With a nod, Jacob began the slow, arduous process of sitting up. He felt like an old man.

"There you go," Ian encouraged. "Just like that." He took out a small device and tapped it against the patch on the side of his neck. "Let me just make sure your vitals are synced up properly... yep. All signs point to you being a healthy young man."

"But?" Jacob asked, hearing the slight tremor in the doctor's voice.

Quirking his lips into a pensive frown, Ian looked straight into Jacob's face. He wasn't one to look away from a bad situation. "We nearly lost you. It was the strangest thing I ever saw. It wasn't quite a heart attack and yet you were quite dead for a few seconds there. No brain activity, your heart stopped... we brought you back but I don't know how many more times we can do that.

"We don't even know *why* it happened. Alice swears that her tech is not causing it but I cannot find a *medical* reason why you're in such duress. First, it was seizures and now this. The next time you're brought back, you might not make it Jacob. I want you to remember that. Not to scare you but to remind you...."

"Remind me of what?"

"You do not have to do this."

"Unfortunately, he does," Alice said, her lilting french tones coloring her words.

"Don't you knock?" Ian asked.

With a shrug, which made her red curls bounce, Alice came forward to stand beside Ian and look at Jacob. She frowned slightly. "I will not force you. Never will I do that. But you are now connected. It is a thread I cannot break and it makes this machine useless to any but you."

Alice gently stroked the curving metal frame of the FIVR pod as if it were a favored pet. "Unless you know of another [Ember of Probability]? I thought not. Still, worth asking, no?"

"I wasn't going to stop anyway," Jacob said, squaring his shoulders resolutely. "Put me back in."

Ian was shaking his head and for a wonder, so was Alice. "We know so very little of what we do," she said, lips pursed. "The toll it takes on your body must be great. Rest, and eat. While you do, you can brief us. Perhaps you have changed enough things that there are differences."

"What do you mean? I've barely done anything," Jacob said. Then he groaned, realizing Camilla was left all alone in the depths of the asylum.

Alice leaned forward, eyes sparkling. "What is it?"

"When you pulled me out, I was with Camilla. She's... it's hard to explain right now but we were both injured and hoping to find a Pyre. Without me there-"

"She will be fine." Alice shook her head. "We can send you back to her. While the process is not... exact, it will be within a few seconds. To her, you will have simply froze up for a few moments. Perhaps in fear." She patted him on the cheek. "I will go fetch Alec."

Alice swept out of the room, leaving Ian to go sit down on a rolling office chair and put his head in his hands.

"Still think I can just walk away?" Jacob asked, folding his legs beneath him. He felt naked wearing nothing but a pair of thick woolen socks, a shirt, and a pair of sweats. Not that they did anything to ward off the perpetual chill in the air.

There was something *wrong* about the world and it only truly dawned on him how wrong it was after experiencing life before the Collapse. The change came on slowly but no matter how much hot air they forced through the vents, no matter how close he stood to a roaring fire, there was a perpetual chill in his bones.

Kimberly had said it best. It was like the world's fire was snuffed out. Though the more Jacob thought about it, the more he felt it was more internal than that. It wasn't the world, it was them.

As ridiculous as it seemed, it was like each person's soul had grown cold and dark. Not in the metaphorical evil way but physically. Any heat he felt was on the surface.

Ian looked up. "We could leave again, find another place," he offered weakly.

Jacob chuckled and repeated an old phrase among the survivors. "'Run far and hide in deep holes'?" That didn't help anybody.

The doctor merely shrugged his shoulders. For once at a loss. Not that Jacob blamed him. Eventually, even this recent safety would be found and they would be overrun.

Many people would die in the exodus and their numbers were already lower than they had ever been before.

What used to be hundreds of able-bodied survivors was reduced to double digits. Most of which were so essential – or weak – that they couldn't defend themselves, much less anybody else.

They had more armor and weapons than they had bodies to use them. And each month there were more deaths. It had been nearly a year since Jacob saw any other soul beyond his group.

The world was so empty.

"Jacob!" Alec said, rushing over to him and burying him in a brotherly hug, mindful of his IV. He pulled him out to arm's length. "Man, I'm so glad you're okay! Alice told me all about it, you know you don't have to go back in if you don't want to, right?"

Jacob returned the hug with a single arm and nodded. "I know, but it's not like you guys can get another person to do it, can you?"

"Well...."

"Yeah, that's what I thought. So, I can be selfish as hell... or I can suck it up and do my duty. Not much different than raiding a Spider-wasp nest for their medicinal silk, is it?"

A shudder coursed through each of the four people standing there. One of the most horrific mutations to come from the Collapse. But their silk, when wrapped around a wound could dramatically speed up healing as well as ridding the body of any infection or toxins.

"You made your point." Alec shook his head, found a seat, and pulled up the chair right beside Jacob's bed. "Kat's going to join us when dinner is ready, if you don't mind?"

Jacob could only shrug.

"Good," Alice said. She looked over at Ian. "He is in proper health?"

"As far as I could tell," he agreed. "But you will recall, we thought that an hour or so ago too after the first episode."

"Last episode?" Jacob asked.

"You had a mild seizure the first time we brought you back," Alice said, waving away the concern with a slim hand. "Nothing like this. Perhaps it is based on the length of time... the first time we pulled you out, you were in the middle of something, yes?"

"Fighting," Jacob answered.

"And this time?"

"We just finished clearing up a group of Gekks."

"Aw man, those were horrible," Alec said with a groan. "Though, if they drop some Gekk Blood you can use it to recover from their poison."

Jacob nodded. "I learned that from Camilla, would have been good to know going in."

Alec raised his palms in surrender. "Sorry man. I know it sounds like a cop-out but that was over a decade ago. Small details like that are hard to remember but if you can tell us where you are in the game and where you're going it could probably jog my memory some. Are you still in the Steps of Penance?"

"No, I'm out."

The door opened, Kat came in with a large tray of food and a bright smiling face. "Dinnertime!" She was forcing that happiness so hard Jacob worried she might burst a blood vessel.

Alec dragged over a table and they had an impromptu dinner together, just the five of them. Kat hopped up on the bed next to Jacob, nudging him in the ribs and prompting him to tell her more of his adventures in Pyresouls.

She wasn't the only one hanging onto his every word. Alec and Alice were taking down notes, it would be their job to compare the events that Jacob knew to the ones that occurred in their timeline.

Any mismatch meant Jacob had affected things, however slight, and would prove their theory. The problem was, Jacob was still in the beginning stages of the game.

For most people, the undead village of Hollow Dreams was the mid-way point of the game. It marked a sharp increase in difficulty that many people couldn't get over.

In his original timeline, it was just after Hollow Dreams, in the Defiled Cistern that he gave up and left the game. Hardly an accomplishment.

Any changes Jacob was likely to enact would be at that point or later. Or so he thought.

While they were discussing the events of the last few days, Alec said something that startled him with his spoon of canned soup halfway to his mouth. "Who?" he asked.

"Matilda, you know her," Alec said. "You, Matilda, and Kat here disobeyed a direct order and went to meet Caleb as soon as you heard the report instead of defending the bunker. You saved Caleb's life."

"He's got a long road to full recovery," Ian confirmed, "but he'll pull through."

Jacob shook his head. "I never heard of Matilda, and I *failed* to save Caleb's life. He... sacrificed himself to destroy the horde at the base of the path to the bunker, killing himself as well as Sal, Daniel, and Melissa."

Alec nodded, his expression suddenly somber. "We did lose Daniel, but Sal and Melissa are fine."

Alice's eyes lit up excitedly. "You are *absolutely* sure of this?" She lunged over the table, grabbing Jacob's hands in a surprisingly tight grip.

"Of course," Jacob said, offended. "I remember every one of our fallen. Tell me what happened."

And so they told him how he and Matilda had overheard a scout talking about what he saw. Nobody knew what it was but Jacob seemed to know something nobody else did.

Together, now with Matilda, they reached Caleb before he was overrun and they were able to give the majority of the horde the slip.

With Caleb's Sorcery, what few Vacant came upon the bunker were dealt with. Daniel still died but a single death was better than the host that was originally lost.

Alice couldn't contain her glee. Right before her was concrete proof that something was different. Their timeline was altered by Jacob's actions, though nobody quite understood how a new person joining the group would have happened from his actions.

They discussed more than just the recent events, with each of them trying to go as far back as they could remember to find other inconsistencies. There were a lot but most of the results ended up the same.

The Red Plague still came. The Vile Kingdom revealed itself to be the horrible monsters they truly were, and every other apocalyptic event after still transpired.

Whatever effect Jacob had, it wasn't enough to shift the course of the world's events.

So they ate, and they talked. When it was over, Ian came over to Jacob's IV and took out a small syringe. At the alarmed look Ian merely smiled at him. "It's just a mild sedative. You need your rest and I doubt you're going to get it constantly talking about exciting events."

Ian turned to the rest of them. "You don't have to leave but keep your voices down. You appointed me as his guardian, and I intend to make good on that." He looked back at Jacob with a wry smile. "Even if I have to protect him from himself."

Injecting the sedative into his IV, Jacob didn't feel anything right away even though Doc Ian practically forced him to lie down with his head propped up on a gel pillow.

Talk eventually turned away from the differences back to the game of Pyresouls. Kat had far more experience with the game than he recalled her ever having. And together the others discussed where Jacob was and where his next goal should be as the sedative finally kicked in and consciousness slipped through his fingers.

16

When Jacob awoke, he felt much the same as he did before. The only difference was his aches and pains seemed muted. He still felt that icy pit in the core of his being, that chill that never seemed to leave his bones.

Everybody was gone except for Kat who had taken a chair and pushed it up against the FIVR pod Jacob was using as a bed. She had fallen asleep reading a book, some worry creased her brow as Jacob looked over at her.

Was she guarding him? Or was there some emergency that called everybody else away?

Curious, Jacob sat up with a groan and nearly rolled out of the bed.

Kat's strong callused hands were there to brace him and help him sit upright in an instant.

"Sorry," Jacob said with a sheepish grin. "Didn't mean to wake you."

Kat leaned forward, the look in her tender blue eyes stunned him as she kissed his lips gently. "It's okay, I was worried something might happen to you again so I told them I'd stay with you while they got some rest too."

What the- Jacob's mind ground to a halt, the shocked expression on his face only made Kat smile even more.

He didn't have long to ponder the sudden – and very abrupt – change in Kat's demeanor. Were they together in this timeline? He always thought she looked up to him but they had never done... anything.

If Alice and Alec hadn't walked into the room at that moment, Alec snickering at the closeness of Kat and Jacob, he might have done something truly stupid. Like asking Katherine if they were together.

That would be classic Jacob. Insulting a woman that showed feelings for him.

Even though his head was still spinning from the kiss, Alec and Alice came over to greet him. They had a bullet point list ready for him, detailing where he should go next and what they were able to pull from various sources about Pyresouls.

There was still a rudimentary internet of sorts, but it resembled the older version of interconnected servers instead of freely browsed pages. You had to know the exact address and often the password to gain access to them. But it was one of the few ways groups like his had managed to stay in contact.

Some servers had gone silent, the databases were still accessible but nobody was home. And in the years after the Collapse, many universities had the bright idea to collect and document as much information about Pyresouls as possible and spread that information far and wide.

It was a far cry from a wiki, but it still held information about what happened. Archived forum posts hosting both first-hand accounts and those that were embellished by people who couldn't get past the Razorpass who were only looking for fake internet points.

Over the years, the fake accounts were trimmed, leaving a database of collective knowledge about Pyresouls Online. Highly incomplete, some parts were blatantly wrong, but it was better than nothing.

After the initial few years waned, few people bothered to update or alter it. It was included automatically in any distributed repository and often left unopened. Only now, with their ability to send Jacob back was it relevant.

And so Jacob listened with rapt attention as they rattled off potential items near his position, confirmed that there was a Pyre only two hallways away to the south, and gave him pointers on where to go next.

Included in that laundry list was the recommended parameters and level he should have for the coming area, the Desecrated Catacombs.

"Wait," he said suddenly. "I thought I was going into the Corpse Garden?"

That was, after all, where he knew the nearest Spell Gem was from his last playthrough.

"Well, yes," Alec said, "But there's a secret entrance into the Desecrated Catacombs that will allow you to skip the Corpse Garden entirely by going beneath it. I didn't know of it when I played and besides, I cleared the asylum by ringing the bell. Which you told me you didn't have any intention of doing.

"You have enough Souls that you can probably survive the upper levels of the catacombs if you're smart about what fights you pick and move quickly. *Do not linger*, Jacob. You know the reputation that place has."

Jacob nodded. It was one of the most horrible places in the entire game by all accounts. An area he hadn't reached last time. He wasn't looking forward to traversing its cramped warrens filled with unkillable skeletons.

"He will need to return there later, yes? For the…" Alice looked at her tablet, swiping down to read a particular note. "For the Ring of Broken Vows that will let you enter the Smog Rifts. Why does he not save time and get it now?"

Alec was shaking his head from the first sentence. "No, he's not strong enough for that yet. Not only is the Gnawing Hunger down there guarding the ring but there's a Crossing halfway through. He needs at least plus five armor and ideally a plus ten weapon. Otherwise, they'll just one-shot him."

That hardly seemed to disturb Alice who leaned back in her chair stroking her chin thoughtfully. Big surprise there. She wasn't the one who would be brutally murdered.

Kat reached out and held Jacob's hand, lacing her fingers through his. "Just go through the catacombs, make it through to Hollow Dreams and get some better equipment from the merchants there. If you see me there... tell me you know Ryan Thorne and he said I could trust you to trade with. I might have something you can use."

"That's a good idea," Alec said. "But try not to do that with anybody else you already know. You might say something that could have a ripple effect. Nobody's going to believe you about the Collapse, unfortunately. At worse, people will think you're trying to scare others into quitting to give yourself a better chance and they'll attack you for it.

"At best, they'll think you're some kind of doomsayer and laugh at you. Either way, calling attention to yourself isn't a great idea. I had more than one person come out of nowhere and kill me. They only take a portion of your Souls when they do that but I lost a lot of time getting that back."

"Crossings are different. If somebody kills you, they take a quarter of your currently held Souls. That's what makes the areas so dangerous. At the same time, you can find a lot of people willing to trade and there are often merchants there too."

"Why don't people just kill each other then? The two Crossings I went to were surprisingly tame," Jacob asked.

"You were there a little later," Alec explained. "At first, once people realized they could kill each other for a portion of their victim's Souls it was a constant free-for-all. Only, once people realized the losses they incurred did they stop. A lot of people thought it was basically just 'free Souls' since a wisp wasn't dropped. Fear is a powerful motivator in Pyresouls, the fear of losing so much work kept a lot of people in line."

"But the first people to realize they could do it, did so with reckless abandon," Jacob said, coming to understand just how different the game was for Alec than it was for him.

"Exactly."

Not long after that Jacob was lying down, counting back from 100 and getting ready to go back home. He started at the mental slip and had to start counting down from 100 again.

Home? he thought to himself.

But as he drifted off, he had to admit there was a grain of truth to the slip. The world Post-Collapse was, bit by bit, becoming a place he was unfamiliar with.

The constant ache of being there, the cold that never seemed to abate, and even the events he remembered clearly were all unwelcoming. On the other hand, Pyresouls Online welcomed him back with open arms.

He was in no threat of permanent death. The flames of the Pyre warmed his world-weary soul and reinvigorated him. Even after a gruesome death, their comforting flames gave him the determination to get up and go out again.

And Camilla.... He still wasn't sure how he felt about her but he was glad for the company.

With the taste of blue raspberries on his tongue, Jacob opened his eyes.

August 31st, 2035 – 13 days remain before the Collapse.

Camilla straddled his body, weaving his [Longsword] in a clumsy pattern as she just barely managed to hold off three Gekks that were testing her defenses.

The bodies of more Gekks lay scattered around them. How long had passed here?

"Oh good, you're not dead," Camilla said flatly. She stabbed his [Longsword] into the stone right between his legs. Without another word she lurched toward the leftmost creature, leaving the other two for Jacob.

Even though he was still getting his bearings, Jacob had enough training and presence of mind to get up to one knee. Instead of wasting time pulling the sword free from the stone – a feat that was surprising given Camilla's Sorcerous leanings – he dismissed and summoned it to his hand.

While Jacob was in the middle of summoning the blade, he spun in place on one knee, turning a full circuit as ash flashed into the air and his blade appeared in his hand.

Seeing him moving with no weapon the Gekks came upon him with incredible speed. As the blade reappeared in his hand, their surprise was complete as he performed *Reaping the Harvest,* drawing bright yellow lines across their low faces.

Getting to his feet, Jacob planted his foot hard on one blinded Gekk and speared the other through the head. Its companion joined the first Gekk in death a moment later.

> *You defeat the* [Gekk].
> *You defeat the* [Gekk].
> *Awarded 800 Souls.*
> *You gain 2* [Vials of Gekk Blood].
> *Your Sword Skill increases to Level 65.*

Another wisp weaved through the air to strike him in the chest as Camilla finished off her Gekk.

When Camilla turned on him she opened her mouth and then realized it was useless.

"Wait, I heard you!" he said to her.

Camilla pointed to her ears and talked very slowly, clearly trying to get him to read her lips. "I. Can't. Hear. You."

But Jacob could hear her just fine.

It amounted to the same thing, either way. They still couldn't effectively communicate. Looking at the hallway full of Gekk bodies, he must have been out for more than a few minutes.

Limping forward, Camilla begrudgingly let Jacob loop her arm over his shoulder and help her along. Together, they moved quickly through the corridor to a side path Jacob learned about.

Desecrated Catacombs

He was right, there was a Pyre here but it wasn't in the asylum. It was through a broken section of the stonework that opened onto a massive black cavern.

With his hearing restored, Jacob could hear the sticky-footed sound of lizards running about in the dark and the sound of rushing water far below in the cavern they stepped into.

Down the sloping dark path they went. If Jacob didn't know to look for the pile of bones on the floor marking the path to the Pyre he would have missed it. He turned and proceeded into a narrow roughly hewn tunnel.

It bent at such an odd angle that a casual glance would make it seem as if it were nothing more than a dead end.

Jacob knew better.

The tunnel twisted and turned, eventually opening up onto a single room with a pile of familiar ashes in the center. Jacob knelt to it at the same time Camilla did, her hands shook as she reached them over the pile of ash.

"You see it too?" he asked, but there was no reply. She wasn't looking at him and obviously, the silencing enchantment was still in effect for her.

Reaching within himself, Jacob summoned the Fire Oppa by recalling the memory of the Pyre and its soul-warming flames. Something else shot out of his hand, a small flame that fell upon the ash and disappeared.

Wiggling out from the pile of ash came the ferret-like creature, the Fire Oppa. As his dark beady eyes focused on Jacob he seemed to give the man a wolfish grin. In an instant flames blasted forth from his fur and *became his fur.*

The Pyre caught and the flames jumped nearly five-feet high. Much higher than the previous Pyres had. The pleasing crackle and warmth of them had Jacob collapsing into a rough sitting position in front of them.

Pyre Ignited.
Your respawn location has been set to the **Desecrated Catacombs (Upper)***.*

> *The Fire Oppa stokes the embers of your conviction.*
> *Health, Stamina, Ampoules, and Spell Gems restored.*
> *You Kindle the Pyre.*
> *+5 [Cinder Ampoules].*

"That's your third Pyre," the Fire Oppa said, patrolling around the flame. "And you've learned how to Kindle. Interesting."

"What do you mean?" Jacob asked.

"Kindling a Pyre makes it stronger, which allows me to confer better benefits to you. Like your Cinder Ampoules. I can now give you 10 whenever you rest at this Pyre."

"Is it only this one?"

"Any that you Kindle," the Fire Oppa said, slowing his pace and laying down in the glowing embers of the roaring fire. "Which you should be able to do now at any Pyre you visit. Even the old ones."

"Why would I go back there?"

The Fire Oppa just shrugged his burning shoulders.

Jacob could only shake his head. He hadn't even *meant* to Kindle the Pyre, it just *happened*. More than ever, he wished he could see Kim again. He didn't understand how, or even why, but she had helped him. Immensely.

Doubling his [Cinder Ampoules]... he didn't even know such a thing was possible. All of the information combed through the archives had no mention of such a thing being possible.

But now that he had, he felt the knowledge there in the palms of his hands. All he had to do was focus like Kim said. He shut his eyes, recalled her adorable pixie features, and cupped his hands as she had taught him.

A surge of warmth spread from his heart. It raced down his arms into his palms where a ruby-red fire blossomed and danced. Opening his eyes, Jacob stared at the tiny flame in his palms.

He stared at it for a long while. It wasn't damaging, at least not that he could tell. Nor was it like any magic that existed in Pyresouls. This was not a spell inscribed on a Spell Gem.

Good thing too, because if he was going to be skipping the Corpse Garden he would be down a Spell Gem.

Off to the side, Jacob caught Camilla seated in a similar position with a look of serene peace on her face. All the blood was washed free of her and the wounds she sustained were gone.

No longer emaciated and skeletal, her cheeks were full and the faint smile on her face was genuine. Camilla looked like an entirely different person. Beautiful with long curling locks of raven black hair, pouty lips, and a healthy glow about her, she was transformed.

In her hands, she held an emerald bottle. Her lips were moving slowly like she was talking to herself.

"Can she see you?" Jacob asked.

The Fire Oppa lifted his head, lashed his bushy tail, and then regarded Jacob. "That was an unexpected twist. I'll give you that. The answer is both yes, and no. She sees me, but not the me *you* see."

Turning his attention back to the Fire Oppa, Jacob thought about what he meant. Camilla said she needed a Cairn, not a Pyre.

Considering the similarity of their uses – both to inter or honor the dead in some way – the two were likely the same in function if not form.

Which meant there was probably a... a what, a Burial Oppa? "So she sees a version of you?" Jacob asked, and the Fire Oppa nodded. "You can use Souls to strengthen her as well then?" The Fire Oppa gave him a flat look. "Okay, okay, that was probably pretty obvious."

"She's a bit faster than you," the Fire Oppa said with a snort of flame. "Already reinforcing her parameters as we speak while you're asking silly questions."

Grumbling to himself, Jacob pulled up his parameters.

[Status]

Jacob Windsor
Covenant: None
Race: Kemora - Fae-touched (Human/Fairy)
Level: 13

Health: 124
Stamina: 86
Anima: 0
Souls: 15,731
Required Souls: 1,238

Parameters
VIT: 3
AGI: 6
END: 3
TMP: 9
STR: 10
DEX: 10
INT: 8
FTH: 3

Curse: Fractured Sight
Curse Level: 2

Spell Gem: No Spell Inscribed

Jacob double-checked his armor as he took out the [Repair Kit]. He placed each piece of equipment into the bottomless box, repairing everything he had at once. It cost him just shy of 300 Souls, a small sum compared to what a merchant would charge.

If he could even find one.

He had nothing short of an astounding amount of Souls but he had to remind himself that he needed to upgrade his armor. And yet, something stopped him from doing that immediately.

With 3 [Bright Sparks] and 6 [Dull Sparks], he could easily reinforce two pieces to +3 or one to +8 if one piece was left at +1. But what if there was a better piece of equipment out there?

The knight armor was simple, its metal was thin but worked with ridges that helped to turn attacks aside, yet it was far from the best armor he'd ever seen. It was, however, very good early on.

Spending all of his upgrade materials, not to mention the Souls, would be a waste. The problem was holding enough Souls that Jacob could purchase or upgrade any improvements he came across.

Loot in Pyresouls was rare. Merchants sold low-quality equipment most of the time unless you got lucky like he did with Brother Aker or you knew how to gain their favor.

For the most part, bosses, treasure chests, and the wisps of the dead were the only ways to get decent equipment. And that meant knowing where they were. Alice and Alec looked into the archives to provide him with some good options, but they also were trying to make sure he stayed on mission.

He could range all over Lormar for the most epic weapon and armor but he would fail in his mission to defeat the Burgon Beast before Alec reached it.

This was more of a speed run than anything. He had to have just enough strength to get through it to the end, but not so much that he wasted time growing stronger.

The clock was ticking. He was still several days out from Hollow Dreams, and already there were barely 13 days left before the Collapse. Even if he didn't reinforce his parameters here, by the time he pressed on it would likely be the next day.

Regardless, he should be following Camilla's lead and reinforcing his parameters. After a good rest, he would feel right as rain. Rain, now that was something he dearly missed from Earth before the Collapse stole such simple pleasures.

Frustrated, Jacob turned back to his parameters. He could probably reinforce roughly 8 parameters by his guess.

If he wanted to get rid of his Stamina and Movement penalty from his current Guilt tier, he would have to reinforce Temper up to about 16. Spending most of his Souls in the process.

He wasn't keen on doing that, not when his Health and Stamina were so low. On the other hand, he could raise his AGI to counteract the Movement penalty. It would technically be a waste of a point or two but those points should bring him back to rough parity to his old speed.

If Alec was right and anything in the catacombs would one-shot him, then he'd need to have just enough Health to survive a single hit.

That way he would have the time to use a [Cinder Ampoule] and carry on. Which meant he needed to know exactly how much damage the creatures below did.

Having over 15,000 Souls really felt like a lot until he started to plan out how he was going to spend them. He was keenly reminded that his Souls wouldn't last very long and that each time he reinforced a single parameter those remaining Souls would stretch less and less.

Stamina was a must-have. As soon as he placed a point into END and confirmed it, he groaned. His Stamina went up by 2 points, the green bar in the top-left quadrant of his vision stretched ever-so-slightly. And now the next parameter reinforcement would cost 1,445 Souls.

Maybe he was overly optimistic about getting 8 parameter reinforcements. Jacob raised his END a total of 4 points, bringing it up to 7 END and his Stamina up to 94. Just 2 points shy of where his Stamina was back on Earth.

It was easy to forget just how slow stat growth was in Pyresouls. Rather than feeling bloaty like a lot of games, every point of Stamina felt like the precious resource it was.

Eventually, he wanted it at 100. There was a Sword Form that he hoped to unlock – one that he never could use since the highest his Stamina ever reached was 96 – that cost 100 Stamina to execute. In exchange for depleting so much Stamina, it dealt a decisive blow.

As tempted as he was to go all-in at the moment, he still needed to see to his Health. Unfortunately, it would waste a day but he figured with the shortcut they found through the catacombs, he was ahead enough. It took Alec 3 days just to clear the asylum.

With a glance across the Pyre to Camilla, he saw that the elven woman was already fast asleep. Jacob shrugged, shut his eyes, and joined her in peaceful slumber.

No dreams of Kim came to him, just restful sleep. He felt revitalized and full of energy when he awoke to see Camilla stretching and yawning.

September 1st, 2035 – 12 days remain before the Collapse.

So, with 9,505 Souls left, Jacob stood up.

Camilla caught the motion and looked at him curiously. "I'm guessing the Cairn dispels the enchantment. What are you doing?"

"I'm going to die," he said brightly. "Want to come watch?"

This is going to suck.

17

"This is ridiculous," Camilla said, struggling to keep up with Jacob's determined stride. "You know this isn't a *game* right?"

She kept up the constant talk ever since they left the Pyre.

"I'm aware," Jacob said. Even though he *knew* he would be fine, dying was still going to *hurt*. But he needed to know how much damage those things did and so he donned his knight's armor and descended into the upper levels of the Desecrated Catacombs.

An area that most people sprinted through, going so far as to shed their armor so they could run faster and longer.

"You're going to willingly die, just to learn how much damage they deal to you?"

"That's the gist of it," Jacob agreed. As the sloping path evened out, Jacob found what he was looking for in the distance. A plain pile of bones lying on the ground, not too dissimilar from the ones that marked the entrance to the Pyre.

Except, Jacob knew that these bones weren't harmless decoration.

"Just stay over there," he warned. "I'll be back in a moment to pick up my wisp."

Swallowing hard, he dismissed his shield and took his [Longsword] in a two-handed grip. He had to quell every survival instinct as alarm bells rang in his head, warning him of impending danger.

Teeth grit, knuckles white beneath his gauntlets as he strangled the grip of his sword, Jacob walked forward onto the dark cavern floor.

The first thing he noticed was how oppressively dark it was. His body, which naturally gave off a small radius of illumination was severely weakened. Darkness held fast even five feet away and at double that all he could see was a blanket of black velvet.

As he approached the bones he saw several loculi, shelves roughly hewed out of the cavern walls to house the remains of the dead. Just as he thought, the bones in front of him began to quiver.

Normally, he would have enough time to run past before they reassembled. But his goal wasn't to run into the warren of twisting, confusing tunnels with as many dead ends as fatal drops into the abyssal darkness. He was here to die and to learn.

Rattling bones gathered together and formed a complete skeleton, its bony hand already gripping a rusted saber. Foregoing any Sword Forms, Jacob bashed his [Longsword] against the thing's ribs.

Several cracked, the blade swept through the creature's spine and broke apart the thing before it could bring its saber to bear. The two halves hit the floor a moment later, breaking apart into disparate pieces.

It only took a few moments for them to rattle again, rejoining faster this time. The skeleton was back on its feet and more eager than ever to visit some revenge on Jacob. It cut sideways with the saber, a blow he instinctively parried with his blade.

The ring of steel on steel echoed in the chamber, waking up more skeletons. Jacob cursed himself and dismissed his blade, spreading his arms wide. He was terrified but remained resolute.

No matter how many times he might die in Pyresouls Online, it would hurt every time and was a truly frightening experience that nobody in their right mind would want to repeat.

In sacrificing himself this once, he would prevent further deaths. That thought alone gave him a measure of solace that instantly evaporated like fog before the noonday sun when the skeleton's saber took him in the throat.

The brief spike of fear and pain was blessedly short as the rusted blade of the saber severed his spinal cord and everything went dark.

You Died.

Jacob awoke at the Pyre with a start, his hands immediately flying toward his throat. The Fire Oppa gave him a curious expression. "Find what you were looking for?"

"I did," he said shakily, pushing to his feet. "I'll be back soon."

Camilla was where he left her, from her vantage point she watched as he approached the emerald wisp that held his Souls. Jacob leaned forward to grasp it and the wisp suddenly attacked.

It shifted between two different forms, the harmless wisp ahead of him and this strange puffy thing with sharp teeth.

"What the fu-"

"Jacob, hurry up!" Camilla cried.

Looking over his shoulder, he saw her point. His gaze traced the source of her distress to the rattling pile of bones that had reset in his absence.

The two images of the wisp shifted and shimmered, and Jacob reached forward regardless. The second image of the wisp faded into a puff of smoke and he felt the reassuring presence of his wisp as it was absorbed.

Souls Retrieved.

He beat a hasty retreat soon after, running up the sloping ramp of stone all the way back to the Pyre. Even if the skeleton followed him, it couldn't enter the immediate safe zone of the Pyre so long as Jacob was there.

"Did you find out what you wanted to know?" Camilla asked, crossing her arms and staring at him. It was clear she was trying to decide whether or not he was crazy.

Bringing up his log, Jacob saw that he wasn't that far off from preventing a one-shot. The skeleton dealt 148 damage to him, well over double what the Graceful Penitents did and they hit pretty hard. And back then he was wearing the robes with horrible defense.

No wonder people were scared of that place. Add on the fact that the skeletons *didn't die or award Souls*, and the whole place was downright terrifying.

"I'm only twenty-five points of health off," he said, staring into the Pyre and thinking about his next move. The Pyre shifted, a faint wispy second image of it danced at the periphery and Jacob realized what happened with his wisp.

How could I have been so stupid to forget about my curse?

Looking around, he could see the hazy dreamlike quality of the room around him. Everything looked far less substantial than normal and he knew it would only get worse if he didn't curb it right now.

Even if he could find a secret pathway by using the curse to his advantage, he'd be a hindrance to Camilla. Even if he was able to walk on a bridge she couldn't see, without the same curse, he wasn't sure if she would be able to use it.

Fractured Sight gave the afflicted a view onto an alternate plane of reality. At curse levels of 1 or 2, it was mild and rarely triggered. Starting at 3 the hallucinations grew more severe.

Eventually, around curse levels of 3 to 4, you could see hidden pathways and alternative routes that weren't visible or even possible for anybody else.

The curse would allow Jacob to not just view into an alternate plane of reality but to walk it where the barrier between was especially thin. Doing so, he could walk upon a bridge of light over a chasm that would require hours of backtracking.

Unfortunately, as he just witnessed the hallucinations were not friendly. At higher levels, the creatures on the other plane were able to not only hurt him but cross over as well. And then they would be a problem for Camilla as well.

For now, he had no choice but to expend an [Anima] to reset his curse. Summoning the black piece of coal in his hand, Jacob plunged his arm into the fire. The [Anima] crackled and shattered, its soothing energy rolled over his body and rid him of his curse.

While they were rare, a single [Anima] would reset his curse back to 0. At least he didn't need to use one *every* time he died.

Camilla seemed content to lean back against the nearby wall and shut her eyes while Jacob finished with his business at the Pyre.

Reinforcing VIT by 1 would raise his Health by 8 and cost 2,114 Souls. He needed to not only meet the bare minimum of 149 Health, but have over it to account for damage variance.

With the number of Souls he had left, he wasn't sure that was possible.

He would need at least 4 reinforcements to bring it up high enough. Only doing 3 would have him equal to the strike that had killed him which meant he would die in a single hit again if hit in a similar manner.

At the rate the required Souls was raising per parameter reinforcement, there was no way he could increase VIT 4 points.

Taking a look at his armor gave him an idea. Armor was, by all accounts, pretty simple in Pyresouls. It resisted a set amount of damage and anything over that damage would hurt you. Otherwise, it would do nothing.

Physical damage was the most common to receive and was split between the three major types; blunt, slashing, and piercing. While his [Knight's Armor] claimed 90 physical protection, that wasn't entirely true.

Its total physical protection was nothing more than the total sum of its individual protections. Medium armor like that, especially plate mail, excelled at slashing protection and to a lesser extent piercing.

His [Knight's Armor] had 40 slashing protection, the most common type of damage, and the damage that had killed him. He could up his VIT high enough to have enough HP to withstand the damage, or he could improve his armor enough to lower the incoming damage.

Raising his armor was raising his "effective HP," since each point of reduced damage was, in the end, little different than raising his HP by 1.

While upgrading his armor would likely cost fewer Souls, it would cost him [Dull Sparks] which took time to acquire. And if he ever found better armor, it would be a waste.

There was a good reason why most people ran naked through the catacombs. The damage you took was so high that even with a hoard of Souls like Jacob had, it was still hard to get enough Health to survive a single hit from even the weakest enemies.

Most people ran through, spending as many of their Souls as possible so that if they lost it all it wasn't a waste. If they died, they would return to the Pyre to try it all again.

It was somewhat insane but made sense. This was undoubtedly the fastest way to Hollow Dreams where he could not only find plenty of loot but merchants and the start of the quest that would point him toward the Burgon Beast and how to awaken it.

Not that he needed it.

Everything hinged on Jacob getting to Hollow Dreams as fast as possible and that would be easier done if he accepted the loss and sprinted through. After seeing how swift Camilla was, he doubted she would have any trouble keeping up with him. In her lighter robes, she wouldn't be slowed down.

And now that she attuned to a Cairn, she was in no danger of dying. But if he could get the [Ring of Broken Vows] on his first pass, he could avoid coming back to the catacombs entirely.

That alone would shave off days of time. And the last time he ignored Alec's adamant advice, he had died. But it turned out for the best in the end.

If Jacob had never gone inside the bridge - regardless of whether or not he had a choice, which he didn't - he would be in a vastly different predicament now.

So maybe there was something to the Doc's suggestion.

"What do you know about the Desecrated Catacombs?" he asked Camilla.

Without opening her eyes, she said, "It is a horrible, horrible place. The interred dead no longer stay dead and necromancers wander the halls raising up armies as their playthings. You only go there if you want to join their army." She opened her eyes and looked at him intently. "You aren't thinking of going *deeper* down there, are you?"

Jacob nodded.

The look she gave him was at once deeply concerned and terrified. "Then you'll be going on your own."

Whether she meant it as a way to goad him into abandoning his plan, or she was simply stating her limits, Jacob wasn't sure. Perhaps a bit of both.

The ruby-eyed elf was a great companion. With her magic and his swordsmanship, they were a potent foe to contend with. But even together they would not be able to fight their way into the darkest depths of the catacombs.

He understood it as a simple truth and there was nothing he could do to change it. But he also knew there was no way he wasn't about to try it. "I have to try," he said as much to himself as to Camilla.

A flash of hurt crossed her features but she recovered quickly enough. "I had hoped we would stay together a little longer," she said. "When we first met, you told me you had a duty to the countless souls of another realm. Your dedication to them is laudable. I hope they are worth it. My own obligations are no less, and while I am loathe to leave a debt unpaid-"

"You stood guard over my unconscious body while I was... indisposed," he interjected. "You could have left. I would not have faulted you for that. Neither did I ask anything of you. All you have given, I am thankful for. You owe me nothing, Camilla."

Camilla clenched her jaw, her eyes softened with emotion. "Very well, then you will go alone and here we shall part ways." She stood up. "Come here and give me your hand."

Surprised, Jacob got to his feet and offered his gauntleted hand to her.

"I am not supposed to do this but I do not believe you will survive the affair without this gift. I cannot go with you, but perhaps you can take a little of my magic with you. I can sense the capacity within you – weak though it is."

Camilla placed her hand atop Jacob's and shut her eyes. Flames, golden and gentle twirled around their joined hands. They spiraled across her forearm and made their way to Jacob, snaking up his armor and diving into his breastplate as if it didn't exist.

You learn the Sorcery: **Heat Blade.**
Wreathe your weapon in deadly flame. Effective versus Undead. This Sorcery was granted to a specific order of Knights of the long-ago kingdom of Asalin. Sorcerers and Knights were paired for life, sharing both strength of arm and Sorcery alike. The Heartbinders were the pride of the kingdom, before its tragic betrayal and fall.
Requirement: 7 INT
Uses: 3

He was speechless. Though he doubted that Camilla gave it to him for the same reason listed in the description, he still felt honored. "Thank you," he said as solemnly as he could.

Before he could say anything more, she wrapped him in a tight hug and was gone in a flutter of parchment robes. No goodbye, she was just gone. He could have gone after her but he knew he would never convince her and it would be wrong to try.

Sitting back down at the Pyre, once more alone with the Fire Oppa, he said, "I really hope I see her again."

"Perhaps you will," said the Fire Oppa slyly. He always seemed to know more than he let on. "You want me to inscribe that spell onto your Spell Gem?"

"If you don't mind," Jacob said, obviously distracted. He hardly paid attention as he found his thoughts drifting back to Camilla. Did he make the wrong choice in splitting up with her?

It would have been unfair to demand she go with him, and that might have been why she was so quick to leave. But a small part of him hoped that was not true. He felt, he hoped, that she was afraid of agreeing to accompany him despite her protestations.

Camilla had her own goals and desires that were apart from his. He told her the truth when he said she owed him nothing, that he wanted nothing from her.

In the face of being alone again, he wondered if it would have been so bad to force her to come along to repay her debt to him. It was a dark thought, one he immediately threw away.

But he missed her. Despite how little they spoke, they had formed a wordless bond. They fought well together, developed ways to communicate, and clearly, they looked out for one another. All without a single word.

How much better might they have been....

She reminded him so much of Kim, and yet it was more than that.

Lormar was a lonely, broken world. It helped to have even one other person by your side. It was why he caved on his first playthrough and agreed to let Emily come with him even though he felt something was off.

And he trusted Camilla. He knew that she wouldn't suddenly turn around and stab him in the back. She surely had enough opportunities. It would have been much easier if she left him when he was pulled to the future than to stay with him at great personal risk just to defend him.

For her, the risk was permanent death. If Jacob died there, he'd return to the Pyre back at the Steps of Penance. It would be a major setback but minor compared to hers.

Maybe that was why she didn't stay.

As much as Jacob liked Camilla, she didn't seem to be the selfless type. Jacob shrugged and swiped his hand down his face, smelling the rich leather of the worn glove.

He sighed and pulled himself together. Camilla was gone and he had to accept that.

Now he needed to focus on what he could do to get the [Ring of Broken Vows] and get out of the catacombs. If he could reach it and retrieve it, he would gladly accept death. He wouldn't even bother trying to collect his wisp. It would be well worth the price.

But to get there, he had to survive the gauntlet of nigh unkillable creatures and dark pathways that were shrouded in darkness. All without a map, not that he could have remembered any directions that Alec gave him.

"How much can you improve my Knight's Armor?" Jacob asked the Fire Oppa.

"If you've got the Souls and the right type of spark, I can improve it up to around plus five, why?"

"Not plus ten?"

The Fire Oppa shook his head. "Nope, need a special ember to strengthen the Pyre for that. Not enough heat."

"Any idea where I might find one?"

"Now that you ask... I do have an idea," the Fire Oppa gave him a wolfish grin. "I can't tell you precisely but there's nothing prohibiting me from saying I heard there are quite a few treasures down in the catacombs. Adventurers and brave knights who lost their lives and their very valuable items. Coffins often contain more than just bones."

Taking off his [Knight's Armor], Jacob put it within the flames of the Pyre, careful to avoid the Fire Oppa. He took out a [Dull Spark] and looked at the Fire Oppa.

With a wave of his bushy, flaming tail, a prompt appeared.

[Equipment Reinforcement]

Knight Armor [Chest] -> Knight Armor [Chest] +1
Cost: 200 Souls

Physical Protection: 90 -> 102
Blunt: 20 -> 22
Slashing: 40 -> 46
Piercing: 30 -> 34

Magical Protection: 70 -> 80
Arcane: 30 -> 33
Fire: 15 -> 16
Water: 10 -> 12
Earth: 15 -> 17

Harmony: 0 -> 1
Chaos: 0 -> 1

Resistances
Bleed: 22 -> 30
Poison: 9 -> 11
Curse: 0 -> 0

Stability: 20 -> 22
Durability: 550/550 -> 600/600
Guilt: 1 -> 1

It was less than he hoped for, but the price was less than a tenth of what it would take to increase his Health.

Health was better, but for half the Souls he could +5 his [Knight's Armor] and assuming it was roughly the same increase each time, he would have a significant defense boost.

There was no reason to think he would get a new piece of armor and even if he did, reinforcing his [Knight's Armor] would increase the chances that he could survive long enough to discover something better.

Deciding upon his course of action, Jacob upgraded his [Knight's Armor] to +5. The Fire Oppa took the [Dull Sparks] and the Souls as fuel for the process. The Pyre surged and flared, its long flames licking the ceiling as the Fire Oppa worked his magic.

Curling coronas of flame leaped across the breastplate, strengthening it and giving the ridges a dull gleam. The tattered leather accouterments darkened back to their original, lesser worn color.

It was as if the Fire Oppa was peeling back layer after layer of time, rejuvenating the [Knight's Armor] and returning some of its former glory.

When the Fire Oppa was done, the [Knight's Armor +5] gleamed like it was freshly polished. Its asymmetrical ridged pauldron caught the firelight in its gilded curves.

It was beautiful. For as simple and thin as the metal was, for the first time in forever, Jacob felt a sense of pride as he donned the armor.

Out of all his equipment, the chest piece had the highest defenses and would improve the most. But he was still surprised at the results.

It seemed that the more it was reinforced, the more it improved. Going from +4 to +5 was almost as large an upgrade as +0 to +3.

[Equipment Reinforcement]

Knight Armor [Chest] +5

Physical Protection: 90 -> 212
Blunt: 20 -> 48
Slashing: 40 -> 94
Piercing: 30 -> 70

Magical Protection: 70 -> 193
Arcane: 30 -> 71
Fire: 15 -> 40
Water: 10 -> 26
Earth: 15 -> 40
Harmony: 0 -> 8
Chaos: 0 -> 8

Resistances
Bleed: 22 -> 55
Poison: 9 -> 21
Curse: 0 -> 5

Stability: 20 -> 40

Durability: 550/550 -> 800/800
Guilt: 1 -> 1

And it only cost him 1,000 Souls and 5 [Dull Sparks].

With the extra 54 protection against slashing, the attack that had killed him would do less than 100 damage. Even if it was at the lowest end of the damage the skeleton could do, he still should have enough Health to weather any single blow.

The extra 5 [Cinder Ampoules] would come in handy, with 10 total he would be able to withstand 11 hits. That last hit would bring him down to critical Health but it might be enough to make it where the [Ring of Broken Vows] was stashed.

He didn't need to kill the Gnawing Hunger if he could slip in, nab the ring and take a one-way death trip back to the Pyre.

Deciding that he should go all-in on this strategy, Jacob spent every last available Soul he had. He added 1 point to VIT, and 2 went to reinforce his AGI, leaving him with 1,437 Souls.

[Status]

Jacob Windsor
Covenant: None
Race: Kemora - Fae-touched (Human/Fairy)
Level: 20
Health: 132
Stamina: 94
Anima: 0
Souls: 1,437
Required Souls: 2,857

Parameters
 VIT: 4
 AGI: 8

END: 7
TMP: 9
STR: 10
DEX: 10
INT: 8
FTH: 3

Curse: Fractured Sight
Curse Level: 0

Spell Gem: Heat Blade (3/3)

Reinforcing weapons was costlier, but with a single [Dull Spark] left, Jacob decided it would be better to upgrade *something*. It wasn't likely he would get to keep any Souls he had on him. Though he favored his [Longsword], he already knew it was notoriously ineffective against skeletons.

Anything besides blunt type damage was severely impaired, which made his choice relatively easy. It was between his [Mace] and his [Kite Shield], the latter was technically considered a weapon under certain conditions.

Jacob heard more than one account of a player dual-wielding shields to varying degrees of success. They were still stuck in the lower level areas compared to those who went with more traditional setups but they seemed to be promising.

If only there had been enough time to figure out the mechanics.

Entrusting his [Mace] to the Fire Oppa, Jacob reinforced it to +1, exhausting his supply of [Dull Sparks] and spending 500 Souls in the process. It was painful knowing that his dramatically lower [Mace] would be superior to his [Longsword's] damage.

[Equipment Reinforcement]

Mace [Weapon] +1

Physical Damage: 100 -> 109
 Type: Blunt
 Scaling: STR [B] -> STR [B+]
 Light Attack: 15 -> 13 Stamina
 Heavy Attack: 40 -> 35 Stamina

Magical Damage: 0 -> 0
 Arcane: 0 -> 0
 Fire: 0 -> 0
 Water: 0 -> 0
 Earth: 0 -> 0
 Harmony: 0 -> 0
 Chaos: 0 -> 0

Status Infliction
 Bleed: 10 -> 12
 Poison: 0 -> 0
 Curse: 0 -> 0
 Stagger: 50 -> 55
 Break: 30 -> 35

Durability: 400/400 -> 450/450
 Guilt: 1 -> 1

Just like that, 15,000 Souls were spent. He easily felt the physical effects of more Health, in the sturdiness of his body and the sensation of calm that came over him. His higher END and AGI made every motion both faster and less tiring.

He was now within striking distance of the Level he was at when he quit Pyresouls.

Folding his arms, Jacob nodded off to sleep, confident that things were going to be different this time.

18

"Where did you learn to do that?" the Fire Oppa asked when Jacob awoke. "Kindling, I mean."

Jacob thought back to the dream or... whatever it was. Even now, thinking back on it he couldn't be sure what it was all about. Was that actually Kim? If he was technically dead for a short period, had she found some way of contacting him?

They had been close. It was one of those silly pacts that some people made. Post-Collapse most people swapped pacts of contacting the other person from the beyond for the practical promise of making sure they wouldn't return.

After all, everybody knew that the dead didn't stay dead for long. And the whole concept of contacting somebody after death took on a much darker tone Post-Collapse.

But not Kim. She was fascinated with the beyond. Always into mystical junk that worked about as much as it failed.

Not surprisingly, Kim was gifted in the Clemency arts which required FTH. He shouldn't have been surprised when she said she'd find a way to talk to him from beyond the grave, but only if he kept an open mind about it.

Where Kim was concerned, Jacob would always try. He owed everything to her but as the years went on and there was no sign, he eventually gave up.

"The living owe it to the dead to continue living," was her favorite saying. Unsure about the dream, or the talk with Kim... whatever it was, Jacob recounted the events to the Fire Oppa.

He lapsed into a contemplative quiet afterward. All he could think about was how he agreed with her. *If only we had more time.*

"Very interesting," the Fire Oppa said. "It sounds like you had a brush with death."

"And you're going to tell me that it was just wishful thinking? Random synapses in my brain firing as it begins to die?"

"Do you want me to?"

Jacob looked down at his hands and shook his head.

"I would be lying to you anyway," the Fire Oppa said, crossing his paws beneath his muzzle and resting his head upon them. "I can't tell you what precisely, but there is more than just this one life you have. Or, in your case the two lives you have."

There were so many questions he wanted to ask but Jacob held them in check. What little the Fire Oppa shared with him made him feel better even if it wasn't true. It felt good to believe it anyway.

"You wanted me to light all the Pyres I could, didn't you?" Jacob said, getting to his feet.

"That would be nice, but I only require six to be relit."

"How many more do I have to go?"

"Three," the Fire Oppa said around a yawn. "There are, however, nine Pyres in total that you could light. That's a pretty strong number around here."

"You said you could give me more information if I reignited more Pyres," Jacob said, looking at the exit to the room then back at the Pyre. "Was that part of your hint about the treasure down below?"

He wasn't sure but it looked like the Fire Oppa nodded.

"Can you tell me where the next Pyre is?"

"Every major area has one but there are specific Pyres, those with particularly strong roots. The next closest one? There's one on the Ashen Flood in the middle of the lake."

"How do I get to that? I can't exactly swim in heavy armor and I doubt the lake is friendly besides."

"Quite. You might want to go looking in the Drowned Halls for a pretty pearl ring. It could come in handy."

"You're not going to give me more than that, are you?" Jacob shook his head.

"My paws are tied," the Fire Oppa said. "I've given as much as I can. But I'll have a treat for you if you can reignite the Pyre in the Drowned Halls." He winked at Jacob then shut his eyes and took a nap.

He knew he was stalling. What mattered right then was getting into the catacombs and making it to the very depths of its dark heart where the Gnawing Hunger resided. Considering the caginess of the Fire Oppa he doubted the creature could give him directions to his objective.

Which meant he would need to search and flounder on his own. The prospect wasn't particularly appealing. Though he did have a Pyre close to the upper levels of the Desecrated Catacombs, his treasure was at the deepest levels.

Isn't it always? he thought to himself with a snort.

No treasure or goal was ever on the ground floor. It was always at the tallest peak or the lowest valley. No in-betweens.

Swapping his [Longsword] for his [Mace +1], Jacob left the Pyre behind and ventured down into the catacomb, his heart hammering in his chest.

Camilla's absence was a keen loss he couldn't help but lament. Every so often he looked over his shoulder, hoping he might spot the raven-haired woman but knowing at the same time that it was an impossible hope.

He might as well turn around to find Kim, alive and well. She was alive too, but he didn't know where in Lormar she was. And even if he did, what would he say to her to gain her trust?

Thoughts swirling in his head, Jacob reached the first bone pile without realizing it. The rattling drew him from his reverie and he cursed himself for getting distracted.

As the bones came alive, he passed one hand over his [Mace]. The spell came easily to him, all the required incantations and motions already ingrained in his mind like the ABC's.

In a flash of shimmering heat, the head of the [Mace] was swathed in thin licking flames. The name, *Heat Blade* was a bit of a misnomer. It could be cast on almost any weapon, regardless if it had a blade or not.

The flames that ran up and down the length the [Mace's] flanged head gave off a pleasant light, throwing back the blanket of darkness as if he carried a torch. For that alone, he was thankful to Camilla.

As he stepped forward, taking the [Mace] in a heavy two-handed grip, Jacob swung at the rising skeleton. In one strike, its ribs shattered. Without halting his momentum, Jacob swept the [Mace] up and over in a clockwise arc.

Before the skeleton could get its bearings after that first strike, Jacob's [Mace] came crashing down on top of its skull. The flaming weapon crunched through the undead thing's skull and powderized a good portion of its spine as well.

He thanked Camilla silently again as he watched the flames imparted from the mace's head char and blacken the rest of the bones.

They didn't rise again.

A wisp flew out of the pile and passed into his chest with a chill.

You defeat the [Skeletal Warrior].
Awarded 50 Souls.

Another pile of bones began to rattle and assemble. Choosing to indulge his curiosity, Jacob dismissed the flaming [Mace] and instead summoned his [Longsword] in a swirl of ash.

Before the skeleton rose to his feet, he applied *Heat Blade* to the [Longsword]. Its entire length alight with curling tongues of flame. Jacob lifted it high over his head not to blind himself as the skeleton raised a blood-stained cudgel and lurched toward him.

They were weak and slow to start with but quickly gained strength the longer they were 'alive'. For now, they provided the perfect test subject.

Down rushed Jacob's blade, *Lightning Cracks Stone* clanged against the skeleton's bony ribcage. The flames darkened the bone but aside from a few chips, no real damage was done.

Undeterred, Jacob pulled back and shifted his weight to his right leg as the skeleton continued to rush him. *Dove Takes Flight* caught the falling cudgel and threw it out wide, the tip of the sword nicking against its ribs again but dealing minimal damage.

Twirling about, *Falling Rain* transitioned into *Moonlight's Edge* catching the skeleton about the clavicle in a blinding one-two combo that would have most enemies dead or dying.

Up came the cudgel and Jacob just barely executed *Sheltering Rain* to counter the blow. His sword bit into the wooden weapon and in the instant of struggle, Jacob kicked out into the thing's ribs and dismissed the blade.

Down went the skeleton, crashing onto its back and struggling to right itself.

Breathing hard, Jacob gave himself a second to regenerate some of his Stamina. The skeleton rose to its feet and made a disconcerting clacking noise with its jaw.

Grinning, Jacob rushed forward to close the gap. He summoned his [Mace] as he swung his arm around. The sudden added weight lent strength to his swing.

A glimmer of awareness had the skeleton raising a bony arm in defense but the [Mace] blasted through the bone and proceeded to take its head from its body.

As the skeletal form of the creature broke apart, Jacob exhausted his last use of *Heat Blade* to cause the [Mace] to burn brightly. Before the creature could reassemble, he drove the burning head of the weapon into the pile of bones.

They caught like dry kindling.

In a flash of heat and light, the bones turned to ash. Another wisp flew out of the pile, granting him 50 Souls. Not much considering how difficult the creatures usually were.

But with the right weapon, they were almost trivial to dispatch. And if attacked early upon their reanimation, they were clumsy and slow. The only danger came from how many there were.

Several more bones were animating and rather than clear the room, Jacob beat a hasty retreat back to the Pyre.

On his way back, he looked over the logs. His [Longsword] should have been doing *at least* 300 damage or more per Sword Form. Instead, it was doing a tenth of that. *Lightning Cracks Stone* did a paltry 37 damage. And his favorite, *Moonlight's Edge* was only 45 damage.

And that was *with* the additional damage from *Heat Blade*. Meanwhile, his [Mace] was dealing a consistent 200 to 230 per hit. Far more than it should be able to do without backstabbing or utilizing riposte.

He shook his head and sat down to rest at the Pyre. The Fire Oppa perked up at his return, watching him silently. Jacob sat down as the flames of the Pyre rose in a bright flare and a ring of light echoed out from the flames.

His fatigue was washed away in an instant, and his Spell Gem was recharged. The skeletons would be back but he now had a definitive way of dealing with them. At least he confirmed that the player advice he had gotten was good.

With a pet and a fond farewell, he was once more heading down into the upper levels of the Desecrated Catacombs. As he descended the stone path into the burial room, he cast *Heat Blade*. The [Mace's] head flared to life and he held it high like a torch, keeping his [Kite Shield] loose and limber at his side.

Jacob smiled as the first set of bones animated and came at him. Not only did he have a proper light source now, but he had a way of putting the skeletons down for good.

Or at least until he rested at a Pyre, which was just as well.

He stepped around a natural pillar splitting the room in half and summoned his [Kite Shield], bringing it up to block a heavy club strike from the next Skeletal Warrior.

Curious if Sword Forms translated to other weapons, Jacob looped his [Mace] out wide and crashed it down in a heavy strike on the skeleton's crown.

The [Mace] crushed its bone to powder, igniting it like a handful of flour thrown over an open flame. Quickly glancing at his log, he was surprised to see that the Sword Form was called something else.

Instead of *Lightning Cracks Stone*, it was considered a Mace Form by the name of *Hammering the Nail*. "Good enough," he muttered to himself, stepping over the charred corpse of the skeleton. He set his shield in line for the next one.

By the time the room was clear, a dozen charred piles of bones and ash littered the ground. Jacob was down a single ampoule and worn out from the constant fighting.

The longer a skeleton was alive, the more skilled it became. Like an expert warrior slowly awakening from a deep slumber, every second they were awake they became a bigger threat.

Kicking a pile of bones, Jacob lamented taking the time and effort to clear the room.

This was only the first of dozens. Perhaps even hundreds.

At first, he thought it would be easier to clear them out room by room. A typical strategy for resource gathering back on Earth. He had to remind himself that this was not Earth. He could die here and return.

Time was more precious than avoiding the pain of death.

Old habits died hard and Jacob found himself using *Heat Blade's* ability to put down a skeleton enemy for good again and again. Clearing the room came naturally to him, it created safety but he didn't need it.

It would take too long and the number of Souls the skeletons awarded was far too little to make it worthwhile.

Raising his flaming [Mace], Jacob rushed forward with his shield up to guard against oncoming blows. It would slow his Stamina regeneration but it would defeat any ambush attacks coming from the dark ahead.

Lit by his [Mace], the catacombs became marginally less terrifying. The silence remained oppressive, but the darkness rolled back beneath the weight of his enchanted weapon, giving him insight into blind corners and small nooks that appeared as viable paths from afar.

For some time he ran on, unmolested by the creatures of the catacombs. They would be hot on his trail, he knew. The skeleton army of the Desecrated Catacombs was slow in waking and relied heavily on the labyrinthine tunnels to confuse and disorient intruders.

Unlike the run-of-the-mill player, Jacob had a vague idea of where he was going. Down. He didn't allow the rattling of bones and the scraping of weapons being drawn that filled the tight corridors to unnerve him.

He kept up a steady pace and remained vigilant, taking every path that hinted at going deeper. The exact opposite of most players, who would be scrambling for an exit.

With a magical light that peeled back the shadows in the dark corners of the cramped, twisting warren of the catacombs Jacob stayed ahead of the horde. But he was just one dead end, one false turn, one misstep away from being swarmed.

They made no noise besides the clatter and clacking of their bones.

Somehow that was worse than if they screamed or wailed at him. The silence was only punctuated by the sound of their gaining bony footfalls. But with the way the catacombs were designed, it sounded as if they were coming from all directions at once.

He kept up a jogging pace most of the time, only sprinting when he came upon a room full of bones. Before they even began to reassemble, he would be out of the room and into the hallway beyond.

On and on he went, one room, one hall blending into the other until Jacob gave up ever trying to map his progress in his head. He was tired, afraid, and the *Heat Blade* spell was beginning to flicker fitfully, signaling it was nearing the end of its duration.

Thousands of loculi decorated the walls. Every space possible seemed dedicated to the dead. There were enough bones down here to build a city. Grinning skulls leered down at him as he broke left through another circular room just as his *Heat Blade* extinguished.

It was like being plunged into the abyss.

The dark rolled back in, stifling him. Fear threaded through his heart and made his hands shake as he recited the rites and passed one hand over his [Mace].

By the time the enchantment took, Jacob could hear the army of the undead marching upon him. A brief glance over his shoulder, fiery [Mace] held high, showed him countless bleached bones staggering toward him.

Dozens of red fiery glowing eyes burned with hatred, visible even as he lowered his source of light and turned his back on them.

He quickly found himself in a large cylindrical room. A narrow walkway corkscrewed down along the edge. Not even the light from his *Heat Blade* spell could illuminate what lay beneath. Even the other side of the room was lost to the dark.

Behind and above him, those twin specks of red glowing hate followed him. They were so numerous it was like looking up at the night sky full of red stars.

Skidding to a halt, Jacob stopped just a few inches from an obvious pressure plate. There wasn't even an attempt to hide the spike trap in the wall. Nevermind that a rotting skeleton was still stuck to the half-retracted spikes.

Not for the first time, he wondered if he was going the right way. What if the skeletons – or the necromancers that controlled them – were corralling him? Without his extra light, he would have been too scared and going too fast to avoid the trap.

Then an idea hit him.

Looking over his shoulder, he could just barely see the first of the skeletons illuminated at the edge of his [Mace's] light. There was enough time.

Leaning away from the spikes, Jacob tapped the plate hard enough to trigger it and retracted his foot quickly.

There was a brief delay as the mechanism activated and then the spikes shot forth with such speed that the air whipped about. The pierced skeleton flew off as if catapulted, he could not hear it hit anything and did not wait to listen longer than it took for the spikes to retract.

Nearly a second, he thought, mentally timing the trap. *It's enough.*

And if it wasn't, he would be dead or slowed to the point that the rattling horde of skeletons behind him would finish him off.

Well worth the risk.

Lowering his shield, Jacob hopped over the plate and took off at a run. He sprinted flat-out, not caring to watch his footing except to place the next over something solid.

Traps triggered and spikes jabbed at empty air. A heartbeat slower and he would be sporting numerous wounds. Stopping meant death. He was far beyond the skeletal undead but they were no longer his main threat.

If his Stamina wore out before the gauntlet of traps....

Pushing the thought from his mind, Jacob continued on until the green bar of his Stamina began to shrink to nothingness. The traps were unending and the dead were without mercy or fatigue.

With nothing but bad choices available to him, Jacob raised his shield just as his Stamina nearly bottomed out. His heavy boot came down on a pressure plate, he twisted his hips to face the wall and the spikes struck out with lethal purpose.

Rather than impale him, they clanged off the shield and sent him flying. With so little Stamina he took a significant amount of damage from the blow. He sailed through the air, dazed and reeling from having his block broken.

Even mid-air, Jacob had the presence of mind to summon a [Cinder Ampoule] and break it open, healing himself back to full just before he landed with a back-breaking *crack*.

Out came another ampoule, healing the damage that nearly killed him from full health. For a moment, Jacob thought the fall had severed his spine and somehow the [Cinder Ampoule] failed to heal it. His legs felt like they were dangling, which couldn't be right.

Lifting himself up on his elbows and angling the fiery light of his [Mace] revealed the truth. The bottom of the room was shaped like a donut, with a massive pit into darkness at its center. Jacob only barely managed to avoid it with his knees right at the precipice, causing his legs to dangle into the dark.

Catching his breath, he watched as a skeletal form lunged at him from on high. It fell short several feet and sank into the void without a sound. Another skeleton followed it, then another.

Up above him, the red stars were falling as the skeletons took the shortest path to him in an effort to claim him as part of their number.

He watched, somewhat amused as skeleton after skeleton fell into the dark pit never to return. He pulled his feet beneath him but took a moment to sit and recover his stamina.

Alive and whole, he couldn't believe he survived. Idly, he wondered just how many of the skeletons he could bait into the pit. He could potentially clear out dozens of rooms making his return that much easier.

Scores of white wisps streaked out and struck his chest with their chilling touch. Even with such a dismal amount per skeleton, his Souls were quickly filling up by the sheer quantity of skeletons plunging to their death.

The thought was immediately discredited when a large skeletal hand the size of his torso reached up and slapped itself down two feet to his right. Joined a second later by another.

It dug its long fingerbones into the stone, filling the chamber with an ear-bleeding screech like nails on a chalkboard. Each of its fingerbones was as thick around as Jacob's thigh.

Scrambling back as fast as he could, Jacob soon got to his feet and did a quick look around the room for any exits. He spotted only one.

Stamina restored, he poured on a burst of speed and made a beeline for it as he cast a glance over his shoulder to see the monstrosity that came out of the pit.

What did I just wake up?

Unfortunately for Jacob, the tunnel was wide enough to admit the bestial skeleton. The blood-red fires in its eyes locked on Jacob with murderous intent and it *galloped* toward him. It did not rear up and run like a person but used all four limbs to chase him like some kind of animal.

But the creature was clearly humanoid, though its massive skull was twisted in a way that was vaguely reminiscent of a canine.

Running blind was not the way Jacob intended to explore the catacombs. But with a hulking monster quickly gaining on him, he had little choice.

Dust shook free of the tunnel and Jacob didn't need to look over his shoulder to know the horrid thing was gaining on him with every furious heartbeat. There was a side passage up ahead, one too small for the thing but he would never make it.

One last look over his shoulder showed it less than three feet from him. As it raised a bony clawed hand toward him, Jacob threw himself hard to the right. Halting his forward momentum was easy with a planted boot but the Skeletal Beast had a much harder time.

It was going much faster than Jacob and was heavier besides. As it reached out to grab at nothing but air, it overbalanced and tumbled forward. Giant mitts raked the sides of the tunnel, digging furrows in the hard stone and arresting its movement.

But Jacob was already up on his feet by then, sprinting toward the side passage that was now between the two.

With a look of utter hatred, the Skeletal Beast lunged forward just as Jacob reached the smaller tunnel. He didn't get his shield up in time and the jagged tips of the Skeletal Beast's fingers tore straight through the armor on his side.

Blood gushed from the savage wound. Jacob pushed forward, staggering to one knee and forcing himself back up again as he put as much space between him and the creature as possible.

Predictably, it tried to reach in but couldn't quite get its whole hand in. The tunnel was barely large enough for Jacob to stand upright in, something he was having an increasingly difficult time doing.

His Health was bottoming out as his side leaked a considerable amount of blood. The quarter of his Health quickly shrank toward a sliver.

Another [Cinder Ampoule] was summoned and crushed, revitalizing him from near-death.

"Six left," he muttered to himself, leaning hard against the wall and keeping an eye on the Skeletal Beast raging in the larger tunnel beyond. "Man I really hope I don't have to go back out there."

Wounds recovered, Jacob straightened and raised his fiery [Mace]. If he had any hope of getting to the bottom of the catacombs, he would have to do it while avoiding that beast.

Eventually, even the scraping and clawing of the Skeletal Beast faded as Jacob followed the tunnel as it bent ever downward toward his goal.

19

"Just another obstacle," Jacob said, staring at the curtain of drifting fog. The sound of his own voice in the dark soothed him. The dead would know he was there well before the sound alerted them. They held a deep hatred for the living that pierced through the thickest shadow.

But it was no undead skeleton that he feared. This was a Crossing, one of the few areas in Pyresouls Online that allowed players to mingle. It also meant it would be more dangerous, usually with several puzzles that were best completed by working together.

Jacob stared at it for several seconds. He could go back and take another path but it would involve a lot of backtracking. The deeper he delved into the catacombs the more refined the structures became. Natural caverns gave way to worked corridors with fitted stone slabs as flooring.

A vague memory of Alec talking about a Crossing deep within the catacombs played in his head. He must be on the right path then. But he was far from ready to face other players.

If they were anything like Alec made them out to be, they would sooner kill him than work together. Approaching the gray mist that fell in a constant sheet, obscuring the room beyond, Jacob couldn't help but remember Kim's face.

He found himself instinctively cupping his hands, fingers – *and thumbs*, he thought with a smirk, remembering Kim's words – pressed together. The red flame blossomed in his palms.

This was no magic he ever heard of. It was not inscribed upon his single Spell Gem. And yet there it was. A warm flame that reminded him of a miniature Pyre. Its soothing heat soaked into his bones and began to grow, enveloping his hands until he could no longer see them.

Worry rippled through Jacob as the ruby flame began to grow still. It had never done that before. A thread of the gray fog separating the Crossing from Jacob's world stretched out to the flame in his palms and began to burn away. Before Jacob could do anything, the flames raced along that thin connection like a fuse.

With a flash of light and an explosion that blew Jacob onto his back, the flames vanished. Coughing through the smoke that filled the narrow corridor, Jacob rose to his feet and summoned his [Kite Shield] and [Mace] to his hands, ready for whatever was about to come through.

His heart stopped in his chest when the face he saw was Kimberly O'Neill. Dressed in a tight suit of scaled mail, she sauntered forward with her signature weapon, a glaive. Though this one looked to be in much better repair than the one he remembered her using.

Her visor was tilted up, her baby-blue eyes regarding him curiously. "What've we got here?" she asked, pointing her glaive at him. Jacob found himself staring at its wicked blade, tracing its length to her mismatched gloves and on to her pretty freckled face.

He couldn't breathe.

She was the last person he expected to see in Pyresouls, let alone so deep already. It had occurred to him that he might be the only one so far into the catacombs at this early juncture.

Kim's appearance thoroughly disproved that theory.

As much as he wanted to tell her he knew her, they hadn't met yet. Not for another year or more. She would have no idea who he was. It was a hard thing to remember.

This version of Kimberly was not a friend. Not yet.

He had to assume she would attack him just like anybody else. But still, he found it hard to keep his guard up. The impulse to walk over to her and wrap her in a tight embrace was stifling.

"Dude, you got something wrong with your tongue?" she prompted. Jacob could see the concern in the way she set her stance and tightened her grip on her glaive.

She was expecting him to attack.

"Sorry," he said with a chuckle, trying to diffuse the situation. "I was going through that Crossing and… well, it sort of blew up."

Kim looked over her shoulder at the empty archway once filled with falling fog. The area was still shrouded in a thin haze of smoke though and she didn't doubt him.

With a shrug, she set the butt of the glaive against the floor and jerked her head toward him. "Let's go." And just like that, she turned her back on him and walked back through the empty archway.

Jacob's head spun, and it took Kim giving him a second look over her polished scaled shoulder to shake himself from his stupor and catch up to her. He expected the archway to stop him, forcing him back for the offense.

He tensed, but nothing happened.

It made no sense. Crossings were protected by strange unnamed walls of drifting gray fog. No other creature in the game seemed to be aware of them. So the players came up with their own name for them, "fog gates."

Fog gates existed only in two places: before a bosses' arena, and before a Crossing. They were impossible for any monster to pass through, only players seemed to have that right. Not that a creature couldn't attack you as you were passing through, but it was rare.

And Jacob had just burned away the barrier. He still didn't understand how and as curious as he was about the ruby flame he summoned, he wasn't keen on doing it in front of an audience.

"You're not going to try and backstab me, are ya?" Kim asked as they continued into the small room. She stepped gingerly around the shattered clay pots in the light of the small rippling blue fires set in twisted iron lanterns on the walls. "Mind the shards, they're covering the traps."

Picking his way in her footsteps, Jacob shook his head. "Not unless you give me a reason to. I'd rather get through than risk fighting and losing Souls, y'know? Lots of time lost getting back down here."

He hoped he didn't sound like a coward. Even though this wasn't the Kimberly he knew, he cared what she thought. As stupid as that might be.

On a more practical level, showing fear meant he was weak. And the weak were easily preyed upon.

The woman that stood before him might have better morals than most, but it wouldn't do to tempt her too much with an easy target.

Chuckling, Kimberly turned to look him in the eyes. "Huh, so you're not as stupid as you look. That's good, maybe we can work together then? Unless you're one of those edgy loners."

"Our chances of surviving are higher together," Jacob agreed.

"Good." Kimberly rested her glaive in one hand and reached the other toward him. Dismissing his shield, Jacob grasped her hand and shook it. "Ya got yaself a partner. For as long as we're together, that is. Call me Kim."

"Jacob."

"Jake, eh?" she said with a teasing grin. "That's an old name. Your parents big eSports fans or something?"

He suppressed a groan and shook his head. "I'm not named after Jacob Callor."

"Sure you aren't," she said unconvincingly, sliding her visor down over her face. "Your parents were probably eSports groupies and didn't want you to know. My parents were nerds too, so's I understand."

Trying once more to lower his visor over his burning face, Jacob finally gave up with a frustrated snort and followed Kim into the next room. Traps were a common element of Crossings, as were merchants. Though he doubted even the hardiest merchant would dare brave the catacombs.

Not after he came to understand that they were thinking beings. The Desecrated Catacombs were legitimate insanity. He never wanted to come back.

The ghostly blue lantern light provided just enough illumination that Jacob didn't feel the need to expend his last use of *Heat Blade*.

Three paths stood before them after the first few rooms of simple pressure plate traps. The first path, straight down the middle, was filled with spikes. The left path was a sheer drop into a room filled with milling skeletons and various undead.

Jacob went to check out the right passage, but just as he poked his head to look inside, Kim grabbed his armor and yanked him back hard. A crossbow bolt skipped off the stone where his head was a second ago, followed in quick succession by three more.

With that little glimpse, he saw a series of floating platforms in a dark room. "Archers and crossbowmen," Kim explained. "Looks like a platforming puzzle."

"Thanks," he said, silently chastising himself for not leading with his shield out. Being near Kim again was scrambling his thoughts. She probably thought he was an incompetent idiot the way he was acting in front of her.

"You got a preference?" he asked.

"I do, in fact, c'mere."

She stood in front of the hall filled with spikes. An impassable network of jagged metal defenses with no way to traverse them. They stretched from the ceiling to the floor in a complex mesh all the way to the far end of the hall.

"Okay, Jacob, here's the thing. We can go left or right but I saw three dudes come through already and I haven't heard a damned thing from them yet. They said they'd come back and open the middle path for me from the other side but they're probably dead already.

"However, see this little lever here?" She reached into a small slot in the stonework, pulling down a metal lever. With a grunt of effort, she shoved it down so it stuck out at a ninety-degree angle.

Jacob distinctly heard the ticking of clockwork machinery within the walls as the spikes retracted to reveal a clear path forward.

"This little baby keeps the path free and open," she said, snapping her fingers to catch his attention. "There's another one on the other side, and there's the rub. We gotta have some level of trust, right? If I hold this down for you to go through, you need to trust that I won't use it to kill you and take your goods."

"And you have to trust that I'll return the favor when I cross," Jacob finished for her.

It was an interesting trap. More a social experiment than anything, when it was in a player's best interest to work together as far as it took them to gain an advantage and then backstab their partner.

She looked at him, trying to read him. A much easier feat since his visor was stuck in the raised position.

Taking her hands off the lever, it stayed in place for a scant few seconds before it began to ratchet back into its original position.

The spikes didn't shoot out immediately. They grew slowly, but fast enough that even if Jacob put all his parameters into AGI, he wouldn't have reached the halfway mark before the spikes impaled him.

Kim held his gaze. "I already thought about charging in, there's just no way. That hall is too damn long."

"I'll hold the lever," Jacob said. It might have been because he felt he had a second chance to help her now. Kim looked at him for a moment longer then nodded.

Whatever she saw in him convinced her she was as safe as one could be trusting another person with their life in Pyresouls Online.

Dismissing his weapon and shield, Jacob took hold of the lever, pulling it down easily and holding it there.

"Listen for my call," she said. Her weapons vanished into ash as she lowered the visor on her helm and took up her position like a track runner waiting for the starting gun. Kim was ready to sprint the moment the spikes cleared. She turned toward him, her angular helm hiding the grinning expression he knew she would have. "See you on the other side."

Once the spikes cleared she took off like a shot, sprinting with all of her effort toward the end of the narrow hall. Even if she trusted him not to let go and kill her, there wasn't any reason to linger.

A familiar, shrill whistle pierced the air soon after. "You ready, dude?" she shouted back at him. Her speed was impressive to have cleared the hall already.

When Jacob let go of the lever, it kept its position. It was too far between the lever and the hallway to see if Kim was still there but he kept faith that she was.

He wasn't nearly as fast as Kim was, but he ran as hard as he could. His lungs burned and his legs felt like lead halfway through and he pushed on. The image of the spikes coming out was a constant motivator.

One that became all too real when he heard a shout of surprise up ahead and the clanging of metal on metal followed quickly by the ominous sound of clockwork machinery in the walls.

No, no, no.

The spikes inched out of their holes.

If he wasn't wearing his armor he might have made it. It would've been a smart idea to stuff his armor into his inventory, but hindsight was 20/20. As it was, he could see the end of the hallway and narrow room beyond. A mirror of the one he just left. The spikes would impale him just as he was within spitting distance of freedom.

"Kimberly!" Jacob shouted, hoping she hadn't betrayed him.

A resounding metal clang echoed through the hall and the spikes stopped for a moment, but only a moment.

Jacob reached forward at the very end of the hallway when the first spike grazed his thigh. He leaped forward, throwing himself as far as he could. The hallway filled with the squeal of the spikes as they scraped against his metal armor.

Halfway through the roll that would have brought him to safety, he felt a searing bolt of pain in his calf. The rest of his body lurched forward out of the hallway, but his calf was speared and held solidly in place. The steadfast hold made his head snap forward into the hard ground, breaking his nose.

He cried out in agony, dazed and with the pain in his leg mounting. Pushing against the stone ground, Jacob stared at the splatter of blood on the stones. Crimson dripped down his nose and onto the floor, spreading the red stain.

One look behind himself and he could see the problem. And the gruesome solution. In his desperate bid to get away from the spikes, he rolled forward but it wasn't enough. His left leg calf was impaled through the muscle by the last two spikes of the hallway.

Terrible luck, he thought to himself as he summoned his [Longsword].

The solution was simple. Cut himself free. The wound wasn't mortal, though it would prevent him from walking properly. The pain made him sick but he reminded himself he had been through worse.

Using the sharp edge of his blade, he dove the [Longsword] between the spikes to cleave open the twin wounds in his calf. His scream was long and horrible as the muscle split and blood poured freely from the ruined leg.

Pulling it free of the close-knit spikes hurt worse, the torn chunks of his calf sent dizzying waves of nausea and mind-blacking pain whenever they brushed against a spike.

Finally freed, he wasted no time summoning a [Cinder Ampoule]. He crushed the thin glass container and set the glowing cinder free to do its work.

Jacob watched his dwindling Health freeze then fill up once more. Getting to his feet he tested his newly healed leg. It was too bad there were no [Cinder Ampoules] back on Earth. A lot of good men and women would still be alive if they were.

Looking around the room, he noted several bloodstains retreating into the only path that continued out of the area. Kim was nowhere to be seen.

Jacob took off through the exit, ready for battle. If Kim betrayed him, he would deal with her when he found her. If somebody interfered, they were going to wish they hadn't.

The first room was nothing more than a simple storage area full of ceremonial wine barrels, lit with black candles flickering in groups of three and four spread throughout the room.

But no Kimberly.

Three rooms later, running at full speed, Jacob came to the edge of a large room that opened up into a spacious chamber. He immediately threw himself down to the ledge as he caught the glint of an arrow streaking through the air at him.

"Come to save the damsel in distress? How twentieth-century of you!" taunted a deep voice from below. "You wanna take away the girl's agency by coming to her rescue? Did you even ask for *consent* to rescue her?"

Jacob belly-crawled as quietly as he could to another area on the ledge. His brief glance had shown a large room below set with runes carved into the floor in a familiar pattern. Several tables were set up in the middle of the runic symbols with altars nearby.

While he never saw it himself, he recognized the room from Alec's stories. This was a sacrificial chamber. The way you passed the "puzzle" was to spill enough blood to fill up all the symbols.

Only then would the large doors on the other end of the room open, letting the players out of the Crossing. Running all along the circular room was a massive holding cell about seven feet above Jacob's head. The holding cell stuck out a few feet beyond the ledge, making it impossible to see what was above him.

A few other voices tried taunting him, but he wasn't going to give in to the obvious bait. He spotted six people, and those were the only ones he was able to mark quickly.

Vastly outnumbered, he wasn't going to give away his location so easily. They already knew he was there, best not to let them know *exactly* where.

"Oh, you better hope this is a permadeath because when I come back I am going to *gut you like a fish!*" Kimberly shouted, her voice dripping with vitriol.

"Will somebody please gag her?" came the first voice again, the deep bass marking him easily. He lifted his voice, clearly talking to Jacob. "Listen, man, I've got a fresh spot on my crew. We're splitting off in pairs to push through after this. There's no way you're getting out of here alive but if you join me you've got a good shot at taking the prize."

Jacob shook his head and continued around the ledge. *Typical carrot-and-stick approach.*

Among all the offers of "unlimited power," or "ungodly strength," that was by far the weakest one he could remember. No hint of what he could achieve with the group. Hell, the guy didn't even have a name for his little band of degenerates.

He probably found a few people, convinced them they could work together - with him at the top, naturally - without any understanding that after they left the Crossing each of them would return to their shard.

Movement across the way made Jacob freeze and pulled him from his thoughts. Directly below the jutting lip of the holding cell above, he was hidden. But across the room, he saw a familiar shape that made his blood run cold.

The Skeletal Beast was stalking behind the bars, burning ruby-red "eyes" filled with hate, looking for anything alive to punish. A wicked smile came over Jacob and a plan began to take shape.

It hadn't seen him yet, which was good. If he could circle around until he was beneath it, he might be able to rouse its anger enough that it broke open the bars. After that, he wasn't really sure what would happen.

Either it would manage to crawl down to the ledge he was on, or the creature in its violent rampage would overshoot the ledge and land in the room below. Slaughtering everybody – including Kim.

As Jacob made his way around the room, he peeked his head over the edge, removing his helm so that the metal didn't glint in the light and give him away.

Five tables in total filled the room, their use was obvious from his vantage point. Strap a person down, bleed them out and let their blood flow into the channels carved into the table and the floor.

Barbaric and stupid.

The solution was obvious. If each person sacrificed a little of their blood directly over a rune, each of them would light up and with little use of their cinder. With even two people possessing a single mote of cinder, it was child's play.

Kim was strapped down onto one table directly below his ledge halfway to the where the Skeletal Beast roamed. He *might* be able to make it down unseen, but then what?

He couldn't fight six players all at once. Even with Kim's help, they'd both be killed and the group would continue on their merry way.

Two other tables held bodies squirming and fighting against their bonds. The leader, dressed in gleaming white plate with a lion's head helmet on, was making his lackey's draw straws for the last two tables.

"By your sacrifice, we will all prosper," he was telling them. He seemed to have dismissed Jacob's presence out of hand. And judging by the number of players he had on his side, the man had a right to be unconcerned with a single player.

"This is the first major step toward winning the competition," he continued. "Remember what you're doing this for: not for the billions of dollars in controlling stock in Altis but because we'll have a *controlling interest* in the company.

"Imagine it, any game owned by Altis as your personal playground. Yearly dividends in the hundreds of millions. Your families will never want for anything. Anybody who willingly sacrifices themselves will have a guaranteed share of five percent."

"I don't know, Mack," said a woman in close-fitted leather armor and a bow slung over her shoulder. "Five percent doesn't sound like a lot."

"Do you even know how much money we're talking about?" the leader, Mack, said. "Even if the dividend is as low as two hundred million, that's ten mil for you. Otherwise, it's a single percent if you survive until the end, more depending on contributions.

"And that's what you'd get *in one year* at the current valuation of the company. Imagine how popular they're going to be after Pyresouls Online goes live."

Jacob found himself nodding along despite himself. Not that he necessarily agreed or bought into the sale's pitch, but it was a decent one given the circumstances. Better than the one he gave Jacob.

Aside from the blatant lie about the controlling interest, Mack was right.

Even after the large bouts of inflation in the '20s, a million a year was nothing to scoff at, let alone ten times that.

While they were arguing amongst themselves, Jacob made his

move. Shedding his armor so he could be as silent – and swift – as possible, Jacob picked his way down from the ledge.

Without five years of rock-climbing experience, he would never have been able to do it. Years spent in the Appalachian mountains of North Carolina and Virginia had forced Jacob to adapt to the harsh environment.

Climbing was among the fastest and most secure way of avoiding the Vacant and other horrific creatures that roamed Earth looking for victims. And those few creatures that could climb? They were much easier to deal with when they were clambering over the edge after you.

Jacob made it to the floor silently, wearing nothing more than a drafty loincloth to cover his modesty. He padded over to Kim, covering her mouth with his hand as he pressed a finger to his lips.

On the ground floor, Jacob could see how much the group that faced him outnumbered them. There were at least a dozen people in varying states of armor, but none of them seemed as opulent as the leader's.

How did he get such nice armor so fast? I've never even heard of armor like that.

Jacob's [Longsword] was summoned in a swirl of ash, blissfully silent. He used the sharp edge to cut through her leather bindings and together they turned to make the climb back up to the ledge.

Halfway there, Kim jerked her hand from his and summoned her glaive. She pointed it threateningly at the group. With their backs turned they would be easy prey. With Kim's skill, several would be killed before they realized the threat.

Jacob shook his head and they glared at each other, her in polished scale armor, while Jacob was practically naked. Their silent argument was broken when a voice called out, turning all heads toward the pair.

Kim pushed him forward and took her glaive in both hands. "Go, I'll hold them."

There wasn't much use in arguing. Without any armor, he wasn't going to last very long in a fight. Jacob made it up to the ledge in short order as Kim backed herself up to the base of the wall.

An arrow sank itself in his side but he managed to pull himself up, gritting his teeth the entire way. He rolled toward the wall as arrows skipped off the stone and struck sparks where they hit near the edge.

If Kim wasn't already an experienced climber, there would have been no way she could have made it in full armor. Even still, she took more than one arrow as she climbed and Jacob had to reach down grab hold of her and haul her up.

"Great," she panted, pushing up close to him to avoid the volley of arrows being sent their way. "Now we're stuck. Why did we do this again?"

"Follow me," Jacob said, wincing as the arrow in his side shifted with each motion. Gritting his teeth, he reached back and yanked the arrow out. His Health fell another ten points down to 77, and a thin stream of blood leaked out from the wound.

It wasn't enough damage to warrant wasting a mote of cinder. Not yet.

Kim wasted no time summoning a [Cinder Ampoule] and using it after she yanked out the arrows with a hiss of pain. "This is ridiculous," she started to say but with a sharp look back at her, she stopped her complaint.

Arrows arced through the air, most of them didn't come close to hitting either of them. By that point, the archers were guessing where they were.

Jacob could hear Mack below trying to organize them, shrugging off the loss and offering his sacrifice deal to another.

"The faster we get the hell out of here the better, yeah? So stop wasting time and volunteer!" he bellowed.

"I'll do it," said the woman in tight leathers. "None of your other members have the stones it seems. Five percent, right?"

Mack came forward and clapped her on the shoulder. "This is what I'm talking about. Yes, five percent to you." He motioned to a sword-wielding knight nearby. "Take her to that table. Hurry it up."

Despite her attempt at being stoic, the woman still screamed when they strapped her down and the bloodletting began. Her screams doubled when another sacrificial victim was cut open.

By the time Kim and Jacob were below the Skeletal Beast, three victims had been chosen and killed to feed the runes. The archers hadn't given up on finding them. A few of the members of Mack's group were trying to climb the walls with varying degrees of success.

The girl finally stopped screaming. "She'll probably get more than most of us," one of the men said.

"Who?" Mack asked.

"The woman that-"

Mack let out a low bassy chuckle. "I didn't even catch her name. More money for you guys, right?"

The dark laughter filtered among the group, even as the next victim was chosen, realizing that there would be no compensation he started to fight back.

If he was going to make his move, now would be the time.

"I need your flail," Jacob said, his voice a hoarse whisper. "We're going to get some help from that thing prowling around above us."

Kim stared at him. "How did you-"

"No time, just give it over." Jacob held out a hand to her and she summoned the weapon, handing it over.

It was one of the first weapons she picked up in Pyresouls Online. She abjectly hated it. But kept it just in case she needed it. Which, as far as he could recall from their talks, she never did.

Flail in hand, Jacob dug his fingers into any handholds he could find and leaned out over the ledge. He swung the flail as hard as he could up and over until it rang against the metal bars.

The Skeletal Beast shifted above him at the noise and lunged at the bars. Jacob could hear them squeal with the effort to hold the monster back. Unfortunately, it meant the archers now knew where he was.

Jacob banged against the bars a few more times before he had to retreat from the archers' renewed attention.

But it was enough.

The Skeletal Beast threw itself at the bars again but this time they couldn't hold back its unbridled fury. The creature sailed through the air. Jacob turned to see Kim lift her visor and gape in wide-mouthed shock at the sheer size and ferocity of the thing.

It landed with a heavy crash, scattering the stone tables and sacrificial altars. As it did, Jacob crawled forward to peek out from the ledge.

He had a front-row seat to the slaughter. Mack, to his credit, tried to organize a defensive line against the thing but its raking bony claws were too great. It swept aside an entire row of defenders, disemboweling them on the backswing and leaving them to die a horribly slow death.

They never stood a chance.

The Skeletal Beast had no lungs, no ability to roar or make terrifying bestial sounds as you might expect. The only thing Jacob and Kim heard were the sounds of men and women dying.

Those few that managed to make it halfway to the ledge were pulled down, impaled on spear-long fingerbones, and then ripped apart.

Rolling back to the cover of darkness, Jacob donned his armor once more and didn't dare look. Understanding that the show was at its end, Kim inched her way back until she was pressed up tight against him.

Neither of them said anything for a while as the beast rampaged around the room looking for something else to kill. Jacob knew it could detect life but with so much blood and viscera around he hoped that it would get confused and wander off.

The stone trembled beneath its assault as it demolished what was left of the room and any poor soul still left alive. A whirring sound filled the room followed quickly by a flash of red and the squeal of old rusty hinges swinging open.

For several long, tense minutes, they stayed together silently. At any other time, Jacob would have appreciated the closeness. He could only hope that the Skeletal Beast, finding no further victims, had left.

Making his way as quietly as he could, Jacob peeked over the ledge. The floor shimmered wetly with blood, not a single inch was spared. None of the bodies were recognizable, they were little more than lumps of meat.

But there was no Skeletal Beast.

The exit was easily visible, wide rust-flaked iron doors stood open to a large corridor beyond. One last look to make sure the way was clear, Jacob lowered himself down to the floor.

"That's one way to solve the puzzle," Kim said at his side, a clear tremor in her voice. "It's like somebody had a balloon fight with blood." She squinted her eyes at the exit. "Shouldn't that be a fog gate?"

Jacob nodded. Something wasn't right. With great care not to slip on the slick bloodied floor, they picked their way to the metal doors. He looked back at Kim. "The way is clear."

She had stopped halfway to the door, staring in queasy horror at the carnage around her. The same carnage that Jacob merely shrugged off. He'd seen worse.

Kim hurried up next to him and poked her head into the hall. She snapped her visor down. "So it seems," she said doubtfully. "You're pretty cold, you know that?"

Jacob turned to regard her. "They were going to kill you."

She shrugged. "Who am I to you? How did you know I had a flail, which I would like back now," she said, holding out her hand expectantly.

He handed her back her weapon, which she dismissed with a thought. "I guessed you picked it up early on. I saw one and decided to leave it since I can't stand how unwieldy they are."

Kim nodded along in agreement but still remained suspicious. "Well, it looks like we're stuck together a bit longer then, huh?"

"It would seem so," Jacob said distractedly.

There *should* have been a fog gate here. He remembered Alec telling him about it clearly. Did he do something to *all* of the fog gates when he burned away the first one?

He swallowed hard, trying to work through the implications.

With the fog gate destroyed, and the appearance of the Skeletal Beast, they had been pulled into Jacob's shard. His semi-private instance of Pyresouls Online.

Each person was given their own little world, not quite solo and not entirely private either. You could make a pact with somebody at a Crossing and invite them over to your world but if they died they were sent back to theirs so most people didn't bother.

Those that did often backstabbed the one who invited them, like Emily did to him. That way they could take the spoils while resetting the progress of the naïve player.

The list of player interactions was decidedly short. Cooperative opportunities even less so.

Without the Skeletal Beast, he would have had to sit by and watch Kim die, or else get pinned down and eventually slaughtered alongside her. Though he didn't appreciate the thought of following behind in the beast's path, Jacob did admit that without its help he might not still be standing.

"Want some free Souls?" Jacob asked with a grin, pointing at a nearby pile of meat. A red wisp floated over the remains of the body. Now that he took a moment to take stock of the ruined room, several more wisps were visible. They were hard to pick out amongst all the blood.

Kim looked at him, then at the red wisps. "I don't follow."

Motioning her to follow him, Jacob went to the nearest corpse and reached toward the wisp. It quivered, then flew into his chest. A quarter of the player's Souls went into Jacob.

Since it was a monster and not a player that had killed them, Jacob didn't automatically acquire the Souls.

He explained as much to Kim. Even with her visor down, Jacob could sense the waves of nausea from her as she understood what he was proposing. She clearly didn't want to be around the lumps of gore that were once people. Even if those people had been about to kill her.

Her practical side won out, however, and they agreed to split the bounty 60/40 with the lion's share going to Jacob.

Most of the players didn't have many Souls on them. Not as many as he thought they might, anyway. But Mack did. He must have been holding well over 20,000 to drop that wisp of 6,125.

The leader was only recognizable from the battered and caved-in red-smeared white metal lion's head helmet. Altogether, Jacob gathered 12,255 Souls.

Not a bad haul considering I didn't have to do anything.

"Let's go," he said to Kim. "Time's wasting."

20

"Jake... *Jake!*" Kim hissed at him.

"What?" he whispered back, hiding behind a pillar as he searched for the switch that would open the next section.

This area of the catacombs was worked with cunning traps and countless levers, pulleys, and other contraptions that moved or altered the rooms around them.

Thankfully, there weren't quite so many undead and the Skeletal Beast was quick to absorb any into its disturbingly spacious frame.

Whenever it came upon a skeleton it would immediately absorb it, integrating the creature into its growing bulk and becoming all the more deadly for it. The upside was each skeleton it found, slowed it down.

Until there were no skeletons left.

That small reprieve gave them enough time to locate two out of four switches that would open the large stone door.

The Skeletal Beast was prowling around the expansive hallways looking for them. They already narrowly escaped it three times so far. Jacob wasn't sure how much longer their luck would hold.

"He's back," she said, trying to keep her voice low.

They stood on a high platform with a sheer 40-foot drop between them. Down below in the main room, there was a large stone door with all the hallmarks of the area boss that would be guarding the [Ring of Broken Vows]. But first, they had to find a way to open the damn thing.

Jacob leaned over the side of his platform, watching the Skeletal Beast prowl around the area. Several black scorch marks decorated its grotesquely expanded bony frame.

He needed to get into that room. What imagery Jacob could make out on the massive door depicted an amorphous beast battling a great towering knight with a hammer almost as big as he was.

Much of the carving was destroyed or scratched out, making the tale's end hard to discern. As dark as most of the lore for Lormar was, Jacob was fairly sure the knight died a horrible death but somehow managed to seal the amorphous beast away.

For a brief moment, he was afraid it was the Burgon Beast. While he never saw the creature in person, Alec was a passable artist and showed him what it looked like.

A feral black creature with six limbs, countless red-glowing eyes that wrapped around its jagged-toothed maw and down its long serpentine neck. The way Alec drew it looked like a horribly mutated and enlarged wolf made out of black vines instead of fur.

When he asked Alec which it was, the man only shrugged, unsure himself.

"Maybe it'll go away," he whispered back, knowing it wasn't likely.

Even if it did, the hallways and chambers nearby that it patrolled were too close. By the time one of them descended a ladder it would be back. Its life sensing ability seemed muted at a distance of more than thirty feet. If they tried to go down too soon, it would know where they were.

While Jacob didn't think it would be able to reach them, in making an attempt it could very well destroy the thin metal ladders. He was already down to 2 [Cinder Ampoules] after their last brush with the thing.

It had come upon them when they were distracted by a treasury, one of many no doubt. And while Jacob had no desire to fill his pockets with gold and riches that were overflowing like gilded water from the various coffers, he *did* want some of the relics and armor in the room.

That was until the Skeletal Beast found them.

There was a gorgeous set of golden armor he had been forced to leave behind that he desperately wanted. Hammered plate mail that looked sturdy and light, ridged in such a way that there was no need for leather or chainmail underneath to form adequate protection.

"Yeah, and I'm going to sprout wings and fly down there," Kim said in reply. "You have to distract it."

"Why me?"

"I did it last time."

"Not willingly."

Kim turned to him, but with her visor down he couldn't tell why. "If you can't tell because of the visor, I'm giving you *such a scathing look*, Jake."

"Rock, paper, scissors for it," Jacob suggested.

He could practically *feel* the eye roll coming from Kim, even if he couldn't see it. "*Ugh, fine.* No best of three bullshit. First wins all."

Turning toward her, he tapped his fist to his palm to a count of three then threw scissors, to which Kim put forth rock. Soundly beating him.

Despite the gravity of the situation, she gave a husky chuckle. "You're so easy to read, dude."

Grimacing, Jacob glared at her. "Easy because my janky-ass visor is busted."

"Excuses, excuses. Get a move on, we're only going to get one shot at this."

Steeling himself, Jacob pulled on the lever set into the floor. It made surprisingly little noise as it pulled back easily and stuck in its position. If they were right, the doors would open if Kim threw her lever.

But they were far too weak to handle the boss within. Seeing how useful the Skeletal Beast was before, and considering its annoying proximity they agreed it would be best to have a repeat performance of the Crossing.

By using the Skeletal Beast to attack whatever was behind the door

– presumably the Gnawing Hunger – they could kill two birds with one stone. Even if they didn't kill each other, it might provide enough of a distraction for Jacob to slip in and pilfer any items they could find.

Likely their Souls would be forfeit but any items they found would stay with them. And if the [Ring of Broken Vows] was down here – an item necessary to beating the game – Jacob had to at least try.

Even if he died, despite the horrible gauntlet it would be to return, he knew the way now. Next time he would do his best not to trigger the Skeletal Beast. While the monster took care of the players, it was a severe threat now.

Just as the Skeletal Beast was stomping away, Jacob hopped on the ladder. He gripped the vertical bars of the ladder tightly and set his boots against the outside of the same bars.

Taking a deep breath, Jacob relaxed his grip and started to slide down at an alarming pace. Modifying his grip and the pressure of his boots he was able to control his descent so that he touched the ground just as the beast left the room, none the wiser.

He took a moment to shake out his overheated hands before he took the southern exit to the room. With any luck, he could snag a few items before he ran into the Skeletal Beast.

The goal would be to run it straight toward the door at the northern end of the chamber then dive aside and hope he was fast enough not to be caught between the two deadly titans.

Tall decorated pillars marched along the middle of the spacious hall with bright flames set in the hollows of the pillars, casting long shadows in each direction. It would not have been out of place in a dwarven hall, or in any one of the many reboots to the Tolkien VR franchise.

Jacob managed to spot an azure wisp and raced for it hovering over the armored body of a knight. He crept to it as quickly and quietly as he could, very aware that the beast was probably just around the bend.

It wasn't the golden armor in the room filled with treasure, but it had its own charm with blue cloth, ridged steel plate, fine chainmail, and sturdy leather.

He managed to kneel and touch the wisp just as the gleam of bone caught his eye. The beast saw him, or sensed him – not that it mattered – and immediately barreled straight at him.

> *You gain* [Elite Knight Helm].
> *You gain* [Elite Knight Armor].
> *You gain* [Elite Knight Leggings].
> *You gain* [Elite Knight Gauntlets].
> *You gain* [Ring of Boundless Fury].
> *You gain* [Cloven Phoenix Tree Crest Shield].

Swiping his item notifications aside, Jacob ran for all he was worth, trying to keep close to the center of the hallway. Predictably, the beast charged straight through the pillars instead of weaving around them. The floor shook as it crashed into each of the stone supports, slowing it just enough that Jacob could keep ahead of its many new swiping claws.

"Now, Kim!" Jacob cried as he passed between the two ladders.

If he was going to die, it would be here. The room ahead was large, like a purpose-built arena it was wide and had no obstructions save for the two ladders.

The Skeletal Beast promptly charged into the room. Jacob was halfway to the large stone doors when an explosion warmed his back. Looking over his shoulder, not daring to stop or even slow, he saw another [Firebomb] explode on the Skeletal Beast's back.

It didn't hurt it, but it distracted it enough that it was torn between chasing Jacob and looking around for the new threat. "Thanks, Kim," he said, even though there was no way she could hear him at that distance.

The pressure in the room dropped, Jacob's ears popped and a great sucking wind pulled him toward the stone doors that were beginning to swing inward. If all went according to plan, he could get in while the opening was still small and dive aside to avoid the worst of whatever was to come.

Obviously, nothing ever goes according to plan.

Just as Jacob neared the doors, the Skeletal Beast lashed out. He was only brushed but the blow had staggering power behind it, enough to send him flying into the darkness ahead.

Jacob hit the ground in a tumble, his armor making enough of a racket to wake the dead. And whatever horrible monster they just unsealed.

Scrambling about in the dark, Jacob heard the Skeletal Beast break through the doors, shattering them with colossal strength. Debris rained everywhere, by some stroke of luck Jacob avoided getting crushed by tons of broken stone.

He was up on his feet rushing to the rear of the half-circle chamber. A figure stood there, tall and imperious. It wielded the same large hammer as it had on the carvings on the now-broken door.

Ducking to the side, Jacob veered around the suit of immobile armor and to the small altar behind. He spotted the ring immediately, an amazingly intricate band of gold and silver threads with a single cracked black diamond at its center.

Jacob reached for it, only to have his arm crushed beneath the grip of the knight that wasn't actually just a suit of armor at all. He screamed as his bones turned to powder under the knight's strength.

That would have been the end for Jacob if the Skeletal Beast didn't collide with the knight and distract it. With the edges of his vision rapidly darkening, Jacob reached his other hand forward and grabbed the ring.

You gain [Ring of Broken Vows].

At that point, he thought he would be killed. But to his surprise the two ferocious beasts battled it out, giving Jacob enough time to not only flee the chamber but snag three more rings on the way out.

You gain [Ring of Calamitous Intent].
You gain [Ring of Covetous Breath].
You gain [Ring of Opportunity].

By the time Jacob left the room, Kim was already sprinting toward it. Jacob pulled her aside to stop her from running to her death. She resisted long enough to see his ruined arm, the metal gauntlet crushed like a tin can around his forearm.

She gasped staring in horrified shock at it. "Your arm... it looks like a smashed can of tomato chunks."

Releasing her with his free hand, Jacob took out a [Cinder Ampoule] and restored his Health. The armor expanded but was badly damaged. When the thrashing and shaking finally died down, Jacob expected to get a surge of Souls from the death of one or more of the creatures.

When nothing happened he moved cautiously toward the broken doorway. A dark shape snaked out, gleaming red eyes opened along its dark vine-filled shape. Followed closely by a zipper of jagged teeth.

His heart stuttered in his chest and Jacob froze in fear as recognition slammed home.

He was still standing there, trying to process what he was seeing when another coiling tendril of black vines shot out from the room and impaled him through the stomach.

The tendril snaked through the air as if gravity was a mere suggestion. Desperate to cling to life, Jacob popped his last [Cinder Ampoule]. The force of his regenerating flesh pushed him off the impaling limb and onto the floor.

By then the tendril had carried him partway across the room. Instead of the knight as Jacob expected to see, it was the Skeletal Beast. Only the beast was being consumed. Black vines whipped across the bones giving it a feral, lupine shape.

Red glowing eyes popped open all along its body and its maw lengthened into a wolfish equivalence. The last thing Jacob saw before it opened its zippered maw to bite him in half was the spitting image of the Burgon Beast.

You Died.

21

September 2nd, 2035 – 11 days remain before the Collapse.

Jacob thrashed awake at the Pyre, kicking and flailing with fear. The Fire Oppa regarded him idly. Eventually, as Jacob calmed and his thudding heart stilled, he looked to the Pyre, that symbol of hope that would soon be guttered.

What have I done?

"I set it free."

"Set what free?" the Fire Oppa asked, tilting his head in confusion.

"The Burgon Beast... I- how did I set it free so much sooner? I thought I had to open up the door to its chamber?"

Taking a deep breath, Jacob exhaled through his nose to calm himself further. Something wasn't quite right. The Burgon Beast was held in place behind the massive gates at Journey's End.

There was nothing about it coming out from the Desecrated Catacombs.

The Fire Oppa shut his eyes and flickered for a moment. The Pyre flared then died down. "You did not release the Burgon Beast," he said in all confidence.

"But it looked-"

"Appearances can be deceiving. What you released was the Gnawing Hunger. The Gnawing Hunger takes the shape of the thing you fear most and uses it against you." The Fire Oppa looked down and sighed. "Knights of greater power than you could know have been fooled by it. Do not be so hard on yourself."

Once he calmed down and sorted through everything rationally, he guessed it had to be true. At least partially. When Alec was killed by the Burgon Beast he was ejected from the game.

The working theory was that the Burgon Beast destroyed Pyres, forcibly logging out players across all shards of Lormar associated with that Pyre. And the first thing it did was seek out the nearest Pyre.

Alec had fought it right in front of the Journey's End Pyre. As soon as he was killed, the Burgon Beast destroyed the Pyre fast enough that Alec didn't have a chance to respawn.

To the best of his knowledge, it systematically destroyed one Pyre after the other, intentionally destroying those closest to the latest sections of the game and working its way to the first areas.

Only once the Burgon Beast reached the first Pyre in the Razor Pass did it break free of the game. By then, nobody was alive to see what happened and all first-hand accounts ended there.

The Burgon Beast was the most powerful monster in the entire game. Its ability to wipe out Pyres aside – and the horrible fate that might await the Fire Oppa as a result – made it far too early in the game's life to be awakened now.

If he did, *nobody* stood a chance.

Alec had been in the low 40s when he faced it and with gear that far outstripped Jacob's. Not to mention it was about two weeks into the game's competition. By Jacob's reckoning he had been in Pyresouls for just over 3 days, give or take a few hours.

Looking around, Jacob couldn't help but wonder if the Fire Oppa was wrong. Even as he doubted, the fiery ferret walked out of the Pyre and curled up in Jacob's lap. The soothing presence of the Pyre burned away his fears, his worries, and his anxiety, leaving nothing but a still sense of peace.

Without them clouding his thoughts, Jacob could see the truth of the matter clearly. The creature had appeared *exactly* as Jacob imagined the Burgon Beast. He dreamed of it often enough, though probably not as much as Alec had.

Out of every person Jacob knew, it was Alec who could most benefit from the soothing effects of the Pyre.

It was a shame he wasn't here.

"Thanks," he said, absently petting the Fire Oppa. "Did... Camilla ever come back?"

"No."

What small fragment of hope that he might run into the curious woman again vanished. He doubted Kim made it out of the Desecrated Catacombs alive either, which meant she would be sent back to her own shard.

"So I'm alone again," he said more to himself than to the Fire Oppa.

And then he remembered all the items he managed to get right before he died. Despite what the Fire Oppa said, he didn't see much treasure on the way down into the catacombs.

Then again, he was focused on getting the hell out of there. Not looting the place. Even still, he expected there to be more than he found. Considering the many dead ends he turned away from, maybe that's where the treasures were.

Sprinkled bits of sapphire wisps hidden just out of sight that would have given an item to him but at the cost of his progress. A single dead-end would have allowed the hordes of skeletons to catch up to him.

And that would have certainly spelled his doom.

As it was, he lost over 20,000 Souls. Not a small sum, and for once he wasn't keen on trying to retrieve them. The depths of the Desecrated Catacombs had nothing for him anymore.

They could keep whatever treasures lay buried deep within. He was done with that place. He would travel the upper levels to continue on and no more.

Jacob pulled out the [Cloven Phoenix Tree Crest Shield]. The fact that it was broken was obvious from more than the item's title. Never before had he known an item's title to change when it was broken. The item, upon examination, offered no stats.

In fact, it acted like it was an item and not a piece of equipment.

[Cloven Phoenix Tree Crest Shield]
Shield once belonging to a knight of the Phoenix Covenant. The shield symbolizes a high amount of trust given to the knight, suggesting he or she was on an important mission when they perished.

The Fire Oppa perked up at that. "Where did you get that?" he asked.

"I found it down in the catacombs outside of the room with the Gnawing Hunger."

"So she failed," he said softly. The flames that made up the Fire Oppa began to cool and darken, the little furry thing sullenly slinked back to the Pyre as his coat turned as dark as coal.

"Who failed?" Jacob asked, setting the shield aside.

"A friend."

"Do you know what the Phoenix Covenant is, then?"

"It is the covenant of the Pyre," the Fire Oppa said simply. "Extended to those trustworthy individuals who were tasked with assuring the Pyres stayed lit."

"I take it they didn't do so well?" Jacob hedged, not wanting to flat-out state the obvious. Judging by the state of Lormar, and the lack of any Pyres when players first arrived that covenant was likely wiped out.

"Unfortunately so."

Glancing at the shield, Jacob lifted it and placed it into the Pyre beside the Fire Oppa. "Here, this isn't going to do me any good in its current state and it sounds like this has some sentimental value to you. Why don't you keep it?"

The somber, reflective Fire Oppa looked up curiously at him. His little rounded ears perked as he regarded Jacob in a new light. "That is... unexpected of you. Thank you."

With a swish of his tail, the Fire Oppa summoned a swirl of flame to consume the shield, leaving nothing in its wake. Jacob inclined his head and took out the rest of his loot.

While he didn't get to keep his Souls, the items he found were more than compensation.

Few people were able to say they plundered 5 rings, one of them a key component to the Burgon Beast's release, and a full new set of armor. All from a single foray into a highly dangerous area that the vast majority of the player base would never survive, let alone see with their own eyes.

When Jacob looked over the set of armor, his jaw nearly fell to his chest. The elite knight armor set was something that even Alec never managed to find. It wasn't precisely ground-breaking but for the protection it offered it was amazing. It could punch well above its weight.

But the cost was high.

[Equipment]

Elite Knight's Helm [Helm]

Physical Protection: 60
  Blunt: 20
  Slashing: 20
  Piercing: 20

  Magical Protection: 50
  Arcane: 15
  Fire: 15
  Water: 5
  Earth: 5
  Harmony: 5
  Chaos: 5

Resistances
Bleed: 15
Poison: 8
Curse: 0
Stability: 15

Durability: 600/600
  Guilt: 4

Elite Knight's Armor [Chest]

Physical Protection: 134
  Blunt: 40
  Slashing: 54
  Piercing: 40

  Magical Protection: 113
  Arcane: 32
  Fire: 25
  Water: 18
  Earth: 15
  Harmony: 11
  Chaos: 12

  Resistances
  Bleed: 33
  Poison: 19
  Curse: 0
  Stability: 29

Durability: 600/600

Guilt: 8

Elite Knight's Gauntlets [Gauntlets]

Physical Protection: 54
Blunt: 18
Slashing: 18
Piercing: 18

Magical Protection: 48
Arcane: 15
Fire: 15
Water: 8
Earth: 8
Harmony: 1
Chaos: 1

Resistances
Bleed: 15
Poison: 8
Curse: 0
Stability: 10

Durability: 600/600
    Guilt: 3

Elite Knight's Leggings [Leggings]

Physical Protection: 103
Blunt: 32
Slashing: 36
Piercing: 35

Magical Protection: 84

Arcane: 30
Fire: 18
Water: 10
Earth: 10
Harmony: 8
Chaos: 8

Resistances
Bleed: 24
Poison: 17
Curse: 0
Stability: 15

Durability: 600/600
  Guilt: 6

Despite superior protection, the cost of guilt was high. Far too high for Jacob at the moment. Even donning the gauntlets, among the lightest at only 3 guilt, would bring Jacob fully two tiers of Guilt up to tier 4 or even higher.

And that he knew he could not withstand.

Tier 4 was a 50% penalty to both movement and stamina drain. Even if he switched exclusively to his [Longsword], which had its own drawbacks against certain enemies strong to slashing and piercing, the drain would be too much to bear.

But the defense was enticing. For medium grade armor, it was surprisingly sturdy and well-balanced with a hefty amount of magical protection.

Curious, Jacob swapped his current helm for the elite version. It would still be far too much for him to withstand but he remembered that the [Ring of Blameless Guilt] was lightening his burden somehow.

If his burden increased by the difference of 3, then he knew the ring was static. Good for early game but he would soon want to increase his TMP the old-fashioned way.

On the other hand, if it reduced that value as well then he might have something worth more than he knew. With so many rings in his possession, his 2 slots suddenly became hotly contested.

Once I figure out what those rings do, he reminded himself.

Dark thoughts settled deep into his bones. A sense of loss that was not his own stole into his heart and without even bothering to look at his parameters Jacob could tell he had significantly slowed.

The effect of so much Guilt weighed heavily on his soul.

Not quite doubled, he thought as he moved his arms around with familiar effort. He didn't bother to get up, tier 3 Guilt was what he was used to back on Earth. *Tier 3 then, not tier 4. Interesting. Adding 3 more Guilt onto the 7 from my equipment should have put me over 100% Guilt.*

But it hadn't, and that meant the [Ring of Blameless Guilt] was not a static reduction.

A glance at his equipment painted a clearer picture. Originally, he should have been at 7 points of guilt. Which the ring reduced to 4. With the addition of the [Elite Knight's Helm], he was adding 3 guilt onto that 7. But his guilt only increased to 5.

He knew, without a doubt, that he would never take off the [Ring of Blameless Guilt]. Without testing it further - which he had no inclination to do – it appeared that it lowered the guilt of equipped items by *half.*

That was a massive boon that nothing else in the game could come close to equaling. Armor and weapons all had varying amounts of Guilt but the best ones were soaked in it.

The amount of guilt was, after all, what made the weapons effective. Items had a way of soaking up the experiences and memories of their wielders. In particular, it was the guilt these people possessed as they fought, lived, and died with the items in hand.

Guilt strengthened the items, nobody could ever quite figure out how. Only that it did.

Without any Souls to reinforce TMP, Jacob was left with a strong set – he still couldn't believe he had the entire set – of armor but without the parameters to wear it properly. No matter what pieces he tried to swap around, there was no getting around it. The Guilt on each piece was simply too high.

Grumbling to himself about his lack of reinforcing TMP when he had the Souls, Jacob turned his attention to the rings.

One of them, he knew he would need to wear before long, but the other four he could only guess at.

[Ring of Broken Vows]
Intricate band of gold and silver threads with a single, cracked black diamond at its center.
The once-great Sir Gailsyn wore the ring of his betrothal into mortal combat with the Gnawing Hunger, so confident that he would be the victor and return to his beloved. A promise he, in depths of his pride, broke by falling to the creature. Allows the wearer to survive harsh environments.

[Ring of Calamitous Intent]
A heavy black metal ring with sharp spikes that prick the owner. A red jewel is set beneath narrow bands of metal that give the ring an appearance of an angry red serpentine eye gazing out.
Ring belonging to Sir Gailsyn, an overly prideful knight of great renown. It was this pride that was the man's downfall when he sought to clash with the Gnawing Hunger. Increases damage to the wearer while increasing Counter, Riposte, and Backstab damage.

[Ring of Covetous Breath]
A ring fashioned into the likeness of a silvery serpent coiled about itself, a peerless pearl grasped in its mouth.
The Slyhalthans were an ancient enemy of Lormar, often striking from the depths of various waterways to ravage and plunder ships and to raid towns reliant on the waterways. An ambitious enchanter created this ring in their silvery serpentine image, mocking them as it provided its wearer the capacity

to pursue the slippery creatures into their watery home where they were utterly destroyed. Provides breath.

[Ring of Boundless Fury]
A ring fashioned from cracked black stone. Ruddy light peeks out from the cracks in a wave of unbearable heat.
In times long past, Lormar was host to the Eternal Pyre. When that fabled flame went out, many tried to replicate it. This ring was fashioned from the dying embers of that flame and imbued with the anger of a people betrayed. Imbues the wearer with great strength even as the dying embers burn them.

[Ring of Opportunity]
Gold ring with deeply etched symbols running on the inside of the band, leaving a perfectly smooth exterior.
The old faithful believed gold to have extraordinary powers to channel the miraculous prowess of Clemency. The many faiths also believed that ostentatious display of wealth was a sin of pride and thus kept their empowering and flashy sigils hidden from view. Increases power of Clemency spells.

Jacob held up the silvery serpentine ring to the Fire Oppa. "Is this the one you were suggesting I find?"

"It would appear you have found quite the treasure trove," the Fire Oppa said, eyeing him. Jacob thought the small thing still looked rather forlorn and sad after taking the shield. "But yes," he managed to say after a lengthy pause. "You found that in the catacombs? Strange. I had it on good authority it was within the Drowned Halls...."

He guessed he would too if he was in the Fire Oppa's place. Reaching into the comforting fire, Jacob pet the Fire Oppa and took a moment to draw comfort from the Pyre's strength.

The Fire Oppa stokes the embers of your conviction.
Health, Stamina, Ampoules and Spell Gems restored.

Each ring he found was useful, except the [Ring of Opportunity], he'd sell or trade that away as soon as the opportunity arose. If it had boosted Sorcery instead of Clemency, he would have instantly equipped it.

That left only two rings that had any discernible effects, the [Ring of Calamitous Intent] and the [Ring of Boundless Fury]. He didn't like the look of the former, and he liked the description of it even less.

He didn't understand the exact mechanics behind it, but taking more damage when he could barely survive a single hit seemed idiotic at the present.

The [Ring of Boundless Fury] was something known to him, though. It caused a constant health drain but increased the damage output of the wearer.

That might be useful before going into a big fight but it would be useless for his purposes, which now that he thought about it, he wasn't sure what his purpose was.

To heat Alec to the Burgon Beast and to defeat it, yes, but that was still some time away. Given that he couldn't pull himself out of Pyresouls to speak with Alice or Alec again, their earlier plans were now altered by Jacob's foray into the pit of the Desecrated Catacombs.

The fairly detailed plan hinged on Jacob only skirting the upper levels of the catacombs, to return later once he was much stronger. But that wasn't necessary anymore.

Arriving at Hollow Dreams early might not be a bad idea, it would allow him to capitalize on the growing market and the flocking merchants before everybody grabbed all the good items.

But in order to do that, he would need an ample supply of Souls and the strength to protect that supply while in Hollow Dreams.

Decisions, decisions.

Jacob knew where another Spell Gem was, but to get it he'd have to backtrack. And it wasn't like he had another spell to use either. As much as he would like the extra gem, it didn't fit into the goal of getting to the Burgon Beast first and destroying it before it could destroy everything.

And on top of it all, the Fire Oppa had a task for him. To reignite as many Pyres as he could. Some were, apparently, more valuable than others.

With a significant task completed early, he could venture out to the Drowned Halls to relight the Pyre there. If he could go beyond to the Ashen Flood - quite the way out of his projected path - that would be 5 out of 6 Pyres lit.

When he lit the final Pyre in Hollow Dreams, he would have satisfied the minimum number of Pyres that the Fire Oppa asked to be relit.

While Jacob had never been to the Ashen Flood, it seemed as good a destination to him at the moment.

Retrieving the [Ring of Broken Vows] so early allowed him to cross that particular item off his to-do list, which meant he could focus more on farming Souls and growing stronger.

Despite the annoyance of having an empty ring slot, Jacob kept his newly acquired rings firmly in his inventory. None of them directly helped him at the moment. As with many rings in the game, they held niche uses that he could exploit later.

What he really wanted, was a ring that affected his stamina. Which meant he would likely never find such a ring without great trouble. That seemed to be the way of things.

If he was practiced in Clemency, no doubt the [Ring of Opportunity] he found would have increased the power of Sorcery instead.

"Some Pyres are what... stronger than others?" Jacob asked the Fire Oppa.

"You could say that." The Fire Oppa didn't even lift its head, barely even responded to the petting like before. "Each Pyre radiates a strength to the surrounding regions. Igniting a Pyre where it is darkest provides the largest benefit. You could, if you so chose, ignite all of the Pyres. It would increase my strength, and the strength I could lend to you but that would be time-consuming."

"And so the Ashen Flood is the closest Pyre of significance?" he asked.

The Fire Oppa shut his eyes and seemed to go to sleep, ignoring Jacob's question. He was about to repeat himself when the Fire Oppa spoke. "Yes. There are six total Pyres that need to be lit. Though each region has more than a single Pyre, lighting any will do.

"The Ashen Flood is so named for one of the darkest betrayals the Phoenix Covenant ever experienced. It is a bleak, horrid place that I would greatly wish could be lit with the warming strength of the Pyre.

"You have already reignited the Pyres of the Razor Pass, the Steps of Penance, and the Desecrated Catacombs. Twelve Pyres in this area remain cold and dark, though only three of them need to be lit.

"To the north and west, the Drowned Halls and Ashen Flood. Northeast is Hollow Dreams and the Defiled Cistern with the Blind Sisters far to the east of those two. To the southeast, the Corpse Garden, and Mercy Tower. Directly south of us is the Stalking Wood and Fogdrift Garden.

"Southwest is Weslyn's Watch, and finally to the west is the Smog Rifts, and Journey's End. Which you choose to relight is up to you."

While there was no map to be had, Jacob had a general mental layout of the areas given to him by Alice and Alec in his briefing. That meant Weslyn's Watch, the Stalking Wood, Corpse Garden, and Defiled Cistern could all be skipped.

If his goal was to help the Fire Oppa, that is.

Each of the areas was fairly far from the other, and Jacob could guess well enough that lighting the Pyre in the Stalking Wood and Corpse Garden was less effective as they bordered one another.

With a list of destinations in mind, Jacob started to rise. "Looks like I better get a move on, then." Though he didn't really want to get up. It was harder each time to pull away from the comfort of the flames.

For the first time, Jacob saw just how lonely the Fire Oppa must be as the little animal opened its eyes and watched him with a sense of resignation.

Jacob didn't know what to say. So he returned to the Pyre to offer the ferret-like animal one more sympathetic pet. "Would that somebody could stay by your side and give you a home and love that you deserve," he said, only then aware of how belittling and demeaning that might sound.

What if the Fire Oppa was a god, or some creature far beyond a simple magical animal? How offensive might his words be then?

The Fire Oppa merely shrugged his narrow shoulders and snorted a tiny jet of fire from his nostrils. "It is a nice sentiment," he agreed.

Unable to stand the sad look in the Fire Oppa's eyes, Jacob quickly left to search out a way through the upper levels of the Desecrated Catacombs.

22

Jacob veered left, pivoted on his back foot, and cracked through the ribcages of two [Skeletal Knights], sending their bones scattering into the dark. Completing his turn, eyes focused on the sapphire wisp at the dead-end, Jacob sprinted forward while the skeletons recovered from the blow.

He didn't bother to ignite his [Mace] for the blow. Jacob abruptly threw himself forward when he noticed the discolored flooring below him, diving and rolling with a clatter over the trap without triggering it.

Up in a run, Jacob made it to the sapphire glow of the wisp just as the two knights came after him. Ignorant of the trap, the two [Skeletal Knights] were immolated in a burst of white-hot fire.

There were only three things that could destroy a skeleton: fire, harmony-based spells, or chaos-based spells. The first destroyed the body, turning it to useless ash. Harmony consecrated the bones, preventing their reanimation. Chaos performed a similar rite but rather than sanctifying the bones, it controlled them and ordered them to stay down.

Without even looking over his shoulder, Jacob reached out and touched the wisp. The flames warmed his back, but he was far enough away for it to be a distant concern.

You gain [Soul of a Wandering Knight].
You gain 2 [Anima].

It was the third such soul he found so far in the upper levels of the Desecrated Catacombs as he made his way northward.

Tucking it away, Jacob turned to regard the piles of ash as two white wisps streaked out and hit him in the chest. Not for the first time he wished they dropped more Souls.

He didn't know much about the catacombs, it was an area beyond him originally and spoken of in hushed horrified tones even by his brave friend. It was not an area to be traveled lightly and one that should be crossed with all haste.

Great treasures tempted and lured the unwary – or the greedy – into winding tunnels that were filled with death. Jacob had already narrowly escaped two such death tunnels already, abandoning the prizes that glowed tantalizingly in the dark.

He didn't dare ignite his [Mace] again, because he found that it had a rather ironic effect. The skeletons were drawn to it. Flame offended them, and they sought it out with all the ferocity of a rabid animal.

By keeping to the dark, he struggled to navigate the tunnels but less than half the skeletons that had arrayed against him before rose against him this time. And they were much less likely to follow him indefinitely.

Putting enough winding tunnels between them was sufficient for the monsters to give up the chase. Useful information that he hoped he would never need to make use of again.

Retracing his steps, Jacob joined the main tunnel he was using to get out of the catacombs. Dodging traps and skeletons for the better part of an hour had put him on edge. Every shadow, every sound grabbed at his attention and refused to let him go.

Sparks flashed out into the dark when he crashed his [Mace] into the dark fold between two natural juts of the stone tunnel. There was nothing hiding there, of course.

This was the reason they cycled out their watch back on Earth. Tasking any human to ward against such horrific threats took its toll.

Either the person on watch would lapse into carelessness, or they suffered from what Jacob did: hypervigilance.

Every bump in the night, every crunch of a dry leaf, even a glint from the ruddy moonlight, would cause the person to call out the alarm. More often than not their noise and ruckus would attract undue attention that would have passed them by.

Alone, hours without rest, or being able to drop his guard, Jacob tried to get a grip on himself.

There hasn't been an enemy in some time, he reminded himself.

Looking around the natural tunnel, he began to realize the truth. He wasn't safe, never that. Only the Pyres were safe. But he could loosen his grip on the [Mace] a little bit.

His hand cramped from the effort of relaxing it, and a thousand aches assaulted his worn-out body. The few hits he took passing through the Desecrated Catacombs had worn through two of his ampoules but he still had an ample supply left.

Centering himself, Jacob breathed in deep through his mouth and forced several slow exhalations through his nose. The rhythmic, calming breathing quieted his raging thoughts.

Moments later, he was on the move again, aware but not overly so. He soon came to a split in the tunnel. The one on his left stayed relatively flat and even, while the right tunnel curved away and to the right at a sloping downward angle.

The left would take him to Hollow Dreams. While the right led to the Drowned Halls. He didn't much like the sound of that place, and while arriving at Hollow Dreams early might give him an advantage, he had a Pyre to light.

Just to be safe, Jacob equipped the [Ring of Covetous Breath].

Clean, fresh air filled his lungs on each breath. The faint fetid stench that pervaded the tunnels vanished in that same instant.

I guess it really does provide breath. Man, I wished I had this back in the asylum. Camilla reeked.

Even the memory of the stench nearly made him gag. Though the thought of Camilla covered in gore did bring a wistful smile to his lips. He hoped she was okay.

Taking the right path, Jacob set off at a steady jog, armor rattling the whole way. With any luck, the next area would have a Pyre sooner than later.

He didn't fancy the idea of having to make the hours-long trek through the upper levels of the catacombs again.

He hoped to never see the rotten, bony place ever again.

Sloping downward and curving, Jacob noted how the walls became less natural and more manmade. Blocks of stone replaced the sloping walls. The deeper he went the colder it became.

The Drowned Halls

A slick pervasive dampness filled the halls. Droplets of water that glittered in Jacob's faint illumination deposited puddles on the floor that he found harder and harder to avoid.

It wasn't long before he came upon a circular room, with three sealed exits. At the center of the room was a suit of armor on a pedestal. Jacob lifted his shield and cast his gaze about the dim room to see if anything else was lying in wait for him.

He came forward in a rush and shield-smashed into the suit of armor, not at all surprised when it didn't topple and instead lifted its rusted sightless head toward him.

"Yeah, thought so," Jacob said. And despite the enemy before him, he found himself relieved to finally have a fight. The tension of waiting was broken and he launched himself at the suit of armor again before it could attack.

On came his [Mace]. Jacob fell into a deep crouch, turning his hips to add force to the swiping attack at its knee. *Breaking Rocks* took out the rusted armor just above the knee and the suit of armor overbalanced as it attempted to counterattack.

A reversed backswing was enough to break its Stability and set the animated armor crashing to the ground. Unfortunately, the attack angle was all wrong and had no real force behind it to deal much damage.

Wasting little time, Jacob lifted his [Mace] over his head as the suit of armor began rolling back and forth in an attempt to get up. He had a momentary thought that it looked like a turtle on its back before he snapped every muscle in his body and sent his [Mace] arcing forward.

Hammering the Nail shattered the armor's breastplate and cracked the stone beneath, sending up a spray of suspiciously briny water against his face.

The suit of armor seemed undeterred by this and swept out a broken sword at Jacob's ankles. He wasn't fast enough to leap back nor was he skilled enough with a [Mace] to bring it back in line like he could with his [Longsword].

Still, he tried and took a sharp jolting hit to the lower quadrant of his shins. The armor held but the bone had nearly cracked from the casual swipe.

Pushing the pain away into a tiny compartment made for the sensation, Jacob jumped over the returning strike. He tried to time it to land on the gauntlet, halting future attacks but he wasn't fast enough and missed it by an inch.

Foregoing all form and finesse – not that he had much with a [Mace] – Jacob straddled the armor and struck at the thing's helm in a series of brutal, denting blows.

The air filled with the red flaking rust and Jacob fell back from a sudden searing pain in his side as the white wisp of the defeated creature streaked into his chest.

You defeat the [Animated Armor].
Awarded 400 Souls.
You gain 1 [Dull Spark].

Thinking he pulled a muscle, Jacob reached down to rub the stitch in his side and found, to his surprise, a jagged blade stuck there. It wasn't in too deeply, just barely penetrating the leather armor padding beneath his breastplate.

That he was stabbed in the middle of the fight wasn't surprising. But it *was* surprising when he realized it wasn't a blade that he was stabbed with. It was some sort of tentacle made of stone.

Worse, when Jacob went to extract it the thing wriggled and burrowed deeper. He tightened his grip for a moment, trying to extract it by main force but the waves of nausea and pain that wracked him as the thing tore deeper into him made him stop.

So long as he didn't try to remove it, whatever it was didn't move. It remained solid, though now another quarter of his Health was gone, leaving him at roughly half. Disturbingly, the half of his Health that was missing had turned gray and stony.

This was a creature he never heard of before.

Just to be sure, he looked at his logs and found no prompts telling him what happened. He was not afflicted with any disease or toxin and his Curse Level wasn't high enough to cause a hallucination yet.

Getting to his feet, Jacob winced as every movement caused the thing in his side to shift. It dug no deeper but having a solid piece of stone impaled in your side was not so easily shrugged off.

As tempted as he was to use an ampoule, something about the thing in his side told him that it would react violently to the action. Not to mention the way his Health bar was half-filled with gray. And so Jacob limped on, careful to move as gingerly as possible.

The doors to the rooms had a disturbing amount of tentacle iconography, the sort he hoped he would never see again. The Vile Kingdom used such religious symbols.

Was this where they got the inspiration for their kingdom?

Even now, as he laid eyes on the twisting carved tentacles on the faces of each of the stone doors, was he looking at the impetus for the Vile Kingdom?

Jacob couldn't help but wonder if he might find something that would help him undo their terrible reign. Humanity was already limping along, mostly dead, by the time they came to power but what hope was left turned to ash when the Vile Kingdom revealed themselves.

Kim's bloodstained grin flashed into his mind.

It let off a bone-deep spark of anger that flared into a towering inferno. Without thinking, Jacob lunged forward and bellowed. He spent his fury, his rage, on the twisted iconography on each door.

Breaths coming in short gasps of exertion, Jacob looked at the ruined imagery with grim satisfaction. Weary from the anger and the effort, he didn't bemoan the wasteful act.

He would break every image of their twisted design he could find and be glad for the opportunity.

A shrill noise caught his attention. The sound ratcheted up out of human hearing but being Fae-Touched, he could still hear it as it climbed the octaves.

Only then did he realize the absence of sharp pain in his side. Looking down at the floor he saw, coated in his own blood, the writhing thing that had impaled him.

A tentacle made out of gray-blue stone that shriveled as lines of cinder glowed within, consuming it from the inside. The creature writhed in deep pain before the flames leaped out from the glowing cracks in its stony skin and turned it into a charcoal husk.

You defeat the [Leviathan Spawn].
Awarded 200 Souls.

Out came a [Cinder Ampoule] and Jacob crushed it, reveling in the soothing sensation of a Pyre as his wounds were knit. He kicked the dark, twisted thing at his side but remained troubled as he went to the left-most door.

He didn't know why that happened. Was it destroying the imagery? Or did the thing simply not get a deep enough hold on him to sustain itself?

Those thoughts filtered through his mind as he pushed the heavy doors open and felt the ground quake beneath his feet, followed by a guttural, otherworldly roar from deep within the complex.

Walking into the dark corridor beyond, Jacob heard the wet sloshing sounds of something moving ahead. Normally the stench of such a large, rotten creature that slinked out of the dark ahead would have clued him in but the [Ring of Covetous Breath] prevented any of the area's scent from reaching him.

The bloated thing shambled forward, skin sloughing off its bulbous frame. Its eyes were not red and glowing like a Vacant. This was something else.

Milky, sightless eyes stared at him and a rasping, rattling breath of excitement escaped the gills hidden beneath its three chins.

Most disturbing of all was the writhing tentacle creature fastened to the corpse's rotund belly.

Unarmed as the man was, Jacob wondered if he should even bother. The doors were likely sturdy enough that if he left now he could turn about and check the other passages.

It didn't seem likely that the monster before him was capable of enough thought to pull the doors inward to open them. Even as Jacob backed up slowly to stay ahead of the sluggish threat, he found himself readying his shield and weapon.

He held a hatred for the Vile Kingdom and all of its eldritch machinations that was unlike anything he ever experienced in his entire life.

There was so much anger that despite the disgusting thing in front of him, he was already charging toward it, yelling curses at the unhearing monster.

Hammering the Nail split its forehead wide open. The blubbery skin curled disgustingly, like an unseen pair of hands was peeling an orange. But the way his [Mace] rebounded from the strike had Jacob curious.

Pulling it back, he lifted his shield to block a harmless-looking reaching pale arm. Several barnacles on the underside of the man's arm opened and out lashed half a dozen spiny tongues. They rang against the shield in one long note and pushed Jacob back with surprising force.

He wasn't stunned for long and he pressed on ahead, sure to keep his shield up to absorb the coming blows. More barnacle attacks came but his shield held and they did no real damage.

But neither did Jacob's next strike. A heavy winding sidelong swipe of his [Mace], *Ringing the Bell* clocked the Drowned Wretch in the side of the head but again seemed to do less than it should have.

Jacob rushed forward around the wretch, clipping it with his upraised shield to set the thing spinning about like a drunken ballerina. In a flash and swirl of ash, he dismissed his [Mace] and brought forth his [Longsword].

Without breaking the momentum, Jacob spun and dropped to one knee letting his blade arm go out to full extension. *Reaping the Harvest* cut the wretch's legs out from under him in a clean slice.

As the bloated man continued to turn, his ankles and feet remained where they were and he uncerimoniously toppled to the side.

Rising to his feet, Jacob was there. He pumped his arm up and with a twist let go of his blade, reversed his grip on it, and in the same twirling motion snapped his arm down just as the blubbery creature hit the slick floor.

Planting the Flag took it in the heart, a twist of the blade stilled its twitching. It was good to be using a sword again.

You defeat the [Drowned Wretch].
Awarded 250 Souls.

Looking deeper down the corridor, Jacob could hear the wet sloshing sounds of more would-be victims. It wasn't common to find an enemy type that was resistant to blunt weapons like maces. But he was happy for the change in pace.

A flick of his wrist and a roll of his fingers brought his [Longsword] back to its proper upright grip. He had trained with straight swords for nearly a decade Post-Collapse. That skill, gratefully, transferred into Pyresouls and gave him an extreme advantage.

But only if he was wielding a sword. Even then, it wasn't enough that he could use a sword the entire time. Using the right tool for the job was just as important, if not more so.

Despite that, Jacob flashed a savage grin and strode toward the wet sounds. He had reached a level of swordsmanship that he was proud of and he never felt more confident than when he held a sturdy shield and a good sword.

The image of Kim's last moments echoed in his mind again and he tightened his grip on his blade. It didn't matter to him that these creatures before him were from a time and place so far removed from the Vile Kingdom as to be practically blameless.

He hated them all the same. Every slain abomination was a balm to his wounded soul.

The Drowned Halls would fill with the briny opaque seafoam blood of the grotesque creatures when he was done.

23

Wind Parts the Grass, Stag Rushes Through the Field, Hummingbird's Kiss, Moonlight's Edge. Jacob flowed from one Sword Form to the next in a dance of fiery death. Wherever he struck with his flaming sword, viscera spilled to the floor, limbs went flying, and an abomination died.

He only stopped when his Stamina demanded it and occasionally to pop a [Cinder Ampoule] from the few strikes that managed to slip past his defenses. Jacob rampaged through the Drowned Halls with a single-minded determination to slay every creature he came into contact with.

The halls were serpentine and massive. Jacob could easily imagine a creature the size of a house slithering through the place. As always, the sense of scale of Lormar stunned him.

Bioluminescent flora lit the way with deceptive beauty that Jacob was quick to cut down. He needed only his own illumination and that provided by *Heat Blade* to light the way.

His violent display only ceased when he came upon the first Pyre of the area. It was surrounded by calcified coral and the strange shapes that decades upon decades of slowly dripping water made on stone.

It was the first time he smiled in that damnable place that wasn't followed by a murderous spree. Jacob reached his hand over the cold pile of ashes and reignited the Pyre.

Before the Fire Oppa could crawl out from the ashes, Jacob cupped his hands and focused on Kim's face.

Not the one he remembered from her last moments but the smiling face from his dream. A ruby flame blossomed in his cupped palms and he tipped his hand so it rolled down into the growing Pyre.

It struck the gathering flames and caused the whole thing to rush up, scorching the low ceiling.

Pyre Ignited.
*Your respawn location has been set to the **Drowned Halls (West)**.*
The Fire Oppa stokes the embers of your conviction.
Health, Stamina, Ampoules and Spell Gems restored.
You Kindle the Pyre.

"That was quick, four down, two to go," the Fire Oppa said. Seeing Jacob's determined face, he chuckled. "I take it you wish to press on." The Fire Oppa raised his head proudly and though Jacob sat cross-legged in front of the fire in a dank briny hole underground, he addressed Jacob as if they were in the court of a king. "How might I assist you?"

Even though he killed a host of various drowned men and women, his total Souls were still less than a quarter of what he had lost in the Desecrated Catacombs. With a total of 4,350 Souls, he could only afford a single parameter reinforcement.

He increased his TMP to 10. It wouldn't be enough to wear the [Elite Knight's Helm] but it was a step toward it. He would still be left with 5 Guilt in any case.

The only way to keep his lower Guilt tier would be to remove his [Mace] as part of his loadout.

He would be able to use the [Elite Knight's Gauntlets] if he did that, but it would mean losing a potentially valuable weapon. And he didn't know enough of the area to take that risk.

Just because one type of monster was resistant to blunt damage didn't mean that there would be one that was weak to it.

Jacob took a look over his parameters once more.

[Status]

Jacob Windsor
Covenant: None
Race: Kemora - Fae-touched (Human/Fairy)
Level: 21
Health: 132
Stamina: 94
Anima: 0
Souls: 1,493
Required Souls: 3,122

Parameters
VIT: 4
AGI: 8
END: 7
TMP: 10
STR: 10
DEX: 10
INT: 8
FTH: 3

Curse: Fractured Sight
  Curse Level: 1

  Spell Gem: Heat Blade (3/3)

Considering the sorry state of his armor, Jacob deposited it into his [Repair Kit] and gingerly set it within the Pyre.

It would take many more uses of the kit to make the relatively high cost worth it but without any merchants since the Steps of Penance, he would have been forced to detour to Hollow Dreams or else suffer broken equipment.

Neither were good choices.

Repairing everything took more than he expected, 323 Souls, but several items were in a very poor state. He was fast approaching the point where each parameter was harder and harder to reinforce.

After fixing his gear up to full durability he was about to leave when he remembered the 3 [Souls of a Wandering Knight] he picked up in the Desecrated Catacombs on his way out.

Never managed to find many of these. If they're anything like the Soul of a Loving Father they aren't worth much. Still, better check just to be sure.

Jacob took the first shimmering white wisp in his hand and crushed it, infusing the Souls held within into his body. His eyes shot open at the staggering number.

You use [Soul of a Wandering Knight].
Awarded 1,250 Souls.

Without hesitation he popped the remaining 2, granting him another 2,500 Souls for a total of 4,920. It was enough to bring Jacob's TMP up to 11.

[Status]
Jacob Windsor
Covenant: None
Race: Kemora - Fae-touched (Human/Fairy)
Level: 22
Health: 132
Stamina: 94
Anima: 0
Souls: 1,798
Required Souls: 3,396

Parameters

VIT: *4*
AGI: *8*
END: *7*
TMP: *11*
STR: *10*
DEX: *10*
INT: *8*
FTH: *3*

Curse: Fractured Sight
    Curse Level: *1*

Spell Gem: Heat Blade (3/3)

Jacob wasted no time in swapping his current helm out for the elite variant.

The difference didn't seem like much at first glance but the overall protection was nearly doubled from what he was used to.

Since most enemies didn't use a single type of damage, with many using multiple types in the same swing at times, the overall protection was a valuable metric.

Even if it meant he only took 10 less damage from a blunt hit. If that attack was both blunt and fire damage he would take 25 less damage from the single hit. Though, considering the area, it was more likely to be chaos or water.

Two elements that the flimsier [Knight's Helm] didn't have any protection against. Somewhat more importantly to Jacob, was the working visor. He reached up and flicked the grated plate down to guard his face.

The helm was valuable for that alone. Dealing with people and not giving away any facial expressions was hard. An intact helm would help him since he had such an "honest face" as Kim used to tease.

With his [Elite Knight's Helm] on, his Guilt jumped up 10 but with the effect of his [Ring of Blameless Guilt], it dropped to 5. At 11 TMP, that placed his Guilt at 45%. Still well within Tier 2.

He was getting used to the speed increase over his previously heavier Guilt tier back on Earth. It was amazing how much lighter and nimbler he could be.

He still had a lone [Dull Spark] and figured he should spend it. As much as he wanted to upgrade his [Longsword], he was all too keenly aware of his own frailty.

Instead, he spent the [Dull Spark] on getting his [Elite Knight's Helm] to +1.

[Equipment Reinforcement]

Elite Knight's Helm [Helm] -> *Elite Knight's Helm [Helm] +1*
   Cost: 600 Souls

Physical Protection: 60 -> 72
   Blunt: 20 -> 24
   Slashing: 20 -> 24
   Piercing: 20 -> 24

   Magical Protection: 50 -> 60
   Arcane: 15 -> 18
   Fire: 15 -> 18
   Water: 5 -> 6
   Earth: 5 -> 6
   Harmony: 5 -> 6
   Chaos: 5 -> 6

   Resistances
   Bleed: 15 -> 18
   Poison: 8 -> 9

Curse: 0 -> 0
Stability: 15 -> 18

Durability: 600/600 -> 650/650
Guilt: 4 -> 4

He shouldn't have been surprised by the high cost of reinforcing the armor, but the increase was larger than what the other set allowed. Taking the upgraded helm back from the Fire Oppa, he donned it once more.

Unlike the rest of his armor which was made of thin, ridged metal plates interspersed with chainmail and leather padding, the helm felt sturdy and solid.

It was clearly of good make and the way it fit onto his head was a perfect fit for him, though that seemed to have more to do with the equipment of Lormar as a whole.

There also seemed to be an enchantment of some sort on the helm. He should have had a much harder time seeing out of the thin vertical slits that made up the protection but he had his full field of view.

Satisfied with the changes he was able to enact, Jacob reached over and pet the Fire Oppa who seemed to burn just a bit brighter than he remembered.

Jacob shut his eyes and relaxed, getting some rest after reinforcing his parameters. It was a stroke of luck that he remembered to check the [Soul of a Wandering Knight] *before* he took his rest after the first reinforcement.

September 3rd, 2035 – 10 days remain before the Collapse.

When Jacob left the Pyre, the cold dampness of the Drowned Halls seemed a few degrees warmer than he remembered. He didn't get much time to appreciate it as just a few steps out of the room had Jacob tasting the familiar blue raspberry flavor on his tongue.

Knowing what was imminent, he turned and began to spring back to the Pyre. His legs, already numb, flopped uselessly beneath him.

A sharp tug at his navel pulled him away from the wet tunnels of the Drowned Halls so quickly that he didn't even hit the puddle-strewn floor.

May 7th, 2045 – 10 Years Post-Collapse.

Sunlight struck his shut eyes. The warm glowing rays felt good on his skin and he smiled reflexively, forgetting his recent memories. "C'mon sleepy-head, wake up!" Kim's voice called to him, she gripped his wrist and pulled him to his feet easily enough.

Jacob's eyes flashed open and the scene before him dazzled and confused him. Kim was tugging on his hand, pulling him along in a stumbling gait through the thigh-high vivid green grass somewhere out in the country.

The hills rolled by like furry globes, dotted here and there with splashes of color. The skies were blue and filled with fluffy, cottony clouds.

In the distance, the trees of a nearby forest shimmered as their leaves danced upon the warm breeze that rippled the long grass all around them.

"Where am I?" Jacob asked. Was this another memory of his? He couldn't recall such an idyllic setting.

Jacob's parents hadn't been well off and they were city-dwellers like him. There was no way this was one of his memories, which begged the question: Whose was it?

"Caught on to that, have ya then?" Kim asked, her auburn hair shining in the midday sun as it bounced around her shoulders. She twitched her freckled nose at him and smiled. "All your memories are so dark and those that aren't dark are *boring*. So I figured I could loan you one of mine."

She tugged him along to the top of the nearest hill to look back down at the grass that swayed in the wind. Birds chirped somewhere nearby and he swore he spotted the red coat of a fox dart into a row of hedges not too far away.

"I guess you're right," he admitted with a chuckle. Something felt wrong, but he couldn't put his finger on it. "I didn't really start living until after the Collapse. That feels weird to say."

There was no judgment in Kim's bright blue eyes. She wore a very un-Kimberly-like outfit, a simple sundress that went halfway down her shapely thighs and a white, wide-brimmed hat she held in her free hand.

"Don't judge," she chided, leaning against him and watching the sun make its graceful arc from high above toward the west. That felt significant to him. But just like the feeling of wrongness, he couldn't say why. "My memory put me in these clothes."

Jacob wanted to ask why he was there. But just thinking the question made him shy away from it like it was a flame that would burn him. He didn't think he wanted to know the answer to that question.

The more he thought about it, the more he was sure. The sun slipped through the sky, its motion visible to the naked eye.

"Isn't this a beautiful view, Jacob?" Kim asked, looking up at him with tenderness. "Wouldn't it be nice to see this every day?" Her tone took on a pleading edge that was very unlike her.

He wanted nothing more than to agree with her but found that he couldn't. He found that he couldn't do anything. Every muscle in his body seized up. His hands cramped painfully.

Kimberly slid her hand into his, and no matter how hard he crushed her hand she didn't pull away.

A soft hand, softer than any he had ever known Kim to have brushed his cheek. "Just look at me, okay? You'll be all right, Jacob. This will pass. Don't worry. Just keep looking at me."

Her eyes shimmered but they stayed resolute and held his gaze firmly. "I thought being here would-" A terrible wrenching feeling twisted his guts and everything around him faded into mist.

For a moment, Kimberly's face drifted in the mist and then it too was gone.

Jacob came awake in a start, his heart jackhammering in his chest. Two strong pairs of hands held him down on the familiar gel bed of the FIVR pod. It took a moment to gain his bearings and when he did, he relaxed.

The hands stayed on him a few seconds more before he felt them tentatively release him. "Hey, man," Alec said with a forced grin.

"How do you feel?" asked Ian, sliding into Jacob's view. Rather than his signature pencil mustache, he had a ridiculous goatee in the shape of an upside-down T.

"How long have I been out?" Jacob asked. "Why did you get rid of your mustache?"

Ian started, cast a worried look to the side, and began examining Jacob. He flashed lights in his eyes, tested reflexes, and asked him basic cognitive tests such as what year it was, what his name was, and the names of those in the room.

Satisfied that Jacob seemed well, Ian backed off and was immediately replaced by Alice. Her hair was tied up in a bun and she had on a pair of black-rimmed glasses. "Tell us everything," she said with a manic grin.

24

Jacob told them all he could about what he'd done, the people he met, nearly everything. Nothing was left out to his knowledge. Nothing at all, except the dreams with Kim.

Those were personal.

Throughout it all, Jacob tried to push aside the ache in his soul from being back in a Post-Collapse world. Everything was so much colder than he remembered. Even the Drowned Halls were welcoming compared to the perpetual chill in the air that laughed at the laws of thermodynamics.

No matter how hot they turned the heaters, it would still feel achingly cold. He could lie down in a burning fire and it would do nothing to melt the frost that crept into his bones.

Alec blew a long, low whistle. "Man you've got some brass ones on you," he said, shaking his head. "That would definitely cut off some time. I took my time getting to the depths of the Desecrated Catacombs. That place was a nightmare."

"He already has this ring he needs, yes?" Alice asked, consulting a tablet in her lap. "That means he needs only the ember."

"Right," Alec said. "Except, he's nowhere near where he should be. I guess he's far enough ahead that it doesn't matter though. Dude, are you sure this Fire Oppa is legitimate? Something about him seems a little sketchy but if you trust him I won't say another word."

"I trust him," Jacob said without hesitation. He didn't think the Fire Oppa had ever lied to him. He was cagey sometimes, and didn't seem capable of giving him full answers most of the time but that didn't seem intentional. "It's almost like he's just another player trying to work within the rules of Lormar."

"Still, it's strange."

"Did you ever see him?" Jacob asked. From all of their talks by the campfire, he couldn't remember Alec ever talking about the diminutive creature.

"Never."

That was odd. Jacob surely remembered the Fire Oppa from the first time. How did anybody else interact with the Pyre?

"Let us see," Alice interjected, scrolling through her tablet with a flick of her finger. "Drowned Halls, yes. Many fleshy, flabby creatures. Water affinity, no surprise. But you said you already lit the Pyre there, so you are about to leave, no?"

"Soon as you send me back," Jacob agreed. "The place and its eldritch leanings remind me too much of the Vile Kingdom." Alice shivered at the name and Alec's jaw clenched. "I can't get out of there fast enough."

"Doesn't it seem a little strange that this Fire Oppa is asking you to light Pyres nowhere near where the Burgon Beast will show up?" Alec asked.

"Not really. He explained it well enough. The darkest areas need the most light. By lighting a Pyre in the Drowned Halls it does more good than if I were to light three Pyres in Hollow Dreams, for example."

Jacob was intent on lighting the 6 Pyres, even if it was only as a favor to the Fire Oppa. He remembered the sad, dejected look of the fiery ferret. It broke his heart. And as Alec said he was quite ahead of the curve already.

He could spare a few days to do something for the Fire Oppa. Something he hoped might bring the Pyres back to Earth in the meantime. How many lives might he save if he completed the Fire Oppa's 'quest' and the Pyres came to Earth?

"If you retrace your steps out of the Drowned Halls, you'll be able to take a pretty straight path directly to Hollow Dreams," Alec said, pacing back and forth. It was a common habit of his when he was trying to remember.

"Yes," Alice said, swiping across her tablet a few times. "But..."

"But what?" Jacob asked. The look on Alice's face didn't sit well with him.

"He needs to be stronger, yes?" she asked Alec, who nodded and continued his pacing.

"Then there is a path to power you could use," Alice said, looking into Jacob's eyes with uncharacteristic concern. "But it would be your choice and yours alone."

"What is it?" Jacob asked, sitting upright and sliding his legs over the side of the opened FIVR pod.

"The Vile Covenant is located within the Drowned Halls," she said quietly.

Alec immediately stopped his pacing. "No. That's... Alice, that's wrong on *so* many levels. That's unacceptable."

"Even if it means saving billions of lives?" she asked, her jaw set. When she turned to Jacob, her features softened in sympathy. "I know you lost people close to you because of the Vile Kingdom's actions. But if you join them, they could provide-"

Jacob couldn't believe what he was hearing. Join the Vile Kingdom? "No."

"There is more at stake here-"

"No."

"Be reasonable-"

Alec placed a hand on Alice's shoulder. "Alice. Let it go." He shot Jacob a sympathetic glance over her head.

Of all the people, Alec understood Jacob's hatred for the Vile Kingdom. He was there when they attacked, when Kim died saving him.

Some avenues of power were off-limits.

"Where are they located?" Jacob asked.

"The Covenant?" Alice asked, an edge of hope creeping into her voice. But she quickly caught on to the dark look in Jacob's green eyes. "What do you intend on doing?"

"I am going to destroy them," he said simply, already in the process of lying back down. "Tell me where they are and any notable areas nearby and then send me back in."

The very air in the bunker hurt his skin. The bone-deep weariness that he felt was even worse than last time.

More than anything he wanted the comfort of Lormar again. Even without the Pyre nearby, Lormar had a warmth to it.

Granted, it was like the warmth of a recently dead thing that was fast cooling. But it was better than the stone-cold corpse of Earth.

"Yeah, about that, dude." Alec came over to the side of the pod. "Pulling you out every hour is placing a lot of strain on your body. We're going to lengthen the amount of time you're inside, for your safety."

Jacob started. "What do you mean, placing a strain on me? What happened this time?"

"There is a disconnect," Alice said, trying to downplay the severity. "We do not know what is the cause but whenever we recall you... there is a momentary pause when we... lose you."

"As in, I die?"

"No, we lose you."

Jacob turned to Alec, hoping for some actual answers. His friend offered a shrug. "It's just as Alice said. You're lost. She can't find where you go or how long you're gone for relative to your sense of time. You just... disappear.

"You should go straight back to your body but without a connection to your past, and with you no longer inhabiting your current body you kind of...die. Like, braindead. Your heart stops working, you seize up. It's terrifying."

"We are working on it," Alice said, placing a gentle hand on his arm. "By extending the time you are inside Pyresouls, we will limit the stress of pulling you out. However, that means you will be without our aid for longer. So ask what you will and we will gather the information for you now."

"And hey," Alec said, playfully slapping Jacob's shin. "With any luck you'll only need one more trip back here before you clobber the Burgon Beast! Man, I won't have any idea how much of a screw up I was, would I?" He chuckled. "Oh right, before I forget, there's this sword you might want to be on the lookout for. It'll be down a small cul-de-sac in Hollow Dreams...."

It was another hour of discussing his path forward and trying to find anything that might be used to help him along his way before Jacob went back in. Alec had been stronger than him, but not by much.

And the sooner he could release the Burgon Beast the better. There were ripple effects from his actions. Already several reports in the archives spoke of the Steps of Penance being utterly ruined.

Paths that people had taken were changed and each interaction Jacob had in Lormar changed more. His romp in the Crossing deep in the Desecrated Catacombs was a horror story that became more insane and terrifying with each retelling.

Each day closer to the Collapse meant another chance for somebody to get there before him. And that, he could not allow.

The fewer times he was recalled to the present the safer it would be. Though, they confessed they didn't understand the underlying mechanisms that caused the problem.

Physically, he was healthy until the recall procedure pulled him back. Then all bets were off.

It made sense why he was able to see Kimberly again. For just a moment, they were both dead and whatever veil that separated the two was briefly lifted.

Despite the danger to himself, he liked seeing her. He missed her. And he hoped he would get the chance to see her past self at least once more.

With memories of Kim and the violent retribution he would visit upon the Vile Covenant once he was back in the Drowned Halls, they sent him back.

Pyresouls Apocalypse: Rewind

September 4th, 2035 – 9 days remain before the Collapse.

Jacob woke up tasting blood and brine.

Opening his eyes, he could see he was unmoved from the hallway he was last in. It was later than he thought. Inside Pyresouls it was harder than usual to gauge time.

Without the need to eat, or drink, and sleeping was only needed when reinforcing a parameter, it was remarkably easy to while away the hours while thinking only a few minutes passed. Lormar demanded so much attention, for your own safety most of all, that the time just slipped away.

But this was more than usual.

Getting to his feet, he wiped away the blood where he split his lip on the hard brine-soaked stones of the floor. His first piece of business was to revisit the Pyre for a quick top-off before going out to seek the Vile Covenant.

Fully healed from the Pyre, and with a fond farewell to the Fire Oppa, Jacob took off deeper into the Drowned Halls. Being a Covenant faction within Pyresouls Online, he doubted there was much lasting damage he could do.

At the least, he could vent his frustrations on whatever poor fool they had recruiting.

He found his quarry a few hours later in a round waterlogged chamber. Tentacle iconography filled the room in various states of wear. Upon a dais at the back of the room, in front of a blood-stained altar was a strange-looking man in dark green-and-gold robes.

The colors of the Vile Kingdom.

As much as Jacob wanted to rush through the room of knee-high water, sword raised in a promise of death, he sublimated his rage and calmly walked forward.

Wading through the water seemed to awaken the priest at the altar who looked up, his face hidden in the dark of the cowl. Jacob knew that the man would be "modified." A pleasant way of saying he had tentacles, perhaps mouths growing in weird places, fins, gills, or some other such watery adaptation.

It was unsurprising then, as Jacob slogged through the water, when the man lowered his hood and had a too-wide fish-like face. He pushed the briny water out of his way with every forceful step while being careful to avoid the darker sections of the water where he couldn't see the floor.

Now the brine made sense. It was one of the many oddities that presaged the Vile Kingdom's arrival. Freshwater turned brackish and briny. The horrendous creatures of the Vile Kingdom were not suited to freshwater, they thrived in the lightless depths of the ocean.

The man spoke in a watery voice. His eyes were several sizes too large, his skin sweaty and glistening like it was melting candle wax. Most telling of all was the mouth that split his face in half. "You have come to pay ssssuplication to our great Covenant?"

The hint of suspicion in the man's voice reminded Jacob to keep his sword down and low. In his recognition of the man's features, he had instinctively tightened his grip on his sword and began to raise it.

His original plan was to get close enough that he could kill the monstrous thing before it could slip away or worse, call for aid. This was, after all, a holy place to the Vile Covenant.

Jacob looked at the dark spots of the water, wondering how deep they went. There were several other paths just beneath the brackish water that vanished out of sight.

The saltwater was an oddity, but hardly unexpected. Especially considering the only body of water nearby was the Ashen Flood, a freshwater lake.

Now that he looked at the fish-faced creature sweating nervously as Jacob stalked toward him without answering, another idea came to him.

A blurring streak of ash made his shield and sword vanish. "I have heard that Covenants could make me stronger," Jacob said, doing his best to sound like a typical greedy player. The sort that looked for any shortcut or boost to power without any regard for the long-term implications.

"Ahhh." The priest grinned happily, greedily. The wide mouth taking in all of his wide face. "Yessss, we have much you might wissssh to sssavor." With a gesture of his wide billowing green sleeves, a small egg-shaped gem appeared on the altar.

Jacob's surprise was real when he climbed the dais and eagerly reached toward the spell gem. A tentacle slithered out of the man's robes and smacked Jacob's hand away. Not enough to hurt him but more than enough to chastise.

It made Jacob's skin crawl. A blinding rage filled his chest like a growing white-hot fire. It was all he could do not to snarl and slay the creature where it stood.

"After you have sssigned the Covenant," the priest explained. "Then you may have the sssspell gem. Many more giftssss await the loyal disssssciples of the Vile Covenant." Another flourish and a simple prompt appeared.

Join the Vile Covenant?
Yes / No

He never managed to join a Covenant before but he knew enough about them that there was a specific set of rules governing each. Rules, that like most of Pyresouls Online, nobody was told about.

While any Covenant – if offered – could be joined, it was impossible to join more than one. And often joining one Covenant prevented another Covenant from being offered later.

Jacob was free to accept and then betray the Covenant but in doing so he would be declared an enemy and any players that belonged to that Covenant could seek him out for a bounty.

In essence, it would incentivize players to invade his shard and kill him.

Rejecting the Covenant had similar, but less severe, consequences. The Covenant looked unfavorably upon the person and interactions with its members was viewed through a negative lens.

Staying completely neutral, however, was not an option. Many Covenants looked down on those without *any* convictions at all. And it was often a requirement to turn down certain Covenants in order to gain access to another.

The Lightblade Covenant, for example, required one to be tempted by the Blacksun Covenant and reject them.

If Jacob chose to remain within the Vile Covenant – fat chance, that – he would be able to receive more boons and greater prestige if he climbed the Covenant's ranks. A feat that involved performing tasks set out by the Covenant.

There was an incomplete list of Covenants in Pyresouls and the question of which was better was a hotly debated issue. Learning more about the Vile Covenant, even just what tasks they preferred would be useful.

Not to mention, he could get a spell gem out of the deal. He wasn't so committed to his morals that he couldn't use the Vile Covenant to further his own strength a little bit.

Especially if it meant betraying them. The irony was too delicious to pass up.

Jacob accepted the Covenant. The priest grinned stupidly at him and generously offered the spell gem to him.

"Hail the Vile Covenant," the priest intoned.

*You join the **Vile Covenant**.*
The purpose of the Vile Covenant is to invade other shards, defeat the champions that reside within, and carve out their hearts to be gifted to the Great Old One. Once you have proven your worth, you will gain access to the gift of transformation to be closer to the Great Old One.
You gain [Sacrificial Knife].
You gain [Spell Gem].

"Great Old One?" Jacob muttered, but apparently loud enough for the priest to hear.

The man-fish gasped and a tentacle lashed out, slapping across Jacob's closed helm. It did little damage but it startled and enraged him all at once.

He barely heard the priest shout, "You sssshal not speak of Him!

You worm! You filth! A Neophyte ssssuch as yoursssself is not worthy to know His-"

Jacob lunged forward, wrapping the priest in a tight hug. Focusing, Jacob summoned the [Sacrificial Knife] to his right hand. As he squeezed the priest, he drove the blade into the thing's back.

Twisting the blade, Jacob wrenched it out to the side, tearing through its lung. Seafoam froth bubbled out of his mouth mixing with black blood familiar with those aligned to the Vile Kingdom.

Easing the dying man to the stone, several tentacles flopped about on the floor. They curled and weakly tried to hit Jacob but could hardly fight their way out of the folds of the priest's robes.

Without sympathy, Jacob knelt on the man's chest, eliciting a gurgling groan of agony. The dark, tainted blood spread into a wider pool beneath them. Jacob flipped up his visor. His dark green eyes filled with hate aimed at the flailing, dying creature.

He wanted to see the horror on the thing's face, wanted it to see his face and know its doom. All he could see was the red flash of bloodied teeth from Kim's final smile.

Jacob's grin was more of a feral grimace as he dove the [Sacrificial Knife] into the man's chest, working to cut out his still-pumping heart. He sawed through the soft, cartilage-like bone with ease.

When he was done, he lifted the bloated black thing out of his chest so the priest could see it in his last moments.

"Hail the Vile Covenant," Jacob said with a sneer.

It took a surprisingly long time for the man to die without a heart. Several full seconds passed as the horror and life began to drain from the man's ugly features.

Jacob dropped the heart to the stones and stood. "Your tainted god isn't getting this sacrifice," he added, crushing the misshapen thing under his boot and grinding his heel against it.

A look of pure mortal terror filled the man for the last flickers of his life as he realized he would be severed from his god. The act, unsurprisingly, was viewed as a betrayal of the Covenant and he was summarily kicked out.

You defeat the [Vile Priest].
You have betrayed the **Vile Covenant.**
You are marked as an Enemy and can never attempt to rejoin the Vile Covenant.

Awarded 1,500 Souls.
You gain [Soul of a Devout Priest].
You gain [Antediluvian Ring].

"Fine by me," Jacob said, spitting on the corpse and sliding his visor down.

Dark threads of the priest's blood wound their way through the cracks and seams of the stones until they found their way into the dark waters of the room.

Wherever the blood touched, the water churned and frothed.

All thought of further desecrating the room flew from Jacob's head. *Time to go!*

Jacob swapped his [Ring of Covetous Breath] for his new one immediately, hoping that it might give whatever creature was coming for him pause. Just enough confusion that he could slip out of the room without fighting the damn thing.

As soon as the rings were swapped he was hit with a sickening brackish, rotten fish stench so heinous he tasted bile in the back of his throat.

When a black tentacle with purple suckers split the water in the middle of the room, Jacob knew it wasn't confused by the ring he wore. He had no time to swap the rings back though.

Praying he wouldn't vomit in his helmet, he surged through the water, surprised at how little it bothered him.

No matter how the reeking brackish fluid churned and filled the chamber it didn't slow him one bit. He ran at full speed, sprinting through the room even as it filled up to his waist with water.

Dodging the swaying tentacles that sprouted from the water was even easier without the slowdown that water normally inflicted. Two quick, successive rolls had him at 30% Stamina and at the foot of the stairs to the drier hallway.

A tentacle slammed him in the back, doing more good than harm as it propelled him up the stairs and into the hallway beyond in exchange for a quarter of his Health.

Jacob staggered to his feet and continued to flee down the tunnel. A glance over his shoulder revealed reaching dark tentacles that couldn't quite fit through the narrow doorframe.

Slowing down to let his Stamina regenerate, Jacob heard the cracking stone as the tentacles behind swelled and forced the stone doorway apart.

The deep guttural, otherworldly roar that rumbled the stones and filled the halls with ancient rage chased him out of the Drowned Halls.

Puddles grew exponentially in size. Sprays of briny water erupted from seams in the walls, filling up the halls with seawater that thankfully did little to impede his escape.

By the time Jacob passed the room with the Pyre, he saw a wall of steam flooding out from that room. "Go!" the Fire Oppa cried from beyond the veil of mist. "Not even the Vile God can stifle my Pyre. Do not linger, Jacob!"

He didn't stop running until he returned to the fork in the tunnel.

25

While Jacob took the path toward Hollow Dreams, he looked up the [Antediluvian Ring] in his equipment. Without it, he still felt confident he could have escaped. Even if he was killed he would have been sent back to the Pyre and that was clearly still safe even as the tunnels filled with seawater.

[Antediluvian Ring]
An ancient ring of rough, unpleasant stone with mind-bending carvings in an indecipherable language. Tentacle carvings appear to move whenever salt water is near.

This ancient ring is older than the first Covenants. It is a testament to the Vile Covenant's lasting ambitions and is given only to those who have fully dedicated themselves to the Great Old One.
Its name is inscribed upon the ring, and reading it aloud begins the slow process of change required to become one of the Anointed. Until that time comes, the ring grants greatly improved mobility in areas of rough terrain such as swamps, water, or tar.

Jacob took off his helm and shook out his wet hair, glad that the stench of the Drowned Halls hadn't seeped into his armor. Though the seawater had.

It didn't seem to cause any immediate issues, so he dealt with the deep discomfort of a whole-body wet-sock sensation.

The ring was niche in its usefulness, but considering his other options he decided to keep it on. He didn't remember any rough terrain leading into Hollow Dreams, but then again he never came through this path before.

And for all their discussion, the specifics were never - or very rarely - known. Aside from Alec's memories of a game he played ten years ago, the archives were notoriously spotty.

Discussing and planning what to do was more like streetlights in the dark. There were bright spots with accurate and verified information. But between those spots was utter darkness where neither Alec nor the archives had any helpful information.

It was left to Jacob to navigate the dark to find the light.

The path ahead split again, prompting Jacob to slow down and summon his armaments. Shield lifted, sword out to the side at the ready, he came into the rough circular chamber.

A lone knight's body with a sapphire wisp was laid in eternal rest to his left, and a Snake Sister was to his right, staring at the earthen wall.

Realizing his fortune at sneaking up on a Snake Sister, Jacob moved as slowly and quietly as he could. [Longsword] poised for a backstab, he got within two steps before he lunged forward with all his might into her naked torso.

He jammed the blade up to the hilt. The Snake Sister let out a shrill sibilant cry and her too-long neck twisted about in a series of sickening cracks and pops.

Oversized serpentine eyes glared at him between curtains of oily black hair. Her jaw unhinged, showing fangs several inches long dripping with venom.

Repulsed, Jacob planted a boot on her pale scaled back and forced her to stagger forward. With her head turned around, most people would take the opportunity to chase her and strike.

That was a rookie mistake. One that was likely to end in death.

Jacob waited, shifting his back foot to be perpendicular to his right. He knew what was coming and kept his sword pointed low to the side in hopes of baiting her.

True to their name, the woman's neck elongated by several feet. Mouth wide and fangs dripping with venom, she struck with the lightning quickness of her namesake.

But Jacob was expecting it and at the slight twinge foretelling of the strike, his blade was already arcing to intercept the attack. *Moon Crests the Horizon* severed her neck before she could bite him.

Her head toppled to the ground, and her body a moment later. Dismissing the monster from his attention, Jacob bent to the sapphire wisp.

You defeat the [Snake Sister].
Awarded 500 Souls.
You gain [Dull Spark].

Jacob walked to the entrance of each split in the tunnel and listened. He knew the left path was the one he wanted to take. Alec had told him the path he took and Alice confirmed that – as far as they could tell – there was nothing useful down the right path.

But if he heard shuffling, he might be able to gain enough Souls to reinforce a parameter by the time he hit the first Pyre in Hollow Dreams. Which should be coming up fairly soon, considering the distance traveled already.

Not hearing anything, Jacob decided his curiosity wasn't worth the cost in time and took the left path.

Luckily, there were a few more Snake Sisters littered throughout the earthen tunnel. By the time the tunnel began to slope upward and Jacob saw the first hints of light at the end of the tunnel, he was 1,500 Souls richer.

He came out into the weak, watery sunlight of Lormar, still sopping wet from the Drowned Halls. As stifling as it was, he didn't remove his helm. Just because it was a town didn't mean it was safe.

Hollow Dreams

Hollow Dreams was a maze of tight turning corridors and tall leaning buildings. Most of which were utterly abandoned or filled with Infested Rats or Vacant. Considering the meager Souls killing them would net, Jacob gave those places – and their suspiciously stacked crates – a wide berth.

The rats liked to spring out from the crates and surprise the unaware. Their bites were poisonous and painful. Not quite deadly but being poisoned was no fun, even with the vials of [Gekk Blood] he had on him.

Winding through the dirt roads, Jacob came within sight of a tall burned-out husk of a building. It had once been a guard tower. The blackened bell hung at a sharp angle on its flat-topped roof where he knew a Pyre awaited him.

But first, he had to clear out the Vacant that were milling about the courtyard in front of it.

They saw him – or perhaps heard him, he wasn't really sure since he made no effort to quiet his loud clanking and squelching armor – and turned to face him, broken weapons raised threateningly.

The first came at him with a club studded with nails. Jacob caught the blow on his shield as he swept it up and around, opening the monster up to a vicious riposte that tore out what little desiccated organs it had left.

As the first attacker lay dying at his feet, the next came on too fast for Jacob to parry. He threw himself into a roll, coming up and around the Vacant's axe swing.

Hummingbird's Kiss took it in the unguarded back but he didn't have time to finish it off as he heard the third Vacant coming up behind him.

Ripping out his sword, Jacob spun on the balls of his feet. Shield raised, he accepted the triple-jab of the Vacant's rusty spear. The blows gonged off the metal, his arm tingled from the reverberations but the only loss he suffered was a tenth of his Stamina.

When it had spent its initial fury, Jacob dismissed his [Kite Shield] in a whirl of ash and took his [Longsword] in both hands.

He quick-stepped forward to bridge the gap and to get inside the longer reach of the spear. *Falling Rain* shattered the creature's frail skull.

Up and around Jacob lifted the sword and it fell upon the creature's head with a resounding *crack* that split the air. The red glow of fire in the Vacant's eyes winked out, leaving only the recovering axe-wielding Vacant.

Turning on the still-staggering Vacant, Jacob could only shrug in disappointment. He took a few casual strides toward it, blade tipped low that drew a line in the dirt as he walked to it.

By the time the creature turned around, *Wind Parts the Grass* carved a lethal wound from groin to chin.

> *You defeat the* [Vacant Shambler].
> *You defeat the* [Vacant Spearman].
> *You defeat the* [Vacant Axeman].
> *Awarded 300 Souls.*

With the way clear, Jacob headed into the tower and took the laborious climb up to the roof. On the way up, avoiding the rotten boards that would surely send him falling to his death, Jacob reflected on the difference between himself now and the young man he was when he first visited Hollow Dreams ten years ago.

Those Vacant would have presented more than the trivial challenge they posed to him now. With unsteady hands, he would have battered, blocked, and dodged aside all while expending at least 2 [Cinder Ampoules].

Fear of pain was a powerful motivator. Especially to a young kid barely old enough to look out for himself and who had never endured any true hardships.

Ten years of nothing but horror and death made the pain of Pyresouls inconsequential. He dealt with pain every day. Getting a gash in Pyresouls was just another Tuesday to him.

The Vacant within Hollow Dreams were of varying difficulty. Particularly those of the western side of town, there were Vacant Assassins that would leap out of the shadow and take off half of your Health or more with a single blow.

Few people went out that way. To the best of his knowledge, there was nothing out to the west of Hollow Dreams. Only a strange pair of rents in the ground and a location called The Blind Sisters. Likely named after the two impossibly deep crevices.

Nobody knew what it was for or how to get past them. To the north was a sheer cliff face that rose more than three hundred feet skyward and a massive city that could be seen from most places in the valley. To the south was a steep canyon and Journey's End.

And the gap between the two massive cracks in the ground was too far to jump.

Reaching the second-to-last floor within the tower, Jacob turned from the stairs to the opened room filled with tall clay jars. The temptation was too great to resist.

With large sweeping two-handed motions, Jacob shattered several pots in a single swing. A few items revealed themselves as sapphire wisps but mostly the room was empty.

You gain [Anima].
You gain [Rusted Spear].

While he had never come to *this* Pyre, he knew of it well enough. Placed at the southern side of Hollow Dreams, it was often considered the exit Pyre.

From the south side of town, he could venture into the canyon where the Smog Rifts and Journey's End were located.

His original path had taken him to the center of town, down into the Defiled Cistern. A place he never intended to venture again.

This time, his path would take him to the south and to the Smog Rifts. Provided he didn't take too long at the Crossing in Hollow Dreams, he should make the rifts within 2 days.

He hoped.

Time was weird in Pyresouls Online. Most especially when moving between areas.

Sometimes the sun seemed to be in a set position, other times it seemed to move. Not many people appeared to care because the few people who pointed it out never bothered to look into it.

Not that most players would. It was irrelevant to the contest, and any player who explored more than was necessary found themselves falling behind.

And with such a juicy prize dangled in front of their faces, nobody was going to waste time researching and testing things that didn't directly have an impact on their ability to progress.

The cool wind of the rooftop chilled his sodden armor. When he looked at the Pyre, a pile of cold ashes situated directly beneath the tilted black bell, Jacob felt a pang of disappointment.

Did I really expect to see Camilla again?

For just a moment, he realized that he did. Somehow, he thought she might be here.

He missed the company.

Reigniting the Pyre, Jacob gathered the ruby flame of Kindling into his palms and tipped it once more into the Pyre. The flames leaped high into the bottom of the bell and then stilled.

This time, the Fire Oppa didn't emerge from the ash and coals. He arrived in a flash of flame and light, floating in the air between Jacob and the Pyre. "Still soaked, are we?" the Fire Oppa asked with a wolfish grin.

Jacob sat down, resting at the Pyre. The comforting warmth washed over him. It wouldn't dry his armor but it made the soggy outfit matter less. It almost felt like he was floating in a warm bath.

His weariness faded and as always, he felt rejuvenated in mind, body, and spirit.

Pyre Ignited.
*Your respawn location has been set to **Hollow Dreams (East)**.*
The Fire Oppa stokes the embers of your conviction.
Health, Stamina, Ampoules and Spell Gems restored.

You Kindle the Pyre.

With a playful swish of his fiery, fluffy tail, the Fire Oppa swept a corona of flame over Jacob. The flames were harmless, and he looked curiously at the Fire Oppa before his mind caught on to what happened.

His armor was bone-dry.

Jacob took off his helm and set it aside, then reached forward and pet the Fire Oppa gratefully. "I appreciate that."

"As does my sensitive nose."

"That's fair," Jacob said with a smirk.

"One more Pyre to go," the Fire Oppa said, he almost sounded hopeful. "You really had to thumb your nose at the Vile One, didn't you? You couldn't simply have gone on your way?"

"Had to be done," Jacob said with mock sorrow.

"Be that as it may." The Fire Oppa clearly didn't agree but he had the good sense not to argue the point. "You would do well to avoid any of the Vile Covenant. They will be out for your blood, quite literally."

"Duly noted."

The Fire Oppa's whiskers twitched as he leaned toward Jacob and sniffed. "I take it you want to do some reinforcing?"

Jacob nodded but he wasn't quite sure what he was going to spend it on. He had enough Souls for a single parameter reinforcement and a few upgrades to his [Elite Knight's Helm] but that was it.

Reinforcing TMP wouldn't do him much good. In a way Temper was a breakpoint parameter that was only useful once it cleared certain thresholds.

Increasing TMP from 11 to 12 wouldn't allow him to equip anything new. Even the [Elite Knight's Gauntlets] with 3 guilt would still push him over the edge into the next tier.

After getting used to being so light and swift, Jacob wasn't about to go back to the 25% penalty to Stamina and Movement. Every point of reinforcement he could achieve would help, eventually. But this wasn't a game that he planned on playing for years.

This was a race, and one he intended to quit as soon as he was done. As soon as Earth was safe and the Collapse was averted.

Thinking about the Collapse reminded him of the item he got from the priest. He took out the [Soul of a Devout Priest], meaning to inspect it but was startled by its shape and size.

Usually, when Souls were solidified as items, they were shimmering white wisps. Sometimes they danced like a white flame but they always had a similar look.

The priest's Soul was different.

It was taller and larger than anything Jacob had seen before. It flickered and shimmered in the air with a dark green tint to its edge that darkened into a ragged blackness at the center.

It looked like a tear in reality.

"I wouldn't absorb that," the Fire Oppa suggested. "Wasteful business taking an Ascended Soul and using it for raw Souls."

"I'm listening," Jacob said, putting it back into his inventory and looking curiously at the Fire Oppa. He had never heard of an Ascended Soul before.

"You can use Ascended Souls to imbue greater strength to your arms or armor. While they provide plenty of Souls when absorbed, you will lose their unique properties. Properties that – more often than not – are rare and powerful."

"And what will this Ascended Soul do?" Jacob asked.

"Examine it and see."

Jacob pulled it out again, examining it further.

[Soul of a Devout Priest]
Soul of an "enlightened" priest already undergoing their transformation to become closer to their Vile God. As one of the rare devouts, this Soul contains a fragment of the Vile God's dominion over the sea and its transformative powers.
Special beings such as this Devout Priest have unique Souls touched by a higher being. Used to acquire a huge amount of Souls, to imbue the Vile God's strength into a weapon, or its protective enchantment upon a piece of armor.

Eyes popping at the description, he looked at the Fire Oppa. "Can you tell me what the enchantment is without forcing me to do the process itself?"

"Place the Soul into the Pyre."

Jacob complied. The flames shifted and swirled around it as if repelled. The Fire Oppa alighted onto the Pyre and circled the Soul.

"Perhaps your selfish desire to mete out justice bore fruit after all," the fiery ferret said with a snicker. The Soul floated back to Jacob's waiting hand. "If placed within a weapon, it will transform it into a Vile Weapon. A rare and uniquely powerful sort that, as the description no doubt told you, uses the transformative powers of the briny Vile God."

He was about to ask what the Fire Oppa meant by that when he caught on. "Will it cost anything?" he asked greedily.

The transformative powers of the Vile Kingdom were well-known. It was the power of decay and destruction. Madness made manifest as even the strongest shields and armors were turned to brittle, rusted junk under the magical assault.

If the Fire Oppa was saying he could wield that power, he was right. It was *well* worth the effort to go out of his way and kill the priest.

"Yes, only weapons that are plus-ten can be transformed by an Ascended Soul. As well, it requires an item of significant magical strength to reinforce the item."

"Wait," Jacob said, remembering when he was reinforcing his chest piece. "I thought you could only reinforce up to plus-five?"

"Before you learned how to Kindle the Pyres, I could only reinforce an item to plus-five," the Fire Oppa agreed with a hint of chagrin. "Now I can increase that to plus-ten. However...."

"However, what?"

"As I said, only a powerful magical item can be used to ascend the weapon. I don't mean to be presumptuous... but you are barely scraping by with Souls. It doesn't seem like you're exactly overflowing with rare and bountiful treasure."

With a grin, Jacob pulled out the [Minos Horn]. His last one. The look of shock and awe on the Fire Oppa's face was priceless.

Once he managed to find his voice the Fire Oppa said, "I stand corrected. My, you are simply full of surprises, aren't you?"

Stuffing the item back into his inventory, Jacob turned his attention back to what his next steps should be.

With only 2 [Dull Sparks] to his name, he was a long way from getting his [Mace] to +10. Even though [Dull Sparks] could be purchased from one of the undead merchants in Hollow Dreams, they wouldn't come cheaply. He would have to hold onto his Souls until then, risking losing them all in the process.

The weapon that he would ascend would have to be the [Mace]. His [Longsword] was good but it was significantly less effective against heavily armored enemies.

With the rusting, weakening power of the Vile God ironically – and unwillingly – bestowed by the dead priest, it would be a significant advantage against the stronger enemies he was about to face.

But first, he needed 7 more [Dull Sparks]. With his [Mace] already upgraded once, he just needed 9 more reinforcements to bring it to +10.

With such a high requirement, farming for them would be a waste of time. He didn't know the drop rates of the various monsters well enough. The game was simply not out long enough for people to delve into its mechanics to understand things like that.

His best bet was to continue on to the Crossing of Hollow Dreams, find the undead merchant and get the hell out before he was attacked. Considering the path *most* players took, there shouldn't be too many Vile Covenant members running about.

If there were, he was in serious trouble.

Most people would be coming to Hollow Dreams through the overland routes. Those that were able to somehow survive Weslyn's Watch and navigate the deadly Smog Rifts blind, came from the direct south while those from the Corpse Garden and Stalking Wood from the southeast.

Few people came belowground as Jacob did from the east.

Which gave him a unique approach as he entered the village from the east and would arrive at the Crossing closer to the center of town from a different direction than most.

He looked up at the Fire Oppa. "I'm going to hold onto my Souls until I can make that weapon." Jacob reached forward and pet the Fire Oppa from his fiery ears to his thrashing, flaming tail. "One more Pyre," he said with conviction. "You better be waiting for me at the Smog Rifts, Fire Oppa. Just a few days and I'll be there to reignite your Pyre."

The look of sweet love and adoration startled Jacob for a moment. He smiled at the tenderness, at the wash of warm emotions that came over him.

The Fire Oppa looked directly into his eyes and said, "I believe you, Jacob. Out of millions of humans, you were the only one who not only took me up on my request but have gone above and beyond in doing so. I look forward to seeing you in the Smog Rifts."

Steeling his conviction once more, Jacob stood up and put on his helm. He had a merchant to see.

26

Jacob approached the Fog Gate in the distance slowly. Towering moss-covered brick walls of nearby buildings blocked the sun down this alley and created perfect hiding spots just above as the alleyway widened.

Just the perfect spots for Vacant Assassins to ambush him.

The problem was, being undead they had infinite patience. As Jacob drew nearer, he kept his shield raised and constantly glanced over his shoulder to make sure nothing was sneaking up behind him.

As he neared the edge of the closest building he could see a tattered leather pant leg. It wasn't a good enough angle to see the Assassin itself, but he knew it was there.

Being undead, they didn't even need to breathe which made them perfect ambushers.

Rather than fight two or more of them – because they were never alone – Jacob came around the corner in a diving roll. Tucking his shoulder he hit the dirt hard in a clattering roll. A blade swiped at the air where he would have been if he hadn't fully committed to the roll.

As soon as he felt the ground beneath his feet, he sprang up and twisted about. His sword came flashing up in a sharp curving arc. *Moon Crests the Horizon* took off the Assassin's left arm, a wickedly curved dagger held in its hand.

Jacob knew it would have two such blades. Even as his sword completed its arc he raised his shield to absorb the coming blow. The ring of steel echoed off the closed space around him.

The stench of the rotting Assassin assaulted him as Jacob pressed forward, shield-charging the first Assassin into a second Assassin behind the first.

A third Assassin burst out of the shadows. Too invested in the shield charge, he could do nothing as the Assassin stuck a blade in his hip and ripped it out with brutal efficiency.

Luckily, he moved too far for the wretched thing to get in a backstab but that cruel blow still took off a quarter of his Health. A few more points dribbled out as his blood flowed from the pulsing wound.

Pushing the pain away, Jacob continued his charge until both bodies crunched against the building on the opposite side of the alley. Stunned and disoriented, Jacob could have taken one of them out then and there.

He pivoted on his leading foot, leaned into the stacked pair of Assassins against the wall and rolled across their stunned bodies just in time for the third Assassin to lunge forward with both daggers out.

They plunged deep into its cohort's leather jerkin and the red fires in the first Assassin's eyes winked out. Still turning, Jacob raised his blade high and snapped it down on the outstretched arms of the third Assassin.

Lightning Cracks Stone severed them at the elbow. They stuck out of the dead Assassin at a comically awkward angle, their bony hands still clutched tightly to the daggers implanted in the first Assassin's chest.

Reversing the stroke, *Moon Crests the Horizon* took out the unarmed Assassin's throat.

Up came his shield, Jacob fell back a step as the second Assassin – the only threat now – pushed off the corpse of its companion and came at him. Its daggers twirled faster than he could keep track but he felt confident with his [Kite Shield] poised to absorb any blow.

As soon as it struck, he would counter in the moment it took the Vacant Assassin to recover.

But the Assassin seemed more than happy to menacingly twirl its daggers about in a complex and... distracting weave.

Realizing his mistake, Jacob set his feet apart. While his leading leg stayed put, his left leg slipped further behind him. He snapped them together, quick-stepping backward at the same time as he reversed the grip on his sword and jabbed it behind him.

The slight bowing motion he gave the Assassin in front of him gave the Sword Form its namesake.

Courtier's Bow took the sneaking fourth Assassin in the chest even as it crept up behind Jacob. Leaving his sword impaled in the creature's chest, Jacob raised his shield and bashed aside the glinting, diving daggers of the second Assassin.

Without a weapon to take advantage of the parry, he instead drove the edge of his [Kite Shield] into the withered, cowled face; aiming for the twin ruby glow of its eyes.

The blow made a sickening crunch as it caved in part of the creature's withered face. Its cowl fell back, revealing a mostly bald head with patches of scraggly hair still clinging to its jerky-looking skin.

Twisting about, turning his back to the second Assassin, Jacob snapped his hand forward and took hold of his [Longsword] impaled in the fourth Assassin's chest.

As he pulled it, the Assassin jerked forward as well. It must have gotten wedged in the bone.

The Assassin, feeling no pain, took the opportunity to get close and stabbed Jacob in the shoulder with one dagger. The other dagger Jacob managed to deflect with his shield.

Rather than dismiss the weapon to ash, he had another idea. Jacob let go of the handle and took a step back, launching a heavy boot at the [Longsword's] pommel.

He put as much power as he could behind the kick and was more than a little surprised to see the effectiveness of his action. The weapon, hilt and all, punched straight through the creature's brittle ribs and tore out the other side.

It landed with a dull thump on the dirt behind it. Surprisingly, the Assassin was still alive and standing.

Jacob dashed to his right and turned to face the two Assassins. At nearly half Health, he took out a [Cinder Ampoule] and crushed it. His wounds knit in the blink of an eye.

But it was long enough for the two wounded Assassins to come at him once more. Summoning his sword to his hand in a burst of ash, Jacob met them head-on.

Sunflower Faces the Sun picked off two dagger strikes but he didn't have time to take advantage of the opening. He turned his attention to the Assassin with the hole punched through its chest.

A swift block blunted the initial strike and Jacob had to be quick to lower his shoulder to catch the second that tried to get under his blocking shield.

Sword flashing, *Dove Takes Flight* opened up the Assassin's throat and the backswing liberated its head from its shoulders.

By a stroke of luck, the head rolled off into the Assassin's chest to Jacob's right and distracted it long enough for Jacob to perform *Twin Forked Lightning*. A heavy Stamina Sword Form that took a third of his Stamina in its impossibly quick double-strike.

Two hefty, 450 damage strikes in the blink of an eye meant the last Assassin was dead before it hit the ground.

Breathing hard, Jacob took a moment to himself allowing his Stamina to regenerate. The number of times Vacant Assassins had killed him in the past was embarrassingly high.

He knew their tactics well enough to face them, but even with years of experience fighting, taking on more than one was a challenge.

One that he was only too happy to overcome. Too bad the Vacant Assassins gave such a pitiful amount of Souls.

You defeat the [Vacant Assassin].
You defeat the [Vacant Assassin].
You defeat the [Vacant Assassin].
You defeat the [Vacant Assassin].
Awarded 600 Souls.
You gain [Small Buckler].
You gain [Assassin's Cowl].

Jacob turned toward the Fog Gate and paused just before it, wondering what he would find on the other side.

Briefly, he wondered what would happen if he used his ability to Kindle on the Fog Gate again.

If he wanted to sow the same amount of chaos – which was a tall order, considering how destructive that damn Skeletal Beast was – he would need to return to a Pyre then lead a train of Vacant to the wall.

And hope that he could burn it again before they descended on him.

As good as Jacob was, being outnumbered made dying incredibly easy. If he had made a few mistakes more or the Vacant Assassins had gotten lucky, he would not be standing after that encounter.

It was a sobering reminder of just how hard Pyresouls was. Even with his high sword skill and intimate knowledge of both the area and the monsters, it didn't mean he was invincible.

Far from it, he thought with a snort of derision.

There were still decent players, people like Kim who weren't out to screw everybody over. Even if he did manage to burn the Fog Gate and lead monsters inside, and they only attacked players he wanted, the merchants would still flee.

And then his whole reason for visiting the Crossing would be for nothing.

He pressed through the Fog Gate.

Time slowed down. Drifting mist fell over him and the doorway as he slowly moved through the thick gelatinous air. He felt cold for a split second as if all the heat in the universe winked out and then he could see the other side of the Fog Gate.

When he exited the other side, time resumed smoothly enough that his next step wasn't a stumble. The transition, for all its slowness, wasn't jerky or disorienting enough that he was incapacitated for a moment afterward.

Which was a good thing, because as soon as he stepped through a blood-stained club swung for his head. A shrill ululating cry rent the air.

"Fresh meat!" the voice cried.

Jacob moved too fast for thought. Countless hours of training kicked in at the sense of a threat he didn't consciously register yet.

In a shining arc, his sword swept up. *Moon Crests the Horizon* batted the unwieldy club out wide. A snap of his muscles sent the blade in a reversing direction back at the unarmored Savage. *Diving Falcon* took him in the throat.

A quick withdrawal had the Savage dropping bonelessly to the cobbled stones, his spine severed. It was over before Jacob realized what had happened.

You defeat [Gregory].

The other Savages hiding out at the edge of the market square ahead saw the lightning-fast exchange and went to go find easier targets elsewhere.

By the time he looked up to notice them, all Jacob could see were their flapping, retreating loincloths.

Staring in surprise at his bloodied blade, Jacob didn't even give a second glance at the body of the player as he walked down the street except to scoop up the crimson wisp containing a measly 50 Souls. He could feel the rough, familiar cobbles even beneath his hard-soled boots.

There was a perpetual smell of smoke and fire in the air and not the pleasant campfire kind. It smelled of recent destruction and a town just barely holding on.

He had to remember to stay on his guard. The Crossing at Hollow Dreams was among the most deadly of them all. He could only hope that he was early enough to avoid Emily.

Having to deal with his ex again was one of the last things he needed right then. But if he had to, he would put her in the ground again without a second's hesitation.

As Jacob stepped into the circular marketplace, several merchants had set up shop with big burly guards by their stands. Others had unmoving statues, Golems that would come alive in the blink of an eye, for their protection.

Golems and any enchanted entity would be nearly impossible to take out without significant magical firepower or a heavily enchanted weapon. Like what he wanted to turn his [Mace] into.

Only about a dozen players were visible, bartering and talking quietly. Some with each other, others with the undead merchants. None of them seemed outwardly aggressive, but each clearly marked the other. And as the newest player in the area, Jacob felt each of their stares fall upon him.

For a game with millions of players, he expected there to be more people here already. Even if he was ahead of the curve, he didn't hope that he was *that* far ahead.

Most of the merchants were unknown to Jacob. It originally took him several more days until he was able to make it to Hollow Dreams. By that time most of the merchants were sold out.

He spotted a few selling poisons, others armor and weapons, but the merchant he wanted was a simple undead man with a gap-toothed smile and a floppy hat.

"Ah, hello good sir!" he cried, upon seeing Jacob wander up to his spread. Unlike the other merchants, he sat on the floor with a large tattered blanket spread out. Most of the items on display were junk. "Care to partake in my humble wares?" He struggled to keep his tittering quiet.

Jacob knew this man. Undead, but not a Vacant somehow, he was a unique merchant. Not unkind necessarily but he was far from benevolent.

The man always seemed on the edge of giggling with the way his voice hitched up several octaves. He found selling to players to be some sort of joke that nobody else was in on.

None of that mattered though, because this undead merchant could sell upgrade materials.

With 6,248 Souls, Jacob came prepared to spend every last Soul if he had to in order to get those 7 [Dull Sparks] he was missing.

Jacob sat down comfortably across from the man, placing his sword and shield to the side. "I'd like to see Melinda's wares," Jacob said, using the correct phrase to open up the merchant's unique list of items.

The man's dull-brown eyes lit up at that.

Somewhere in Hollow Dreams was the man's home, or what was once his home. With enough time and searching, a player could find letters between himself and his mother.

The specifics of the story weren't told anywhere on the archives that Jacob could find but invoking his mother's name was enough for him to offer a different set of items. Rare upgrade materials that were difficult to find. He could also repair gear at roughly three-quarters the cost of another merchant.

Not that Jacob needed a merchant to repair his equipment.

"Well then, *fine sir*, have a gander!" he tittered.

[Undead Merchant's Shop]

[Repair Service] -- *(2 Souls per point of Durability Restored)*
    [Dull Spark] -- *1,000 Souls*
    [Bright Spark] -- *3,500 Souls*
    [Brilliant Spark] -- *10,000 Souls*
    [Prismatic Spark] -- *8,500 Souls*
    [Blue Dull Spark] -- *5,000 Souls*
    [Blue Bright Spark] -- *9,000 Souls*
    [Blue Brilliant Spark] -- *12,500 Souls*
    [Red Dull Spark] -- *5,000 Souls*
    [Red Bright Spark] -- *9,000 Souls*
    [Red Brilliant Spark] -- *12,500 Souls*
    [White Dull Spark] -- *5,000 Souls*
    [White Bright Spark] -- *9,000 Souls*
    [White Brilliant Spark] -- *12,500 Souls*
    [Black Spark] -- *7,500 Souls*
    [Dragon's Breath] -- *12,000 Souls*

He also sold a lot of other common items. Arrows, bolts, poisons, all of varying quality. The types of things that didn't matter much to Jacob. Ranged players had their work cut out for them since Stamina was used to not only aim and fire the bow but also to run away.

As they would have to do since ranged attackers were typically frail with their light armor.

Jacob was glad for the visor hiding his face when he saw the price of the [Dull Sparks]. All of them were ridiculously expensive, but he had hoped that he would have enough Souls for 7 [Dull Sparks].

With a sigh, he tilted his head at the merchant. "Do you buy items as well?" he asked.

The undead merchant stroked his leathery, long-dead chin for a moment. A bit of white gleaming fingerbone stuck out at the tip of his index finger. "If you got something *interesting* I might be convinced to give you a discount. But you should know, most merchants don't even do that. If you're looking to sell for Souls then you're shouting at the wrong grave!"

He giggled for a long moment, enough for Jacob to digest his words and understand his meaning behind them.

It was well-known that in Pyresouls there wasn't a functional economy as in most games. Players could trade items but not Souls - not unless they were in item form - and merchants would sell items for Souls but would not buy for Souls.

Altogether, it made getting items a greater task than normal. Many items could be purchased but most items couldn't be sold.

You either used what you managed to find or you stuffed it in your [Boundless Box] and left it there.

What the undead merchant was saying, was something altogether different. If Jacob intended to buy something, he could put up items against the value and get a discount.

Considering no other merchant did any such thing, it seemed as if he stumbled upon a bit of information that not even the archives had back on Earth.

Jacob took out any loot of potential value that he found along the way. Out came a collection of rusted armaments and armor shards, a [Small Buckler], and the [Whisper of Insanity].

The merchant looked over the items laid out on the cloth, picking each one up and examining it. When he got to the [Whisper of Insanity] he made a warding motion with his left hand, and what was left of his fingers on his right. "Put it away, I beg! Do not show such profane things out in the open, are you trying to tempt the...." He looked around and pitched his voice into a barely heard whisper, "*Twilight Council* to free your stupid head from its shoulders?"

Heeding his advice, Jacob took the item back and looked expectantly at the rattled merchant. He hadn't the faintest idea what the Twilight Council was but that was far from his concern at the moment.

Leaning forward, palm pressed to one knee Jacob continued to say nothing as the merchant gathered himself. If he thought Jacob was some sort of dangerous or perhaps unstable person, he might be more willing to trade with him at a favorable rate.

If only to make him leave faster.

That suited Jacob just fine since he wanted nothing to do with the area. At any moment somebody from his past could show up. Alec, Emily, or any number of other players that might wish to do him harm.

If that group from the last Crossing was still around, they certainly had a bone to pick with Jacob and he wanted to be far from the Crossing whenever they came through.

Not that he feared them, but you didn't face 6 opponents and live to tell the tale. That only happened in stories and fantasies.

He would have scoffed at the thought that Lormar was realistic not too long ago. But having lived a life very similar to Lormar in all the worst ways for a decade, he didn't find it so silly now.

"What are you looking to buy, son?" the undead merchant asked.

"Seven Dull Sparks."

"Hmmm... might be that we can work something out." Looking over the items once more, he added, "Normally that would run you around seven-thousand Souls. Considering your... proclivities and these items I'm willing to part with them for the paltry sum of five-thousand, nine-hundred Souls."

Jacob leaned forward, handing over the items in exchange for the [Dull Sparks]. "Deal."

Transaction concluded, Jacob couldn't help but grin. He was about to get up when he remembered the mention of the Twilight Council.

"Yes?" asked the merchant, sensing his unasked question.

"What is the Twilight Council?"

The undead merchant's eyes went wide. "Never speak their name aloud like that, you fool! You will doom us all."

He leaned forward, lowering his voice once more. "They are not to be trifled with, that much you should know. They confiscate such profane items as that you hold and liberate the foolish holder of such items of their life.

"If your goal - like so many of these fools around you - is to head into Camon, the Forbidden City, you will find their power there is absolute. And you will run into them when they choose."

"I appreciate it," Jacob said, rising.

"Show your appreciation by never mentioning them around me again. Now be gone or buy something."

Grinning, his core objective complete, Jacob turned to leave.

He gave the few players nearby a wide berth. There were more people than he remembered upon first coming in and there was something familiar about them that he couldn't place his finger on.

None of them dressed the same, there were metal-clad knights, sneaky rogues, robe-wearing magic-wielders, and even a few well-behaved Savages.

But still, something nagged at him. Something that he couldn't figure out and so he pushed it from his mind to focus on the task at hand.

Deep in thought, Jacob only heard snippets of what those around him were talking about. But he caught the word "bounty" more than once and everywhere he walked people milled about nervously.

While it might be more prudent to go back to his set Pyre, Jacob felt confident enough to press on to the southern exit of Hollow Dreams and make his way to the Smog Rifts.

He could wait to upgrade his weapon. With only 348 Souls to his name, he wasn't much of a target. Even if he did die, not only would the attacker get next to nothing but there was no way to rid him of his [Dull Sparks].

The worst-case scenario was if he died before he reached the Smog Rifts and that was a small issue. Transported back to the last Pyre, he would lose a lot of time but it couldn't be helped.

Plotting the course through Hollow Dreams that would get him out as fast as possible while avoiding the worst of the monsters, Jacob noticed how quiet everything suddenly became.

He should have been paying closer attention to his surroundings. Only now that he took the time to look around the barren street did he see other players speeding away.

He saw no monsters about. The marketplace of Hollow Dreams was fairly safe. There were a bunch of boarded-up houses that a few ill-intentioned players might break open for a brief bit of chaos but nothing more threatening than that.

Certainly no reason to be running anywhere.

The confusion sorted itself out soon enough when Jacob turned his head back to the winding, sloped cobblestone road ahead of him. A lone figure in gleaming white armor stood in the center, wearing a familiar lion's head helm.

Lovely.

27

Jacob tightened his grip on both shield and sword. He came within ten feet of the lone knight. He couldn't remember his name for the life of him. "Mind moving aside? I've got a hot date."

"Oh, no, I won't be moving," the lion-knight said with a sneer so deep he could hear it. "It took a bounty of eight thousand Souls to draw you out but I knew If I was patient-"

Jacob shifted his weight to one leg and sighed impatiently. "I'm sorry, what?"

That took some wind out of the man's monologuing sails. He recovered quickly, puffing his mailed chest out with some effort. "Ever since you wronged me, I have been looking for a way to properly repay you."

From the periphery of his vision, Jacob could see archers and several more armor-clad knights inching in from the alleys between the leaning buildings. There were already three moving out into the street behind the guy in front of him.

And he knew without turning around that they had cut off his escape so he didn't bother showing his concern.

In truth, he didn't have much of an option but to fight. He doubted there was any way he could talk himself out of this.

His attention back on the lone knight seemed to bolster the man's confidence. "Joining the Vile Covenant was the best thing I ever did. Yes, you made quite the enemy when you betrayed them. They offered me power, more power with each follower I brought to their glorious cause."

The man placed his palm over his armored breast and when he moved it away, a familiar - and hated - symbol appeared. A red hooked tentacle circumscribed by a black circle.

The symbol of the Vile Kingdom.

One by one, the men and women around him did the same. Each showing their allegiance.

"So you see," the leader continued, every word dripped oily smugness. "Through the Vile Covenant's magic, I was able to track you down. And not just track you down, but bring along those who have pledged their lives and souls to the Great Old One!"

He would defend himself and take down as many as he could. There was no way he would give them the satisfaction of surrendering. Jacob had heard of more than a few reports of particularly sadistic players extorting others.

Though this was something else. Something personal. He recognized the man, though he couldn't bring his name to mind. The fact that he was part of the Vile Covenant made things harder on Jacob.

He didn't realize the depths the Covenant might go to in order to exact their vengeance. He wasn't sorry for what he did, never that. But he was beginning to see why the Fire Oppa hadn't thought it was a good idea.

No good deed goes unpunished, Jacob thought with a wry grin hidden behind his visor.

If they were intent on extracting maximum suffering, they would do as many of the other extortionists in Pyresouls did. They would surround him, order him to take all of his equipment and items out, effectively robbing him of all his possessions or they would torture him to death.

The pain in Pyresouls was real, just like everything else was. And so, people were naturally afraid of it. On most people, it worked quite well.

Jacob spotted the white-hemmed robes of a Cleric doing his best to stay out of sight in an alley peeking out around a pile of boxes off to Jacob's right.

As one of the rarest types, they were one of the few capable of inscribing a healing spell to a [Spell Gem]. Though the uses were limited, with somebody that could heal, a person could be brought to near-death several times.

He'd met enough of these bullies in his life, where the stakes were much higher. He knew how to deal with them. They preyed on weakness and expected it in everybody.

With so many obvious players arrayed against him, any normal player would be deeply nervous if not downright frightened. They couldn't steal anything from him. No items would drop from his corpse except a fraction of his held Souls - which wasn't much at that point.

It was a silver lining that he had already spent his Souls and did what he came to the Crossing to do. Not much of one, considering the odds were exceedingly high he was about to die very painfully.

At least they would get less than 100 Souls for the effort. He would lose time being sent back to his Pyre, but there was no getting around that. Once he returned, he would have to waste even more time to avoid the Crossing and head south into the Smog Rifts.

At least he would be free of these idiots who didn't realize that by detaining him they were jeopardizing billions of lives. Worse, they were allying themselves with one of the most heinous enemies of humanity.

With a beleaguered sigh, he pointed the tip of his sword to the cobbles and rested it there gently, point-first. He set his palm atop the pommel and looked around himself, counting the number arrayed against him.

Thirteen players, really? That's a little ridiculous.

"What do you want?" Jacob asked.

"I want you to pay for what you did to me!" he roared. The fact that Jacob didn't understand what this was all about seemed to set him off. "Don't pretend you don't recognize me! You may have lowered your visor but you still wear the same equipment *Jacob!* Yes, I know your name."

Of course he did. The game told you the name of the player who killed you unless the player was using a few specific items to hide their identity. Even though Jacob didn't *directly* kill the man before him, the system clearly identified him as the instigator.

His name would have shown up alongside the skeletal abomination that did the actual deed just as if Jacob had set off a trap that killed him.

If the guy thought using Jacob's name was going to elicit some sort of horrified or shocked reaction, he was sorely mistaken.

The whole thing was just *so silly*. Jacob's shoulders shook with honest laughter and once he got going it only intensified. The man sputtered and raged as Jacob bent over double, laughing all the harder.

The damn irony of it all! I'm going to be killed by a whiny player who feels personally wronged while I'm trying to literally save his life and nearly ten billion more. It was too much for him to get mad at.

He was far enough ahead of Alec that he could still get through the Smog Rifts and Journey's End before his friend did. But all the backtracking was going to cost him time he should spend farming Souls.

With a deep breath to steady the last chuckles that bubbled up from his belly, Jacob stood up and shook his head. "Oh man, that's rich. Thanks for that."

"Why are you laughing! This is not funny!"

"It kind of is," Jacob countered. He would have lifted his visor and wiped the tears that were squeezed out from all the laughing if he had a free hand. "I don't even know who you are dude."

There was a faint snort of laughter from one of the lion-headed man's subordinates. When he whirled around in a whining rage, the offender was silent.

"Don't try to act aloof with me, I know you *Jacob*."

"Why do you keep using my name like that?" Jacob asked, honestly curious. "The game tells you who killed you. Even though I didn't do it myself, I'm not terribly surprised the game informed you. What, did you think I would get spooked that you *knew my name?*"

He shook his head with a chuckle. "Listen man, you do you. You wanna fight, bring it. You want to be a coward and use your friends? Whatever. I got places to be, things to do."

The white armor on the man rattled as he shook with uncontrollable rage. Apparently, he never had anybody speak back to him. The worst this little stain could do to Jacob was kill him.

He had been through worse. Ten years of it. Nothing this guy had up his sleeve could ever compare to those horrors.

A silvery halberd appeared in the man's hand. He gripped it so hard, Jacob was surprised he didn't crack the wood. "How pathetically frail is your ego that you get *this* bent out of shape over some guy killing you? *In a game designed for PVP* at that!" Jacob said.

"Nobody disrespects me!" The man's voice jumped several octaves. "My name is Mack McKinnon. Yeah, *that* McKinnon."

Jacob manufactured a shrug. He made no move to ready himself for the impending fight aside from putting the toe of his boot against the backside of his blade.

"I still don't know who you are," Jacob tilted his head to the side. "Oh. You think you're famous or something don't you? Poor guy. Must suck not doing anything notable enough on your own. So, let me guess... you rely on mommy and daddy's name to open doors you can't? Damn dude, I feel bad for you."

"Kick this bastard's ass!" Mack ordered, raising and leveling the point of his halberd at Jacob threateningly. "But don't kill him." Jacob didn't need to look over his shoulder to see that Mack had clearly looked to the Cleric hiding in the nearby alley.

That would be his first target.

For a moment, everything held. The street had become so quiet that Jacob could hear the creak of the first bowstring tighten.

That's my cue.

As much as Jacob wanted to lunge at the leader, he needed to take out that Cleric. Just because he *could* withstand the torture didn't mean he wanted to. It would also mean more time lost.

If he could kill the Cleric - and any others he found - he could probably force Mack to kill him. He seemed easily manipulated and had the most fragile ego Jacob had ever seen.

There was no way Jacob was coming out of this alive, he knew that well enough. With so many players arrayed against him, it was a pure numbers game at that point.

But he could put a little fear into the rest of them. Make it memorable.

Grabbing his [Longsword], Jacob twisted on the balls of his feet with his shield raising at the same time as two arrows flew for his back. They pinged harmlessly off the shield and with it raised, he rushed the pair of archers.

Their surprise was complete when he bowled into them, knocking them to the hard cobbles with a grunt of pain from each. Another arrow clacked against the cobblestones on his right, narrowly missing him.

By the time anybody realized his goal was the Cleric and not to flee, it was too late.

The mousey looking red-head opened his mouth and raised his hands ineffectively. He didn't even try to cast. Locking up wasn't an uncommon reaction, especially if the person was used to staying in the back.

Wind Parts the Grass drew sparks from the cobbles and cut a bloody vertical line up the man's chest. Jacob rolled around behind him as he let out a shrill scream of pain.

His robes were surprisingly reinforced. That blow should have nearly killed somebody as physically frail as most casters were. Then again, damage from one player to another was weird. It seemed drastically reduced compared to what could be done against a monster.

Reversing direction mid-roll, Jacob came up behind the wailing man and hamstrung him with *Reaping the Harvest*. Again, his blade didn't bite quite as hard as he would expect it to but it was enough to do the job.

Convinced the man - if he ever stopped that infernal crying - wouldn't flee, Jacob stood and cast *Heat Blade*. A shimmer of light and heat warped the air around the blade as it ignited with long curling tongues of flame.

Hummingbird's Kiss took the man in the heart from behind, more to quiet his wailing than any desire to kill him quickly. The effect of *Heat Blade* more than doubled his damage against another player.

Instead of the drastically reduced 40ish damage he was doing before, *Hummingbird's Kiss* did 87 points of damage.

You defeat [Allen].
Awarded 2,500 Souls.

Damn, Allen. You were hanging onto a lot of Souls there.

With a mental command, he disabled further death notifications. Now wasn't the time.

With their healer out of the way, and several melee fighters closing in, Jacob darted to the side and hopped up the crates set against the nearby building in the alley. A quick leap and he was up on the loose tiled rooftop with two archers turning at his loud approach.

With his shield raised, they had a hard time landing a hit. One arrow grazed his thigh but hardly did any damage. He closed the distance easily. *Falling Rain* took out the first archer's throat as he struggled in vain to nock the next arrow. *Dove Takes Flight* severed the other archer's right hand at the wrist just as he was drawing back.

The arrow made a pathetic flop once the tension of the bow relaxed and with a reversing cut, Jacob took the other hand from the man. A boot to the chest sent him careening over the edge to the main street below into a group of players.

His only hope was to use the overwhelming odds in his favor. Contrary to popular movies, real fighting made it hard for a large group of people - particularly melee fighters - to gang up on a single opponent.

Swords got crossed, people took collateral damage, and a smart opponent could use that against his or her attackers. After all, the lone fighter could swing nearly anywhere and hit an enemy. Not so for the others, who had to be as mindful of their ally's weapon as their target's.

Grasping at the rapid flow of blood from his torn throat, the first archer gurgled in pain and fear. His eyes were wild with it and Jacob was all too happy to use that to his advantage.

A hard kick into the man's knee snapped it backward with the sound of somebody biting into celery. Arrows from below skipped off the loose tiles, sending several slipping and sliding to crash on the stones below.

Another hard boot to the first archer's chest sent him sailing over the roof. Knowing that he was making a point more than being effective, Jacob jumped after him.

Reversing the grip on his flaming [Longsword], Jacob timed their fall so that he would perform *Planting the Flag* at the same moment as they landed. The archer's body actually bounced a little, forcing him to cry out and impale himself even deeper on his blade.

Already half-drowned in his own blood, Jacob didn't bother to finish him off.

Three down, ten to go.

The next two arrows struck him in the thigh and shoulder respectively. Jacob gritted his teeth through the pain. It only took off a quarter of his health.

As the knights rushed toward him, clearly much slower than he was, Jacob reached the reloading archers. They wisely split up, forcing him to choose a target.

Jacob broke left, *Lightning Cracks Stone* severing the man's left arm at the bicep. He dropped the bow with a shout of pain and in that brief moment of stunning pain, he reversed the motion. *Wind Parts the Grass* didn't quite sever his right hand but since it was dangling from a thread of scorched muscle and sinew, he felt it was good enough.

He didn't have time to be perfect.

A heavy bolt thudded into his back, draining his health by half and forcing Jacob to cough up blood inside his helmet. He staggered to one knee, dismissed his sword, and crushed a [Cinder Ampoule].

He was back to full Health by the time his knee tapped the cobblestones. Jacob committed to the motion and used it to propel himself forward in a roll that pushed him forward and around the archer who conveniently took the next bolt in the chest. A bit of the heavy quarrel stuck out of his back.

And that brings us down to nine.

Dashing back and forth drained his Stamina more, but it was the only way to avoid the relentless bolts and arrows. *How many ranged attackers does he have?*

Diving Falcon impaled the next archer, but that killing move earned Jacob two bolts in his ribs. Crushing another ampoule he pressed on.

The three knights that came to face him were almost as easy as one of the Vacant. He rolled through their clumsy attacks as he came up spinning. *Falling Maple Seed* lamed two of them, the third escaped the worst of it but *Hummingbird's Kiss* took him in the heart.

The man died before he could conjure a [Cinder Ampoule].

But no matter how well Jacob fought, there were simply too many of them. He used the ampoules without the slightest hesitation. They went fast, almost as fast as he flowed through his Forms, laming, crippling, or outrightly killing those who came against him.

But his opponents also had [Cinder Ampoules]. And as their numbers dwindled, they formed a fiercer defense.

Metering his Stamina to within a hair's breadth of emptying and leaving him vulnerable, Jacob went through their ranks like Death itself. Five men were dead, three were moments away too blinded by pain to use an ampoule, and he was closing in on his next victim.

Three bolts struck him as he stabbed down into one of the pesky crossbowmen. *Planting the Flag* took his life, bringing the total remaining to four. With only one [Cinder Ampoule] left, Jacob thought he might as well take one of those annoying crossbowmen out.

They remained spread out while the melee fighters came in at him. The so-called leader stayed back and watched it all like the true coward he was.

No matter how badly he wanted to kill the man, one look at that armor suggested he wasn't going to be a pushover like the rest. Better to thin the herd, more than half of them would think twice when they saw him again.

Dismemberment tended to leave a lasting impression.

And since everything felt real in Pyresouls - there was a reason the waiver was as thick as a brick - the players would no doubt wish to avoid a repeat performance and look elsewhere for their victims.

As Jacob tried to dismiss his [Longsword] to summon the last [Cinder Ampoule] nothing happened.

*You are **Paralyzed!***

Well, shit.

That was unexpected. Paralysis powders and poisons were hard to find and didn't have a terribly high chance of working. Had they been using paralysis bolts the entire time on him?

It hardly mattered if they were. There was nothing he could do.

Arcs of yellow lightning chased up and down his limbs, binding them in a net of painful spasming. He couldn't drop his sword if he wanted to. Nor could he summon or dismiss any item.

He was, for all intents and purposes, screwed.

Mack wasted no time shouting out orders. The paralysis effect wouldn't last very long. Maybe a full minute if he was particularly unlucky.

A wiry little man sprang out from the shadows. He shied away from Jacob, tapping him with a foot to make sure he couldn't actually move.

Jacob would have grinned at the obvious fear in the man if he could have.

"The paralysis isn't going to last forever, do you want to still be in front of him when he comes out of it?" Mack barked at him.

The smaller man nodded and fit something around Jacob's neck. There was a sharp metal *click* and the smell of ozone filled the air.

The hell is that?

Without his permission, both Jacob's shield and sword vanished in a swirl of ash. His hands were dragged behind his back, though he noted it was done carefully, as if the man was afraid of hurting him unnecessarily.

A pair of manacles clicked into place around his gauntleted wrists. When the paralysis finally wore off, two people came around either side of him and looped their arms under his, lifting him to his feet.

He didn't bother to support himself as they expected. If they were going to force him to his feet they could hold him up. He wasn't about to do their work for them.

A grunt from either side told him that they hadn't expected that. Few people did. This wasn't the first time he was taken hostage. The easiest way to avoid being taken or otherwise used as a proper body shield was to go fully limp.

Humans were weird, unwieldy creatures that were surprisingly hard to carry if you didn't do it a specific way. And holding a person's back to your chest while you tried to threaten them, using one hand to hold them up didn't work so well for keeping them on their feet.

Often the choice came down to holding them and forgetting the weapon, or dropping them and fleeing. For the few people who were strong enough to do both, it tired them out enough that an opening could be made in the future.

Not that Jacob thought he might get that lucky. He was resigned to his fate of dying. His point was made. Once those last two died, that would make nine kills.

Nine out of thirteen was better than he expected. Though he would have preferred an even ten. *Oh well, life is full of small injustices.*

Making sure he could talk without spluttering like he just came back from the dentist's after having some work done, Jacob said, "How many bolts did it take?"

The two on either side of him looked to each other with more than a little alarm at his clinical attitude. He did well to keep from laughing out loud.

"Twelve," said the man on his left as if embarrassed.

"Lot of wasted Souls," Jacob commented off-handedly. It really was. To craft a paralysis bolt or arrow cost several hundred Souls.

Even if they killed Jacob, the most they could get was a little over 3,500 Souls after the men and women he'd just killed. He chuckled to himself at the thought that, when they did kill him, they would only be getting back their own Souls.

How's that for ironic? They try to kill me and I'll still walk away with over ten grand in Souls.

"Something funny, *slave?*" Mack asked, standing in front of him.

Jacob turned to the man that held him up on his left. The one that talked to him. "What's it like having a man-child for a boss?"

That earned him a solid smack to the helm and a hiss of pain from Mack. Jacob chuckled again at the man's stupidity.

Smart enough to get you in cuffs, came the unbidden thought. *Touche.*

"You're coming with me," Mack said, barely containing his rage. He looked around the street at the dead bodies. "Somebody kill off Jim and Percy. I'm tired of their mewling."

Aside from Mack and the two men holding up Jacob, there was only one other person left, that wiry little man. He slinked off out of sight, silencing the two men's weak cries of pain.

"Hey! I thought I would get the Souls when I touched their orb!" he cried in a nasally voice as two crimson wisps streaked out somewhere from Jacob's left and absorbed into his side.

It goes to whoever dealt the most damage to them, Jacob wanted to say but he kept his mouth shut. No use in giving them any information they might be able to use.

"I claimed their Souls with my spell, *Soul Devourer*," Jacob lied. "Whenever any of you die now, I'll get a portion of your Souls. Unless you kill me to break the spell."

A hush settled on the street as they digested that. Of course, no such spell existed to Jacob's knowledge. But that didn't mean they knew that.

"Time for you to see what happens to people who mess with me," Mack said, turning his back on Jacob.

Despite himself, Jacob began to worry.

28

They took him through several back alleys. A few Vacant were milling about but they proved of little consequence to Mack and the wiry man at his side that slipped in and out of the shadows like a ghost.

That one was worth watching.

It wasn't until they brought him into a circular building that Jacob understood their true motive. A part of him was impressed. It was a solid strategy and a surprisingly cruel one as well, all things considered.

He was taken down the crumbling steps into the sub-level of the guard tower where a trio of dank cells awaited. One of the doors was opened by the wiry man and Jacob was shoved in. The cell door locked behind him as he stumbled in barely keeping himself from pitching over.

Turning around, Jacob bowed to the four men. "Not the best accommodations but it'll do." He picked a spot on the filthy ground and sank into a crosslegged position despite the collar and manacles that made it difficult with his arms secured behind his back.

Mack glared at Jacob through the bars. "I'm going to find your little girlfriend too and I'll make sure you have some company in that other cell. The both of you can sit out this whole affair and after I win the competition I'll come back for you."

Jacob could hear the lie in Mack's voice. It was incredibly unlikely Kim was as stupid as Jacob and had done something to get on the Vile Covenant's bad side. Considering what Mack said earlier, it wasn't so much the man's ability to track him down as the Covenant's magic that allowed him to find Jacob.

Despite it being a clear consequence for his reckless, vengeful behavior against the Vile Covenant, Jacob wasn't about to let it go.

If the Vile Covenant wanted to escalate things, he would be more than happy to oblige. Every single one of them would fall to his sword when he was done.

Mack lifted his lion-faced visor, his face was flushed and twisted with rage. Face pressed tight to the rusting bars of his cell, he added, "And I haven't forgotten what you've done. I'll make you beg for me to kill you. For each of my men that you've killed, you will suffer."

"All this because I hurt your feelings? Whatever, Matt," Jacob said turning his head away.

Mack spluttered and went apoplectic at the slight. It was oddly amusing watching his face turn progressively darker shades of purple. If he ever found him again, he would go out of his way to kill him. Slowly.

Before Mack could open the cell to kill Jacob, he managed to calm himself down. *Damn, really thought that'd get him. Oh well.*

Jacob ignored him, turning his head away. Just about the biggest middle-finger to an egomaniac like Mack.

The man ranted and raved for a little while, costing him precious time in getting ahead. But after nearly thirty minutes of monologuing, Jacob had enough.

He turned back to Mack. "Listen, Mort, or whatever your name is, just kill me now because all this cheesy bad-guy monologuing is more torture than you could ever imagine.

"I *get it*. Mommy and daddy didn't love you enough. You're acting out in the only way you know how. Nobody respects you, blah, blah, blah. Just shut the hell up, dude.

"Or better yet, give me a dagger and I'll cut my own throat so I don't have to listen to your whining. Don't you have a competition to win or something?"

That was enough for Mack to snap.

Unfortunately, one of the crossbowmen had been given the key to the cell with explicit orders to leave. There would be no luring the guard into the cell to kill him or stealing the key from him somehow.

So as much as Mack bellowed and raged, trying to get into the cell, he couldn't. Tantrum played out, he composed himself and flipped the visor down over his pretty-boy face.

He was about to leave when Jacob called out to him, "Hey, guy."

All three men in the room turned to Jacob, which only made Mack angrier. "No, not you guys. That dude in the middle. Yeah, you. When you get to the Burgon Beast, I hope you don't choke. That would be *super* embarrassing for you."

Jacob's laughter chased all three of them out of the guard tower and he was left utterly alone. As he wandered around the room he realized he only had two options available.

He could wait and let everything fail which was utterly unacceptable or he could kill himself. Whatever heavy metal collar they had snapped onto his neck had removed his ability to take off his armor or summon his weapons. He didn't think something like that even existed.

And that meant with even a quarter of his Health remaining, it would take a while to reduce it to zero.

And it was going to *hurt*.

Pressing his back to the wall, Jacob pushed to his feet. He lined up with the opposite wall and charged head-first into the stone. A jolting, shocking pain rippled through his head and neck taking off a grand total of... *1 Health*.

One Health down, thirty-two to go.

No matter how he did it, he simply could not harm himself more than a single point of Health. The cell was not big enough to get a running start. With his arms pinioned behind his back and that horrible collar on his neck, he couldn't move around properly.

The pain and dizziness from slamming his head into the wall made it hard to keep going. It went against every instinct he had.

More than an hour of ramming into the wall to chip down his Health and he was hardly able to stand. At least two vertebrae in his neck were crushed but by some stroke of luck, he could still stand.

It was too much to ask that he sever his spinal cord and die that way. More than likely he imagined he would be left paralyzed but alive. Forced to stay where he was without any way of getting out.

With only 2 Health left to go, Jacob got to his feet and turned around. He lined up once more with the opposite wall and charged. Except, this time when he hit the wall he rebounded and felt a warm wave of comfort pass through him.

His Health jumped up by half, then half again until he was at full. Jacob cast a murderous look around to find the man in white-hemmed robes sitting on a simple stool facing the bars.

In his stupor and haze of pain, he didn't even notice his arrival. How long had he sat there, watching Jacob bash his Health away 1 point at a time?

"Already here, Al?" called a voice from up the stairs.

"Yeah, just watching this guy try to kill himself."

One of the crossbowmen came down the stairs, his weapon held in the crook of one arm already loaded with a bolt. "How's that possible?"

"Ran into the wall over and over, taking a single point of damage each time. He must have been at it ever since Mack left him here," Al said. There was a hint of respect in his voice. "I got you a seat, Dan."

"That's some dedication," Dan said, sitting on the other stool.

They both touched their breast with a hand, revealing the symbol of the Vile Kingdom - the same as the Vile Covenant's - as a form of greeting. "Hail, *Vilis,*" they said in unison.

"Yeah," Jacob said, falling to a sitting position facing them. "And I would've gotten away with it too, if not for you *meddling kids.*"

Neither of them seemed to recognize the ancient joke and Jacob just shrugged it away. He shifted about, bringing his cuffed hands beneath him and then out in front to rest with some level of comfort.

He had to think of another way out now.

Or so he thought.

"All done with the theatrics?" Dan asked, casually aiming the crossbow his way.

You have got to be kidding me.

Before Jacob could answer, the crossbow fired. It was a tiny dart coated with a very potent - and expensive - sleeping poison. *Where the hell do they get so many Souls from?*

Darkness closed in and Jacob knew no more.

He had no idea how often he was struck with the sleeping toxin. Without the need to eat, sleep, or otherwise keep track of time, the hours bled away like the hopes of Earth.

The few times he found himself awake and cognizant he tried, in vain, to explain what he was doing. The future he was trying to prevent. They looked at him like he was crazy and stuck him with another dart.

Jacob slowly came to consciousness, still groggy he saw the Cleric nudge his friend in the side. "He's up again."

"Yep-yep," Dan said, standing and fitting another bolt to the crossbow. "I'm on it. Hey, Al, what're you going to do with your share-"

Jacob squinted at the sight before him. He couldn't make out the shape behind the crossbowman as two black-gloved hands reached up to either side of the man's face.

He froze there for all but a heartbeat before roaring flames sucked the air and heat from the room as they cooked his skull to a blackened crisp.

The Cleric turned toward his friend, more annoyed than concerned. That moment cost him dearly. The black-garbed form *stepped* across dozen or so feet in a single motion and was upon the chubby man in an instant.

A familiar jagged cleaver flashed through the air. Blood sprayed and the man's shrill cries brought Jacob to full consciousness as he struggled to get his uncooperative legs beneath him.

"Camilla?" he dared to ask.

Once the man was dead, she stowed the cleaver and turned to him. It *was* Camilla. She wore a set of tight-fitting black lacey robes with a large conical hat that had an egregiously wide, floppy brim.

Those ruby eyes were unmistakable. She pulled out a key and undid the lock.

Camilla fell to her knees beside him. His legs were still numb and try as he might, he couldn't get them to support him. So he sat and looked at her. "Fancy meeting you here," he said.

"I could leave, you know," she said, staring at his helm. She reached forward and lifted it off his head, setting it aside. "I really thought I would have run into you several days ago. Now I guess I understand why I didn't. Hold still, this is going to hurt."

Jacob's groggy mind was still trying to process that she was there, let alone what she just said.

Searing, scalding pain that felt like somebody had wrapped a hot curling iron around his neck pushed all thought from his mind. He screamed in pain, letting it wash over him.

Somehow, he managed not to blackout.

When it was over, the collar was off and his manacles were broken. Both were half-melted heaps of slag on the floor. The pain was so intense on his neck that he didn't even recall his wrists hurting.

Jacob wasted no time using his last [Cinder Ampoule] to recover from the severe burns.

Without thinking, Jacob surged to his feet, wrapped his arms around Camilla, and pulled her into a tight hug. "Thank you, Camilla."

Taking a step back, he summoned shield and sword into his hands again, feeling a measure of calm settle over him until his sluggish mind finally caught up to what she had said. Panic surged in his chest.

When he bent down to retrieve his helm, he nearly fell over.

"Wait, what did you mean by *several days*?"

"I mean that it's been many days since I've seen you back at the entrance to the catacombs," she said, folding her arms and looking at him with a mixture of concern and another emotion he couldn't place.

Jacob nearly choked. He hadn't seen Camilla in days, he couldn't even remember how long it had been since he saw her last. Just how long was he held prisoner? He tried to get a grip on his spiraling thoughts.

Jacob took a look at the only time-keeping allowed in Pyresouls, a simple clock that gave the date and time in the real world. It was already September 9th, a few hours before midnight.

September 9th, 2035 – 4 days remain before the Collapse.

All of that time spent getting ahead, using shortcuts, and getting here *days ahead of Alec* were for nothing.

While there were already players in Hollow Dreams, there was no way they had already been to the depths of the Desecrated Catacombs. Even if they had, they would need to contend with the Crossing there, as well as the Gnawing Hunger once they reached the bottom levels.

And even *after* that, they would need to find the one ring among many that would allow them to navigate through the Smog Rifts.

But now much of that advantage was gone.

"Jacob, are you all right?" she asked. "You're free, you realize that, yes?"

He staggered toward the stairs in a stupor. How was he supposed to get ahead now? Once they were out in the open air, Camilla placed a hand on his shoulder and forced him to spin around.

"Tell me what's going on, Jacob."

"It's hard to explain," he answered.

"Uh-uh," she said, cutting him off when Jacob tried to keep walking. "That's not going to cut it. Tell me what has you so bothered, and why you were *imprisoned* by the Vile Covenant, or this will be the last you ever see of me."

That brought Jacob up short. Partly because he didn't want to be alone with his own thoughts, partly because he enjoyed her company, and most of all because Camilla clearly thought that was a strong enough bartering chip to make him talk.

He stuffed that tidbit of information away for another time. Right now was neither the time nor place to be examining how Camilla viewed whatever their relationship was.

"All right, but we walk at the same time."

Camilla stepped aside as Jacob hurried along the winding alleyways. In her lighter garb, it was easy for her to keep pace with him as he filled her in on everything about the Collapse, Earth, and his bitter entanglement with the Vile Covenant.

Finding a small pile of crates, Jacob clambered up them, pulled himself up onto the roof, and offered a hand to help Camilla up. He needed to reach the southern Fog Gate but the last thing he wanted to was to get ambushed by any of Mack's goons if they were still about.

As he crept slower on the rooftop, scanning the nearby tiled roofs for threats, he continued to fill her in. "I know it sounds crazy, time travel and all that but it's-"

"I believe you," she said earnestly. "Time entanglement is not an unknown concept to my people. Nobody has had the power or proper ritual to pull it off, however. And if they did, they saw fit to tell nobody about it and left no witnesses."

Jacob chuckled. "Well, that's the bulk of what's going on. I had nine days to get to the Smog Rifts, then to Journey's End, and to kill the Burgon Beast to stop this whole thing.

"Now I only have about three. If I don't get there before Alec, he'll summon it first and it'll destroy the Pyre at Journey's End before I ever get a chance to fight it."

"Why does it matter?" she asked. "If all you need to do is kill it, why not work with Alec?"

"Because... well, I don't know how this works for you but people from Earth are fragmented into copies of Lormar. Only at the Crossings - the areas covered by Fog Gates - can we easily interact. I could try to invade his shard but it would be a shot in the dark, using an item I don't have.

"Plus, he doesn't know me in this time. He has no reason to believe me. Worse, he would likely think I'm a rival trying to screw him over."

"Okay, so you can't work directly with him. Well, even if you *do* defeat it, who is to say you didn't just beat a single aspect of it? What if all of your humans in this place have to beat their own version of it?"

Jacob shivered at the thought. It wasn't like nobody thought about that but at the same time, there was not enough information. Their best guess was that if it was defeated once, it would be defeated everywhere.

Its ability to leap from one Pyre to the next and destroy it, removing any players bound to that Pyre across *all* shards, lent a bit of credibility to that theory.

He explained as much to her, and added, "The greatest reason? It follows a very particular path. From what we were able to piece together, it follows the inverse path that the player who summoned it took to reach it.

"I didn't follow Alec's path directly. I took a more circuitous path. And I won't be bound to the Journey's End Pyre when I summon the Burgon Beast. It'll be a chore, but if I can constantly bind myself at the next Pyre in its path then go out to meet it, I should be able to stay ahead of the Burgon Beast.

"It might kill me a dozen or more times, but I'll keep coming back, wearing it down. Or, that's the plan at least. Unfortunately, it's the best I have."

"Sounds like you don't have enough information to know whether or not it will work," she pointed out.

He conceded her point with a nod. "It's better to try with partial information than to accept the slow decay of our world."

It was Camilla's turn to nod, her ridiculous black, wide-brimmed hat flopped as she did so. "It focuses my magic," she said defensively, watching Jacob tilt his head up to look at the brim.

"I didn't say anything," he reminded her.

"You didn't need to."

Jacob turned to scout the alleyway on the southern side. It all seemed clear so far. If they both hopped down and made a run for it, they should make it. Even if people were lying in wait to ambush them.

The clinking of armored feet caught Jacob's attention and he ducked back behind a crumbling chimney. Running down the alleyway about to pass directly below him was a familiar set of gold armor. Its owner was a knight he knew well.

It was Alec. And he could only have that armor if he had already been to the Desecrated Catacombs.

At that moment Jacob's mind whirled back to a story of Alec's. One he liked to tell about Hollow Dreams and the time he was randomly killed. He never saw the person who did it, he just died as he was trying to exit the Crossing.

It was a particularly brutal death because the last place he had bound was in the depths of the Desecrated Catacombs. The death had cost him, by his estimation, at least a day.

Across the alleyway, another figure was watching Alec's jogging figure with interest.

Jacob's instincts told him to warn Alec but he knew he couldn't. Alec was at least on par with him by this point. If Alec was sent back to his Pyre, that would at least give Jacob a *little* advantage on him.

But he wasn't going to let that sneak stab his best friend in the back. Motioning for Camilla to come over, he pointed at the dark figure across the alley. The figure kept their head bent and eyes glued to the gold armor of Alec's.

Most people thought you could steal armor from a downed enemy and so people with particularly beautiful and rare armor were targeted frequently. At least, until people realized that this wasn't a normal game where you could loot the items of dead players.

He knew what he had to do. Jacob removed his [Elite Knight's Helm] and tugged on the [Assassin's Cowl]. It was one of the few items that was not a consumable that would hide his identity from another player.

Which meant he could kill Alec without the man ever knowing.

It also had decent boosts to riposte and backstab damage. With only 2 Guilt, it wasn't a bad piece of equipment but its defense was abysmal.

Jacob gave Camilla the sign to attack the man on the other rooftop. One of many that they had developed while they were under the silence effect in the Asylum of Silent Sorrows. Jacob dismissed his shield and started to run.

Even though he wore only a single piece of the [Assassin's Attire] set, his normally clanky and loud footsteps were decently muffled.

It felt good to have somebody to fight alongside again.

You mean it feels good to have Camilla by your side again. Jacob nearly missed a step at the errant thought. He pushed hard at it, focusing on the task at hand.

The assassin across the way, however, still heard his footsteps and looked up just as a ball of writhing fire slammed into their chest.

Launching himself into the air, Jacob took hold of his [Longsword] in both hands as he used *Heat Blade* to limn it with shimmering fire.

With the explosion distracting Alec, turning his gaze to the opposite roof, he never saw Jacob's attack coming. It was somewhere in between the grace of *Falcon Dives* and the brutal strength of *Planting the Flag*.

With the many stacking bonuses from Jacob's use of a Sword Form, the cowl's bonus to backstabs, and his *Heat Blade*, the damage was higher than it should have been.

Jacob's flaming sword pierced Alec's armor just to the side of the neck, right through the meat of his shoulder. His blade sunk to the hilt, puncturing Alec's lung. Even with Alec's impressive armor, the attack still did 115 points of damage.

But Alec like Jacob - had more Health than that.

The man crumpled beneath Jacob's assault, and Jacob was thrown from Alec with the force of the collision. He tumbled forward in a clatter that left his flaming blade inside Alec, but even the continual bite of the flames wasn't enough to finish the man off.

Reeling from the attack, Alec began to stir against the threat. Before he rose another inch, a column of fire immolated him, finishing off what little Health remained.

"Sorry, buddy," he said to the corpse once he got to his feet and touched the crimson wisp that floated above it.

You defeat [Alec].
Awarded 4,500 Souls.

He felt a pang of guilt and wondered if Alec would have treated him differently if he knew that it was Jacob who had killed him.

He shook his head, that wasn't important, unfortunately. Alec's setback was for the good of all.

Camilla gingerly picked her way down from the roof and together they fled Hollow Dreams. He was hardly surprised when Camilla came along with him through the Fog Gate without issue.

29

September 10th, 2035 – 3 days remain before the Collapse.

They walked in silence for a while across the dusty plains that slowly sloped downward. Their path was filled with tall rocky outcroppings hiding shambling Vacant that, while threatening, were slow in their heavy armor.

Despite the Souls they offered - 800 each - Jacob urged Camilla to let them be. The pair sprinted when they needed to but kept up a steady jog the rest of the time to keep ahead of their potential adversaries.

"They're a trap," Jacob said as they descended into the canyon. A black wall of rising smoke greeted them to the south nearly a mile away. The smoke was easily visible in the bright moonlight of the night as it rose and blotted out the stars above.

The western side of the canyon leading to Journey's End was hidden by the rising gray stone walls on either side of them.

Scrub brush clung to the walls here and there with stunted trees vying for whatever foothold they could gain. With the Vacant far behind them, it was almost peaceful.

"How do you figure?" she asked, placing a hand on her floppy hat as a mournful breeze groaned through the canyon. "I killed a few on the way into Hollow Dreams. They give decent Souls and aren't hard to kill."

"Both true," Jacob agreed. "But they were heavily armored. They would have taken a long time to kill even if they were relatively easy to do so."

"Don't you think it's weird that a bunch of heavily armored, slow, and bulky creatures were between Hollow Dreams and one of the most important regions in Lormar?"

Camilla shrugged her shoulders. "Not really, no."

Jacob was glad his visor was still down so she couldn't see him rolling his eyes at her. This was real to her, he had to remember. It *is* real but it was also built up as a game.

And as a game, it would make plenty of sense to put easy - but time-consuming - targets as a tantalizing distraction right before the final goal.

Those that were strong enough or felt they might be, could bypass the creatures with little trouble.

People who stopped to farm them - with no Pyre for miles - would have to return to Hollow Dreams, rest to respawn the monsters, and then repeat. Even if they didn't bother to rest at the Pyre, it would take them a long time to flush out all the monsters.

Killing them would net a large number of Souls. That wasn't the issue, it was that while those players were busy killing the tanky monsters, others were slipping ahead of them.

It put pressure on the players to try and press on for fear of others doing the same. If everybody agreed to grind as much as possible in order to reach the final boss with as much strength as they could muster, things would have turned out very differently.

He explained as much to Camilla. The confusion on her face was evident but she accepted the explanation. "Humans are weird."

Jacob couldn't disagree.

The canyon narrowed quite a bit the deeper south they progressed until they were within striking distances of those deep pits that belched forth noisome black fumes.

"We're going in there?" Camilla asked.

"I am," Jacob said. "I don't know if you'll be able to breathe in there." He replaced his [Antediluvian Ring] with the [Ring of Broken Vows], which would allow him to navigate the Smog Rifts and survive their choking fumes.

After a moment of hesitation, Jacob handed her the [Ring of Covetous Breath]. "Take this, it should help. If you still want to come."

Camilla arched a black brow at him, her lips quirked into a wry grin. "I've seen what happens to you when you are left on your own. I'm coming along."

Turning to the curtains of flowing black smoke that drifted toward the night sky, Jacob took a step forward. They parted before him, turning translucent like a thin gray mist once he entered.

Smog Rifts

The air reeked of burning oil and sulfur.

It burned his lungs but didn't seem to cause any actual damage or ill-effect aside from the mild discomfort. He was a little jealous of Camilla's ring. A swirl of clean air kept the smoke away from her, though her visibility seemed to end at the edge of that bubble.

All around them were small depressions in the ground that gushed forth gouts of oily black smoke. Touching the stuff directly burned a few points of Health off.

The thick miasma that hung in the air was - relatively, speaking - harmless with the ring equipped.

Jacob took the lead, navigating around small pockets of spewing smoke while avoiding the larger rents that were too large to jump over. They made slow, but steady progress through the Smog Rifts.

There was a lot more platforming than he thought there would be. No creatures reared up out of the pits to fight him - yet - but he kept up his guard all the same. Camilla kept one hand pressed between his shoulder blades as he led the way forward.

Jacob had no idea how any player ever managed to navigate through the Smog Rifts up from the south of Weslyn's Watch. Especially not without the [Ring of Broken Vows] or, at the very least, the [Ring of Covetous Breath].

And by all accounts, there did appear to be some players that made the journey somehow.

The Smog Rifts was a maze of cracks and pits that would easily swallow any other player without the ability to see. Even Camilla's borrowed ring severely limited her perception to only a foot or two around her.

While her ring pushed away the oily miasma and allowed her to breathe, Jacob's made it harmless and translucent. To Jacob, the thick black miasma appeared as light fog with thicker patches bursting forth from the cracked ground.

Without Jacob guiding her, she would have easily fallen into a pit. Jacob nearly tripped into one that yawned open in front of him. The ground was more soot than soil, coming up to his calves and shifting like sand.

Worst of all was the *sound*. Every time the vents that littered the canyon floor poured forth their oily smoke it sounded like a deep guttural roar from within the core of the planet itself. Like some ancient demon was trapped below their feet, straining to break free and the smoke was its breath.

That felt a bit too close to the truth for comfort.

If not for Camilla tugging at him, he would have missed the Pyre. It was coated in the same black soot but to Camilla, it must have been a more noticeable Cairn.

"Thanks," he tried to say, but his words were swallowed by the roar of a nearby vent sending black oily smoke into the air less than three feet away.

Never had Jacob seen a Pyre so near to danger before.

Camilla came around him at the same time as Jacob knelt at the ashes. He brought forth his ruby flame to reignite the Pyre and Kindle it at the same time.

Pyre Ignited.
Your respawn location has been set to the **Smog Rifts**.
The Fire Oppa stokes the embers of your conviction.
Health, Stamina, Ampoules, and Spell Gems restored.
You Kindle the Pyre.

The fire caught in a flash and its blaze pushed back the smoke in a ten-foot radius. The air immediately warmed and smelled cleaner.

What cracks and pits that invaded on the space closed up and the oily soot was turned into floating embers that drifted all around like fireflies.

It was a beautiful sight.

But not more beautiful than the beaming grin of the Fire Oppa or the way his fur seemed to burn white-hot with excitement. Camilla's face brightened and her lips moved but he could make out no words.

She looked so much better than when he found her. No longer gaunt or thin, she filled out with strength and resolve that had been stretched to the breaking before.

It struck him then how disastrous it would have been had she accompanied him into the Desecrated Catacombs. She wasn't strong enough then and, as she said, she had her own battles to fight.

Battles, it would seem, she won.

"Well," Jacob said, removing his helm and grinning at the Fire Oppa. "I said I'd be here."

Stirring a paw idly into the ash, the Fire Oppa didn't immediately look up at Jacob. "I expected you sooner. When you didn't come... I thought maybe you had thought better of your goal.

"After all, you don't need to light this Pyre. Most don't." He looked up, tiny beady black eyes shining. "I am sorry for doubting you. It will be the last time."

Reaching a hand forward, Jacob scooped up the Fire Oppa,

unafraid of the raging flames on his body or the way the tall flames of the Pyre surged when he stuck his hand within.

"I was regrettably detained," he said. "I wanted to come sooner." He jerked his chin toward Camilla who likewise seemed in communion with her version of the Fire Oppa. "Without her help, I would still be locked up."

"I should have known that would be the only way you would have been missing," the Fire Oppa said. He clambered up Jacob's forearm and perched on his shoulder. "Now that you have reignited six Pyres, I can offer you something I have offered none other of your kind."

"What's that?" Jacob asked.

"My Covenant."

Join the Phoenix Covenant?
Yes / No

The Fire Oppa scampered down his arm and into the Pyre. As he dug around in the ash he spoke, "You have the heart of one who would do more than just the right thing because it rewarded them. I have seen in you a sense of justice and righteousness that I find disturbingly lacking in many of your kin.

"You are, of course, under no obligation to accept. But as my gifts are many, you would be foolish to reject the offer out of hand without-"

"I accept," Jacob said, cutting him off.

The Pyre surged with heat. Coronas of white-hot flame encircled Jacob like twisting snakes. They sank into his armor, into his flesh. The heat was almost unbearable as it soaked into his bones.

Peaceful warmth radiated not only from the Pyre, but from *within himself*. The comfort and warmth of the Pyre was *inside* of him.

There was nothing quite like it. Rather than a sensation of peace and much-needed comfort from the Pyre in front of him, he felt a kinship. A bond with it that went deeper than his conscious mind could grasp.

*You join the **Phoenix Covenant**.*

The sole purpose of the Phoenix Covenant is to restore the Flame of Life to all realms from which it has been extinguished. As a member of the Phoenix Covenant, each Pyre you reignite increases your strength within the Covenant and awards a [Vestige of Flame].
You learn the Sorcery: **Flame Blade.**

<u>Flame Blade</u>
Sorcery passed down to those bound by the Phoenix Covenant. Calling forth the purifying flames of the Pyres to mind, you form a simulacrum of their magnificence to coat the weapon of your choice in the cleansing flames. These flames are unlike traditional fire and are exceptionally potent against corruption or dark-based threats.
It is said a piece of the Fire Oppa's soul is given to each of his warriors who vow to protect the Pyres and reignite the Flame of Life. Through the Fire Oppa's gift, even the darkest, coldest realms cannot steal the warmth from his chosen.

Jacob was stunned. He immediately inscribed it upon his second Spell Gem, only slightly concerned that it had a single-use before it needed to be recharged at a Pyre.

Busy reading the prompts, Jacob missed what the Fire Oppa was digging out of the ash. Propped up against the base of the Pyre was the previously broken [Phoenix Tree Crest Shield] Jacob returned to the Fire Oppa.

"I want you to have this," the Fire Oppa said. "It once belonged to a great hero. A Phoenix Knight. I have repaired it and imbued it with a bit of my power. It will guide your way when all other lights fail you."

You gain [Phoenix Tree Crest Shield].

[Phoenix Tree Crest Shield]

A resplendent, large shield with a glowing design of the leafless Phoenix Tree proudly on display.

The damage that was done to this shield has been repaired by the Phoenix Covenant's patron but it still carries the scar of that loss. When Merina the Fearless struck off to the depths of the Desecrated Catacombs to rescue her former mentor, Sir Gailsyn, she never expected to meet her end in those cold, desolate tunnels.

Though she succeeded in sealing the proud knight corrupted by the Gnawing Hunger, she sustained mortal wounds during the encounter. With the Pyres unlit, her journey ended alongside the resting place of the once-great knight. Her only lament was that she could not say goodbye to her dearest friend, Fenris the Fire Oppa. The guilt of her failure soaked the shield, strengthening it against magical attacks but weighing it down with the previous owner's sense of loss.

Phoenix Tree Crest Shield [Unique Shield]

Physical Damage: 92
   Type: Blunt

Balance: 85
   Physical Reduction: 100
   Arcane Reduction: 60
   Fire Reduction: 100
   Water Reduction: 50
   Earth Reduction: 90
   Harmony Reduction: 45
   Chaos Reduction: 45

   DURABILITY: 800/800
   GUILT: 8 (4 if bound by the Phoenix Covenant)

. . .

That was one hell of a shield.

The Guilt nearly made his eyes pop out of their sockets. Even at 8 Guilt, it would be a massive improvement. "Thank you," Jacob said, taking it reverently and immediately replacing his [Kite Shield] with the [Phoenix Tree Crest Shield].

Bound as he was to the Phoenix Covenant, the Guilt was halved but it was still enough to weigh his soul and body down. He would need at least 2 reinforcements of TMP, maybe more depending on how the rounding was done behind-the-scenes, to get back to tier 2 Guilt.

A problem he could remedy by spending some of the Souls Mack and his lackeys were kind enough to offer to him.

He winced a little, remembering how he cut down Alec in cold blood. Even if he was already going to be killed by somebody else, it still felt a little wrong. That single betrayal for the good of all - or so he hoped - had earned him enough Souls to reinforce a parameter.

"It is a shield of fine make," Fenris said. "I take it you understand a part of its history?"

Jacob nodded, feeling a little unsure. The item's description - like most items in Lormar - held an echo of their history. By examining them he could find out information that was normally not possible to know.

"You may call me Fenris if you wish," the Fire Oppa said, bowing forward a little on all four paws. "It is a pleasure to finally make your acquaintance. But that is not all that I have to give to you."

"I'm certainly not going to say no to anything else," Jacob said with a chuckle. Though he had to admit, this had all the hallmarks of a buildup to a devastating boss fight.

Which, he supposed, it was. Getting better gear, reinforcing his parameters, getting special buffs, refilling his spells, and [Cinder Ampoules], was all indicative that he was about to need every last increase to his strength just to survive.

The Pyre's flames shifted from red-orange to an intensely hot blue for a moment and then cooled. Fenris padded alongside the flames, shifting the ashes with his paws into little designs as he went. "Place your hand into the Pyre and think of another whose flames you have lit."

Jacob did as he was instructed. He thought of the Steps of Penance Pyre and to his surprise, the flames shifted to show him a vision of that place. It was from the perspective of the Pyre itself but he could clearly see Brother Aker seated off to the side looking quite bored.

He could feel the connection between himself and that Pyre. The prompt that flashed across his vision only served to confirm his suspicion.

Travel to Steps of Penance Pyre?

A shake of his head was enough to disengage from the spell and he sat back down. The ability to move between Pyres was an incredibly powerful ability.

It changed everything about how he planned to fight the Burgon Beast. Already, a new plan was taking root.

Petting the Fire Oppa, Jacob smiled. "That is amazing, Fenris. Thank you. Is this all because I joined the Phoenix Covenant?"

"Partially," he said, gently pressing his head a little harder into Jacob's palm. Even petting Fenris felt different. Jacob could feel the connection he had to the Fire Oppa, it brought a perpetual smile to his face. "Igniting the Pyres as you have allowed me to offer the Covenant to you. And while it is true, only members of the Phoenix Covenant may travel between Pyres, I still would have offered the shield to you."

"But everything else?"

"Yes, everything else was because you joined the Covenant. I would have thought you understood the importance and strengths of Covenants by now," Fenris said, giving Jacob a knowing look.

After witnessing the lengths the Vile Covenant went to in order to exact their revenge, he certainly did.

What the Phoenix Covenant offered him was worlds beyond what the Vile Covenant did. *And this Covenant I have no intention of betraying.*

"If I'm going to be able to wield this shield, I'll need to reinforce my

Temper quite a bit," Jacob said, his voice taking on a wheedling tone. "There anything you could do to help me with that?"

Fishing for a discount couldn't hurt.

Fenris snorted twin jets of white-hot fire at Jacob's palm. Despite the intensity of the flames, it only tickled. The Fire Oppa turned around and padded back to the Pyre. "Unfortunately, no. I am not running a business. These things have rules, Jacob. Just as I could not offer you a Covenant without you lighting six Pyres, I cannot give you a discount on reinforcing your parameters."

"Ah well," Jacob said, setting the shield to prop up against his helm. "It was worth a try."

In order to equip the [Phoenix Tree Crest Shield], Jacob would need to balance out the extra 3 points of Guilt it carried over that of his [Kite Shield]. The easiest method was to reinforce TMP by 3 points. That way he could keep his [Mace] handy, which he still needed to reinforce and ascend.

Reinforcing TMP 3 points would halve his Souls down to 11,228. He might need to reinforce it a fourth time if, for some reason, it didn't drop him down to tier 2 Guilt. Though it pained him to spend so many Souls at once, he knew it was the right thing to do.

Committing his Souls Jacob immediately felt lighter, free of the oppressive Guilt equipping the [Phoenix Tree Crest Shield] had imposed.

When Jacob put his helm back on and picked up the [Phoenix Tree Crest Shield], however, he noted that it didn't seem to weigh him down any more than the [Kite Shield] did.

[Status]

Jacob Windsor
Covenant: Phoenix
Race: Kemora - Fae-touched (Human/Fairy)
Level: 25
Health: 132
Stamina: 94

Anima: 0
Souls: 11,228
Required Souls: 4,271

Parameters
VIT: 4
AGI: 8
END: 7
TMP: 14
STR: 10
DEX: 10
INT: 8
FTH: 3

Curse: Fractured Sight
Curse Level: 1

Spell Gem: Heat Blade (3/3)
Spell Gem: Flame Blade (1/1)

Just to be sure he didn't need to reinforce TMP again, Jacob got up and walked a tight circle around the Pyre. Camilla looked up at him curiously.

"Just checking something out," Jacob said, answering her unasked question.

It wasn't slowing him down more than the normal 10%, he was sure of it.

Rather than needing to reinforce TMP a fourth time, he could save 4,271 Souls for something else, like STR.

Even with the glut of Souls he recently acquired, it was ridiculously easy to blow through them all without a significant change in parameters. However, each parameter was quite potent.

Simply being able to wear the equipment he was while moving

with only a slight penalty was a massive improvement over his life back on Earth.

Next, Jacob took out his [Mace] and the 9 [Dull Sparks] he needed to reinforce the already upgraded weapon to +10. "I need this upgraded to the maximum."

The Fire Oppa looked at the weapon curiously but said nothing as he took both the [Dull Sparks] and the requisite Souls for each reinforcement. For the first 5 reinforcements, the cost was 500 Souls.

[Equipment Reinforcement]

Mace [Weapon] +1 -> *Mace [Weapon]* +5
   Cost: 2,000 Souls

   Physical Damage: 109 -> 171
   Type: Blunt
   Scaling: STR [B+] -> STR [A+]
   Light Attack: 15 -> 12 Stamina
   Heavy Attack: 40 -> 35 Stamina

   Magical Damage: 0 -> 0
   Arcane: 0 -> 0
   Fire: 0 -> 0
   Water: 0 -> 0
   Earth: 0 -> 0
   Harmony: 0 -> 0
   Chaos: 0 -> 0

   Status Infliction
   Bleed: 10 -> 20
   Poison: 0 -> 0
   Curse: 0 -> 0
   Stagger: 50 -> 70

Break: 30 -> 55

Durability: 450/450 -> 600/600
Guilt: 1 -> 1

"Why didn't you reinforce it the entire way?" Jacob asked.

"The process is a little different beyond the first cap. It will be more expensive as well, give me a moment," Fenris said, gathering the [Dull Sparks] into a specific arrangement around the glowing metal of the [Mace].

[Equipment Reinforcement]

Mace [Weapon] +5 -> Mace [Weapon] +10
   Cost: 3,500 Souls

   Physical Damage: 171 -> 349
   Type: Blunt
   Scaling: STR [A+] -> STR [S]
   Light Attack: 12 -> 10 Stamina
   Heavy Attack: 35 -> 30 Stamina

   Magical Damage: 0 -> 0
   Arcane: 0 -> 0
   Fire: 0 -> 0
   Water: 0 -> 0
   Earth: 0 -> 0
   Harmony: 0 -> 0
   Chaos: 0 -> 0

   Status Infliction
   Bleed: 20 -> 40

Poison: 0 -> 0
Curse: 0 -> 0
Stagger: 70 -> 100
Break: 55 -> 80

Durability: 600/600 -> 975/975
Guilt: 1 -> 1

Jacob's jaw hung open as he watched the Fire Oppa work his magic. Leaping white-hot fire surged through the Pyre and was infused within the metal of the [Mace].

All vestiges of use and wear were stripped away. The metal practically glowed with vitality and power. There was a brief pang of loss as he realized just how much stronger his [Mace +10] was now over his [Longsword].

Unless the creature flat-out resisted blunt based damage, he would never have a reason to use his [Longsword] again. Not until he either upgraded his [Longsword] or similarly found a better weapon.

Only then did he remember that Alec reminded him about a cul-de-sac in Hollow Dreams that might have something for him there. So much had happened that it had entirely slipped his mind.

Even though his [Mace +10] was more than 3 times stronger than his [Longsword], his 76 Sword Skill helped to close the gap. His Mace Skill, in contrast, was barely 26. Somewhere around the low 20's it stopped increasing as fast.

And despite the hefty investment of Souls, sparks, and time, his Stamina drain while using a sword was still slightly less. That wasn't so much of a disappointment as a surprise.

A decade of studying and practicing with a sword had given him an incredible advantage beyond just his knowledge of Pyresouls Online. That he could - within two weeks - have a weapon that he was poorly skilled with equaling the Stamina drain of his sword was astounding.

It made him wonder how much his [Longsword] would benefit from hitting +10.

"Do you have the items for the Ascension?" Fenris asked, pulling Jacob from his thoughts.

"Oh, yes. Sorry. Here you go," Jacob said, taking out the [Minos Horn] and the Vile Priest's Soul.

The [Soul of a Devout Priest] squirmed and shimmered, the dark tear at its core writhed as the Fire Oppa lashed it with shimmering flames from the Pyre. The Soul was chained, bound within the twirling confines of the Pyre's flames, and slowly dragged into the mace that rested at its heart.

As the Fire Oppa drew the Soul deeper into the mace, the [Minos Horn] began to crumble to ash. Motes of purple magical essence floated toward the Fire Oppa. Jacob didn't understand what it was for until he saw the effect the Vile Priest's Soul had on the weapon.

The steel mace bulged and shifted weirdly in a way that no solid thing should be able to. It contorted like a tortured thing. Cracks of light in the metal bled shimmering green that began to draw heat from the Pyre.

For the first time since returning to Lormar, Jacob watched as the Pyre began to flicker as if in a high wind. Unconcerned, the Fire Oppa drew on the purple motes from the [Minos Horn] and sealed the cracks in the weapon.

Every time another appeared, more of the horn broke down into ash and its essence healed the weapon. The Pyre fought against the transformative power of the Soul. When it was over, the core of the Pyre burned so hotly that it was like staring at the sun.

Averting his eyes, Jacob blinked to rid himself of the afterimage.

"It's done," Fenris said. "Reach into the Pyre and claim it."

Jacob leaned in and without looking at the blazing brilliance of the Pyre, wrapped his fingers around the weapon's handle. It felt different.

Lifting it out, metal still glowing like it was freshly removed from the forge, Jacob could see why. It was an entirely different weapon. Instead of a simple leather-wrapped handle and a steel flanged head, it was a work of art.

Grotesque, tentacle-themed art, but beautiful in its own dark way. The handle was long, made of black metal shot through with green threads. From the top of the mace's head erupted several thick tentacles that flowed over the side and halfway down the handle.

They looked remarkably life-like, enough that Jacob was surprised when they didn't move after staring at it for several seconds. Once he was sure it wasn't going to start moving on him, he examined it further.

[Vile Mace]

Weapon created from the [Soul of a Devout Priest] belonging to the Vile Covenant. Within that Soul was the transformative power of the Great Old One, the patron of the Vile Covenant. Those transformative properties have been transferred in part to this weapon, imbuing it with the destructive power of its corruptive origin.

Mace [Weapon] +10 -> *Vile Mace*

Physical Damage: 349 -> 200
Type: Blunt
Scaling: STR [S] -> STR [A], INT [A]
Light Attack: 10 -> 20 Stamina
Heavy Attack: 30 -> 60 Stamina

Magical Damage: 0 -> 200
Arcane: 0 -> 0
Fire: 0 -> 0
Water: 0 -> 0
Earth: 0 -> 0
Harmony: 0 -> 0
Chaos: 0 -> 200

Status Infliction
Bleed: 40 -> 0
Poison: 0 -> 80
 Curse: 0 -> 0

Stagger: 100 -> 100
Break: 80 -> 80
Corrode: 0 -> 500

Durability: 975/975 -> 500/500
Guilt: 1 -> 2

His grumbling brought a curious glance from Camilla who seemed to be watching him with a look of concern. "I need to reinforce my Temper *again*."

Her lips twitched in a knowing smile.

Though the physical damage of the weapon dropped, its overall damage went up, considerably. The doubled Stamina cost was a shock but he had to remind himself that he functionally created a brand new weapon. Secretly, he felt a little better with that huge downside.

As weak as the simple [Longsword] was, it still had a purpose. He could flow from one Form to the next with the [Longsword] but the [Vile Mace] would chew through his Stamina in two to three swings.

There was nothing stopping him from being able to upgrade it further at a later date. And though the damage was now split between physical and magical, it gave him a rare magical type of damage he didn't have before: Chaos.

Not only that, but the weapon could now cause stagger, poison, break, and whatever corrode was. He never heard of it before but the word, combined with the description of the weapon and what he knew of the Great Old One painted a good picture.

With a grumble - glad that he hadn't rested yet after his last parameter reinforcement - Jacob reinforced his TMP by 1, raising it to 15. Immediately he felt the weight of the [Vile Mace] lighten in his grip.

With no more [Dull Sparks] to reinforce anything and only 1,457 Souls to his name, Jacob curled up next to the Fire Oppa and fell into a deep restful sleep.

There was no way to tell the time within the Smog Rifts since it plunged the world into a smoky eternal night, but a glance at his clock showed that it was still September 10th. Though it was later in the day than he would have hoped.

Jacob got to his feet. He shook his head. Over a thousand Souls and there was nothing he could do with them. Already his next parameter reinforcement would cost him 4,581 Souls.

"Are you ready to go, Camilla?" he asked.

The ruby-eyed elven woman eyed his mace apprehensively. "So long as you watch where you're swinging that thing, yes I'm ready."

With one last check to make sure everything was in order, Jacob hefted the [Phoenix Tree Crest Shield] and stepped out into the wall of smoke.

30

"Oh man! Did you see that, Camilla?" Jacob bellowed with a hearty laugh.

You defeat the [Rot Soldier].
Awarded 450 Souls.

That last Rot Soldier went flying, in four different pieces. It wasn't too long until lanky creations of exposed bone and skeleton reared out of the pits around them.

Jacob had managed to convince Camilla to hold off until he could try out his new [Vile Mace]. It was completely, hilariously broken. He could trigger the corrosive effect but it chewed into the durability when he did so, costing 50 durability each use.

He would be able to use its unique ability 10 times before the weapon broke and he would need to repair it. But even without using its special function, it was so heavy that a single-handed swing carried enough power behind it to blast through these strange monsters.

[Vile Mace] swinging with abandon, Jacob laughed gleefully as he blasted apart one bone-and-sinew creature after the next. Some took a few hits but with his new shield he could weather more attacks.

It was an interesting give-and-take. The [Vile Mace] ate up his Stamina like a man dying of thirst while his new [Phoenix Tree Crest Shield] was splendidly efficient with its Stamina usage.

Combined, he was still expending more Stamina by a country mile compared to his sword but he didn't need his high skill here. Raw power, unfortunately, trumped his skillful swordplay when attacking unthinking, fodder-like monsters that didn't parry or dodge.

A Rot Soldier clambered out of a hole in front of the pair as a blast of noxious black fumes erupted from the cracks to either side. Shield raised to fend off any clawing attacks, Jacob rushed the creature and with one mighty swing of his [Vile Mace] crushed its exposed ribs into powder.

It wasn't even fair.

A part of Jacob mourned the loss of his finely-honed skills. It was replaced with brutal strength that while addictive in its own right, was shallow and lacking.

Heat Blade and it's big brother, *Flame Blade* didn't work with the [Vile Mace]. That *Flame Blade* didn't work was unsurprising considering the [Vile Mace] was technically another Covenant's alignment. Naturally, the two didn't play nice.

But *Heat Blade* also didn't work and he could only assume it was due to the already enchanted nature of the weapon.

He didn't need to parry and take advantage of tiny lapses in an opponent's defense.

He could smash aside any defense thrown at him like the breaking tide. A rather fitting mental image considering the empowering Soul's origins.

The next two Rot Soldiers that opposed him were crushed beneath his unrelenting assault. One's skeletal face was crunched down into its chest with a heavy overhand chop, a sloppy rendition of *Hammering the Nail*.

Jacob stepped back, raising his shield to cover the slow backswing of the unwieldy weapon. Two clawing strikes scraped against the shield but he accepted the blows, biding his time to get the [Vile Mace] back under his control.

He would need to reinforce his STR the next chance he got. While he wasn't below any requirements for the [Vile Mace], its power was unwieldy with his current STR. Raising it - or dramatically increasing his Mace Skill - would help him to control the weapon better.

Twisting, Jacob let his body's momentum do most of the work as his tentacle-headed mace whipped around, his arm at full extension. *Breaking Rocks* shattered the creature's upraised arm and shoulder.

Up went his shield to cover the backswing. After two hits and blocking two more, he was almost out of Stamina. While the [Vile Mace] was fun to blast things apart with, a single miss or glancing blow required him to bide his time and recover his Stamina.

With only 94 Stamina, a single light attack of the [Vile Mace] took off nearly a third of his Stamina, 30 total. A heavy attack, on the other hand, consumed double that.

Using Sword Forms and taking proper advantage of any and all openings with his [Longsword], he regularly hit for 300 to 400 damage.

The [Vile Mace's] light attacks did at least that much while dazing the opponent more often than not. And its heavy attack smashed aside any defense arrayed against it, doing nearly 700 damage at once.

Of course, he still needed 20 to 30 points of Stamina to weather the blows of the enemies before him. They hit hard but with the [Phoenix Tree Crest Shield], he came out of the exchange unscathed. Provided he had the Stamina to absorb the damage.

The Rot Soldier crouched like a feral creature and Jacob recognized the first stage of the leaping attack. His [Vile Mace] was far too slow to intercept it... but his [Longsword] was not.

With only 24 Stamina left, Jacob risked lowering his shield and dismissed the [Vile Mace] with a flurry of ash quickly lost in the black smoke. He replaced it as he stepped forward with his [Longsword] in one unbroken motion.

Just as the Rot Soldier pushed off the ground, Jacob was there, sword leading. *Hummingbird's Kiss* took it right in the heart and its springing leap impaled it the rest of the way.

Letting go of the blade, Jacob watched as the creature half-heartedly continued its leap and flopped to the sooty ground. Camilla leaned down with her rusty cleaver and finished it off as he dismissed the [Longsword] and swapped back to the [Vile Mace].

They continued on in much the same fashion. A monster would rear up out of the roaring pits and Jacob would batter it down if there was only one. He didn't have the Stamina to deal with two at once.

That was the major drawback to the powerful weapon. But there was nothing stopping him from swapping weapons after landing a crushing initial blow to finish them off.

Camilla kept her hand on Jacob's back, allowing his enhanced vision, courtesy of the [Ring of Broken Vows], to lead them through the deadly maze. Even with the [Ring of Covetous Breath], he would have been nearly blind in the black smoke that filled the Smog Rifts.

The smoke began to thin somewhat and they came upon their first clearing. Though the miasma was all about them, the blinding - and painful - blasts of noxious oily fumes were blessedly absent. As were their sources, the large cracks in the ground that were more often than not hidden under a layer of soot.

At the center of the clearing were the barest hints of an old structure. Its blackened bones listed dangerously to the side as if the slightest breeze might cause the ancient stones to come tumbling down.

To the side of the structure was a dais upon which a large stone skeletal hand held aloft a black lump of coal. The coal floated an inch or two above the skeletal hand.

Everything about it told Jacob to be wary, the place had all the hallmarks of a boss fight arena. Alarm bells rang in his head but he could find no danger.

Not until he approached it.

The ground suddenly shook with a terrible rumbling. A vicious roar echoed through the smoke, seeming to come from everywhere and nowhere at once. It was met by another roar, this one much closer and to his left.

Jacob barely got his shield up in time to meet the coming rush of the tall demonic creature. Like the Rot Soldiers, it had no skin. Only sinew and bone.

In place of armor, it had an exoskeleton of bony plates overlaid upon the red muscle. Its skeletal head was that of a deer's, complete with broken horns. Red glowing pits of flame flared out from its eye sockets as it chopped down with a large femur fashioned into a club.

The heavy blow numbed Jacob's arm but he managed to keep his footing. Camilla cast a wheel of fire at the thing's back, garnering its attention. Jacob took the momentary lapse in its attention to swing his [Vile Mace].

Breaking Rocks took it in the bone plates along its side, by activating the mace's special ability a thick oozing green sludge coated the Defiler Demon's armor.

Even as Jacob leaped back and out of the way, his Stamina depleting to a thin sliver, the transformative sludge ate away at the bone.

Snapping its attention back to Jacob, the Defiler Demon struck with lightning speed. One, two, three hits crashed into his shield.

The first blasted through what was left of his Stamina after the leap and heavy attack of the mace. Dazed, Jacob was unable to stop the other two blurring strikes.

One came low, and Jacob could only wince at the coming agony. He could see the intelligence in the creature's measured actions. If he couldn't shake the dazed status preventing him from moving he might not survive the assault. His femur was crushed from the blow and stunned as he was, he was knocked off his feet to the side.

Even as he began to fall, the Defiler Demon swung the club around and up high, bringing it down in a fast chop to Jacob's right arm. The bone splintered to dust and he crashed to the ground with a guttural shout of pain.

As he laid there, dazed and reeling he knew there was nothing Camilla could do to stop his impending death.

Expecting the final blow to fall any second, Jacob could only blink in confusion as another ground-shaking roar split the air. The Defiler Demon raised its club up high for the finishing blow and... then it was just *gone*.

The whole chain of events only took a couple of seconds. When

Jacob's dazed effect wore off, he crushed a [Cinder Ampoule] to heal up to full and rolled to his feet looking around in confusion.

"You have *got to be shitting me*," he said as he realized the truth of what happened.

Back in the lowest levels of the Desecrated Catacombs the Skeletal Beast had doggedly pursued Jacob and Kim. His idea to have the Gnawing Hunger and the huge skeleton battle while he slipped in and grabbed the [Ring of Broken Vows] seemed like a bright idea at the time.

But the Gnawing Hunger had quickly bested the usurper and incorporated its bony body into itself. Jacob thought - and hoped - that would be the last he saw of the gruesome thing.

He was very wrong.

The Gnawing Hunger, reared up with the Defiler Demon clamped in its massive jaws, shaking it like a dog would a favorite toy. Jacob cringed, watching parts of the Defiler Demon's body shake free in a spray of gore.

Wasting no time, Jacob rushed to the dais and scooped up the coal in his hand. He pocketed the [Black Ember]. The last item he would need to call the Burgon Beast from its cage.

He turned to Camilla, knowing that the Gnawing Hunger wouldn't be satisfied with just one kill. Wasting precious seconds, Jacob wrenched off the [Ring of Broken Vows] and tossed it to Camilla. "Take this! Get back to the Pyre and continue heading north out of the Smog Rifts. Go west as soon as you can, there will be a dead blackened tree up on a rise. Wait for me there."

Camilla snatched the ring out of the air easily enough then stared curiously at him as she put it on.

When it became clear she was deciding whether or not to heed him or help him in the coming fight, Jacob bellowed, "Go. Now!"

He turned back to the Gnawing Hunger as it was reaching out a bony hand toward him. Jacob rolled to the side, narrowly avoiding the grab but was unable to do anything about the black tendril that separated from the bone and threw him across the clearing.

The force of the throw was staggering. He crashed into a pile of stones and flopped over them as his ribs cracked and his breathing became shallow.

Crushing another [Cinder Ampoule] so he could breathe, Jacob got to his feet. Tightening his grip on his [Vile Mace], he stared down the Gnawing Hunger.

It watched him, prowling on all four limbs as it slowly circled him. Jacob didn't have any time to be sure that Camilla left.

He hoped for her sake she fled into the black smoke. Without either the [Ring of Covetous Breath] or the [Ring of Broken Vows], he had no chance of following her.

But that was a problem for future-Jacob. If, and only if he managed to survive against this horrific thing that didn't understand when it wasn't welcome.

Jacob stared in mounting fear as he saw the Gnawing Hunger... change.

He had a glimpse of it back in the Desecrated Catacombs but now he saw it happen before his very eyes. The black coiling tendrils of the Gnawing Hunger were still there. Angry red eyes opened along the inky black vines that wrapped parts of its newer skeletal frame.

And now there were large bony plates and sinew growing between the bones and black tendrils. Its bare skeletal head grew impressive, wickedly sharp horns draped with the black stringy vines of the Gnawing Hunger.

"What the hell *are you?*"

It answered with a frigid roar that blasted the miasma aside for a full second.

It was long enough for Jacob to slip on the [Ring of Boundless Fury]. He felt the heat of the ring burn him the second he put it on. But there was also a newfound power coursing through his veins.

The Demon rushed at him, attempting to gore him with its large horns. Jacob dodged to the side and came up swinging the [Vile Mace] with both hands at the Demon's ankle.

Bone and sinew cracked beneath the assault but it was not like the other enemies he faced. Its defenses held and Jacob was caught out. Yet as large as the Demon was it couldn't just stop its quarter-ton bulk and swipe at the much smaller Jacob.

That was the only thing that saved him as the Gnawing Hunger struck out at him with a black whipping tendril. The blow staggered him back, taking off a quarter of his Health but otherwise wasn't a crippling attack.

The corrosive effect of his mace ate at the bone and sinew on its ankle, causing the creature to stumble as it turned to face Jacob. Dismissing his shield entirely, Jacob held the [Vile Mace] over his shoulder, poised to strike as soon as the opportunity presented itself.

He had to weaken its defenses. Against the lesser monsters in the Smog Rifts, Jacob's heavy attacks were doing over 700 damage. But against the Gnawing Hunger, he was hardly doing 400 and that was *with* the damage boosting effect of the [Ring of Boundless Fury].

Against a monster so large as the Gnawing Hunger, blocking with anything less than a great shield was worthless. And even then, a single full-force blow would drain his Stamina and leave him dazed.

That wasn't an experience Jacob planned on repeating.

But with the [Vile Mace's] extreme Stamina consumption, it was a losing battle. No matter how careful he was with his Stamina usage, he would only ever have enough to dodge and use a single heavy attack.

And one missed dodge would be the end of it.

Crushing a [Cinder Ampoule] to counteract the Health drain from his [Ring of Boundless Fury], Jacob lunged forward. *Hammering the Nail* caught the Gnawing Hunger in its outstretched hand.

The satisfying sound of cracking bone echoed in the clearing a moment before the monster bellowed and tried to crush Jacob with a coiled up ball of black vines.

Jacob dodged into the Gnawing Hunger, going beneath its rib cage and swung again. He could manage two light attacks and a dodge, with a sliver of Stamina left over.

Without his shield raised, he regenerated Stamina much quicker. He needed every point to deal as much damage as possible.

Most enemies would be restored to full Health upon dying or resting at a Pyre. But Jacob didn't think the Gnawing Hunger was a normal enemy. If it was, it would have been reset like every other monster was when he rested at the Pyre.

It had clearly been following him for a long time. There was no other way to explain how it managed to track him down.

Even though the Defiler Demon had nearly killed Jacob, at least that fight was one he thought he could win. If he died, he would have returned and with a better understanding of the quick creature.

But this? The Gnawing Hunger was unlike anything Jacob ever heard about, let alone faced. Alec never had to fight a boss that *ate other bosses.*

He hoped Camilla was safe.

As the Gnawing Hunger's ribs cracked, black fissures opened in the bone. Sinew was crushed beneath the heavy assault of the [Vile Mace]. The mace's corrosive ooze shriveled muscle and turned sturdy bone into brittle styrofoam.

Finally catching on to Jacob's game, the Gnawing Hunger dropped to the ground, crushing him beneath its bulk.

His body exploded in pain and agony. A ruined hand summoned a [Cinder Ampoule] and crushed it just as the monster lifted off him and prepared to do it again.

Spitting out the blood in his mouth, Jacob got to his feet and swung with all his might as the crushing force of the Gnawing Hunger came down upon him again.

"I can take as much as you can dish out!" he roared in defiance.

The explosive crunch of ribs and sinew splattering filled the clearing. A sizeable crater of crumpled bone and oozing flesh appeared on the creature's chest. Its newly acquired bone plates on that side were practically powder.

But it had crushed Jacob as well. He wasted no time using another [Cinder Ampoule] to get back to his feet.

This time when the Gnawing Hunger came down, Jacob rolled out from beneath it and as the dust blasted out from the crushing attack, he swung again. *Breaking Rocks* took the Gnawing Hunger in the elbow joint, knocking it the wrong way with a sickening pop.

The bare muscle and coiled black vines of the Gnawing Hunger snapped, spraying red blood and black ichor all over Jacob. He tried reversing the strike but the mace was too unwieldy and he didn't have the Stamina for another heavy hit.

So he threw himself back, popping up to his feet just as the ground was split by a splintered bone that broke free from the Demon's forearm. The black vines of the Gnawing Hunger snapped around the broken bone and pulled it back into place, buying Jacob enough time to recover his Stamina.

Wading into the Gnawing Hunger's range again, Jacob twisted and swung with all his might at the wounded elbow. Out popped the bone again, cutting through the vines that flailed in the air like garden hoses with the water pressure on high.

Rolling with the hit, Jacob spent the last of his Stamina to obliterate that free-hanging bone. The sound it made was like a crumbling tower of pottery. Shards of glistening white bone fell free to the ground.

Jacob managed to scoop up three while he was trying to get out of the way with the sliver of Stamina that had regenerated already.

Explosive pain blinded him and he was flying through the air. The Gnawing Hunger snapped its head to the side, sending the blunt sides of its steel-hard horns into Jacob's side.

He hit the ground in a heap of broken bones and internal bleeding. Jacob managed to get another ampoule into him but he was too slow to get to his feet.

On came the Gnawing Hunger, goring him through the middle with one of those streetlamp sized horns.

It thrashed around, and Jacob had to use a quick succession of [Cinder Ampoules] to stay alive through the agony even as the darkness crept closer and closer to the center of his vision.

Abandoning his two-handed grip, Jacob took advantage of his unique position and slammed his mace against the horn stuck through his middle with all his might.

But there was only so much a [Cinder Ampoule] could do while currently impaled. Even as his muscles and organs were healed, they ripped again.

Several heavy hits of the corrosive [Vile Mace] freed Jacob from the horn. Freed from the Gnawing Hunger's head, Jacob fell with the horn still impaled in his middle.

Hitting the ground on his back blasted the broken horn out through the gaping wound. Jacob hurriedly rolled to the side to avoid a follow-up attack and used his last [Cinder Ampoule] to get back to full.

He couldn't help but grin as he wiped the blood from his face.

The Gnawing Hunger was *busted up*. There was no way he could beat it, not without having any idea about how it moved or what its attacks were. But he thought he did a good job for his first attempt.

One side of the thing's head was cracked and bits of its skull was missing. The horn on its right side was entirely gone, broken off at the base, and still glistening with Jacob's blood just a few feet away.

Several more of its bones were heavily cracked and it was clear from their fight that the Gnawing Hunger's black vine-like body was being used more to hold its body together than to defend it or attack.

The black whipping tendrils had stopped coming at him as he continued to beat on the monster. A puddle of gore dripped from the thing's chest as it turned to charge at Jacob.

Raising the [Vile Mace] high, grinning through blood-stained teeth, Jacob roared in reply and met the charge head-on. At the last moment before he was gored - again - Jacob dove forward and tucked his shoulder into a tight roll until he was beneath the creature.

He broke to the side and swung with all his might into the Gnawing Hunger's leading and broken forearm. Black ichor sprayed as he crushed through the tendrils protecting the bone and shattered what was left below.

At that instant his hands felt suddenly empty as his [Vile mace] vanished into a puff of ash, broken. That second of confusion was instantly seized by the Gnawing Hunger. Though its forearm could no longer hold it up.

Rather than fight against it, the monster leaned into the fall, rolling right over Jacob and crushing the life out of him in the process.

You Died.

Dying was never something that a person could get used to. Jacob bolted up into the sitting position, reaching out for the [Vile Mace] that would not heed his call.

It took a moment for his mind to catch up to the warm, soothing sensation of the Pyre. To recognize he was safe.

"Well, that's four grand of Souls I'm never getting back." He pulled out the [Black Ember] and studied it. "At least I have what I came here for."

It looked no different than any other lump of coal. Perhaps a little more spherical than was normal.

The more he studied it, however, the more he noticed. There was a subtle aphotic property to it that sucked in the light around it.

The Pyre's light seemed diminished when he held up the ember. Not liking the implications of that, Jacob stuffed it away. If he was going to take advantage of his death putting some distance between himself and the Gnawing Hunger, he would need to get a move on.

"I need these repaired really quic-" Jacob started then cursed.

"Mhm," the Fire Oppa said sympathetically.

Without his Souls, he couldn't repair his [Vile Mace] or his armor.

"You better get going," Fenris reminded him. "Your new playmate is looking for you. And here, Camilla left this for you." From within the ashes of the Pyre, the Fire Oppa dug out a familiar ring. He scooped up the [Ring of Broken Vows], replacing the dulled burn of the [Ring of Boundless Fury].

He gave the Fire Oppa an affectionate pet then hopped up to his feet.

"At least Camilla made it out." Summoning his [Longsword] and [Phoenix Tree Crest Shield], Jacob cast one look back at the Fire Oppa. "This should all be over soon."

The look Fenris gave him didn't seem so sure.

31

Jacob ran into a lone Rot Soldier on his way out of the Smog Rifts, but the experience was enough that he was no longer sure of the [Vile Mace's] supremacy.

When Jacob used his [Longsword], he sipped his Stamina, leaving more than enough to absorb a heavy blow or dodge aside if he needed. While it did take considerably more hits to down a Rot Soldier, he could still pinpoint their weak spots and exploit them, increasing his damage.

Using his well-known Sword Forms, his [Longsword] was capable of dealing an average of 350 to the Rot Soldiers. About half of what the [Vile Mace] could do with a heavy attack.

But Jacob could execute three such Sword Forms with just enough Stamina left over to absorb an attack with his shield raised. True, one or two hits of his [Vile Mace] was slightly faster, but if another Rot Soldier appeared he couldn't deal with it without swapping to his sword.

After he factored in the cost of having to recover his Stamina after two hits with the [Vile Mace], one light and one heavy, he was fairly sure it came to a wash.

In the time it took him to swing the [Vile Mace] twice he could flow from *Moon Crests the Horizon* to *Lightning Cracks Stone* then reverse to *Wind Parts the Grass*.

All three Sword Forms combined consumed less than the staggering 90 Stamina those two mace strikes cost.

Now that he had some Souls, he would repair the [Vile Mace] but keep it in reserve for stronger monsters. Like the Burgon Beast.

From what Alec told him, there was a single Pyre at Journey's End to the west. That Pyre was in front of the Burgon Beast's cage and it was the first one the monstrosity would attack.

With less than a tenth of the Souls he had on him, Jacob would have just enough to repair his [Vile Mace] and probably his [Knight's Armor]. Having a gaping hole in the middle invited an uncomfortable breeze across his stomach as he hurried through the narrow canyon to the west.

He pulled up short when he came to a raised section of the canyon with a charred black tree. It was a marker Alec had told him about. Behind that tree, he would find a dead mage with another [Spell Gem] and a Sorcerous set of armor.

But where was Camilla?

The woman stepped out from behind the wide tree, wearing a set of flowing black robes hemmed in gold. They were tattered in such a way as to give the appearance of rolling smoke.

Camilla kept the cowl down, electing instead to keep her floppy black hat on. She did a little twirl, the ruffled edges of gold caught the perpetually wan light of Lormar and glittered like the scales of a fish leaping out of the water.

Jacob was glad the visor of his helm kept him from spoiling the mood with his goofy grin. "Looks good. I take it you found the Spell Gem?"

She started at that and put a hand to her mouth, letting a slight gasp escape her lips.

Before she could say anything, Jacob continued shaking his head. "Don't worry. It would suit you better than me." He looked up and down her. The robes looked good on her, they flowed and fluttered with the perpetual breeze caught in the canyon.

"Are you ready?" he asked. "You can still back out if you want," he reminded her.

Camilla raised two fingers. "Twice now I've left you alone. The first because I chose to, the second because you asked me. And twice you have died. To the same monster no less. I think you need me."

Jacob couldn't argue with that, nor did he want to. He would more than gladly accept the help. He was going to need it.

Together they walked the few yards to the west where the canyon floor suddenly dropped out.

Journey's End was aptly named. The way down was a sheer slope with no discernible handholds. One more step and they would descend into the deepest part of the canyon below with no conventional way back.

"Wait," Jacob said.

Rolling her eyes, Camilla turned to him. "Yes?"

"Will you be able to get back up here?"

"I have my ways," she assured him. Then, before he could say anything else, she took a step forward and slid down the steeply sloped stone.

It was a long way down. Jacob wasn't afraid of heights, but he also wasn't confident enough to stand going down a quarter-mile-long ancient slide made out of smooth stone.

Sitting at the very edge, his legs dangling over onto the slope, Jacob gave a little push and went sliding.

By the time he came to the end, Jacob's fear had abated. It was almost fun. The rush of air that flew past him was exhilarating even though it reminded him of the hole in his armor.

For a brief moment, nothing was coming to kill him - not in that immediate vicinity at least - and he could see the end of his goal in sight.

Bracing for the impact he knew was coming, Jacob hit the bottom of the canyon floor going much faster than he would have liked. He pitched forward and committed to the motion, tucking his shoulder and expending the energy of the impact into three somersaults.

He popped up to his feet and looked to the side to find Camilla staring wide-eyed at what lay before them.

Journey's End

Journey's End was not filled with monsters, tight winding corridors, rooms filled with deadly traps, or impassable terrain like everywhere else.

It was filled with graves.

Everywhere they looked there were grave markers, ancient and rotting. Nothing grew, there was no greenery down in Journey's End. No life.

"It's... barren," Camilla said looking around. Like Jacob, she was on guard.

"Nothing but death," Jacob agreed, tightening his grip on his sword. He hoped he had enough Souls to fully repair the [Vile Mace] for his fight with the Burgon Beast.

With only ten charges for its corrosive attack, he would need to save every one of those hits for the savage monster that caused so much death and destruction.

The canyon narrowed considerably as they pressed on. Its walls were so high that they were plunged into darkness soon after entering Journey's End.

"Whoever's job it was to dispose of the bodies had apparently stopped caring," Jacob pointed out, as they stepped around towering obelisks cracked and worn with age.

"Or there were simply too many bodies to properly inter," Camilla pointed out, motioning to a nearby crevice like one of those in the Smog Rifts. The only difference was, instead of smoke it contained an untold number of corpses.

"It feels like the ground is made up of more bones than earth."

"Ever has that been the way when the fires fade and death comes for all," Camilla said, striding forward. Though she kept well away from the dead-filled pits that seemed to grow in number with every step, she no longer seemed wary.

"Have you seen this before?" Jacob asked, eyeing the nearest corpse pit with concern. He *swore* something just moved.

"More than I would like. I came here, hoping to find answers. And instead, all I find are the dead."

"Camilla, they're moving," Jacob warned, pointing his blade at the nearest pit not more than ten feet away. The bodies inside were slowly writhing as if their presence awakened them.

"Leave them be," she said. "They are unable to leave their tombs, mind your step and they will be unable to harm you."

Jacob nodded and fell into step beside her. Despite her words, he continued to scan around, keeping the pits in his sights. Camilla was right, their presence did seem to cause the dead to awaken.

Try as they might, something stopped them from climbing out. It was as if the whole morass of limbs and withered flesh was too entangled for any one body to escape.

Camilla stopped just ahead of him and Jacob looked around, curious as to why she stopped. His eyes fell upon the sight immediately and he knew that their path was at its end.

Ahead, the black earthy soil flattened out without a single grave marker leading to the end of the canyon. The path was littered with rusting swords, broken shields, tall spears with tattered, muted banners flapping in the breeze, and all manner of armament known to man.

It was a graveyard of a different sort. One for the men and women who went to meet a challenge and failed.

Set within the far canyon wall was a massive black metal door several stories high and thirty feet wide. The cluster of broken and rusted weapons was thickest at the base of that door. And right in front of the door was the telltale ash of an unlit Pyre.

The path leading straight to the door was just as wide. Its sides sloped down to two gargantuan pits of death to either side. Even from where they stood, Jacob could see the claw marks of those who had tried to climb up and failed.

Even now, there were desiccated limbs reaching from the deepest reaches trying - and failing - to climb back up to the path.

If either of them slipped from the weapon-strewn earthen path ahead they wouldn't be coming out again.

"Are you ready?" Camilla asked Jacob.

In the face of such a simple question, he nearly broke down. The enormity of what he was doing finally slammed home.

Of course I'm not ready! If Alec couldn't do this what chance do I have?

He wasn't strong enough. Alec was so much stronger than he was when he faced the Burgon Beast and by his own admission, he never stood a chance against the thing.

Even with little more than 2 days remaining, Jacob realized he couldn't trust the original timetable. What if something he did caused Alec - or somebody else - to reach the Burgon Beast sooner?

He was out of options and out of time. It would be too much good fortune to wait and hope that Alice pulled him out of the machine. At least then he could ask for the precise date of the Collapse.

Maybe he had two days of grinding to do, or maybe somebody was an hour away from opening the Burgon Beast's cage.

He cursed the Vile Covenant, and he cursed himself for being so reckless. He had allowed his emotions to cloud his better judgment and paid the price. If he alone suffered the consequences, he could live with that.

But his hatred had allowed events to spiral out of control. Days were lost that could have been spent gaining Souls and finding better equipment.

What sat heaviest on his soul was knowing that if he failed, billions of innocent lives would pay the price.

Once again, he was glad to have his helm covering his terrified expression. He nodded at Camilla, not trusting his voice to stay firm.

It was really happening.

He was going to face the Burgon Beast. The creature that started the Collapse and doomed billions to a fate worse than death.

Camilla set out ahead of him, but Jacob was quick to join her stride-for-stride. His resolve firmed with every broken blade they passed. Every rusted helmet or discarded gauntlet from ages long past.

By the time they reached the Pyre in front of that looming gate of black, Jacob was ready to fight.

Pyre Ignited.
*Your respawn location has been set to **Journey's End**.*
The Fire Oppa stokes the embers of your conviction.
Health, Stamina, Ampoules, and Spell Gems restored.
You Kindle the Pyre.

"So, you're here," Fenris said, padding forward into Jacob's lap.

"Think you can repair this?" Jacob asked, getting out his [Repair Kit] and the broken [Vile Mace].

"You've got the Souls for it," the Fire Oppa said, turning to trot back to the Pyre and leap into the [Repair Box] with the mace.

A few bright flares of green fire broke free from the gap in the wooden box and the deed was done.

Having it fully restored normally would have been a pain. And though Jacob had no intention of staying, he didn't want to be running all over Lormar looking for a merchant that could repair his stuff.

Not to mention, even at a cost of 300 Souls for the full repair it was still cheaper. Jacob put the rest of his damaged armor into the box, with only 150 Souls left he didn't have the ability to repair everything to full. So he chose to repair everything he could up to at least 50% durability, including his [Longsword].

Soulless, Jacob reached out and pet the Fire Oppa one last time. "I have an idea but I'll need your help," Jacob said. "I don't know how much you can assist-"

"I cannot help you directly fight the Burgon Beast," Fenris said, though his eyes suggested there was more to his words than he could say.

"Are you bound by some law or rule that prevents you from helping?"

"You already know the answer."

"But you can help indirectly."

"In any way I can," the Fire Oppa said, his fiery fur burning brighter.

Jacob turned to Camilla. "Can you move between your Cairns?"

"Of course, do you take me for an initiate?" came her acerbic reply. She colored and ducked her head, softening her tone, "Yes, I can. Why?"

"Bind yourself at another Cairn, one that is farthest away from here." Then, on a whim, Jacob added the Pyres he had ignited so she would avoid them, hoping that his theory about the Burgon Beast was correct. "Meet back here when you're done."

He had no idea if it would destroy every Pyre in Lormar or if it specifically followed his path. In the end, it didn't much matter.

If Camilla had a Cairn that was as far away from this one as possible while not being one of those that he listed then perhaps she stood a chance. He had no idea what would happen to her if the Cairn she bound to was destroyed.

He didn't think she would wake up safe and sound like the millions of players in Pyresouls Online. That safety wouldn't last for long, he knew.

"Take me to the Razor Pass Pyre." As the words left Jacob's mouth, the flames of the Pyre swirled and expanded to consume Jacob in their twisting brilliance.

When the flames receded he was sitting at a much smaller Pyre than he remembered, its flames burning lower and cooler. *Oh right, this was the first Pyre I ever lit. I didn't know how to Kindle... not that I really understand it now.*

Even as he put his cupped palms together, he didn't know how he willed the ruby flame into them. Or how it empowered the Pyre that suddenly leaped with strength and heat.

You Kindle the Pyre.

The Fire Oppa appeared within the flames and looked curiously at him. "Why are we back here?"

Jacob knelt by the Pyre and placed his hand within the warm embrace of the flames.

> *Your respawn location has been set to the **Razor Pass**.*
> *The Fire Oppa stokes the embers of your conviction.*
> *Health, Stamina, Ampoules, and Spell Gems restored.*

"If I told you my theory of the Burgon Beast, could you tell me whether or not it was true?" Jacob asked, already guessing at the answer.

When Fenris shook his fiery, furry head, Jacob was hardly surprised.

"Just as I thought."

"What about a simple question? Like, 'will the Burgon Beast kill me?'"

"It will."

"Can the Burgon Beast jump from Pyre to Pyre?" he asked.

The Fire Oppa tried to make a motion but seemed unable to. Instead, he remained silent.

"So much for that theory," Jacob said with a snort.

He was hoping that he could find a loophole around whatever binding magic that was placed on Fenris. Clearly, the Fire Oppa had some sort of rules he had to obey.

Rules so powerful that he couldn't even openly explain them or talk about them. Asking him questions when the poor thing desperately wanted to provide an answer but couldn't, was torturous and cruel to Fenris.

It wouldn't even work since the Fire Oppa couldn't reply to him in any way. It wasn't like he could use his silence as an answer in itself since every answer regarding anything regarding the Burgon Beast the Fire Oppa was asked presented the same silent response.

With a shrug, Jacob had the Fire Oppa take him back to Journey's End.

Camilla was there waiting for him.

Jacob had meant to offer the Fire Oppa one final pet, but the furry - and incredibly fast - creature zipped up his arm and onto Jacob's armored chest.

He gave the tiny thing a soft squeeze and could feel the Fire Oppa's warmth radiate into his armor and within. That connection, the answering heat of his own soul felt empowered.

"Good luck," Fenris said, slinking back to the flames.

Switching to his [Vile Mace], Jacob stood and glanced at Camilla, then the gate. "Are you ready?" he asked her.

"Probably not," she answered truthfully with a shrug of her shoulders. The gold-edged robes shifted with the motion.

Taking a deep breath, Jacob removed the [Black Ember] from his inventory and dropped it into the Pyre. The Pyre immediately turned black, just as Alec said it would.

"Let's kill us a beast," Jacob said with more resolve than he felt.

The flames flared and climbed higher, higher, until they were fifty feet tall. As tall as the door in front of them. The prison of the Burgon Beast. Black flames crackled and sparked with purple arcs of magic as the curling fire thinned.

As it did, it stretched out toward the door, inexorably slow. Once it touched the base of the door, sigils and markings carved into it began to glow with red-orange heat.

Hidden to the naked eye until that point, Jacob recognized a few of the symbols as extremely powerful wardings and protections. The fire climbed up the gate, lighting symbols along the way and somehow darkening the world around them.

Stormclouds gathered overhead, rumbling with thunder. Angry forks of stabbing lightning rent the air. The hair on the back of Jacob's neck stood on end just as the black door swung open, split down the middle by the black flame.

The gust of fetid wind that rushed toward them nearly guttered the Pyre. The Fire Oppa gave a squeal of pain and Jacob had to dig in his heels to prevent being blown back. The sound of the Fire Oppa in pain redoubled Jacob's resolve and stoked his anger.

Camilla slapped a hand to the top of her hat, holding the flopping brim to her head. "I'm not so sure about this anymore!" Camilla cried over the roar of the wind.

Swapping his [Vile Mace] in place of his [Longsword], Jacob turned to her and said, "Me neither."

32

As the foul wind abated, Jacob slipped on the burning [Ring of Boundless Fury]. He already knew he was going to die. What was important was to take as much of the Burgon Beast's Health off with each revival.

If they were wrong about their theory of the Burgon Beast, then humanity stood no chance. There was no way anybody was strong enough to stand against the Burgon Beast when it could destroy the Pyre you used to rest at.

That had been Alec's fatal mistake. One he made clear to Jacob. It was why Jacob had bound himself to the Razor Pass Pyre. From there, he could move to the next Pyre in line and strike again at the Burgon Beast.

If he was correct.

Health burning away, Jacob took a step forward ahead of Camilla. The roar that echoed off the canyon walls did not come from the black depths beyond the gates ahead.

It came from behind.

"You have *got* to be kidding me!" Jacob groaned.

As he turned around, Camilla put a hand on his shoulder. "I have seen how you fare with this creature. I had hoped to help you in your struggle against the Burgon Beast... allow me to lend my aid by making sure your fight stays uninterrupted."

With that, she strode off toward the pits of bodies where the Gnawing Hunger was gaining ground toward them.

A dark furry form, a wolf more than twice Jacob's height and several times that in length strode out of the gates. Its black fur sucked what little light there was from the Pyre and darkened the space around it as it padded forward.

It made no sound. No growl. No roar of challenge.

As the Burgon Beast's yellow gaze met Jacob's, it almost seemed... sad to see him. It looked about, recognizing where it was, and then looked forlornly at a set of armor between Jacob and it.

It must have been beautiful and gleaming once, but now it was rusted through with tarnished silver and corroded gold accents. The shield was broken into several pieces, the helm split, but a many-notched and partially rusted sword was stabbed into the dirt beside it.

Despite the damage to the blade, the hilt was free of the ravages of time. A red jewel gleamed in the pommel, shimmering like a droplet of blood in the light from the Pyre.

The resemblance to the Gnawing Hunger was there but... twisted. This creature did not have vines of black like Alec said or a multitude of eyes. Nor did it have the unbridled hatred he remembered hearing about so often.

Jacob walked out to meet it, keeping his shield ready, and a tight grip on his mace as he watched for any hint of an attack.

The Burgon Beast stopped and took a deep breath. It lifted its head to the stormy heavens, howling. The sound carried strangely within the tight confines of the canyon, doubling and reverberating until it sounded like a pack of wolves all howling out of sync.

It was a mournful sound, filled with sadness and regret.

As the sound hit him, Jacob staggered as if hit by a physical blow. He felt something deep within himself give way and tear. Fear rose like bile in the back of his throat, and before Jacob's eyes, the Burgon Beast changed.

The [Burgon Beast] *has afflicted you with* **Soulworn.**
Untethered and withered, your soul is incapable of binding to another Pyre.

It seemed to do a lot more than that.

Soulworn, that's the debuff Alec still has ten years later... is this what Alec feels every day?

The Burgon Beast's sad, yellow eyes were consumed in crimson hellfire. It opened its maw to thump the air with a bassy snarl, revealing its gleaming dagger-sized teeth.

The Beast's head contorted, and more burning eyes grew in a circle around its fanged maw. Its lower jaw split into two, revealing a barbed black tongue that lashed at the air.

Black ichor dripped off its greasy hide, splattering the ground with dark filth. Shadowy tendrils curled across its form like black flame as it charged at Jacob with startling speed.

He only just managed to raise his [Phoenix Tree Crest Shield] in time to absorb the blow. All but a single point of his Stamina was wiped out in that opening attack. The black, shadowy stuff that persisted after the strike chilled his bones and burned like dry ice, taking off a third of his Health.

His ring constantly sipped at his dwindling Health, burning steadily like a slow fuse.

Without any Stamina to counter-attack, Jacob circled the rebounded creature as it shook away the dizziness from the blow. Considering the size of the thing, he was surprised it didn't knock him down entirely.

The glow from his shield's crest flickered and dimmed momentarily before flaring once more. Dropping his shield to regenerate his Stamina faster, Jacob studied the creature's sudden monstrous changes.

It seemed... wounded. Even as it was empowered, the creature appeared to suffer from it.

His brief sympathy for the beast vanished in a moment when it bared its teeth again and lunged at him. It was a simple, straightforward attack. One that Jacob quick-stepped back and raised his shield to fend off the glancing blow.

This time only a quarter of his Stamina was taken and a fraction of his Health. As he stepped back, Jacob swung his arm back and up in an underhanded swing. Activating the [Vile Mace's] corrosive heavy attack, Jacob struck with all his might into the Burgon Beast's ribs as it passed by.

He heard a satisfying *crack,* and the creature's fur was splashed with the corrosive ooze.

It also left Jacob with only a little more than 10% Stamina. As he let the green bar fill back up, he watched as the Burgon Beast landed awkwardly from the unsuspecting counter.

Black fur disintegrated where the ooze had touched to reveal sizzling skin that was eaten away by the attack. Growling away the pain, the Burgon Beast came on again. It leaped to the side, pivoted, then jumped at Jacob again from an entirely different angle than he expected.

Those gleaming dagger-point teeth clamped down hard on his shoulder and thrashed him about. Luckily, his armor ripped before the Burgon Beast could get a deadly hold on him, and he was thrown to the side, toward the opened black doors.

Jacob hit the ground hard, the breath blasted from his lungs. His arm was broken from the brief attack and likely dislocated as well from the waves of intense agony-laced nausea that assaulted him every time he rolled across the ground.

Spears rotted with age, rusted metal helms, and corroded shields broke or scattered as he crashed through them. Before he fetched up against that sword the Burgon Beast had looked at earlier, Jacob had his shield dismissed and summoned a [Cinder Ampoule].

Just one bite had severely damaged his armor, and taken off more than three-quarters of his Health. He could hardly block a full-on attack; it tanked his Stamina. And because of its elemental damage, it still hurt him.

But the Burgon Beast was so fast that dodging it was almost impossible.

With hardly the time to crush it and resummon his shield, Jacob rolled to the side to avoid the worst of the Burgon Beast's next charge.

The beast snarled. Its low, guttural aggression turned to a surprised yelp of pain. The Burgon Beast swerved to the opposite side of Jacob, suddenly very keen on avoiding him.

Curious, Jacob looked over his shoulder, knowing full well the Burgon Beast wasn't scared of him. The blood-red jewel set into the pommel of the sword glinted maliciously in the dim light.

Getting to his feet, he looked at the sword then the Burgon Beast. Head low, ears back with a low growl, the Burgon Beast circled Jacob looking for an opportunity to strike.

Jacob circled in the opposite direction, keeping that sword and the broken, tarnished armor between him and the Burgon Beast.

Growing upset, the beast leaped to the side only for Jacob to mirror its motion to keep the anchor point of that sword between them.

Jacob stepped up to the sword and reached out with his shield hand. As soon as he got close to the blade, the Burgon Beast snarled, whimpered, and whined while it came forward as if compelled to stop Jacob at any cost.

Taking his hand back, Jacob took several steps away. The Burgon Beast mirrored his movements, but only too late did Jacob see that it wasn't precisely mirroring them. Instead, it was tamping down its rear paws for a springing attack.

It might fear the sword or have some connection to it that prevented it from getting too near, but there was nothing Jacob could do to stop it from sailing *over* the weapon.

Jacob raised his shield awkwardly as the Burgon Beast arced through the air and landed hard on his chest, bearing him to the ground. He managed to wedge his glowing shield into the beast's maw as it thrashed around with all its might.

Metal groaned and squealed. Sparks flashed as the beast's teeth grated across the shield like nails on a chalkboard. With all his might, Jacob struck out with the [Vile Mace] while triggering its corrosive attack.

Its breath was almost enough to knock Jacob unconscious, the stench was so overpowering. Only then did he remember that Camilla still had his [Ring of Covetous Breath].

He grunted and struggled, somehow managing to keep the shield wedged just right between the crunching maw that the beast's lower jaws didn't bite his arm off. As Jacob was shaken from side to side, he struck out with his [Vile Mace] again and again as much as his Stamina allowed.

Four strikes and the creature's lower-left jaw cracked and broke free. Howling with pain, the Burgon Beast released Jacob's shield and staggered back, dripping thick streams of oily black ichor.

Sensing a brief reprieve, Jacob quickly crushed another [Cinder Ampoule] and shakily rose to his feet. The beast didn't give Jacob much time to recover. Still bleeding, it lashed its long, barbed tongue out at him.

Instinctively, he raised his shield to block it. That was just what the Burgon Beast was looking for.

Before Jacob could realize what was happening, the Burgon Beast's long black tongue wrapped around the shield and yanked it from Jacob's grasp, swallowing it whole.

Fiery heat burned the beast's throat, but it remained undaunted by the pain. Black oily smoke flooded from its mouth, its neck glowed from the heat of the shield as it was swallowed.

Anger welled up in Jacob at the loss of the Fire Oppa's symbol, and he came forward in a sudden rush, swinging his [Vile Mace] two-handed. Left, right, went his massive haymaker swings with the mace.

The force of the blows was so severe that most of the Burgon Beast's snout was shattered. It looked even more alien and distorted than before. Its long black and barbed tongue lolled out of the ruined mess.

Belching black smoke at Jacob's face bought the Burgon Beast some time as Jacob retched and staggered about.

*You are **Poisoned**.*

The toxic fumes seared his throat and lungs. Shifting his mace to one hand, he drew out a vial of [Gekk Blood], lifted his visor, and drank the sickly sweet drink.

His Health immediately stopped its freefall from the poison, and he pushed it back up to full with another ampoule crushed in his hand. The mote of cinder rushed through his body, empowering his ability to regenerate and ridding him of his wounds.

Off to the side, a large column of fire lit up the canyon, then another, and another. The three columns were whipped up into towering twisters of flame that caged the Gnawing Hunger.

For all her magical prowess, it seemed Camilla was struggling to contain the creature that had, unbeknownst to him, stalked him for so long. A gurgling snarl reminded Jacob he had his own problems.

Without a shield, Jacob was even more vulnerable than before, *and* he had allowed himself to get distracted. For all the damage he dealt to the Burgon Beast, it was still standing.

And now it was mad.

The Burgon Beast lashed its barbed tongue again, cracking the air like a whip. Jacob dove forward and to the side, feeling the sharp spines dig a gouge across his back. He let out a strangled cry of pain but kept his wits about him to complete the roll.

Up he came, two hands on the [Vile Mace] mid-swing as he put his leading foot beneath him and rose to full height. The arcing swing caught the Burgon Beast on its foreleg, right where it connected to the body.

A distorted cry of pain accompanied the crack of bone. The Burgon Beast twisted away but stumbled when it put weight on that leg. A twist of Jacob's hips brought the tentacled mace around for a heavy follow-up strike.

The Burgon Beast crashed into the ground with the force of the second attack. Its bloodied pulp of a maw hit the dirt hard enough to stun it momentarily. It took Jacob a moment to recognize what he did.

He managed to break the Burgon Beast's balance. By hitting hard enough, often at opportune moments, an enemy could be staggered. The brief window afforded could allow significant damage to be racked up while the opponent was unable to defend themselves.

Jacob wailed on it with the [Vile Mace], using its corrosive ability to eat away at the Burgon Beast's left foreleg. It wouldn't be enough to kill it, but if he could cripple it, maybe he would increase his chances.

Even though he was expecting it, Jacob still started with surprise when the [Vile Mace] broke in his hands on that last swing. He dismissed it, and rather than call for his [Longsword], he stepped back and drew out the sword with the blood-red jewel in its pommel.

The blade the Burgon Beast feared. A blade that Alec never spoke of, and for all intents and purposes, did not seem to exist. He soon understood why.

You gain [Duskblade].

Immediately, Jacob was assaulted by the Guilt of its former owner. Their failure that doomed so many. Paralyzed, Jacob managed to draw it from the ground, but the blade was so *heavy*.

As he pulled the sword free, he saw a dozen shadowy copies of the blade shatter and evaporate as if he had just removed the sword across all other shards.

Was it a trap? The weapon held too much Guilt for Jacob to move properly.

The Burgon Beast shook itself from its stupor and let out a wet snarl at Jacob, the beast's red eyes flared as it lunged at him.

Jacob dove forward, but every movement was weighed down and sluggish. Like Sal back on Earth, he "fat-rolled" with all the grace and speed of an overweight cow. The Burgon Beast clipped him as he attempted the roll and nearly tore his helmet from his head.

The visor was ripped off and left hanging on one side. Jacob's ears rang from the gonging sound the impact had made. Taking another [Cinder Ampoule], Jacob raised the blade to fend off the creature while he regained his senses.

There was strength in it that surpassed his [Longsword] by many orders of magnitude. But he wasn't sure he could bring it to bear. Not moving as slowly as he was, and ridding himself of his currently bound equipment would take longer than he had.

You already knew you were going to die, Jacob reminded himself. Except, he didn't think it would happen because he was overburdened.

Behind the Burgon Beast, Jacob saw Gnawing Hunger rear up and smash a hand down on Camilla's dark form. She darted aside just in time to avoid the worst of it but cried out as her leg was pinned below its bony hand.

Even without being so heavily burdened, Jacob could never make it to Camilla's side to help her. He watched in helpless agony as she was plucked from the ground and thrown into the wall of the canyon.

Right over the sloping pit of the dead.

"Camilla!" Jacob cried out. He lost sight of her as the Burgon Beast came at him again, warily regarding the sword Jacob tried to wave in front of himself.

Green eyes darting between the advancing Burgon Beast and looking for Camilla, he backed away slowly to buy himself some time.

He spotted Camilla amid the clawing dead. A tide of bodies pulled her down into their midst. She fought against them and, for a moment, seemed to be able to climb out.

Instead of saving herself, she shot an apologetic look Jacob's way and snapped her right arm out at the Gnawing Hunger. A whip of flame surged forth from her outstretched arm and wrapped around the creature's throat.

The whip scorched the exposed bone and burnt what little flesh remained to ash. As Camilla was dragged beneath the thousands of grasping dead, the line of fire tightened and pulled the Gnawing Hunger along.

Claw and scrape as the mighty creature did, it could not break the hold of Camilla's last act. The spell didn't fade or waver. As Camilla vanished from sight, the Gnawing Hunger was pulled down into the pit as well, shrieking and raking large furrows in the earth with its skeletal fingers.

That gave Jacob an idea. Possibly the only one he could think of to turn the tide in his favor. He swapped the [Duskblade] to his left hand. The weight of the blade's Guilt was already dipping the tip of the blade toward the earth.

Quickly, Jacob summoned his [Longsword] to his right hand. He was no good at dual-wielding, but that wasn't the point.

Reversing his grip on the [Duskblade], Jacob kept the weapon held high. The Burgon Beast's baleful eyes followed it with a single-minded concern. A concern that Jacob was all too happy to exploit.

The [Duskblade's] notched and rusted edge glinted in the light of the Pyre, Jacob stalked the Burgon Beast. While the wounded monster was focused on the [Duskblade], Jacob tightened his grip on the [Longsword] in his right hand.

With his increased Stamina usage from the higher Guilt and his sluggish movements, there was no way he could keep this up. Just holding the [Duskblade] aloft to draw the beast's attention to it was slowly draining his Stamina.

Only the Burgon Beast's apprehension regarding the [Duskblade] kept it at bay, but already the effect was diminishing. The recognition began to fade from the Burgon Beast's eyes as if something else was controlling it, forcing it to forget the cause of its fear.

He had to strike before it wore off completely.

Jacob bellowed and charged. He stabbed down with the [Duskblade] at an angle, driving the Burgon Beast to Jacob's right. Halfway through the feint, Jacob pulled back to stop the blade from hitting the ground where there would predictably be nothing.

The Burgon Beast's fear of the [Duskblade] placed it in the perfect position for his true attack. One he could never make as slow as he was without the Burgon Beast otherwise occupied. With his right hand poised, Jacob quick-stepped to line up with the Burgon Beast's flank.

Hummingbird's Kiss took the monster right in the flank. While it was momentarily stunned from the strike, he brought the [Duskblade] around, thrusting it into the Burgon Beast's shoulder from above. Both blades were driven up to the hilt in the foul beast's oily hide.

With as much strength as Jacob could muster, he pushed toward the sloped edge of the earthen bridge. Howling in pain, the Burgon Beast's cry was soon joined by Jacob's as the cold burning shadows that gathered around the monster seared his hands.

The Burgon Beast realized what was going on too late to react. Its suddenly scrambling paws - one that couldn't even hold its weight - only sought to further crumble the edge of the dark earth.

Rusted blades snapped off in the creature's hide as it fell to the side and began to slide down the packed earth slope. Jacob, hands burned beyond sensation, pumped his legs with all his might, propelling both of them to the greedy grasping hands of the dead.

The Burgon Beast hit the dead first. Their withered hands and chorusing moans grabbed at its matted oily fur and began to pull it down. Jacob joined it a moment later. Their clawing hands didn't hurt nearly as much as he thought they would. It was barely more than the [Ring of Boundless Fury] did to him.

As Jacob was pulled under, he felt the blades slide free of the Burgon Beast. The cold black flames of the beast burned and licked at the dead until they gave up, focusing on the much easier target that had joined them. Jacob.

The clawing hands of the dead redoubled their efforts on Jacob, while the Burgon Beast struggled toward freedom. The deeper Jacob went into the pit, the worse the pain became. The crushing, bone-breaking pressure would have made him cry out if he had any breath in his lungs.

Even if he had any [Cinder Ampoules] left, he wouldn't have used them. It would have only prolonged his suffering. He made his play, and it had failed.

You Died.

33

Waking up next to the Razor Pass Pyre, Jacob shook his head to clear it. It was a good thing he didn't have any Souls lost because there was no way he would be getting them back.

But shaking his head did nothing for the pain that wracked his body. A glance at his Health showed that it was nearly gone, only a sliver showing he was near death. He crushed a [Cinder Ampoule], but it hardly filled up a tenth of his Health.

It was enough that he was able to take off the [Ring of Boundless Fury] to prevent it from killing him again. But where were the healing effects of the Pyre?

Only then did Jacob notice the chill in the air. The Pyre's flames were shrinking before his eyes.

The Fire Oppa appeared from the flames and whimpered suddenly, falling to the side and letting out a strangled whine of pain. The Pyre guttered and burned low as if it was never *Kindled* in the first place.

Checking his [Cinder Ampoules] confirmed it. Somehow, the Burgon Beast diminished the Pyre's strength, despite being so far away at Journey's End. Even undoing his improvements to it. Jacob rolled forward onto his knees and scooped up the Fire Oppa. His visor swung beneath his chin, still attached but hardly useable.

The Fire Oppa writhed and whimpered in pain. Jacob stared helplessly, infuriated that anything would hurt such a kind and loving soul. The flames that made up the Fire Oppa's fur were dying.

Cupping his hands together beneath the Fire Oppa's small body, Jacob shut his eyes and brought forth Kimberly's face. The strength she gave him, the good times they had.

"Please don't die on me," Jacob said, his voice cracking with emotion.

Ruby flames flickered to life just before the Fire Oppa's went out completely. Nothing happened for several heartbeats, but the Fire Oppa stopped whimpering. His breathing evened out.

The scarlet flames crawled all over the Fire Oppa, reigniting his flames and waking him up once more.

The Pyre surged with renewed strength, washing its welcoming heat over Jacob. Though he couldn't help but notice it was significantly cooler still than before.

Pyre Ignited.
You stoke the embers of the Fire Oppa's conviction.
Health, Stamina, Ampoules, and Spell Gems restored.

"You gave me quite the scare there," Jacob admitted, giving the tiny Fire Oppa a hug.

"It has already extinguished two Pyres, I only just managed to flee before the Smog Rifts were snuffed out. It is *angry*. So very *angry*." The Fire Oppa shivered, and Jacob lowered his hands into the Pyre's flames. "Thank you."

"Will this happen every time a Pyre is snuffed out?" Jacob asked.

"Yes. But I will be better prepared next time."

Jacob stood and nodded grimly. He pulled out the [Duskblade]. "Do you know what this is? The Burgon Beast seems to fear it."

The Fire Oppa looked at it, particularly at the red jewel in the hilt. "That is the Duskblade. The Burgon Beast has a reason to fear it. That is a sealing blade.

"It was used by the creature's cruel former master to teach it 'obedience.' Houndmaster Vyrthis had a preternatural gift for inflicting pain. Take a closer look at the weapon. You will see what I mean."

Jacob did just that.

[Duskblade]

Given to the great Houndmaster Vyrthis, this weapon has a history of bloodshed and cruelty dating back to its blood-soaked forging. As one of five sealing blades in existence, it is remarkably rare. Incapable of being upgraded, this blade drinks the Souls of those it has wounded, empowering itself while causing untold pain to the victim.

Over time the blade loses the gathered Souls, requiring a constant infusion of living Souls in order to keep its edge.

Physical Damage: 200
Type: Slashing, Piercing
Scaling: STR [B], INT [B]
Light Attack: 20 Stamina
Heavy Attack: 50 Stamina

Magical Damage: 100
Arcane: 0
Fire: 0
Water: 0
Earth: 0
Harmony: 100
Chaos: 0

Status Infliction
Bleed: 60
Poison: 0
Curse: 0
Stagger: 40
Break: 10
Siphon: 500

Durability: 300/300
Guilt: 11

"Woah."

The Fire Oppa looked up at Jacob. "It is a very rare weapon, as you likely know. Its bloody history is filled with subjugation, torture, and thievery. And it may just be one of the few weapons that could stand up to the Burgon Beast. Though your abhorrent mace did a surprisingly good job."

"Vile Mace," Jacob corrected, then shrugged. "But it's destroyed, and I haven't any Souls to repair it. The weapon has so much Guilt, I'm not sure I can use it."

"That is one of its drawbacks," the Fire Oppa said with a nod. "It drinks of its victims, and as it increases its power, it draws out their Guilt as well, adding to its own."

Jacob looked over his parameters to see where he stood.

[Status]

Jacob Windsor
Covenant: Phoenix
Race: Kemora - Fae-touched (Human/Fairy)
Level: 26
Health: 132
Stamina: 94
Anima: 0
Souls: 0
Required Souls: 4,581

Parameters
VIT: 4
AGI: 8
END: 7

TMP: 15
STR: 10
DEX: 10
INT: 8
FTH: 3

Curse: Fractured Sight
  Curse Level: 3

Spell Gem: Heat Blade (3/3)
Spell Gem: Flame Blade (1/1)

Tallying up his total Guilt, his jaw dropped. No wonder he was so horrendously slow. At tier 4 of Guilt, he was moving 50% slower and consuming half again as much Stamina as he should have been.

If he was going to put the [Duskblade] to work, he would need to lighten his Guilt. The Burgon Beast hit hard. Even if it was weakened, he was only going to get a few hits in without his....

"Dammit! It still has my shield!" Jacob cried as he attempted to summon the [Phoenix Tree Crest Shield] again and again to no avail. He didn't even know that was possible.

"That may be a turn of luck in our favor," Fenris said, pacing in the low-burning flames. "It cannot snuff out the phoenix tree's crest so long as you remain alive. The shield will damage it from within, though how much I cannot say."

Jacob took off his [Elite Knight's Helm], storing it in his inventory. It was only a few points from being broken anyway. Without its 4 Guilt weighing him down, Jacob was pulled under the 75% threshold. He was back in the comfortable territory of tier 3 Guilt, though still much slower than he was recently used to.

Without a good shield, he would need to be even faster. His [Vile Mace] came off next, stored away since it was useless anyway. His [Longsword] was next, but *still,* he felt sluggish and weighed down.

Something didn't add up. Then he remembered the affliction, *Soulworn*. The same one that Alec had. It prevented him from going back into Pyresouls Online, or at least he made it seem like he wouldn't be able to because of it.

"Fenris, what is Soulworn?"

The Fire Oppa's ears perked up, and he looked intently at Jacob. "I should have noticed it sooner! I was... preoccupied, allow me to cleanse you. It would normally not be removed even by resting at a Pyre. Similar to the Curse affliction, it persists through death and revival.

"Not to mention, you couldn't bind at another Pyre. Though, considering this was your first Pyre, I assume you won't be in either case.

"Soulworn is a nasty thing that only gets worse the longer you have it. It affects each person differently. Some lose the will to fight. Others grow immensely fearful of the tormentor. For you, it seemed to increase your Guilt. But the effect is relatively minor. At most, it would have placed you into a higher tier of Guilt.

"Once it gained enough strength, you would be unable to carry the burden anymore. You likely wouldn't even be able to return to Lormar, the fear would be that great. If you tried or were forced, it might drive you insane.

No wonder Alec couldn't do this.

A swirl of fire lashed out from the Pyre and encircled Jacob in a comforting glow. When it was finished, he felt better, lighter.

He was sitting directly on the 50% Guilt threshold, but he felt faster than he should have, as if he was below 50%, at tier 2 Guilt. He had figured he would need to lose another piece of equipment. He was deciding between his gauntlets and his leggings until he realized it wasn't just a trick of his imagination.

The Fire Oppa watched him with a twinkle in his dark eyes. He did something to him, something beyond cleansing the Soulworn status.

He wasn't about to go into the fight naked. But now it seemed he didn't need to make a choice. The Burgon Beast was quick, and even with its busted leg, he would need to be at his best.

Going Savage would just lead to him dying faster. And he could not afford that.

"Better than I thought," Jacob said, swinging around the [Duskblade] to get a feel for it. Within a few test swipes, he received a new series of prompts.

[Duskblade] *Sword Forms Unlocked:* ***Souldrinker, Abyss Swallows All, Caging the Beast.***

Souldrinker
When the [Duskblade] is embedded in a creature, the sword can be commanded to drink of the victim's Souls. Repairs damage dealt to the sword and increases its parameters. Souls may not be used by the wielder.

Abyss Swallows All
A powerful two-handed overhead strike that deals heavy balance damage to stagger foes and to drive even the hardiest defenders to their knees.

Caging the Beast
A series of swift light strikes that fence an opponent in like a cage, meant to line up an opponent for a powerful finishing attack.

That was new. Nothing in the archives mentioned anybody gaining Sword Forms from equipping a weapon. That would be game-changing knowledge. Most people only acquired them from long hours of training. Which wasn't easy to do within Pyresouls.

Turning back to the Pyre, Jacob knelt at it and reached out to the Fire Oppa. "Where is the Burgon Beast headed?"

"It has your scent and will stop at nothing to devour you. It has already devoured the Pyres at Journey's End and the Smog Rifts. You will find it soon at Hollow Dreams, near the bell tower," the Fire Oppa answered. "If you are ready, I will take you."

Jacob nodded. *Ready to die again,* he thought with a wry grin. He paused a moment, remembering Camilla's brave last stand. "Where is Camilla? Could you get a message to her?"

The Fire Oppa sadly shook his head. "I am... sorry, Jacob. I can't reach Camilla."

That hurt more than he thought it would. With a muttered prayer for her safety, hoping against hope that she was okay, Jacob said, "I'm ready."

The world bent and twisted around him, wreathed in a swirl of flames. When it was over, Jacob stood next to the Pyre beneath the rusted bell. Even here, the light was wan and weak.

Including the Hollow Dreams Pyre, Jacob had five more chances to defeat the Burgon Beast. And unlike him, the beast wouldn't heal. He could whittle it down, bit by bit until he dealt the finishing blow and ended its terror before it could begin.

Placing a hand on the flat of the [Duskblade], Jacob used *Flame Blade,* wreathing the sword in fiercely burning flames. He looked at the Fire Oppa. "Can you abandon the Pyre to avoid getting hurt?"

The terrible sounds the Fire Oppa made... the memory still tore at Jacob's heart. The poor thing didn't deserve to suffer like that.

"It is my sworn duty to keep the Pyre lit," the Fire Oppa intoned. "Come what may, I will keep the flames alive until I cannot anymore. Do not worry for me, I will be fine so long as a single Pyre remains lit."

Jacob had to accept that. There was no other way. Some things were just unfair. Good people were hurt, the innocent died. But if he could stop the Burgon Beast here, then he could save countless lives from suffering.

It didn't make him feel any better about the Fire Oppa being in pain.

Walking to the edge of the bell tower, Jacob could see the large black form of the Burgon Beast in the distance weaving between the narrow dirt alleyways. The Vacant that got in its way were obliterated, vanishing into wisps of black flame until nothing was left.

Is that what it does to the Pyres? Jacob shivered, remembering the biting cold pain of those shadow flames.

The Burgon Beast was clearly making a beeline straight for the belltower but not once did it look up. Instead, its head was bent down to the dirt. Was it following his original trail in reverse?

With a grin, Jacob stepped right to the edge of the crumbling stonework and reversed his grip on the [Duskblade], holding it with both hands. *Better not miss, Windsor.*

With a keen eye, Jacob watched the Burgon Beast's progress, waiting until he judged the moment right. As the Burgon Beast entered the courtyard, Jacob stepped off.

The wind whipped his hair around and stung his eyes, but he never blinked, never took his eyes off his mark.

The Burgon Beast and the ground below rushed up to meet him. *Planting the Flag* hit the Burgon Beast right in the middle, snapping its back with tremendous force and nearly killing Jacob despite the softened fall.

At over a thousand points of damage, it was worth it.

When the Burgon Beast went down, Jacob didn't land as gracefully as he thought he would. As the beast fell to the side, Jacob went down hard and broke his right ankle as he tried, and failed, to hold onto the [Duskblade] to drive it deeper.

Without Jacob holding onto the blade, the flames on the weapon flickered and died. The area all around the sword was scorched and charred.

He rolled away, trying to expel the excess energy of the fall before it killed him. Mid-roll, he summoned a [Cinder Ampoule] and crushed it, restoring himself to half Health. The next topped him off as he rose to his feet.

His [Cinder Ampoules] had never been so weak before. A quick glance showed that he was rid of the Soulworn affliction, which meant it was whatever the Burgon Beast did to the Pyres.

Since the ampoules were a gift of the Fire Oppa - and therefore the

Pyres themselves - snuffing them out was weakening the healing effect of the ampoules.

Instead of removing the [Duskblade] through dismissing and summoning it, Jacob sprinted to the Burgon Beast as it thrashed on the ground, trying to get its legs beneath it.

It would have been too much to ask that he crippled it with that initial blow. Even still, Jacob found himself moving easier. He closed on the Burgon Beast quickly.

The red jewel was shining like a beacon in the pommel. As Jacob put his hands on the hilt, he willed it to pull at the Burgon Beast's life-force. *Souldrinker* brought forth a twisting pattern of white wisps forcibly extracted from the Burgon Beast.

Its thrashing and pained yelping grew more frantic. The Burgon Beast managed to throw Jacob off, and in the process, dislodge the sword.

Jacob hit the ground hard, knocking his head against the stones in a blinding burst of pain.

But he still had the presence of mind to roll out of the way as the Burgon Beast lunged at him, gleaming jaws snapping at the spot he just was at.

Its fury was magnified several times over with the reminder of the painful bite of the [Duskblade]. Jacob could see the unchecked rage burning in its red eyes.

With his [Cinder Ampoules] less effective and diminished in number, he couldn't take much more damage.

Flashing his sword out with a haphazard strike, more to fend off the next attack than to deal any damage, Jacob got to his feet in a rush. *Diving Falcon* nicked the Burgon Beast along the ribs, drawing a pained snarl and a countering bite on Jacob's left thigh.

Moon Crests the Horizon cut off its left ear and forced the beast back before it could sink its teeth too deeply into Jacob's thigh. Blood flowed freely from the wound, and the Burgon Beast's poisonous saliva scoured his veins, dropping him to a third of his Health.

By the time Jacob used an ampoule to recover his Health, and a vial of [Gekk Blood] to counteract the poison, the fierce monster was on him again. Jacob forced his blade up, bracing it with his left hand along the flat of the blade in an awkward rendition of *Barring the Gate.*

When the Burgon Beast snapped its jaws on the [Duskblade] it yelped in pain as the notched blade cut into its ruined maw. The barbed tongue bled freely, but the beast had succeeded in drawing Jacob's attention fully.

Jacob noticed the snaking thread of shadow too late. The freezing bite of dry ice struck at his right ankle and crept up his calf. The numbing agony climbed higher and higher until Jacob could no longer command his right leg at all, and he went down hard.

Try as he might to slash at the Burgon Beast, few of the hits connected. It didn't bother to use its broken maw to finish the job. The crawling shadow flames consumed him, freezing his heart.

You Died.

Waking up at the Razor Pass, Jacob thrust his hand into the Pyre feeling its warm comfort envelope him. It was even colder than before, but the Fire Oppa came faithfully to his side.

Without another word, the Fire Oppa pulled Jacob to the Drowned Halls Pyre.

The *drip, drip* of nearby water, and the briny scent told him that they had made it without issue. The Fire Oppa lay in the diminished flames, forlornly curled up. He reached out to soothingly pet the poor thing.

At the edges of Jacob's vision, dancing lights flitted in and out of view, followed by more corporeal forms. Lithe and angular creatures only vaguely humanoid moved with disturbingly fluid grace.

"The barriers of the shards are breaking down," the Fire Oppa warned. He sounded tired. "Be careful."

Unlike last time, the Pyre was still functioning. Full Health, Stamina, and with a full - albeit diminished - stock of [Cinder Ampoules]. Jacob hesitated as he wondered whether or not to use his curse against the Burgon Beast.

Alec had told him that it might reveal locations to him. Jacob only ever found it an annoyance, one he hardly had time to explore.

Then again, Alec had several days of exploring that Jacob didn't. Held prisoner for much of that time, Jacob was also much weaker than he should have been. Alec was nearly Level 40 when he faced the Burgon Beast.

Jacob was Level 26.

This was the last place he wanted to be. The flooding seemed to have pulled back, but now that he was here again, would the Vile Covenant's god-thing attack him as well?

Four more lives, Jacob thought. He used an [Anima], wiping out the moving shapes that were starting to become dangerously corporeal out in the hall. He didn't have time to be testing something new.

Besides, if it turned out to be useful, he still had enough potential deaths to bring himself back to a high curse level.

Jacob stroked the Fire Oppa, whose inner flames seemed so very weak. Fenris raised his head and pressed his tiny bear ears into Jacob's palm. But even that small motion seemed too much for the tiny thing, and it curled up again, in a deep slumber.

Grinding his teeth, Jacob stepped forward into the hall and turned toward the exit. If at all possible, he wanted to fight it in a wider hallway where he would have room to maneuver around the lupine creature.

He welcomed the fight to vent his mounting rage. The Burgon Beast would pay dearly for every second the Fire Oppa was in pain.

"Did they finally let you die?" came a snide, painfully familiar voice to his left. "No matter. I'll kill you myself. You've caused me enough problems!" Mack came forward, in stained and rusted armor, his gleaming halberd leading the charge.

34

"I really don't have time for this," Jacob said, rolling his wrist and sending the [Duskblade] in a lazy looping motion in preparation for Mack's attack.

It also shouldn't have been possible. But if the barriers between the shards were breaking down, he guessed it made as much sense as anything else in Lormar did.

Which was to say, not much.

Mack lunged forward in a predictable stab at Jacob's gut. *Leaf Circles the Whirlpool* brought Jacob's blade up and around. Sparks flew where the notched edge of Jacob's [Duskblade] met the metal pole of the halberd.

"You should be honored to be killed by me, you know!" Mack taunted. "By killing you, I'll rise to the acolyte rank within the Vile Covenant! You'll help me in more ways than you could ever know."

To his credit, Mack disengaged quickly and choked up on the halberd. He levered it down in a two-handed strike. One that Jacob sidestepped with the aid of an upward arcing swing of *Sheltering Rain*, forcing the halberd to catch on the uneven stone wall to the left.

Jacob grit his teeth and dashed in before Mack could gain control of his weapon. *Wind Parts the Grass* sparked against the floor and drew a gouging line in Mack's new aquatic-themed outfit.

Rather than the gleaming white metal with the lion helmet, he wore rusted chainmail covered with barnacles and tentacle iconography. His helm was a simple affair with a chain veil covering his mouth and a series of metal sculpted tentacles as a faceguard.

Twin Forked Lightning drew forth two blossoms of blood from Mack's armor. Jacob raised his sword up high in two hands, and with a lunge forward, *Diving Falcon* took Mack in the gut. A third bloom of crimson joined the other two.

The halberd vanished in a splash of seawater, not ash, Jacob noted. As soon as Jacob saw the glow of the [Cinder Ampoule], his sword was arcing toward that hand. *Moonlight's Edge* cut the hand off at the wrist.

A quick shift in his footing, a levering twist on the blade, and *Falling Rain* took out Mack's throat in a spray of blood.

Jacob placed a boot on Mack's chest and kicked him over onto his back. The anger roiling in his stomach made him taste bile. It was this selfish idiot that had cost him so many days.

And all because I hurt his feelings!

Jacob still couldn't fathom how fragile the man's ego must be to get so bent out of shape over what he only knew to be just a game.

It was so much more to Jacob, and that only made him angrier.

Twice now, his chance to save humanity was set back - present company, unfortunately, included - all because of this jerk. Billions of lives in the balance, but it was a *player* that likely did the most damage to his mission, not a horrible monster.

Looking down at him, Jacob shook his head. "If only you knew what your actions have cost us all. You might see me as some horrible villain in your story. But you're just a footnote in mine."

Almost as an afterthought, *Planting the Flag* took Mack in the heart.

You defeat [Mack].
Awarded 500 Souls.

If he was quick, he might be able to get back to the Pyre and repair his [Vile Mace] before the Burgon Beast came.

Just as Jacob turned toward the room, a wall of opaque fog appeared, cutting off his access to the Pyre. The Burgon Beast was here. And Jacob was still in a tight corridor without much room to maneuver.

He wasted precious seconds enacting *Flame Blade* to coat the [Duskblade] in brilliant flame. The sword was set in motion, *Wind Parts the Grass* swept up. Though the Burgon Beast leaped to the side, it was still caught on the shoulder by the burning strike.

Its fur burned and crackled angrily wherever the fire touched. Jacob lunged forward, trying to keep up the momentum. *Falling Rain* drew a horizontal charred line right above the too-many eyes of the Burgon Beast, dealing nearly 450 points of damage.

Compared to the Vile Mace's corrosive strikes of 300 to 500, the [Duskblade] was holding its own quite well and continued to deal more damage every time he used *Souldrinker*. The Burgon Beast was surprisingly sturdy, its defenses well-rounded and high enough to severely weaken even his strongest Sword Forms.

Leaf Circles the Whirlpool fended off a powerful swat of the Burgon Beast's paw, which caused the creature to overbalance on its weakened leg from their first matchup.

Dove Takes Flight took out two of its eyes on the left side while a quick reversal and a forward step of *Diving Falcon* took out a third eye and stabbed deep enough to hit bone.

Souldrinker pulled at the Burgon Beast's strength, withering the creature before Jacob's eyes. The flames burned the beast as it howled in agony. Jacob was distantly sorry for the beast, for the things its previous master must have done to it.

Thick tendrils of shadowy flame brushed at him, but Jacob remembered the last time he died and broke off the attack with a backward leap. Recovering his Stamina, Jacob weaved the flaming sword back and forth in a figure-eight pattern.

What he thought was a poor place to fight the creature turned out to be great. The Burgon Beast was just as trapped as he was, and getting past Jacob wasn't easy.

Jacob lurched forward with *Lightning Cracks Stone,* missing only because the ground suddenly shifted below his feet. Likewise, the Burgon Beast was caught off-guard but with four paws - three good ones - it recovered faster.

A lash of its barbed tongue took Jacob in the hip, sending poisonous fire radiating up into his chest. Before he could draw forth an item to take care of it, the ground quaked again.

Thrown to his knee, Jacob heard the distant gurgling roar of rage and cursed his luck.

Water burst forth in mighty geysers all around him. The Burgon Beast turned tail and ran as tentacles leaped out of holes in the stonework. He was lashed in place, unable to break free as the tunnels flooded with saltwater, and he drowned.

You Died.

He came awake with a start, gasping for air that blessedly came to his lungs. Drowning to death was one of his least favorite ways to die.

Jacob looked at the pitiful flames of the Pyre, barely higher than a foot off the glowing embers.

The Fire Oppa looked at him mournfully, he was thinner. His fur seemed less lustrous and full. Jacob reached into the flames and took the Fire Oppa in his hands and pet him, trying to soothe the creature though he had no idea how.

"That last death didn't count," he said, trying for a jovial attitude. "I drowned, the Burgon Beast didn't get me."

Looking up at Jacob with love and adoration, the Fire Oppa winked at him. "That'll stay just between you and me then, eh?"

"Exactly," Jacob answered, petting him gently before setting him back into the flames. "Just a little more. It's already missing a few eyes, and one of its legs is badly damaged. Every time I use *Souldrinker* on it, the blade gets stronger."

Several of the [Duskblade's] nicks and notches were healed. The many tarnished sections of the blade were now giving off a dull gleam in the weak firelight.

"The Burgon Beast returned to snuff out the Drowned Halls Pyre as soon as you died and the tunnels drained," the Fire Oppa said.

Jacob expected as much. He gave a forced smile of comfort to the Fire Oppa. He was running out of chances faster than he thought possible.

Its red-jeweled pommel pulsed like a heartbeat. Reaching into the flames, Jacob willed the Pyre to transport him to the Desecrated Catacombs. A wash of flames scoured his vision and deposited him on the hard stony ground of the Desecrated Catacombs Pyre. Not too dissimilar from the Razor Pass, except for the deeply oppressive air and the dusty rot.

Jacob hurried to the first layer of the catacombs, where he knew several skeletons were waiting. Before he finished going down the ramp, he spotted the glowing red eyes of the Burgon Beast.

Damn, that thing is fast.

Skeletons rose up against it, and for a moment, Jacob wondered how they would fare against the creature.

Not well, it turned out.

Every skeleton that reanimated was quickly crunched into powder, unable to get up again. Several fractures appeared mid-air as other players, just as surprised as Jacob for appearing there, suddenly found themselves in Jacob's shard.

Jacob silently thanked them as the Burgon Beast turned to the nearest threats. They didn't stand a chance. Most of them were already half-dead by the looks of it.

Once they saw the threat before them, something amazing happened. Something Jacob never would have thought to see in Lormar.

They worked together.

He took the time to reapply *Flame Blade* and then rushed forward, hoping that the new players would provide even a slight advantage. He was beginning to run out of "extra lives."

The Burgon Beast looked much worse for wear, but it still bit the motley crew of players in half with ease. A massive paw swatted the head from a man in rusted chainmail. The dark fiery shadows burned a young woman to ash.

Jacob wasn't the only one to score a blow on the Burgon Beast, but after the first few seconds of battle, he was the only one to remain. A collection of axes, daggers, and thrown javelins stuck out of the Burgon Beast's greasy hide.

The damage they caused may not have been considerable, but each wound was one less point of Health that the Burgon Beast possessed.

It bled on the ground in large oily splatters with every strenuous motion. Large swaths of fur were burned away, revealing cracked and charred skin. And every few steps it made, it belched a fiery burp that scorched its tongue and what was left of its broken maw from the shield it swallowed.

By all rights, it should have been dead already. That it could take so much damage and keep coming... no wonder Alec couldn't beat it. There was no way any single player could outlast it. This thing had to have well over several thousand points of Health.

Meanwhile, players like Jacob had Health in the very low hundreds. Even a player that put most of his points in VIT would only be scratching 300 to 400 Health.

For all of Jacob's attacks, only *Souldrinker* seemed to do much damage to it. The physical harm was there, and it limited the Burgon Beast's ability to attack, but it didn't seem to slow it down. Every time he used *Souldrinker*, the beast withered and seemed less... substantial.

Jacob came on with a flurry of attacks. Left, right, left, right, *Caging the Beast* forced the Burgon Beast to stand right before him. Instead of continuing the flurry of light hits that barely scratched its greasy hide, Jacob twisted, pivoted on the balls of one foot, and came down hard in a heavy overhand chop.

Abyss Swallows All cleaved the Burgon Beast's head in half right down the middle. His sword kept going until it sank into the stone, creating a thin cut in it that wedged the blade tight.

Jacob dismissed the blade and summoned it into his waiting palm, watching his nearly depleted Stamina recover. Was it over? The Burgon

Beast was slumped to the stone floor, its head split down to the neck. Nothing could survive that.

A quick brace of the [Duskblade] at the faintest flicker of movement saved Jacob's life. *Barring the Gate* turned the wide blade into an impromptu shield and deflected the harpooning tendril that shot out of what was once the Burgon Beast's head.

Slithering black tentacles crawled out from the mangled mess like black vines dripping oil. They grabbed both pieces of the Burgon Beast's bisected skull and pulled it together.

The result was a Frankensteinian creation that didn't quite match up right. Black vines reformed the beast's lower jaws, and gleaming silvery teeth erupted from the tendrils reforming the mouth.

Swallowing the bile that rose in the back of his throat, Jacob came on again. The Burgon Beast was faster now, whipping black vines cracked in the air as they erupted from its many wounds.

It seemed all that was holding the Burgon Beast together was some kind of... parasite. The beast lunged at him, and Jacob dove forward to the right in a roll. He took a stinging hit that drew blood on his cheek from a passing black vine but avoided the worst of it thanks to his faster speed.

Jacob came up in a rush, twisting and lunging after the beast's hindquarters with *Dove Takes Flight*. The Burgon Beast let out a strangled yelp as the arcing slice lopped off its tail.

Separated from the main body, the tail melted into a black oily goo.

In place of its tail, a coiling segment of black tendrils erupted from the wound. Tipped with a gleaming silver stinger dripping caustic purple poison, it waved the new appendage menacingly in the air.

"You just don't know when to quit, do you?" he groaned.

Sheltering Rain fended off a stinging blow from its new tail just as the Burgon Beast rushed at him. Dodging to the side, Jacob twisted and carved a long wound in the Burgon Beast's flank with *Stag Rushes Through the Field*.

Through the gaping wound Jacob saw writhing black worms, they screeched an impossibly high pitch well out of human's typical hearing - but not his Fae-touched - that had him reeling.

His next few motions were purely instinctual. *Leaf Circles the Whirlpool* transitioned into *Souldrinker* at the 12 o'clock point, suddenly stabbing down into the shoulder of the Burgon Beast's charging form.

Jacob crashed into the ground with the Burgon Beast atop him, but he never let go of the blade or stopped its burning flames or the Soul siphoning ability.

The lashing wounds of the tentacles were punctuated with the deep acidic burn of its poison-tipped tail burrowing into his stomach through a gap in his armor. Even as his Health drained away, Jacob held on and let the sword do its work.

Have to... weaken it.

You Died.

You never get used to death.

Jacob came awake suddenly and started to swing at the air, only to remember he was safe. For the time being.

The Steps of Penance Pyre wasn't terribly far from the Desecrated Catacombs, considering how fast the Burgon Beast was able to travel between Pyres so far. The only shorter path was from the Steps of Penance to the Razor Pass.

As Jacob reached into the Pyre to will himself to the Steps of Penance, the Fire Oppa opened his tired eyes. The Pyre was barely more than glowing coals at that point. A sneeze could snuff it out, and the Fire Oppa too.

Jacob's stomach twisted, noticing how thin and frail the Fire Oppa looked.

As the Fire Oppa shakily rose on all fours, it gingerly padded through the ash to Jacob. Quick to relieve Fenris of his burden, Jacob scooped him up and held him close to his chest. Near one of the holes in his armor where he hoped the Fire Oppa might feel some of Jacob's warmth.

"Do not... go," said the Fire Oppa breathlessly. Jacob didn't have the heart to argue, but he also knew that doing nothing would doom the Fire Oppa to a fate he couldn't bear to let him suffer.

"I have to," Jacob said as softly as he could, looking down at the weak ferret-like creature. His fur barely glowed. He couldn't even feel his warmth anymore.

"Too fast... never make it... weak. So weak..."

"How can I help?"

"Take me... away."

Jacob scrunched up his face. "Where?"

"Village... go now. Beast is coming." And with that, the Fire Oppa suddenly stilled. Jacob's heart stuttered in his chest, his throat closed up.

Then he saw the faintest rise in the Fire Oppa's chest and knew he had only passed out. Without any idea of what the Fire Oppa's real plan was, Jacob set him down in his lap and summoned *Flame Blade* one last time.

That done, he gingerly lifted the Fire Oppa and set him securely in the crook of his left arm. Holding the Fire Oppa there, Jacob stood and held out his flaming [Duskblade] ahead of him as he left the Pyre.

This was no place to fight the Burgon Beast. With sheer drops all about and tight quarters, it would have an advantage with all its newfound whipping tendrils.

The few Vacant that still littered the trail were quickly and easily dispatched, particularly since he came across the archers first before they saw him.

Nobody ever went *back* to the Shrouded Village.

From time to time, the Fire Oppa whined and whimpered, pressing himself closer to Jacob. The glow of his fur went completely out as Jacob came into the Shrouded Village. True to its name, a thin fog hung in the air all about.

Falling Rain and *Sunflower Faces the Sun* took out the two Vacant guarding the entrance from the Razor Pass.

Without any dangers nearby, Jacob wandered into the village, wondering what the Fire Oppa wanted in coming here.

A guttural, triumphant roar split the air, echoing in the vast space of the Razor Pass behind him.

The Fire Oppa shook and shivered. Jacob lifted him up to the burning flames on his blade, trying to warm him up. That seemed to rouse Fenris a little, enough for him to open his eyes. Though breathing still seemed strenuous.

"Pyres... gone. Make this count, okay? I believe in you." With a long, drawn-out sigh, the Fire Oppa seemed to deflate and become less substantial. His fur began to glow again, and Jacob felt his heart lift in hope.

But then the embers broke apart into a thousand tiny glowing motes, each of them pulled into Jacob's armor and body. His armor was repaired in an instant, he felt invigorated, and the flames from his sword burned even brighter and hotter.

Tears stung Jacob's green eyes as he looked at the empty spot where the Fire Oppa had been.

A faint voice came to him on the breeze that ruffled his hair. *Always. With. You.*

35

Tears burned Jacob's eyes and blurred his vision. Heat shimmered over his arms, and for the first time, Jacob felt truly warm. Like he used to feel before Pyresouls Online, before the Collapse. When he was a normal teenager looking toward a bright future with limitless possibilities.

> *The Fire Oppa fuels the Flame of your Soul.*
> [Cinder Ampoules] *now recover full Health and Stamina.*
> *Passive Health regeneration.*
> *Your Guilt is assuaged.*

A glance at his Guilt showed it at a staggering 0%. Not even Savages could attain such a low amount of Guilt. Not unless they were willing to go unarmed.

Jacob could feel the warmth of the Fire Oppa within him, comforting him, guiding him.

Just in time too, the Burgon Beast's roar sounded even closer. Remembering how he dealt with the Vacant upon his return to Pyresouls Online, Jacob hurried up to a side path.

His movements were swift and sure, more than they had ever been before. He reached the familiar boulder at the gravesite overlooking the narrow entrance to the Razor Pass.

For once, he was glad that most things reset in Lormar when he rested at a Pyre. If not for that quirk, the boulder would still be below with two Vacant crushed beneath it.

Setting his shoulder against the boulder, Jacob leaned out just enough to see a sliver of the Razor Pass below. He didn't have to wait very long. The dark form of the Burgon Beast skidded along the rocky path and collided heavily with the tall sheer walls.

The impact was so great that it nearly set the boulder Jacob was braced against rolling before its time. A few moments later, Jacob heaved with all his strength.

Bouncing down the steep path, the boulder crashed into the sprinting Burgon Beast. Seeing it coming but unable to put its bulky form to a stop in time, the creature poured on the speed, going as fast as its legs would carry it.

It wasn't fast enough. The boulder crushed its hindquarters against the far wall with a sickening crunch.

How the Burgon Beast howled! Shrill cries echoed off the high walls of the Razor Pass. As Jacob stepped back to get a running leap and stab into the beast and finish it once and for all, something horrible happened. Again.

The Burgon Beast's head split wide open. Its furry body began to flatten and deflate. Out came a black morass, like a giant ethereal hand was squeezing the Burgon Beast's body like a tube of toothpaste.

A parasite, there was no other word Jacob could think of to describe it, slipped out of the ruined body of the Burgon Beast. It slithered forward on stretching, ropy appendages that were fast differentiating themselves from simple tendrils.

A single great yellow eye like that of a serpent's slid along the bulbous, tumorous body until it fixed Jacob with its awful gaze. Jacob's legs locked up at the sight of the horrible thing.

This was the terrible truth of the Burgon Beast. A parasitic creature that had taken over the poor beast. There was no fear at the sight of the [Duskblade] burning so fiercely in Jacob's hands.

Its name shimmered into being when their eyes locked.

The Incomplete Vessel

As the parasite climbed with surpassing ease up the sheer mountainside, Jacob could feel a familiar warmth emanating from the monster. His [Phoenix Tree Crest Shield] was still inside the disgusting thing.

Breaking free of his own surprise, Jacob lunged forward just as two slimy arms gripped the scrubby ground at his feet. *Reaping the Harvest* cut those two bands of darkness free only for four more to replace it.

The greedy jaundiced eye of the bloated parasite stood before him nearly as tall as Jacob and several times wider. Whipping tendrils cracked the air a dozen times over. It sounded like hail on a tin roof.

Rows of teeth appeared like silver-gleaming zippers all along its body without rhyme or reason to it. Two grasping arms shot out for Jacob and were summarily cut down with a sweeping arc of *Moonlight's Edge*.

Falling Rain took out two more appendages, while *Diving Falcon* went for the massive yellow eye. The creature *blinked,* and its slimy skin became hardened steel. His sword skittered off the eyelid and drew sparks across the black mass.

In fast retreat, Jacob was whipped three times even as his enhanced speed managed to put some space between the two. The attacks brought his Health down to half, but it was already swiftly filling thanks to the Fire Oppa.

The Incomplete Vessel whipped out repeatedly, and Jacob was glad to keep his distance, picking off the stretching appendages with practiced strokes. He was taking a measure of his new opponent. What it lacked in speed from the body of the Burgon Beast, it made up for with an inexhaustible number of appendages.

Diving its many tendrils into the stony ground, glistening black roots snaked their way toward Jacob. Wherever they found a bit of life, like the grass and scrub brush between them, it withered to ash.

It was reshaping the battlefield to its advantage. Which meant Jacob had to change the battlefield, and fast. The Incomplete Vessel was too close to the narrow path that led him up, and he wasn't about to leap down and take his chances by jumping.

All it would take was one tendril to wrap around him, and he was finished. There were no more Pyres. No extra lives. No do-overs.

So Jacob continued to back up, all the while trying to edge to his left to get the parasite away from the only viable escape route. It seemed to know his intent and was content to stay put, guarding the only exit Jacob had foolishly given up in the first few moments of the battle.

Coming forward in a rush, Jacob slashed in a flaming blur with his [Duskblade]. *Stag Rushes Through the Field* batted aside tendrils and appendages that rose up to attack him. He accepted one or two stinging hits in exchange for his soon-to-be freedom.

The way was suddenly blocked by the rotund form of the Incomplete Vessel. Its great yellow eye staring imperiously at Jacob. *Through* him. Jacob leaped back but found tall pillars of dark corruption barring his way.

More and more tendrils coated the ground, he tried to stay between them, but it was becoming impossible. Every squelching step felt like a punch to the gut. The Incomplete Vessel had shaped the battlefield into its own making, literally.

A wide cocoon covered the two combatants in complete darkness lit only by the bright flames of Jacob's spell. A dank, oily foulness filled the air and burned Jacob's lungs. He began to feel the cold embrace of death surround him once more.

The only silver lining was the vast reduction in the Vessel's tendrils. It seemed to use most of its strength to create the hardened shell of darkness around them, it looked a little like a small domed room.

Try as he might to break through the walls, his flaming sword did little but scratch the hardened substance. The Incomplete Vessel slithered closer on its few remaining limbs.

A voice echoed in Jacob's head, like nails on a chalkboard he could not push it out or ignore it. *"Fine form. Finer than the Beast. You will be new Shell. Become complete. We will become complete."*

It continued to repeat the phrase over and over in Jacob's mind until his own thoughts mirrored that of the Incomplete Vessel's. His own mental voice disobeyed him. The two voices, the Incomplete Vessel's and his own, slowly became closer in timbre and pitch.

Every thought was followed and chased by the growing darkness inside his own head. Somewhere in the distance, he heard the Fire Oppa's voice, but it was drowned out by the drumming of pursuit in his mind.

Jacob heard the metallic clatter as his sword fell to the hardened black material of the floor from nerveless fingers. He struggled, fled from the voices that chased him through the caverns of his own mind.

All the while, the Incomplete Vessel crept closer, inexorably slow but assured in its newest acquisition.

Its thoughts bled into Jacob's. It would grow stronger in Jacob's body. It would leave the dying world of Lormar. Within Jacob's mind, it could see the brilliant, vibrant life of another star unsullied by its filth.

Jacob's hand twitched as he desperately tried to fight the intrusion, but it was inside his head already. It knew his thoughts, his defenses as if they were his own. Every thought was copied, mirrored, and used against him, turning his own mental processes away from resistance, toward submission.

Running through the alleyways of his own mind, Jacob saw the dead friends and family he was forced to leave behind. He saw the terrible Red Plague descend once again. The Vile Kingdom's rise to power and its gruesome strength on display.

Off to the side, he spied a flash of light. A small glow of flame. Jacob turned toward it, splashing down a muddy lane between two impossibly tall black buildings.

The light fled before him on swift paws, taking sudden and random turns that Jacob could only just keep up with. Winded and out of breath, he continued on until Jacob could hardly hear the echoing footfalls of pursuit.

The Fire Oppa came around the corner, the puddles of water hissing where his fiery paws touched them. "If it cuts off all of your thoughts, it will consume you. It uses your mind against you, mapping it out with every thought you make. Once it is done, there will be no separation."

Jacob opened his mouth to ask how he could fight it, but he already knew how.

The Fire Oppa looked at him sadly. "I cannot live without a flame. I have kindled your soul as you are part of my Covenant. Anything that my flames have touched, I can abide within. The warmth of your soul keeps me alive. If you die, I will die. For good."

"Stay with me," Jacob pleaded, surprised at how raw his voice was.

The Fire Oppa climbed up him, and Jacob held the small ferret in his hands. The warmth brought a semblance of separation from the sensation of losing himself.

With the Fire Oppa's closeness, he felt more like himself than ever before. But it would not last.

He could feel the approach of the Incomplete Vessel. He would only get one chance at this. Jacob shut his eyes and focused on his trembling hand. Bathed in the warmth of the Fire Oppa's light, Jacob opened his eyes.

Emerging from the mental landscape was jarring and sudden.

A host of slimy feelers coated Jacob's physical body, and that great awful eye was focused with malicious intent on him. Hand still twitching, the only control he had left of his body, Jacob summoned the [Whisper of Insanity] to his palm.

The shifting item gathered there, and just as the Incomplete Vessel was clued in to Jacob's distant thoughts, he crushed the item in his palm.

Swirling shrieking screams filled Jacob's ears. His thoughts careened and spiraled out of control. So close to its goal, the Incomplete Vessel was dragged into the depths of madness with Jacob.

The Incomplete Vessel's every attempt to combat the madness was met with futility. It could not copy what was not sane. The barbed twists of Jacob's rapidly deteriorating mind stymied its every attempt to reestablish a semblance of control.

He saw his mother and father again, not as the people they were, but as the Vacant they became that day out on the lake when the waters boiled and the sky went black. When the Collapse happened.

Broken fragments of his worst memories replayed over and over again. Insanity swirled around him. It was a cyclone with sharp, bright memories of terror and horror like shards of glass which looked onto moments terrible and dark.

At the eye of the storm, Jacob huddled up, pulling his knees to his chest. He was a child again, helpless and weak. Even if he could lift the sword at his side, there was no way he could wield it effectively.

One of the fragments of his swirling memories flashed, and out came the Fire Oppa. "This protection will not last," he warned, padding over and pressing his head gently into Jacob's shin. "You cannot stay here."

"I can't face it again," he replied, though it came out as more of a whine than he intended it to. "Not again."

"It has already happened," Fenris tried to explain, crawling up his leg to perch on his knee. "They are memories. And they cannot harm you any more. But we must leave, now."

Tentatively, Jacob reached out to the Fire Oppa, who merely shook his head. "I cannot join you," he explained. "These are your memories. And only you may face them."

That nearly made the young boy collapse in on himself. He was afraid of being alone. More than anything, he feared abandonment. But he pushed to his feet and even scooped up the [Duskblade] at his side.

He couldn't lift the thing, so he dragged it on the formless ground like some childhood toy in the hands of a toddler.

Jacob walked into the storm of painful memories that would cut and wound him as surely as if they were jagged glass.

Every flash of pain was worse than the last. His first steps were twisted recollections warped by the emotional weight of the memory more than the actual facts.

His first breakup, his first bully, they all loomed larger than life and more terrible than he knew they were. Jacob walked through them, trudged on, and with each memory laid behind him, he grew a little.

By the time he walked into that cabin to find his parents as shambling thoughtless husks of their former selves, Jacob could just barely lift his sword. Conscious thought failed him as he bore witness to his caring, loving mother lunging for him with bloodied fingertips scraped to the bone.

Jacob's mind seized up, but his muscles remembered the forms he studied for years. *Wind Parts the Grass* split her in half. Two steps forward to his kind father whose soft green eyes were now milky white streaked with blood. Jacob was already moving into the next form. *Lightning Cracks Stone* split his father's skull like a melon.

Tears streamed down Jacob's face as he tried to remember the jovial man that always had time for a joke and a laugh. There would be no more laughter.

Flickering memories played out before him. He barely survived his first week alone in the woods, attempting and largely failing to find food and shelter. With his sword in hand, he rewrote the fear-filled memories with blood.

Back then, he didn't know how to hold a blade properly, much less use it. Form after form cut down the fiends that tormented his addled mind. Even twisted and larger than they had ever been in life, Jacob felled them.

And with each victory, he grew stronger.

He fought his way out of madness, one warped memory at a time. Alone. When he emerged, he expected to find something profound, some deep realization of who he was.

Instead, he found the Incomplete Vessel. Its bloodshot yellow eye twitched violently as it reacted to the shared madness within Jacob.

With a great bellowing roar, Jacob tore off the feelers holding him in place. Black ichor sprayed into the air. He leaned back on his left foot, drew back the surprisingly still flaming [Duskblade], and thrust it forward into that unseeing yellow eye.

Hummingbird's Kiss took the Incomplete Vessel in its lone eye, burrowing the blade up to the hilt and beyond. Jacob's hand punched through the gelatinous mass until the tip of the blade made a muffled *ping*.

Abruptly awakened, the Incomplete Vessel let loose a blast of sickly yellow energy that threw Jacob back with such force that it nearly zeroed out his Health. Stunned, he barely managed to twist away from a barrage of spiked tendrils aimed for his head.

Cold seeped into him, and even the fire of his blade was quenched. The Incomplete Vessel lashed about but was clearly blinded. The air whistled with its sharp whipping tendrils.

And then just as abruptly as it began, it stopped.

The Incomplete Vessel shook and quivered. Cracks appeared all over its bulbous body, spilling gouts of fire and bright light. With a high keening cry, the Incomplete Vessel shattered with a brilliant explosion that washed the world in white.

Where the Vessel had been was only Jacob's shield, the [Phoenix Tree Crest Shield] pulsing with golden light. A pair of wisps stood above it. One was golden, the other black as pitch.

Jacob crawled forward, watching the fiery form of the Fire Oppa materialize out of the burning crest of the phoenix tree emblazoned on the shield.

As soon as the little fiery creature saw Jacob, he sprang toward him, and Jacob caught Fenris in his arms. He hugged the warm and healthy creature, overjoyed that he was okay.

Better than okay, the Fire Oppa seemed young and sprightly once more.

Healed to full by the Fire Oppa now perched on his shoulder, Jacob made his way to the two souls and bent to retrieve them and his shield.

You defeat the [Burgon Beast].
Awarded 20,000 Souls.

You gain [Bright Soul of the Burgon Beast].
You defeat the [Incomplete Vessel].
Awarded 15,000 Souls.

You gain [Dark Soul of the Incomplete Vessel].

There were several tense moments when Jacob expected another attack. Something, *anything* that might go wrong. And then the prompt flashed across his vision, and a feminine voice boomed, the same one from the character creation.

"Congratulations to Jacob Windsor for defeating the Burgon Beast and being the first player to complete the introductory area of Pyresouls Online! The Forbidden Lands are now open. Good luck with the rest of the competition!"

Jacob's mouth hung open. *"What?!"* He didn't have much time to ponder what just happened as the taste of blue raspberries overwhelmed him, and he felt a deep tug at his navel.

36

May 7th, 2045 - 10 Years Post-Collapse.

Jacob awoke to the piercing beeping of a digital alarm clock too far away to smack.

As consciousness came back to him, he thought he was back in the room his parents kept for him when he went away to college. Only, he never left the alarm clock so far away.

Smashing the snooze button as soon as it interrupted his sleep was a priority he would not soon relinquish.

But as Jacob awoke and the dry, dusty air hit his throat, he realized he was not at home. The curving, cracked glass of the FIVR pod greeted him. The seals were letting in the air in the room around him.

A dark room Jacob didn't recognize.

With a gentle push, the curving glass top of the pod swung wide, letting him sit up. Jacob ripped diodes and an IV out of his arm. The drip bag was long-since emptied it looked like.

Setting his feet down on the cold stone floor, he suppressed a shiver.

The world was just as ethereally cold as before. Perhaps more. But he didn't feel the same as he usually did.

That bone-deep ache as the cold wormed its way into his body was missing. He hurt, a dozen new pains all vied for his attention at once, but that soul-wearying agony was a distant memory.

He felt a faint warmth within his breast. And he remembered Fenris, the Fire Oppa.

Unsure where Alice or Alec were hiding, Jacob stalked across the dark room to the sharp green glow of the blaring alarm clock. He tripped over a wire once or twice along the way, cursing as he stubbed his toe on some piece of furniture.

With less force than he felt like using, Jacob switched off the alarm instead of smashing it to pieces.

Something was wrong.

"Hello?" he croaked, his throat dreadfully dry.

No response.

Shuffling about the room, with his arms out in front of himself, Jacob finally found the light switch. The room was bathed in harsh flickering white light. The heavy door that led out of the room now sported a massive metal locking bar that extended out from a wheel.

The door looked like it belonged on a submarine.

With more strength than he ever remembered having, Jacob turned the wheel. His only thought at the moment was his dire thirst. Halfway through turning the red wheel with its flaking paint, he spied a bottle of water by the FIVR pod.

Ambling over to it, Jacob sated his thirst, draining the thing dry.

Just to be sure he gave it another tilt, but when no more came out he set it back down. Only then did he notice the dozens of sticky pad notes attached to the FIVR pod.

Bending down to read them, they were all hastily scribbled - in his own hand, no less - instructions on how to use the FIVR pod. How much power it required. How to use the [Improbability Ember], and a lot more he didn't understand.

Wires trailing off of the machine led him to a stand with a computer terminal displaying more code and diagnostic information than he had ever seen in his life. He wasn't a programmer.

With a shrug, Jacob turned away, examining the room in greater detail. Folded neatly on a rolling cart was a set of armor and a chipped longsword out of its sheath.

There was no other way in or out of the room, and the pieces that he was finding did not paint a picture that made him feel very safe.

Taking all possible precautions, Jacob donned the armor. It was far heavier than his usual equipment had been in the future he last remembered and in much better repair besides. Even the sword, which had noticeable chips and cuts in it, still held a sharp edge.

Suited up again, Jacob turned the wheel with one hand, using his other to keep his sword at the ready. It was slow going, but the last thing he wanted was to die *outside* of Pyresouls Online. There would be no coming back from death here.

"What the hell is going on?" he muttered as he came into the hall to find it in a similar state of disuse.

The lights in the rest of the underground bunker turned on as their motion sensors triggered, and Jacob cleared the place room by room. There were some signs that people had once lived there but no longer.

The rooms were barren and without any personal effects - no suits of armor or weapons in the rooms, no mementos. The armory, between the mess hall and the FIVR pod room, held an assortment of well-kept equipment, but none of it was recognizable.

Moving down the hall, Jacob saw the telltale glow of light from under a door on his left. A supply room, if memory served. It was where they kept their non-perishables and anything scavenged that had been deemed safe to bring inside.

Hand tightening around the hilt of his sword, Jacob braced himself and opened the door should anything threatening come out.

What he saw instead, stole his breath and nearly made him drop the sword in his hand.

A Pyre.

There was a Pyre in the middle of the industrial room they once used for storage. Crates and shelves lined the far walls, but the majority of the room was given to the Pyre.

Shakily, Jacob approached and knelt at the Pyre. He reached one hand into the beautiful, warm flickering flames.

> *Your respawn location has been set to **Mount Phoenix (Central)**.*
> *The Fire Oppa stokes the embers of your conviction.*
> *Health, Stamina, Ampoules, and Spell Gems restored.*

"Fenris?" Jacob dared to ask.

The ash shifted, and out came the Fire Oppa, his ferret-like face lit up with excitement when he saw him. "I have been waiting for you," he said.

"What happened?" Jacob asked, looking about.

"Too much," the Fire Oppa said sadly.

"No, I mean with the Burgon Beast and the..." Jacob rolled his wrist, trying to sort out his spinning thoughts. "That *thing* that came out of it."

"Ah, you mean the Incomplete Vessel. Yes, that was quite a long time ago. What did you want to know?"

"I thought you couldn't help me?" Jacob did his best to keep the accusation from his tone, but from the way the Fire Oppa winced and looked down, the fiery fur cooling to glowing embers, he knew he failed.

"The rules that held me... loosened as each Pyre was destroyed," Fenris explained, sitting down on the bed of ashes at the base of the Pyre. "When I fully separated from the last Pyre, I was able to join with you because you were part of my Covenant. A piece of my Flame is now a part of your soul and vice versa.

"When the last Pyre was snuffed out...." Fenris shivered, shaking his whole body for a moment as the memory came back to him in full. Jacob couldn't imagine how terrible it must feel to have his Pyres extinguished.

He could still remember the pained whimpering, and just the memory of that sound tore at his heart.

Lowering his arms and setting his sword aside, Jacob offered the

Fire Oppa a place in his hands. An offer the fiery little creature eagerly took as he scrambled into the palms of Jacob's gauntlets.

Not content to stay there, Fenris scampered up his arm and rested at his shoulder. A pleasant campfire scent of a crackling fire and toasted marshmallows came from the Fire Oppa.

It reminded Jacob of summer camping trips.

"After that Pyre was extinguished," Fenris continued, "I severed myself from the Pyres and my cycle of rebirth."

"You said if I died, that you would die," Jacob said. "For good. Why would you risk that?"

Fenris laid his warm fiery head against Jacob's neck. Even through his suit of armor, he could feel the life-giving warmth of the Fire Oppa's flame. "Because I believed in you. And I knew without my help you would be hard-pressed to succeed. Maybe you could have done it without me, but I could not sit idly by and watch you suffer.

"Not after you repeatedly tried to defend my Pyre from the Burgon Beast. Not after you willingly threw yourself at that tortured beast, again and again, each time dying a horribly gruesome death.

"I have watched countless peoples suffer. I have seen millions of humans suffer and succumb to the ills of Lormar. But never have I seen a human so willingly put themselves in harm's way, to suffer again and again for the sake of others. You are a good man, Jacob."

"Thanks," Jacob said sheepishly. He was never very good at taking compliments.

As he tried to come to grips with the reality around him, he thought back to the last memories of Lormar. He remembered being trapped in his own mind. The horrible intrusion of the Incomplete Vessel turning his own thoughts against him.

A shiver of revulsion passed through him. "I don't think I could have made it without your help," he said to the Fire Oppa. "Is that why you were able to destroy the Incomplete Vessel, because you could leap from me to the shield you created?"

"Indeed, though you hardly needed my help at that point. The thing was on its last legs. But I didn't want to take any chances, and if I'm being honest with you... I wanted some payback too. For myself. For the people it has killed and those it would kill if released. For the Burgon Beast and its continued enslavement and suffering."

"The sword I got in Journey's End certainly didn't make it seem like the beast's former owner was worth saving," Jacob said.

"Houndmaster Vyrthis was a horrible creature, of which you will soon discover. But you did well in freeing the Burgon Beast. It was in great pain and not in control of its own actions, as you might have guessed."

Jacob nodded. "That thing was like a parasite, it must have given the Burgon Beast its shadow flames and other horrible attacks."

"Oh no," Fenris said, "The Burgon Beast is - was - a rare variation of the Shadow Wolves that were commonly raised as faithful hounds of Lormar's elite knights. Those fires were its own making, though it was forced to use them against its will."

A glance at his inventory told Jacob the Burgon Beast's Soul was still there. He wondered what he could do with it, if anything. It didn't seem right to turn it into a weapon... that's what its previous owner did to it.

Could he set it free?

Standing with his thoughts swirling, Jacob petted the Fire Oppa and left the room still deep in thought. He paused after crossing the threshold only to realize that the Fire Oppa was still on his shoulder.

"What?" the Fire Oppa asked him, tilting his head to the side.

"You're still on my shoulder."

"Would you like me to get down?" the confused Fire Oppa asked.

"Don't you need to stay with the Pyre?"

"Not as long as I'm near you."

Jacob felt a warm glow in his chest, answering the Fire Oppa's. What connection he had felt before after joining the Phoenix Covenant was a dozen times stronger now.

It warded off the chill of the world, one he was desperate to check on. Were the skies still red?

He hurried down the winding corridors to the mess hall and then to the exit. It took him a long while on his own to get the bunker's doors opened.

"Fenris... why am I alone?" Jacob asked as each clanking step through the tunnel felt heavier than the last. "Where is everybody? I thought killing the Burgon Beast would stop the Collapse!"

"Perhaps you would prefer to go back inside," Fenris said, his voice solemn. "There is... much to discuss."

"I want to see the sky," Jacob said stubbornly.

Coming around the bend, he saw the ruddy light spilling into the tunnel. He hoped against hope that it was just a sunset. That everybody else was out running supplies. Or maybe they were farming on the rolling hills below.

He needed something - *anything* - that would explain why he had woken up to an alarm and not a team of his friends.

He tried to come up with reasons for everything. But he knew, in his heart, that none of them could be true. And as Jacob came out of the tunnel and stared at the burning red sky, he understood the depths of despair.

Jacob stared at the blood-red skies for a very long time, feeling what little hope and accomplishment he had bleed away like a mortal wound. The Fire Oppa gently nuzzled against his neck, trying to assuage his pain.

Spying a rough stairway of hastily carved stone, Jacob turned and took them up higher onto the cliff face until he came to a small sheltered rise of grass and dirt.

He stopped cold, recognizing the place for what it was - a graveyard.

Dozens of mounds littered the site, each with a marker of stone. His breath came in short gasps. Jacob could barely control himself as his legs moved of their own accord pacing the rows of dead.

Names he knew well. Friends, family, loved ones all.

He spotted Kat's grave, Sal's, Caleb's. In a never-ending parade of death, he found familiar names engraved on the markers. Even Alec's name graced one of the tombstones, he was one of the last.

Jacob was hardly surprised by that point to see Alice and Ian's names next to Alec's grave. But what truly stole his breath away was the last marker. The greatest care seemed to go into this particular grave, and the date was the most recent.

It was Camilla's.

"I'm sorry, Jacob," the Fire Oppa said consolingly. "Please come back inside, you are not done with Pyresouls Online."

For some reason, seeing Camilla's name there broke him more than any of the others. She had no reason to come to Earth. How had she even done it? That she was there meant something had changed, something more than what he could remember. Earth was not Camilla's concern, and yet her grave told another story entirely.

"What do you mean?" Jacob managed to choke out. "I failed, Fenris. There's nobody left. They're all *dead*. The Collapse still happened. I *failed*."

"You stopped one incursion, Jacob," the Fire Oppa said softly, alighting onto Camilla's gravestone so he could face him. "There was another. Jacob, you have to go back."

"I can't," he said, voice barely above a whisper. He was beginning to understand how Alec felt. Jacob didn't know - seeing how much worse things were now after his meddling - how he could set foot in Lormar again.

"You have to Jacob," Fenris said, though his voice was not without sympathy. He looked about the graveyard up high on the sheltered ridge. "Because if you do not, this is the fate of your world. Of more than your world. You must go back to Lormar, Jacob."

EPILOGUE

September 11th, 2035.
Altis Main Campus.

"Johnson, the boss lady wants to see you," Cameron said, poking his head into their shared workspace.

Nodding, but not looking up from the IDE on his screen, Johnson said, "Be right there. Just gotta figure out why I'm getting a segfault here, the memory space isn't reserved."

"Now," Cameron said, with such authority that Johnson looked up and saw the severity on the typically upbeat young man's face.

"Right," he said, swallowing a gulp of black coffee. "See if you can figure out what's causing the error, will you? I can't get it to reproduce in the development sandbox, only on the live server." Standing, Johnson picked up the little rubber duck he had sitting in front of his keyboard. He tossed it to Cameron. "Mister Ducksworth will explain the problem to you."

They both had a chuckle at that. Johnson, running his fingers through his hair, left their workspace, and went to the glass office at the center of their floor.

He had a good idea what Marissa wanted and already had a list of potential resolutions to solve the problem or at least divert blame onto another department.

When Johnson got to the glass box that dominated the center of the 42nd floor of the skyscraper, he paled. Marissa wasn't alone. The Board was in there. All dour, serious faces that turned as one when he gingerly knocked on the door.

Marissa was there, red hair tied up in a bun and a kind smile that could turn into a vicious snarl in a nanosecond. She ushered him in and to the lone seat at the far end of the long table.

Was this a post-mortem? He didn't think they would react *that* soon. Nervous beyond anything he ever felt before, Johnson took the offered seat and scooted it in.

To buy time and to avoid looking at any of the sallow faces of the Board, he fussed with the height of the office chair and took a drink of water from the glass nearby.

Somebody cleared their throat.

Johnson looked up, and a few of the Board grinned at the fear in his eyes. He was dead. There would be no mercy from these curmudgeonly old beings that held his fate in the palm of their wrinkly hands.

A pleading look at Marissa had his direct supervisor offering him a sympathetic smile and a shrug of her narrow shoulders. She was just as powerless as he was.

"Tell us, Mister Johnson," one of the Board spoke, but he couldn't tell who. "Were you the one in charge of the Burgon Beast's origination?"

"Yes, sir," Johnson said, nodding woodenly.

I'm dead, I'm so dead, they hated it.

"And were you also the one who went outside corporate guidelines to add in the Incomplete Vessel?"

Sweating profusely, Johnson nodded again. "I am, yes." And before they could continue, he added, "I did it alone. Please don't punish Cameron. He didn't know what I was doing."

The Board looked at each other and nodded, then another speaker turned to Johnson with an intense stare. "If we were to give you an entire team to yourself, do you think you could improve upon the next phase of the Pyresouls Online competition? We would like to see how you do as a Lead Developer."

His voice stuck in his throat. Johnson couldn't fathom what he was hearing. He wasn't in trouble? He was being *promoted*?

The Boardmember raised a finger at Johnson, catching his attention. "Purely on a trial basis at first, you understand." That received several assenting nods from around the table. "But I see it as nothing more than a formality. With proper resources allocated to your work, we see no reason you won't create something truly fantastic."

Just then, an intern came in bearing a rolling cart full of pastries and a carafe of hot coffee. The young man set it all up, clearly sweating bullets just as Johnson was by being so near to the Board.

Trays set out, coffee cups circling the silver platters full of baked goods, Johnson still couldn't believe his fortune.

"O-of course, I won't let you down," Johnson said, eyeing the coffee cup several feet away.

Without thinking, he summoned a black inky tentacle and slithered it across the table. A grin spread across his face as he wrapped the thin tapered tip of the tentacle around the hot cup and brought it to his lips for a celebratory sip.

The intern let out a squeak of alarm at the sight.

Marissa was there in an instant, arm around the intern's slender shoulders. A black tendril wormed its way out of her pretty red button-up top and locked the door behind her to the glass office room.

Another tentacle slithered through the air and turned the glass opaque. "Now, Johnson," Marissa scolded playfully. "I know you're new to the family, but we can't keep losing interns like this." She placed a hand on the intern's lower back and shoved him forward toward the table.

Johnson understood. "I'll be more careful, boss," he promised as he stalked around the table to the stunned and frightened intern. A dozen or more black inky tentacles sprouted out from behind Johnson as he walked toward the doomed man. They wriggled and snapped in the air. "Terribly sorry about all this," he said. "It'll be over quick. I don't play with my food."

The man's screams never made it out of the soundproof box.

AFTERWORD

Whew, that was a bit of a bittersweet ending, huh? I'm so glad you stuck with it to the end! Thanks for reading Pyresouls Apocalypse: Rewind, it truly means a lot to me. This is the first book in the Pyresouls Apocalypse series, and my second novel in the LitRPG genre.

I wrote Pyresouls alongside writing my other series, Beastborne Chronicles, and working full-time as an EMT. Needless to say, it has not been easy. But through the support of readers like yourself, and my Patrons over on Patreon, I have been able to pull it off.

My goal is to become a full-time author. If I can write two series concurrently, not just one after the other with a delay for each, imagine what I can do when I'm writing full-time!

With your support, I am one step closer to realizing my dream. Whether you read this on Kindle Unlimited, purchased the ebook, the paperback, the audiobook (or all 3!), or support me on Patreon, your generosity is greatly appreciated.

But did you know you can immensely help me to write more of these books that we love so much (and it doesn't even cost a cent!)? If you liked Pyresouls, **please leave a review and rating** to let others know what you thought!

Share it with friends, recommend it to others who aren't as well-

Afterword

read as you, mention it on social media, shout it from your favorite rooftop! None of those things costs anything (though the last one might, depending on your city ordinances!), and they are the very thing that keeps an author like myself writing.

And if you're asking yourself how you can help even more, you could hop on over and check out my Patreon! You'll find constant updates for all my books there, as well as early releases of ebooks, advanced chapters of everything I'm writing, and much more. At the same time, you'll help my books to be released faster as new goals are hit.

I hope you enjoyed reading about Lormar as much as I loved making it. Soulsborne games are some of my favorites, and it was an absolute delight to pay homage to those games.

My goal is to continue writing Pyresouls alongside Beastborne for many years to come. I have a lot of plans for Lormar, Jacob, Camilla, and of course, Fire Oppa. Hopefully, you'll come along and join them on their adventures!

ABOUT THE AUTHOR

My name is James T. Callum, and I'm not going to talk to you in the third person or make it seem like I've got some publisher or editor who has a bio on me.

This is just me, talking to you, the reader. I'm no different than you, I love reading and gaming just the same as everybody else.

In fact, I've loved reading for as long as I could remember. From the very first fantasy book I read, Wizard of Earthsea, I was hooked.

For just as long, I've also been an avid gamer and DND player (as well as other tabletop RPGs). Chrono Trigger, Final Fantasy, Illusion of Gaia, and on through the years as stories and graphics became better and better.

You'll be able to find hints of inspiration from all sorts of RPGs and video games in my works. From the Final Fantasy series to Warcraft, Age of Empires to Anno, and games like Dark Souls and Bloodborne. Because who doesn't love a little cosmic horror thrown in for fun?

These games (and countless others) have inspired me ever since I was a kid, and they continue to serve as my muse now that I'm much older.

Writing has always been my greatest aspiration, and with your help, I hope to make it a full-time job. At the time of this writing, I still work a day job like most people. It is only thanks to Patreon that I was able to dedicate some of my spare time to writing.

So, if you'd like to provide direct support and help me achieve my goal of writing full-time (so I can write even more stories for you awesome people!) you can hop on over to my Patreon page where you'll find tons of content.

Patrons get access to advanced chapters of upcoming books, special discord roles and discussion channels, early releases of ebooks before anyone else, maps, cover reveals, voting, and a lot more.

Become a Patron Today!
(https://www.patreon.com/JamesTCallum)

You can always find the latest information on my website about new books coming up, sales, and more: https://www.jamestcallum.com

And if you spot a typo or error, shoot me an email at: typos@jamest-callum.com, and I will get it fixed and re-uploaded ASAP. I aim to provide the best possible reading experience and as soon as I find an error I fix it. Once it's fixed and updated, your reading device should update automatically with the improved version.

I'm always available to talk, connect with readers, fellow authors, and lovable book nerds:

Discord Server: https://discord.gg/nTvDNFM

Or you can come hang out on my Facebook Page: Beastborne Chronicles.

Looking for more LitRPG series from a wonderful group of people? Head on over to the Gamelit Society Facebook group!

facebook.com/Beastborne-Chronicles-113406063837162

twitter.com/JamesTCallum

ACKNOWLEDGMENTS

To my lovely wife, without whom none of these books would have ever come to fruition. Without your unwavering support and belief, I would have never been able to keep up with my writing.

And of course, if not for my Patrons, I would have never known anybody else cared about my stories. Your support has helped me to not only continually seek to make better, more interesting stories, but to gain a sense of fulfillment I never thought possible.

Of particular note, I would like to thank the following Patrons:

Alex R, Carthel, Cody, Devyn, Dominic Pernicone, Dyoll Rojam, Giuseppe Thibodeau, Jachin Nelson, Johnist, Jørn Håvard Eikenes, Josua Samano, Junior, Kyle J Smith, Larry Baker, Luke Davis, Michael Arceneau, Phllip Rivera, Thomas Wolf.

You are all awesome individuals and I cannot thank you enough for your generosity and kind words.

JACOB'S FINAL STATS

Jacob Windsor
    Covenant: Phoenix
    Race: Kemora - Fae-touched (Human/Fairy)
    Level: 26
    Health: 132
    Stamina: 94
    Anima: 0
    Souls: 35,000
    Required Souls: 4,581

    Parameters
    VIT: 4
    AGI: 8
    END: 7
    TMP: 15
    STR: 10
    DEX: 10
    INT: 8
    FTH: 3

Jacob's Final Stats

Curse: Fractured Sight
 Curse Level: 0

 Spell Gem: Heat Blade (3/3)
 Spell Gem: Flame Blade (1/1)

Printed in Great Britain
by Amazon